TRIAD

By

Mary Holwager

Copyright 2008 by Mary McAteer Holwager
Cover art by Michael Marrujo

No book is complete without a word of thanks to the people who made it possible.

Jesse, David, and Jason are all martial artists of one sort or another. Their skills (and mine) owe a great deal to my Sensei, best friend, and husband, John Holwager, and to my Sifu, Peter Hill.

For three glorious years when I was in college, I was a member of the Army Reserve Officer Training Corps at Idaho State University. Most of what I know of the military, and distilled into this book, came from the cadre of officers who made themselves responsible for educating my classmates and me - Colonel Willard Alverson, Professor of Military Science; Major Bruce Bourgault; Major John Black; Major John Miles; Captain Roger Rucker; Captain Tracy Schoonmaker; Captain James Dhalgren; Sergeant-Major George Wentzel; and Sergeant-Major Ken Henry. My army doesn't bear a lot of resemblance to theirs, but the principle is the same - soldiers go where they're sent and do what they're told to do because their country tells them that's what it needs them for.

I ride with the Patriot Guard Riders, and I carry the memories of Major David J. Reichsteig, USMC, KIA Vietnam; and SFC Steven England, USA, KIA Vietnam.

Prologue

"...Promethean Defense Command Platform 4771, to the designated coordinates, there to establish Border Outpost 4771, to be known as Fort King Kamehameha."

Jesse Larsen looked up from the orders she was reading. Marshall Andranos Solud, overseeing operations in Quadrant Four North, raised an eyebrow, which gave him a quizzical look under the floating cloud of Kondrassi hair. Jesse lowered her eyes again to the specifications she was reading.

"...To include the 227th Border Division, plus research and exploration facilities, scouts, outriders - final complement a garrison between twenty- and twenty-five thousand, with accomodations for family and temporary duty personnel."

Jesse glanced at her companion out of the corner of her eye to make sure he could see what she was doing, then stretched her long legs out, lifted them above the level of the table, crossed her feet in their shiny boots, and set them on the coffee table. Another look showed her the Marshall's eyebrow floating up again, but he didn't say anything.

"He wants something," she thought. "I wonder what." She beckoned with the fingers of her right hand, and the holo display that had been floating above the table came toward her until she raised her hand, palm forward. The display obediently stopped at comfortable eyeball distance. Jesse moved a finger and the plans shifted, moving slowly through the corridors and work spaces of the top level of the five-sided, fifteen-story structure, revealing offices, laboratories, classrooms, recreation areas, library, infirmary - all the functioning apparatus of a full-scale military installation.

She moved the finger again, directing the view down, to the first level of the five "habitat" areas. The cursor floated inward, then settled in the protected center of the area - the triad quarters. Two sets - one for the command triad, one for the operations triad. Jesse pointed her index finger at the living room of the command triad's quarters. The cursor floated down, and the rooms opened up as though the roof had been lifted.

The living/dining room was long, and four doors opened off it - one led to the hallway and three led to three identical suites consisting of sitting room/study, bedroom, and bath.

Jesse replaced the roof on the triad quarters and continued her tour, ignoring her companion. Gymnasiums and training facilities, supply and storage areas, workshops, loading bays, transport systems, mechanical and environmental systems; hangars for fighter squadrons, scout ships, outriders, and transports drifted past, level succeeding level until she reached the bottom - shield generators, weapons platforms, sensor systems.

She pointed her finger at a control and the structure began to collapse, folding into itself until it was no more than five levels, a squat cylinder with a pyramid on one end - the configuration of a mobile command center - the border fort that was being built in the docks overhead, and would eventually transport itself to its designated station, there to resume its original form - fifteen levels; five sides; five rings of offices, laboratories, living quarters, and workspaces on each level.

She waved the holo away and picked up her wineglass, ignoring the reflection of her coffee-cream skin and dark eyes in the surface of the table, and leaned back, uncrossing and re-crossing her feet. "Very nice," she said. "In fact, quite impressive. So how do I rate a virtual tour of Prometheus' newest, largest, best-armed border fortress?"

The quadrant Marshall grinned, a wolf-like flash of teeth that always sent chills up Jesse's spine, the static-filled Kondrassi hair floating around his face like a cloud. "Guess."

"Oh, no - no, you don't." She pulled her feet off the table and sat up. "I have no desire whatsoever to be the next sacrificial lamb. You lost two mobile command platforms and their garrisons before they ever got to Sector 23, Andranos - why would any sane person want anything to do with it?"

He sobered and pulled a data card from the fold of his tunic. "Maybe you wouldn't, Jess - and maybe you still won't after you read this."

It was a set of orders, to take command of Promethean Defense Command Mobile Command Platform 4771 - *King Kamehameha* - transport it to a designated location, and establish an operational outpost - a combination border patrol headquarters, training base, and command center.

Jesse read it, then read it again. The third time one detail screamed for attention.

"These orders are for a triad - a command triad," she said, handing it back to the Marshall, who tucked it into the fold of his tunic. "There are no names on it."

"No, there aren't. There won't be, until I have an acceptance, from you or from someone else."

He pulled in a deep breath and shifted. "I won't minimize the danger. As you said, we've lost two platforms intended for this sector already. And this command has inherent difficulties over and above that - this is no routine walkover any Command School graduate could handle in her sleep. It'll be two years at least, maybe as much as five, before it'll be safe to allow accompanied posting. The garrison will comprise elements from more than one branch, not to mention a large complement of civilians, and whoever commands will have to keep peace and ensure cooperation.

"From the career point of view, it's a gem. Whoever gets *King Kamehameha* into place and operational will automatically take a step up. If the same triad takes it a step further and gets it fully on line and populated, they'll be able to walk into just about any job they choose."

The same triad, Jesse thought. *What Andy hasn't mentioned is that if I take this job, I have to accept a replacement for Thom.* For a moment, a wave of blackness swept over her, and her chest felt as though it was being compressed until there was no room for her lungs and heart.

"I am not ready to replace Thom," she said, gritting her teeth to hold back the scream that was hovering in her mind. She glanced up and Solud was watching her, lines of puzzlement in his face. "Thom wasn't just a working partner, Andy, or just a friend. He was my..." her voice trailed off as her chest tightened again. She cleared her throat. "It's been two months, Andy. How long do they give you on Kondrass before they expect you to replace your mate?"

The luminous yellow eyes widened, and Solud straightened. "I hadn't realized..."

"Apparently no one did. Except David." Jesse reached for her glass, glanced up at Solud's face, then pulled back. "So?"

"So. So the problem, Jesse Larsen, is that Prometheus is at war. We don't have time for you to finish mourning. We don't have time to give the kids coming out of the Defense Command colleges a year or two of seasoning before they hit the front lines.

"There are raiders getting past the ADS, and we don't know how. Any day, they could decide it's time to come across in force, and Sector 23 is a gaping hole in our defenses. And last month we confiscated and destroyed five tons of Crystal, and odds are it's coming in the same way the raiders are.

"You're the best I've got, Jess, and you're who I want as the Command First in Sector 23. And remember, a partner can be a partner and nothing more. Accepting a new partner doesn't mean forgetting Thom Isaacson.

"So make up your mind, and do it fast, Jesse Larsen. I'm offering you Command. I'm offering you the chance of a lifetime. But it has a price, and if you're not willing to pay the price, someone else will."

#

"You're taking the job?" David Christiansen looked up from the data card, his changeable eyes the dark blue that indicated he was relaxed and confident.

"It depends."

"On?"

"You, for a start. And this." She held out another data card.

The big man took it, opened it, and settled back to read. Jesse watched his expressive face change as he read, from neutral interest, to surprise - one mobile eyebrow lifted, to - *I've never seen him look like that before,* Jesse thought. *He almost looks - scared.* The skin of his face had tightened, making the hard bones underneath more evident, and the changeable eyes had lightened from dark blue through steel grey to light grey.

"Jason Ashe," David said. His voice was flat, uninflected. "What do you know about Jason Ashe?"

"What's in that service record," Jesse said. "What everyone knows. I've never met him."

"And he requested this?"

"Marshall Solud asked him, and he responded favorably. I don't think he requested the post. Why, David - do you have a problem with him?"

Christiansen flowed to his feet and began to pace the room, hands in his pockets.

Jesse watched for a moment. David kept pacing, staring at the floor. She'd known him to pace like that for hours when he was working on a problem, when he was upset. When Thom Isaacson died, he'd paced until the medics grabbed him and tranquilized him.

"David, I need an answer," she finally said. "This was Andy's best recommendation, but there are other Sensitives out there - we don't have to take him."

"And you don't have to keep me."

"No, I guess not. But we've been together three years, and you're the best Pathfinder in the service. I lost Thom, David, I don't want to lose you. So if it's a question of not being able to work with Ashe..."

He took two turns and ended up leaning against the bookcase. "No, not at all. In fact, I'd be very glad to work with him - if he's really willing to take this post, and us - me."

"Why wouldn't he be, David?" *What's the problem here? What doesn't he want to tell me?*

The grey eyes had lightened to the color of rainwater. "Because once we were pledged to a permanent partnership. Because after our First was killed, the Point's Commandant had me stationed with a patrol group in Sector 20 - as far from both the Center and the Point as it's possible to get and still be in Prometheus. Because for more than a year, I wrote Jason a letter a week, and called him, sometimes twice if I could get the bandwidth, and I never heard anything. Nothing. Not that my messages were refused, not that there was a transmission error - just nothing.

"Because I've seen him a few times since, and he treats me exactly the way he'd treat anyone he went through the Point with. Exactly."

He pushed himself away from the wall and handed her the data card. "Solud's right, Jess. This is the opportunity of a lifetime. And if you want the best chance of succeeding, you want Jason Ashe. Go for it." He turned and left.

-Chapter 1-
Cry 'Havoc' and let loose the dogs of War
William Shakespeare—Macbeth

"Lock this transport down and evacuate the dock!" Jess Larsen ordered, jumping from the top of the ramp as the first cycle of the alarm klaxon ended. She hit the landing dock's cushiony floor and took off running.

She stuck a hand out, SOP for combat alarm situations to prevent collisions, and ran for the Command Center, guiding herself around sharp corners with the other hand on the wall.

The entire platform shook, and Jesse was knocked to her knees in the corridor outside the Command Center. "By the One, we're taking fire." She grabbed a handrail and pulled herself to her feet. "What in the Name is going on here?"

"Kill that noise," Jesse heard Zephron Bell order as the Operations Command Center door slid shut behind her. The obnoxious shrieking of the contact alarm died.

"Thanks, Zephron, my ears were about to bleed," she muttered. She caught his eye.

"Command."

"Ops." She returned Bell's grave acknowledgement. "May I be of assistance?"

He tilted his chin toward the command console.

Jesse nodded and headed that way, grabbing the backs of chairs and the edges of consoles to keep from being knocked off her feet as wave after wave of concussion shook them. *By the One, what is that and where did it come from? This isn't supposed to be a combat zone.*

"What have you got, Pilot?" Bell said. Jesse stopped where she could see the readout from the forward scanner.

"Bandit approaching at attack speed, Ops," the pilot said. "We took a long-range burst. Screens are on-line now," the floor shivered, "but they're still firing. We've transmitted recognition codes at all frequencies, but received no response. From this distance the profile doesn't seem to fit anything we've got."

Note to self, Jesse thought. *That database just moved to priority one status.*

"Very well, go to Alert Condition One," Bell sa d. The lights went out and the room became dim blue as all possible power was diverted to the defense screens and weapons systems came on line.

The comm officer's smooth voice floated through the corridors. "Alert, alert. Prepare for combat maneuvering. Section doors will close in two minutes. This is not, I say again, not, a drill."

Jesse got to the command console and strapped in. She put her right palm on the sensor plate, and as the system recognized her, pulled her mike down and began voicing commands to *King Kamehameha*'s control systems.

The door slid open and someone stumbled on the threshold.

"Damn! Sorry, Ops." It was the new Command Third, Jason Ashe. He stepped inside and grabbed a railing as the floor shook again.

"Damn it, Pilot, can't you get the system to identify? We need to know what that bastard is." Jesse heard undertones of stress and anxiety in Bell's voice.

"Tragan. Raptor Class." The Command Second, David Christiansen, spoke from the door. Jesse glanced at him, mouthed a command, and watched the outline trace itself on the tactical grid. By the time the others were harnessed, the outline was complete, and the words 'ID match' were blinking on the screen.

Dragon's breath! Combat zone or not, we're about to test this command platform's defense capability. How the hell did a Tragan get through the Interdicted Areas and past the border without triggering every alarm in the sector? And why does David know the profiles of Tragan battleships so well he can identify one from a viewscreen across CC?

"Here? We're three zones from the Interdicted Areas." It was one of the apprentices - Jesse couldn't remember his name - half out of his seat, eyes wide and shoulders tense with incipient panic.

Ashe put his hand on the boy's shoulder, leaned down, and murmured something too soft for anyone else to hear. The youngster relaxed, the horrified stare changing to alert interest. He smiled, nodding as Ashe murmured something else, then turned back to his work.

Good, Ashe, very good. I'm almost impressed.

Bell gestured, inviting the command triad to join their counterparts around the console, then touched the control that created a wall of white noise around them. "We can't get enough firepower on line to stand and fight, we don't have enough speed to outrun him, and we have to protect that transport. And, I should add, we have way too many apprentices on this platform who've never been under fire before. It looks like a no-win situation, and I don't like no-win situations. Suggestions?"

David's big hand came to rest next to James McGowan's on the sensor plate, sending their identification to the core of the platform's computer. Functions came on-line, responding to the Pathfinders' Perception of energy, electromagnetism, radiation currents in and around King K.

"I need some contact, Jason," David murmured, lifting his right hand and extending it.

The segment of the console in front of Ashe and the Operations Third, Mariko Itosu, was active, readouts from the memory cores next to swirling patterns that represented electron flows, photon particles, the life force of King K and her garrison answering the Sensitives' approach to the command link. Ashe lifted his left hand from the console and raised it to David's, allowing the two palms to touch, reinforcing the link and clarifying the information the four were collecting for the Intuits, Jesse and Bell.

"All sections report ready for lockdown," the comm officer's voice came through Jesse's earpiece. "*Ahab* is secure and routing power to reinforce the screens."

Bell glanced at his watch. "One minute, thirty seconds. Excellent."

"Begin lockdown," he murmured into his mike.

The comm officer's voice filled the earpieces and floated through the room again. "Section doors coming down - now. Lockdown is complete."

"Mr. Edmonds, I want all engines on-line now," Bell commanded.

"Coming up, Ops," the chief's warm alto responded. "We're fine-tuning as much as we can. The longer you can give us before the shove, the more oomph you'll have."

"What about randomizing?"

"Not with that transport attached, sorry."

"Understood."

Zephron Bell shifted so he was just behind Jesse and

placed his hand next to hers on the console, his warm breath drifting past Jesse's ear.

The data from the Pathfinders and Sensitives began to appear, showing them King K's and the intruder's relative positions, the nearest inhabited star system, the nearest locator beacon, the patterns of energy flow in this sector...

The console sparked and a body went flying. "Back off!" Ashe snapped. "They're running a trapline."

He slipped his harness and knelt by the small body of Mariko Itosu. "I'll take care of Mari, the rest of you get that..." his voice trailed off. He pulled a capsule from the console's pedestal and broke it under Mariko's nose, then put a pressure mask over her face and placed his hands on either side of her head.

He glanced up, the startling blue eyes hard. "Go on, we can't help you. They're Talent hunting, Ops."

Talent hunting. In the hundred and fifty years since the Tragan Hexarchy had segregated itself from Prometheus, the Tragans had ceased to produce the three major Talents - Intuition, Perception/Pathfinding, and Empathy/Sensitivity. In the hundred years the two had been at a standoff, Talents had become the raiders' chief prey - and of the few who had survived capture long enough to be rescued, none had remained sane, or lived long.

Jesse felt cold fingers creeping up her spine, and the hair on the back of her neck lifted. *Dragon's breath! We don't need this.*

David swore under his breath. Zephron didn't speak, but Jesse saw his lips tighten, and James McGowan went white.

Jesse felt as though every eye in Command and Control was on her. *Up to you, Jess,* she thought. *You're Command. Make a decision, even if it's the wrong one.* "Flight, this is Command. Release the outriders," she murmured.

"Releasing outriders," the flight commander's calm voice responded. Jesse felt a jolt as the explosive bolts that had tethered the outriders to King K's shell blew. "*Mantis* is away, *Spider* is coming up to the pad."

Jesse listened with part of her attention while her hands and eyes were busy on the console, communicating with other stations, adjusting energy flows between screens, and monitoring the bandit.

"All outriders are away."

"Launch fighters," Jesse murmured.

"Roger, Command. Launching fighters."

David brought up a display. "There. See?"

The raider's shields were wavering - ripples washed over the ship as the power levels fluctuated.

"Command, what causes that?" James, the young Ops Second asked.

"Whoever paid for the power contracting let the specs slip," Jesse said. "The shield generator isn't powerful enough to maintain a steady field.

"That's what happens when you have a bunch of warlords contending for power instead of a central authority that's concerned with protecting its resources, including its people.

"*Mantis*, this is Command. We're transmitting a schematic. Concentrate fire on the marked area."

"Wilco, Command."

Bell grinned. "Okay, that's the first move. Now what?"

"Let me see if I can improve our odds," Jesse said. "Can anyone read that sigil?" She let her index finger hover over a small area on the screen where an intricate design was painted on the intruder's nose.

"Sarg of Benetnash," David said. The changeable eyes were rainwater grey.

"I gather whoever Sarg of Benetnash is you don't like him much?" Bell said.

David shrugged and kept his eyes fixed on his section of the console.

Jesse closed her eyes and let her mind wander, while her Talent, Intuition, collected all the tiny things she'd noticed without noticing and heard without hearing and turned them into information she could use. Sarg of Benetnash was a minor warlord known for his stinginess. His eldest son would be commanding the raider - and Sarg's eldest son had a reputation even in Prometheus for stupidity.

"He'll expect us to either run or try to fight, because that's what he'd do. He commands because he's the warlord's son, not because he's competent - in fact we know he isn't the brightest bulb in the box. He'll be thinking of King K as a base under transport, not a mobile command center - he'll think we're slow and clumsy. He'll ignore the outriders and concentrate on us, because he's big and heavily screened and the Talents he's after are here. So we let him get so close he thinks he has us. Meanwhile, the fighters do what they can to attract his firepower and drain his energy reserves, and the outriders concentrate their fire on a vulnerable spot. Then we drop and come up behind him."

"And if *Mantis* hits the right spot, it'll kill his shields, so we can target his engines and leave him drifting," Bell said, eyes half shut as he thought.

"I like it," David said. His eyes had darkened to steel grey and were sparkling.

"I think it's the best chance we've got," the tall, dark-bearded Zephron Bell said. "It's your scenario, you run it, Command." He stepped to the secondary position and put his hands on the console, awaiting Jesse's commands.

Jesse touched the contact that opened the internal comm system, concentrating on controlling her breathing, keeping her voice level and clear. "This is Command. We're about to begin maneuvers. For many of you, this is the first time under fire. Hold tight, concentrate on doing your jobs, and we'll all be fine."

The worst part of a soldier's job is waiting, Jesse thought. *Waiting to hear if you've made it into a Defense Command college, waiting to hear the results of your finals, to know if you'll get the commission; waiting to see what your next assignment will be; waiting for the enemy to attack.* She heard tapping and looked around to see who it was, meaning to silence the offender. It was her own nails, pulsing on the side of the console. She stopped, fisted the hand, slid it into her pocket so no one else would see the knuckles tightened with tension. She forced herself to focus on the console.

Christiansen and McGowan, side by side at the weapons console, seemed cool and composed, their hands a blur as they checked and rechecked data, made tiny adjustments to King K's position, and monitored the outriders and their fighter flights.

"Wait, people. Patience. We have to let him get into position," Jesse said, looking for signs of panic. Faces were tense, some hands shaking, but that was all. This was going to be a baptism of fire for these youngsters - one that shouldn't have happened here and now.

How did that Raptor get past the Interdicted Areas without triggering every alarm in the quadrant and activating the ADS? And how in the name of all the monsters in the Void did he know where and when to find us?

The Raptor drifted in, while centuries passed and Jesse felt sweat trickling down her underarms and the back of her neck and soaking her tunic. The Raptor grew, and grew, and moved closer, until it seemed it was going to run right over them.

"Pilot, relinquish control to Weapons, now. Turning to intercept course and increasing speed," David said, his rich voice calm and uninflected. The dark blonde head leaned close to the red one, and Jesse saw David's lips move. James nodded, touched a control...

A single burst of plasma energy lanced out.

"Turn ninety degrees straight down, now!" Jesse ordered. "Flank speed." *Come on, Chief, give me all you've got.* For a moment it felt as though the floor had dropped away, and Jesse grabbed the console to keep herself from floating into the ceiling.

Then the engines took hold. The increasing Gs pressed her down as James guided King K through the complex maneuver that would bring King K under and behind the Raptor, in position to fire again. Under the whine of the engines and the pounding of her heart, Jesse heard, or felt, joints creaking and straining, conduits groaning as the maneuver strained the compressed base to its limit.

A bolt of blue-white plasma energy sank into the glow from the Tragan's engines. Another. And another. The glow dimmed to red, deepened, intensified, then faded to black.

"That took out at least one engine," Bell said. "They're dead in space."

Jesse heard the beginning of a collective sigh of relief, but a bright flash from the display screen lit the room, then disappeared as the control program dimmed the viewers. Jesse counted seconds, waiting for her eyes to clear.

She wasn't prepared for the concussion wave - as King K rocked, Jesse was ripped out of her harness and skidded away from the console. She grabbed the nearest chair and held on, biting her lip to keep from swearing - or screaming. The apprentice pilot flew from his seat and slid across the floor, coming to rest against the railing. For a few seconds, everything not tied down was airborne, and alarm klaxons mixed with swearing and screaming as people ducked and dodged to avoid being impaled by flying objects.

"By the Many! Did we do that?"

"No," said Christiansen. "They did." The gold skin had taken on a grey undertone and his changeable eyes were lightening with distress, shading from steely to rainwater grey.

The viewer scrolled through infrared, tactical grid, normal space, radar view.

"There. See?" He'd stopped on radar. Instead of the menacing shape of the Raptor, the viewer showed an expanding mass of debris, most pieces too small to be identifiable. "They activated the self-destruct."

"Oh, my God, we had pilots out there," someone whispered.

"All right, people," Ignoring the nausea rising from the pit of her stomach, Jesse took over before things got out of hand, "it's over. You've got jobs to do, get busy and do them." She looked around the room, making sure she'd gotten eye contact and some sort of acknowledgement from every person in CC.

"Mr. Radonov..."

"I'm on it, Sir. Do we need a gunship?"

Jesse caught Bell's nod out of the corner of her eye and let him answer. "Yes. That bastard got through the Interdicted Area without triggering an alarm. We need to know how."

The Comm Officer nodded and turned to his console, the extended fighting nails of a Sliothi male in combat mode scraping the surface.

"Status?"

"Sir, the crash door over the swimming pool on Level Five didn't close and about half the volume came out and replaced itself indiscriminately around the room. We're cleaning it up now. We have a lot of breakage – mostly things falling off shelves and sliding off tables. All replaceable by the mass converter."

Another voice cut into the comm - the flight officer's. "Medical teams to launch bays, stat."

"Status, Flight?" Bell asked.

"Ops, all fighters have been recovered, but we have some severe lacerations and at least one broken leg."

Another deep breath - of relief. "Very well," Bell said. "Maintenance, report when cleanup's finished. Infirmary, status on injuries?"

"Lots of bumps, bruises, and abrasions, Ops. One of Mr. Edmonds' people was in a shaft and her arm's broken. No serious injuries."

Thank the One, Jesse thought. "We need a medic in CC," she said.

"What kind of injury, Sir?"

"Mr. Raschid was torn out of his harness when the shock-wave hit, and thrown into the pit wall. His eyes are open, but he was out for a while. And Mr. Itosu took an energy charge."

"On our way."

"Stand down from emergency status," Bell ordered. "Flight, send rescue drones out, but tell the outriders to maintain patrols until the gunship gets here. Mr. Edmonds, you and your team are to be congratulated on your performance. Comm, maintain scans to be sure that Raptor didn't have a partner, and advise me when the gunship arrives. People, you did good."

He pulled in a deep breath and pulled his mike away from his mouth. "God save me from another afternoon like this one. Mr. Ashe, welcome. I hope it isn't always this interesting."

The Sensitive, climbing to his feet as a team of medics lifted Mariko Itosu to a gurney, glanced up and smiled. "Thank you, Ops. I hope so, too."

Bell caught Jesse's eye, then David's, then Ashe's. "Thank you for your assistance, Command."

He took a slow look around the room, glanced at Jesse, and winked. "Now," he raised his voice slightly, "get back to work and get this place cleaned up. It looks like the back end of a typhoon."

Jesse bit her lip to keep from grinning and headed for the door. "If you need me, Ops, I'll be seeing the transport off."

Alone in the lift down to the landing platforms, Jesse leaned against the wall and concentrated on getting her heart rate back to normal. She was sticky with dried sweat, and glad to be where no one could see the shaking and weakness caused by the adrenalin aftermath.

A burst of profanity in several languages pulled Jesse off the wall, the hair on the back of her head rising. "Chief Cody," she hissed, "you're on the comm."

"Oops! Sorry, Command. Would you and Ops join me on the residential level when you get a chance?"

"Give us about forty minutes, Chief," Zephron said. "Command is seeing transport *Ahab* off, and I've got some stuff to clear up here."

"That works for us," David's voice interjected.

"Us as well," Mariko Itosu said.

"Roger that, Ops, Command. I'll meet you on Level Five, Compartment Thirty-Seven A."

#

Chief Cody held out a big brown hand full of metal fragments.

"What are we looking at?" Zephron asked.

"Some of the bolts that sheared off when we made that drop," Cody replied.

Zephron picked up a chunk, held it close to his face, handed it to Jesse.

"It looks hollow."

"It is hollow. We're going over that section with a fine-toothed comb, and it looks as though about one in every twelve bolts has a hollow core."

"That's pretty bad speccing," Zephron said. "Not to mention lousy quality control."

"This had nothing to do with the specs, Ops. These bolts have been cored with a laser welder - see here?"

He handed Zephron a magnifier and a broken bolt. Bell used it, then passed both to Jesse. Under the magnification, the slick left by the laser was apparent. She handed the magnifier and bolt to David.

"Not something the builders would notice," Cody said, "unless they started shearing when they were applied. They're just strong enough to take that, but any sudden torque after that - crunch."

"I'd have thought the inspectors would notice it," Jesse said.

"Probably. But this could have been done after they were inspected. It could have been done any time in the last three months, right up to this morning.

"The good news is, now that we know they're there, we can find and replace the bad ones."

"And the bad news?"

"The bad news is that we can't lock that section down without expanding it."

"And we can't do that until we reach our station," Jesse said.

The chief nodded. "Unless you want to stop cead for about a month while we do the repairs."

"I don't think so," Bell said. "Unless we're going to cause further damage if we don't?"

"No, but we won't be able to randomize," the chief said. "The vibration when the random space generators come online is just the right frequency to rattle this section to bits."

Jesse and Zephron exchanged glances, and Bell lifted one shoulder.

"I guess your people aren't going to be lacking for something to do until we reach our destination, Chief," Jesse said. "To the extent that it's possible with King K collapsed, start at the top and work down..."

"And check every section we can get at," Chief Cody finished for her. "Roger that, Command. At least it'll keep my guys from getting bored and sloppy."

"Okay, thanks, Chief." The big man nodded and turned away, shoving the handful of metal into his pocket.

Jesse waited, arms folded, until the construction chief was out of earshot. Then she handed the bolt she was holding to David and let her gaze move around the circle of her partners and their operational counterparts. "I doubt we can get anything from any of those bolts the way Chief Cody was handling them, but you might have Security try."

David nodded. "It's a long shot."

"Does this mean what I think it means?" James asked. The youthful Pathfinder's face was pale under its coat of freckles, and the hazel eyes were wide.

"If you think it means we have a saboteur along for the ride, James, you may or may not be right," David said. "If you think it means we're going to spend from now till we get on station hunting for one, you're absolutely right. We're going to comb all the construction logs, all the subcontracts, all the specs, and all the personnel records, both of people assigned to this station and people in the construction yards."

"And we are not going to discuss this with anyone," Jesse interposed. "As of right now, we assume we can trust the five - the six - of ourselves, and no one else. Understood?"

"Understood, Command," James responded.

"How is Mari, Zephron?" Ashe asked. "Have you talked with the medics?"

"She had a terrible headache and she was very cross when she woke up," Bell replied. "Dr. Thassanios told me he put her to sleep and she'd be fine in the morning. And by the way, Command Third, thank you for taking care of my partner."

The blonde shrugged and a faint wash of color touched his face. "Just doing my job, Ops First."

"Anything else?" Jesse asked. She got a round of headshakes and lifted shoulders. "Good. I don't know about the rest of you, but I've had about as much fun as I can stand for one day. I'm taking the rest of the day off."

Zephron glanced at his watch and grinned. "The rest of what day?"

"Yeah, that's what I meant. See you."

Well, things have started well, Jesse thought. *If they continue at this rate, we'll all be dead before we get this base on station.*

Stop, Jesse. That's no kind of attitude for the Command First. She tugged her tunic straight, crossed her fingers in the ancient good luck ritual, and headed for the lift.

-Chapter 2-

For my mind misgives, some consequence yet hanging in the stars... -William Shakespeare, Romeo and Juliet

For almost a month, Jesse's luck held. Her partners were efficient, and more important, unobtrusive - even in quarters, she hadn't seen Jason Ashe more than three times, and that only for moments.

The gaping hole in her solar plexus that had been there since Thom Isaacson had been killed ceased to scream pain at her twenty-eight hours a day. The pain was still there, but time and distance reduced it to a whimper. *I don't like it, but I can live with it,* she thought. *As long as I keep it closed off, it'll be alright.* She never let herself think about what would happen if she allowed herself to feel.

Operational efficiency continued to rise. The bugs inherent in any new system showed up, were caught, and disappeared. The outriders reported the sector was quiet. Jesse began to relax and enjoy the job.

Maybe it'll go smoothly now. Maybe that was the only raider in the sector and we'll get to station and online without any more trouble.

The door signal called her back from her reflections. "Yes?"

The Comm Chief, Valery Radonov, entered, holding a data card. "I think you need to see this, Command."

She held out her hand and he passed her the card. It looked like a routine update from HQ - Sector Reports, news flashes. A section was outlined in red, flashing a warning.

Jesse read it, then read it again. The third time, the words that her brain hadn't wanted to register broke through. "Regret to inform all personnel of a raid on Ansari Colony World Aliria. No survivors found." The rest was unimportant detail.

"How - how many?..."

Radonov's dark face paled and he swayed on his feet.

"Chief, sit down." Jess jumped up and pulled out a chair.

"Sorry, Command. I thought I'd seen it all, but..."

Jess went to the converter and ordered two glasses of brandy. She set one at Radonov's elbow and took the other to her own seat.

Radonov raised his glass to his mouth in shaking hands and she saw his throat move as he swallowed. He set the glass down and looked up. "The last census figure for Aliria - thirty-five thousand." He closed his eyes and rubbed his hand over them. "Thirty-five thousand civilians. Defenseless. I've been on the lines five years, Command, and I've never seen anything like this."

"That's because this isn't war, Chief." The self-possessed, efficient comm chief seemed somehow very young and vulnerable. "It's terrorism. Soldiers don't attack unarmed civilians."

Jess sat back and took a long swallow, resisting the impulse to simply suck down the whole shot, and leaned back while she wondered how many of King K's complement were Ansari - how many had had relatives, friends on Aliria.

She looked up at Radonov. "Chief, can you check..."

"I've run personnel matches with our T.O.O.," he said, before she could finish. "We have fifty-seven Ansari, but only one who had immediate family on Aliria. Other family, friends - there's no way to tell."

He held out a data card and Jesse took it. "Julie Summerthorne. I don't think I know her."

"She's one of Command Two's weapons apprentices," Radonov said. "Not in CC this shift, thanks to the Many, because this report came across in clear and most of them had read it before I realized what it was. I told them to keep their mouths shut until you announce it."

Jesse nodded, rereading the data card. Julie was twenty-two, a graduate of university and Defense Command's weapons school. She'd been selected for the weapons post competitively, and since coming to King K had maintained high marks for efficiency and adaptability.

"She's one of the best of the kids," Radonov remarked. "She rotated through my section last month. She works hard and she learns fast, and whatever you throw at her, she makes the best of it."

"Very well," Jesse put the card down, feeling as though there was a heavy weight on her heart. "Send one of your apprentices to get her, if you would, Valery, and I'll get the rest of the command team here. She deserves to find out before everyone else does. And send someone for the chaplain - we're going to need her."

#

She was tall and thin, her dark red hair cut into short curls that tumbled around her head. The hazel eyes were wide as she walked into the command office, and they widened further as she looked around.

She may never have seen the command team together before, Jesse thought. *Well, most of the command team.* Ashe was late - in the shower, David had said.

"Sit down, Julie," Jesse said, gesturing to a chair. The girl complied, moving quickly around the table and seating herself with no fuss or wasted movement. Except for the wide eyes, she seemed calm and composed.

She has enough self-confidence not to think she's done anything wrong, and enough grasp on reality not to think she's come in for special commendation. That's good - she'll make a good soldier someday. If we can get her past this.

The door opened and Ashe slipped in. It slid shut behind him while he moved around to stand behind Julie's chair.

Did David tell him, or is he quick enough to know just from what he sees and Feels?

She pulled a chair over and sat down facing Julie, close enough to touch the girl if she reached out, not close enough to make her feel closed in. As if at a signal, the rest of the command team found chairs.

The wide eyes stayed wide, but Jesse saw Julie lick her lips, then tighten them, and the long fingers twined together and tightened on themselves. "Something bad has happened, hasn't it, Command?" Her voice was controlled, but there was a slight quiver at the end - she stopped and sank her teeth into her lips.

"I'm sorry, Julie. Yes, something bad has happened."

Ashe put his hands on Julie's shoulders, leaning forward a little to bring himself closer to her, and Jesse saw his usual bland expression replaced by one of fear - a reflection of what he was Feeling from Julie?

Jess didn't have time to wonder about that. The girl - she was barely more than a child by Promethean standards - was waiting.

"Julie, raiders attacked Aliria," Jesse said.

Julie sank back in her chair as though her bones were dissolving, and Ashe came around and dropped to his knees in front of her, taking her hands in his.

"My - my parents?" Her fingers had wrapped around Ashe's, even though her eyes stayed on Jesse. Their knuckles were white.

"I'm sorry," Jesse said. *God, why does this have to be so hard? I feel just as sick, just as ready to cry or scream, as I did the day Thom was killed.*

"Dad? Mom? The - the kids? All of them?"

"I'm sorry, Julie," Jesse said. "I think - they were all together."

The pretty face crumpled and she slid forward, to be enfolded in Ashe's arms. He wrapped them around her and pulled her to rest against him. "It's all right, Julie," he murmured. "It's all right. Let it come out, don't try to hold it in. It's all right."

I don't think it'll ever be all right again, Jesse thought, turning away. *Thirty-five thousand people.* She bit her lip, hard, to keep the sobs she could feel in her throat from coming up. "Mariko, you and Dr. Thassanios need to make yourselves available to the other Ansari crew members. If you'd be so kind as to go and talk to him now?"

The young Sensitive nodded and left.

"Do you want me to make the announcement, Jesse?" David asked.

She shook her head. "No, I can do it. The chaplain should be waiting for you - you and Zephron might see what you can do about a memorial service - we'll all need some consolation. James, perhaps you could help the Command Third take Julie back to her quarters and talk to her roommate?"

The redhead nodded. Ashe rose, holding Julie in his arms as though she was a little girl instead of a grown woman. "I can take her, James, but I'd appreciate your company." The girl was quiet, her face resting against his shoulder. He looked up at Jesse and, "I put her to sleep," he said, as if in answer to a question.

Alone in the office, Jesse paced back and forth a bit, delaying the inevitable. Then, straightening her tunic and running her hands through her hair, she touched the control. She pulled in a deep breath. "This is Command..."

#

"Chief, this is Command One. If anyone wants me, you'll need to send someone down to the dojo to get me."

"Roger that, Command."

Jess pulled the comm link from behind her ear and dropped it into the slot in her locker, reveling in the freedom of knowing she could only be reached in person.

A few minutes later, she sniffed hard, enjoying the gym/dojo's characteristic smell - wood, sweat, excitement - curled her right foot up into her groin, extended her left leg, and reached for her toes. She wrapped her hands around her foot and dropped her head to her leg, luxuriating in the stretch, the softness of the heavy gi against her skin, the knowledge that for the next hour, or two, there would be no demands except those she placed on herself.

I wonder if Ashe works out, she thought, then stifled the thought. She hadn't seen much of Jason Ashe, except in passing - she'd gone out of her way to avoid him. *I'm sure he does work out - he's so perfect, he wouldn't skimp on anything. His reports are marvels - prompt, clear, concise, and informative. Well, Thom was very responsible about administrative work, he just didn't make a fetish of it.*

She took a deep breath, changed legs, and put her head down on her right knee. *Don't think about Thom. Not now.* She wrapped her hands around her foot and let all the tension move into her fingers.

We haven't had a disaster. The bugs are minor. Someday, I hope, they'll get them all taken care of. And someday everything on this platform will work and we won't have to worry about the cleaning 'bots stealing people's books and possessions and forgetting to clear the dirty dishes.

Okay, Command, stop thinking about the job and concentrate on the training. She straightened her legs, stood, pulled her gi jacket straight, and took a deep breath.

#

"Command, you asked me to tell you not to skip lunch."

Jesse jumped and glanced at the wall clock. "Thanks, Mr. Ellis."

She made a note on the night log, initialed it, and threw the data card into the basket for her aide.

Lunchtime, Jesse. She pushed herself away from the desk and stood, bending forward and then back to ease her back and shoulders. She headed for the door, fastening her collar as she went, ignoring the piles of data cards and flimsies she was leaving behind her.

No sandwich at the desk today, Command. Get out and walk the hallways, see if you actually recognize anyone in this small city you're responsible for.

"Good afternoon, Command." The greeting followed her as she made her way along the busy corridor. She returned greetings, recognizing a few faces, wondering if her voice was going to last until she got to the lounge.

Who are all these people? You'd think by this time I'd know more of them. She dodged out of the way of a hurrying tech, acknowledging her apology, and slipped through the double doors.

There was Ashe, sitting by himself while the bustle of the lounge at lunchtime went on around him. *What's he doing here? If he's as Sensitive as they say, I'd think it'd bother him to have this many people around. I've never seen him eat before,* Jesse thought. *I almost believed he didn't eat.*

He wasn't eating. He had a cup of - something - on the table in front of him, and he was working his way through his notebook, making marks with his light stylus.

All right, Jesse, it's time you talked to him. He's your Third, he's been here a month, and you haven't even tried to get acquainted. Take advantage of the opportunity to get to know him. Remember, you promised Andranos you'd give him a chance. And you can't really reject him without a reason, she reminded herself.

He didn't look up as she moved toward him between the tables. David had told her Ashe could get so absorbed in what he was doing he forgot to pay attention to what was going on around him. When you combined that with the way Sensitives shielded themselves, you could sneak up behind him and hit him over the head before he ever knew you were there. Sometimes she'd wondered if it would be worth taking a chance to get rid of him.

Not fair, Jesse. All he's done to you is be efficient, personable, everything any Intuit dreams about in a Third, and so beautiful people turn in the corridors to watch him go by. In other words, all he's done wrong is be perfect.

And not Thom Isaacson. Sometimes, late at night, when she woke from one of those dreams where she could feel Thom's arms around her and then remembered he was dead, she wanted to hurt Ashe, just for being alive. It hadn't helped to find out the reason he'd been a month late reporting was that he'd been in the hospital, recovering from injuries suffered in the line of duty.

He still hadn't noticed Jesse. Sensitives didn't like to be looked at - Thom had told her it made them nervous - so she took advantage of the opportunity to look at him when he didn't know she was there. He was a beauty. White-blonde hair, just regulation length, falling around his head as though it was a little long. His features were strong - high cheekbones, well-defined jaw, determined chin - with none of the cragginess one expected of the ordinary human male. Fair skin, with barely a hint of color, and those eyes - people were calling him "sapphire eyes." He was thin, but he looked strong, broad-shouldered and compactly built. His hands were very beautiful - long and slender, the knuckles articulate but not knobby, fingers slim and active. In the time Jesse had worked with him, and lived in the triad quarters with him, she'd never seen his hands still. It was as though he was compelled to be always doing something.

"Hello, Command, I didn't see you come in." He looked up, smiling as though he was delighted to see Jesse. *I'll bet - I don't think you like me a bit more than I like you, Mr. Ashe.*

"That looks interesting," she said, nodding at the cup at his elbow. "May I join you?"

"By all means. I'd be delighted." He stood and pulled out a chair for her. Old-fashioned manners were taught at the Defense Command schools, but Ashe behaved as though he was born with them.

He put a cup of whatever he was drinking in front of her, and she tried a sip. The warmth was pleasant, but there was a bitter overtone that bit her tongue. She made a face and pushed the cup away.

"Here. Try a little sugar. It mellows the flavor and some people like it better that way."

"I don't think sugar will help this." Jesse pushed the cup toward him, watching for his reaction. He picked it up, smelled it, touched it to his lips. Then he grimaced, and shoved it toward the recycler. "Maintenance," he said, touching the comm pad.

"Sheehan." *Chief Sheehan answers Ashe himself?*

"Chief, you'd better have somebody check the food service. The mass converter just put chili oil in a cup of coffee."

"Shit," Chief Sheehan mumbled. "Yeah, thanks, Command. You should have seen what it did to the eggs this morning. When are you going to get to those control codes?"

The corner of Ashe's mouth turned up. "I'm working on them now, Chief. With luck, sometime tomorrow - but we're still going to have to fix all the cleaning 'bots."

"I know, I know," the Chief was still grumbling when his voice was cut off.

So that's what it is - coffee. The Sensitives' drug. Thom didn't like it - that explained why she didn't recognize it. And chili oil -

but she should have recognized that. *Not flying on all jets, Jesse?*

"Try this. It's better without the chili oil." She jerked her attention back to Ashe and realized he'd been watching her. *Turn about's fair play, Jesse. You were watching him.*

"Thanks." Jesse sipped again, and decided a little sweetness to mellow the flavor would be in order. She could see another reason why they drank it - just holding a warm cup in your hands could be quite - comforting. A tiny question about Thom niggled at her, but she pushed it away.

"So, how are you liking King K, Mr. Ashe? Are you all settled in?"

He grinned. "I think so, First, but I'm not sure. The cleaning 'bots keep cleaning my books away, but they've ignored my dirty clothes for almost a week."

Smug bastard. Why don't you clean up those codes, then you won't have anything to complain about? For that matter, why don't you pick up your dirty clothes yourself, you slob. "Are they still at that? I thought Maintenance had that all fixed," she said out loud. She took another sip of the coffee, and enjoyed the warmth in her system.

"Chief Sheehan tells me I'm thirty-seventh on the list. My turn comes up next week. There's a problem in the 'bots' logic circuits, and it has to be fixed by hand.

"David and I have been cleansing control codes as fast as we can, but some of the cleansing seems to be producing glitches of its own. We'd go faster if we could turn some of it over to the analysts, but the only people cleared to work with the system controllers on that level are us and James - and James is too busy with operations to help us."

"Mmm - but are we making progress?"

"Oh, yes. Little bit here, little bit there - you know how it goes. Meantime, I keep replacing my books, Maintenance keeps adjusting the logic circuits in the cleaning 'bots, and I think I have more room than I've ever had before."

His eyebrows and lashes were dark - Jesse wondered how that happened when his hair was so fair. "Really? I'd have thought you'd be used to triad quarters."

One eyebrow lifted a little, but his expression didn't change. "I'm afraid the triad quarters on attack craft aren't very spacious. And when I was teaching, I lived in the BOQ."

Dragon's breath! I'd forgotten about that. Nice, Jesse - put your foot in it again, why don't you?

"This is very pleasant," she said, changing the subject before she could get in any deeper. "Is it addictive?"

He shook his head. "Coffee contains caffeine. It's a mild stimulant. It's also what helps minimize headaches for Sensitives."

"It's unfortunate that your Talent carries that kind of price," she said. "I remember Thom having terrible headaches. I don't remember him taking anything for it, though." *See, I knew you weren't the man Thom was. He never complained, either.*

"Perhaps not," Ashe said. His voice was neutral. "So many things can interfere with the Talent. My father said he'd always found coffee helped without interfering, and recommended it to me when I started to have headaches."

You would bring your father into it, wouldn't you? Except, Jesse realized, she didn't know who his father was. That wasn't in his records. *I wonder why? I could ask David. And he'd tell me to ask Ashe, if I thought I needed to know.*

Ashe put two fingers on her wrist, the pale smooth skin standing out like a bracelet against the matte brown of Jesse's. His hand was warm - that surprised her, because the day he'd reported it had been cold.

Startled, Jesse looked up. *Sapphire eyes*, she thought, as his eyes widened, grew - it seemed she could see endless depths of blue...

It was like a door, opening in her - not exactly her head. He wasn't Touching her thoughts - Sensitives couldn't, she knew. He was absorbing feelings - things about her. She stiffened, and before she could pull away, she could Feel him. It was like tasting clear water running over green plants.

She blinked, and it was gone, and so was his hand on hers. He picked up his cup, and she could see his hand shaking before he caught her eye and put the cup down.

"Sorry. I took a liberty, Touching you without asking. I hope you'll forgive my rudeness."

"I've never known a Sensitive to do anything like that before. I didn't realize you could."

He smiled, that bright flash so like David's. "We usually don't, in circumstances like this," his gesture took in all the bustle of the lounge, "because it would be easy to be hurt. But that was a very shallow touch - sort of a way of saying hello. I thought it might be considered excusable in a partner."

Before Jesse could say anything else, one of the techs came up to the table and cleared her throat. "Excuse me, Command." Jesse nodded.

"Doctor Ngoro asked me to tell the Command Third that data he requested is spooling now."

Ashe acknowledged the information with a nod and a smile, and the girl turned away and joined a group of youngsters at another table.

"Ah, the sneaky devils behind Chief Sheehan's glitches are coming out. Duty calls," Ashe said, rising and gathering up his notebook and light stylus. "If you'll excuse me, First, I need to get back to work."

Jesse nodded, and he turned and left, handing his coffee cup to a cleaning 'bot as he passed it.

Arrogant bastard, she thought, watching the straight back as he made his way out of the room. *'Easy' - to do something that would scare most Sensitives spitless. 'Just a shallow touch.' 'Pardonable liberty.' 'A way of saying hello.'*

Suddenly reminded of what she'd come for, she ordered a salad. She never remembered eating it.

#

"Jason says the clean up of the command systems should be done in about a week," David said, looking down at his notebook. "He apologized for not being here, but he's in the middle of something that can't be interrupted."

Jesse waved a hand, made a mark on her list, took a swallow from the cup of hot tea beside her. "I sometimes wonder why, when they install a system in a new facility, it gets buggy."

"This one's been tremendously enhanced," David said. "And it was built in a hell of a hurry."

"Thank you." Jesse glanced up, noticed Zephron Bell's eyes on her, and bit back the sarcasm she heard echoing in her mind. *Don't take it out on him, Jesse. It isn't his fault the system's still buggy, and it isn't his fault he gets along with Ashe like the second half of a pair of gloves. Just concentrate on getting the job done.*

"Long-range scanner function is optimal as of this morning," the Operations Second, James McGowan said.

"Nav systems function is also optimal," said Mariko Itosu, Operations Third. "Mr. Radonov reports some fade on long-range comm, but we think that's more our distance from Center than a problem with the system. He's trying to enhance the receptors."

You'd think they'd have done that in the docks, Jesse thought. *They knew they were building a distant border fort.* "Combat readiness?" she asked.

"Last drill came up to ten seconds short of optimal activation time," Bell said. "Mr. Christiansen's enhancements to the training schedule are really starting to make a difference."

"Thanks," David muttered, without looking up from his notebook.

"Chief Sheehan reports that the last of the cleaning 'bot problems has been fixed, and they're developing a schedule for routine maintenance."

"Excellent," Jesse said. "I don't know which I hated more - coming back to quarters and discovering the 'bots had undecorated the place, or listening to the complaints from everybody else. Scouts and secondaries?"

"*Spider* and *Mantis* are at optimal readiness, with crews on standby through all shifts. *Scorpion*'s been on station since day before yesterday, *Tarantula* will establish her perimeter during the night shift tonight, and *Black Widow* should reach position day after tomorrow," David said, making a note and putting his light pen down. "James and I will go out next week and make a tour of inspection."

"ETA?"

"On schedule," Zephron Bell reported, waving a hand to display crossed fingers.

"Anything else, people?" Jesse looked around the big table and received a series of headshakes. "Good. I declare this staff meeting over. Go forth and instill terror and efficiency in the hearts of your subordinates."

There were chuckles and grins as the senior staff gathered their belongings and headed for the door.

"I do okay in the 'instilling efficiency' department," Mariko Itosu said, "but somehow the terror just never happens."

"That's okay," Zephron Bell said, motioning her through the door ahead of him. "I'm good at the terror, less so at the efficiency. We're a good team."

"Well, I'm glad they're getting along," Jesse muttered.

"Something wrong?" David came around the table and began massaging her shoulders, the long fingers manipulating muscles Jesse hadn't realized were tense.

"No, nothing. I was just thinking out loud. How are you and Ashe getting along?"

His voice was level, but his fingers tightened. "Fine. He's a superb officer. We're working together very well."

"Good. I'm glad to hear it, David. Thank you."

His hands fell away. "I'd better get back to work before somebody notices I'm not there. Some of the youngsters do fine as long as somebody's watching them, but if you leave them alone too long, they fall to pieces," and he left.

I'm glad you like Ashe, David, because I don't. I don't like him at all, and the longer I know him, the less I want him around. He's nearly perfect, and perfect people make my teeth ache.

#

"Dragon's breath!" Jesse swam up out of the fog of sleep and pushed aside the blankets. "All right, all right, I'm coming. Shut off that cursed noise, will you?" She slapped the telltale on the bedside table to indicate she'd heard the alarm and was responding.

"Tell me again why we're doing this at night," she demanded as she walked into the command systems hub.

"Because there's less going on that could be disrupted," David replied. "And it was your idea."

"You would have to remind me of that, wouldn't you?"

"Okay, I think we're ready," Ashe announced, snapping his notebook closed and slipping it into the fold of his tunic.

Is he so focused he wasn't even paying attention to us?

"Ready here," David said, glancing at the array in front of him.

"Ready here," Jesse said, starting the recorder.

Ashe pulled his mike down and murmured a command.

He's smooth, Jesse thought, watching as the panels began to light up with information - system functions, energy outputs, information through-puts...

It was like being caught by the edge of a bolt of lightning. Jesse fell back and stumbled against the edge of one of the tables that lined the room. She blinked, trying to stop the flashing colors behind her eyes. Her right hand was numb and tingling, as though she'd taken an electrical discharge.

"Jesse, help me," David demanded.

"What happened?" She shook her head, pushed herself upright, and staggered over to where David was kneeling over Ashe.

"I don't know, and right now, I don't give a damn. Jason,

wake up," he shook the Sensitive, slapped the pale face. "Keep trying to wake him up," David said.

Jesse put her hands on Ashe's shoulders and rocked him. "Wake up, Ashe, come back." His body was limp under her hands. His eyelids fluttered and she could see his eyes had rolled back in his head. "Come on, Ashe," she muttered. "Wake up."

David came back and knelt across from her. "Come on, Jason." He broke a small capsule and waved it under Ashe's nose. She caught a faint whiff of something sharp and aromatic, then David crushed another capsule under her nose and she choked on the fumes and felt her head clearing.

"By the One! What was that?"

"An aromatic mixture of herbal stimulants," David replied. "The original combination's used a lot on Sylvanus - this is a variation of the formula Thassanios made up. It's in every emergency kit on the base."

"Well, it works," Jesse said, using the tissue he handed her to wipe her streaming eyes and nose. "I haven't been this awake for days. And Ashe is stirring." She pushed herself to her feet. "You tend to him and I'll see if I can make anything of this."

All the readouts were normal, the steady pulse of King K's 'night,' when experiments were damped down, most people slept, and only a skeleton crew, mostly nocturnal Anharzi, were awake and functional. *The ideal time for system tests.* She keyed the logs for the last hour - no changes, no alarms, no bogies. No abnormal readings anywhere but in this room. *What in the name of the Void happened?*

"Jason, are you all right?"

She turned back to see Ashe with his eyes open, one hand scrabbling behind him as he tried to push himself up.

"Sorry," Ashe murmured, slipping and wincing as his hand slid a little on the polished floor. "What happened?"

David pulled him to his feet, then guided him to one of the chairs. "Do you need me to get you something?"

The Sensitive sat up, pressing his fingers to his temples as though they hurt. "No. Or maybe - help me back to our rooms and get me a pot of coffee."

David raised an eyebrow to Jesse and she nodded. "I'll get him back. Did you find anything?"

Jesse shook her head. "Not yet. No alarms, no irregularities. Whatever it was was confined to this room. I'll finish checking this out, make sure nothing's going to backfire on us and meet you in a few minutes."

David nodded and turned away, his arm around Ashe's waist, the blonde man's arm draped across his shoulders. "We'll be fine."

I wonder. She watched them make their way across the room and through the door, then turned back to continue her investigation.

The recorder showed all systems normal, the control functions being tested coming online just as they should. Then, two minutes into the test, recording stopped, with no indicators of coming problems. No help there.

She turned to other systems. No indicators, no alarms.

Okay, it's got to be something in the hardware. Pulling in a deep breath and letting it out, Jesse opened the panel below the control console.

Two hours later, sweaty, tired, and thoroughly irritated, Jesse finished fusing the last of the circuits that had shorted out and put the access panel back. An array of control crystals decorated the floor behind her - a couple showed peripheral damage; the others looked fine.

To the naked eye. And when I get my hands on whoever did this - she refused to let the image of Jason Ashe's long, clever fingers stay in her mind - *I'll take them apart, limb from limb. If we'd done this test in CC instead of the hub we could have fused enough of the circuits to cause a cascade failure in the control systems.* She gathered up the crystals and slid them into a carrier pack, then headed back to the triad quarters.

As she came in, David's head appeared over the back of one of the couches. "I was beginning to think you weren't coming back."

"Yes, well, sorry I interrupted your nap, David." *You could have come and helped.*

"Sorry," David said, responding to what Jesse hadn't said. "Jason decided I'd taken part of that hit and put me to sleep. I woke up about two minutes ago, and I'd just realized how long it had been when you walked in."

"Oh. Where's Ashe? Gone to bed?"

"Gone down to the systems lab to work on some kind of failsafe. Listen, you look worn out, and I know I am. If there's nothing that requires us to work on it tonight, why don't we both get some sleep, and work through this with Jason and Zeph and the kids in the morning?"

Good idea, Jesse thought, setting the carrier case on her desk and wandering into the bedroom. *Maybe in the morning I won't be tempted to strangle Jason Ashe just for being alive.*

#

Zephron Bell put the largest of the crystals under the magnifier and switched it on. He scanned it for some moments, then switched off the magnifier and sat back. "Whoever did that had a very nasty mind and some idea of how control crystals work. Jase, have you looked at this?"

Jesse sat back, content for the moment to let Zephron take the lead. A few hours' sleep had done wonders for her thinking processes, but nothing for her desire to strangle Jason Ashe. Just looking at him sitting down the table from her made her fingers itch.

The Sensitive shook his head. There were dark shadows under his eyes and on his eyelids, and there was no color in his face.

"Here, take a look." Bell slid the magnifier down the table.

Ashe looked at the large crystal, then pulled it out of the holder and slid one of the others in. One by one he scanned the six crystals Jesse had pulled from the control hub, then sighed and pushed magnifier and crystals to David.

"If I didn't know better, I'd almost think I'd done it," he said. "It took a fair amount of knowledge and skill to cut those circuits without doing the sort of damage that would cause the crystal to fail when it was inserted into the board."

"I take it you didn't do it," Jesse kept her tone light, but Ashe looked over and responded as though the question was serious - as it had been. "No, I did not. None of us has a motive for doing anything that stupid and dangerous. If we want out, all we have to do is tell HQ we want out.

"Whoever did this," he lifted the largest crystal and held it where the light passed through it, "was trying to cause a cascade system failure that could have left us drifting out of control. He glanced from Zephron to Jesse, then looked over at David. "I think it's about time we stop ignoring the evidence that's been shoved in our faces and admit we have a saboteur on this base."

"Are you sure..." James stopped and cleared his throat, glancing around the table as though to make sure no one else had priority. "Are you sure it couldn't have been done in the manufacturing process? Maybe the crystals were damaged when we got them."

David shook his head. "Sorry, James, Jason's right. Those crystals came in a sealed carrier. I broke the seal, checked them microscopically, and re-sealed them. It was done here."

You're right, David, Jesse thought, ignoring the back and forth of argument and planning that was going on in the command office. *I've been wondering how long it was going to take before someone else had the same idea. New base, new crew, new command structure – any terrorist would find it a temptation. And this is the third mobile command platform they've sent into this sector. We expected problems.*

"How long?" The others stopped talking and turned to her.

"What, Command?"

"How long will it take to repair these? Do we have backups? This system isn't vital now, while we're in transport, but once we get on station, we can't do without it for long. So, how long?"

Ashe pulled his notebook out of the fold of his tunic and tapped it with his light stylus. He studied the data it had given him for a few moments, then looked up. "No, Command, we don't have backups. They're expensive and hard to grow, and sensitive enough that MI doesn't want spare sets around that someone might steal. We do have crystals growing, but it'll be at least a month before any are mature enough to etch. And it'll take me at least a month to etch them." He made an entry in the notebook and closed it.

"And we can't have a transport bring us a set?" Zephron asked.

"We could try, but with the situation in Sector 20 I'm not sure HQ would release them. And that would take almost as long as it will to grow them here and do the etching."

"I suppose no one else can do the etching?" Jesse asked.

"Right now, no," his voice was smooth and even, as though he hadn't heard the edge in Jesse's. "I'll start teaching Mari the process with this batch."

"Very well. First, do you have anything else?"

Zephron shook his head. "Not right now, Command."

"Then let's take this up again at a later date. Right now, I think we all need to get back to work."

Jesse filed out with the rest, heading back to her office. *I'm still not certain I want Ashe. Perhaps he's too good – he's too sensitive, too intelligent, too perceptive, too quick on his feet. Too quick to catch all the reactions I'd rather slipped by him. I always feel as though he's about to surprise me in a feeling I don't want him to Touch.*

-Chapter 3-

*Death lies upon her like an untimely frost
Upon the sweetest flower of all the field.
William Shakespeare, Romeo and Juliet*

Jesse looked at the menu, then closed it and ordered what she always did - toast, juice, hot tea. *I don't know why you bother looking, Jesse,* she thought. This time in the morning, even the sight of anything else gagged her.

She glanced around the quiet lounge, populated mostly by youngsters stoking up for their classes or shifts, and marveled. *Even when I was that age I couldn't eat that much. They make me feel old. They all seem so young - what are their parents thinking, letting them leave home so early?*

A noise recalled her from her thoughts, and she turned to see what was going on. At first, she thought the boy was clowning for his friends, but the horrible choking increased. When his face turned blue and he dropped to the floor, Jesse realized whatever was happening was real.

"Stand back, give him room to breathe," she ordered, kneeling beside the now convulsing boy. "You, call the medics. Tell them it's critical, we need them stat, it looks like some kind of allergic reaction. You, and you - move this stuff out of the way and grab his plate and cup for the labs." One of the girls knelt at his head, trying to cushion it as his body thrashed. *Clear the airway, get him breathing again*, Jesse thought, struggling to wedge her thumb into the corner of his jaw to open his mouth. His lips parted and blood ran down over his face and her hands - he'd bitten his tongue. She wiped as much blood from his mouth with her sleeve as she could, then began artificial respiration.

As she followed the stretcher to the infirmary, she felt useless and in the way, but she needed to know what had happened.

#

The usual hospital quiet had disappeared into a cacophony of medics barking commands, techs running to and fro, alarms ringing.

For what seemed like the next three days, Jesse helped lift

people from stretchers to beds, hold them while the medics sedated them, cover sweat-soaked, trembling bodies with sheets and blankets. She felt sweat soaking her clothes, her limbs trembling, but forced herself to keep going.

"Jason, no!"

There was a scuffle behind her. In the center of the floor, several medics and David - *David? What's David doing here?* were huddled around two still figures. As Jesse watched, her mind as numb as her body, a group rose, lifted one, and moved away. That left David, the chief medic, Nick Thassanios, and one of the techs kneeling around a long, still body. *Ashe?*

She moved closer, trying to hear what they were saying.

"Jason, come back. Hear me, Jason, I'm calling you. Come back." It was almost a litany, and as he spoke, David shook the slim shoulders, and once slapped Ashe's face. "Jason, come back," he demanded. Behind and around him, the medic was doing things with injectors – probably stimulants, Jesse realized.

Finally, the blond man's eyelids fluttered and opened. The dark blue eyes were cloudy. David shook him again and said something Jesse couldn't hear. Ashe responded, and the corner of David's mouth lifted. He said something else, again too soft for Jesse to hear.

As though it was very heavy, Ashe's hand lifted and touched David's cheek. He murmured something, and Jesse heard David respond, "always."

One of the medics came up to her then with a question, and she turned away. The room kept turning, and the next thing she knew she was looking up at the ceiling.

"Command? Can you hear me?"

"What happened?"

A face interposed itself between her and the ceiling - Nick Thassanios, the head of the medical section. He put two fingers on Jesse's throat and held them there briefly, then backed away and ran a medical scanner down her body.

"You've got blood around your lips, Command. Did you bite your tongue when you fell?"

Jesse ran her tongue behind her teeth, then lifted her fingers to her mouth. "No. It must be – that boy who was choking – he bit his tongue."

"Well, at least you haven't added an unknown factor to the problem," he said. The injector was cold against her neck. "This will make you drowsy. Go ahead and sleep." The word was more command than permission, and before Jesse could ask again what had happened, she slid down into the comforting darkness.

#

The bed under her didn't feel familiar, and she could hear voices murmuring in the background. She opened her eyes without moving, and looked up in dim blue light at a ceiling of grids of acoustical tiles. There were green, gauzy curtains around the place where she lay, and somewhere behind her and over her head there was a soft, regular beep.

Where the hell am I? Jesse thought, returning to full consciousness. She pushed herself up on her elbows, surprised to feel shaky, and an alarm began beeping as she dislodged the contact of the IV infuser that had been positioned over her left arm.

An hour later, clean, damp, and still a little wobbly, Jesse walked into CC.

"Command. I didn't expect you so soon," Zephron Bell exclaimed.

"First," she acknowledged. "May we consult?"

Bell nodded, and Jesse saw him expel a long breath. "Second, CC is yours," Bell said. James McGowan nodded without looking up from the console he was monitoring. "I have it, First."

"All right, Zephron, start at the beginning and tell me everything you know. Assume I don't know anything." *You won't be far wrong.*

Zephron ran a hand over his well-trimmed black beard. There were deep lines around his mouth. "Well, this isn't the beginning, but - that boy you resuscitated died about ten minutes ago."

"Oh, God," Jesse whispered. She dropped her head into her hands and let the darkness wash over her mind for a few moments. "I can't remember his name," she said, raising her head.

"Ali Nagani Raschid. You remember, he's the boy who got thrown into the pit wall in CC the day the Command Third reported in." Bell moved behind Jesse and she heard the soft gurgle of liquid from the mass converter outlet. He put a glass of brandy in front of her, seated himself across the table, and took a sip from his own glass.

Jesse shook her head. "We were calling him, trying to get him to respond to us, and it didn't even register." She straightened, trying to get herself thinking again. "Please, tell me he's the only one."

Bell shook his head. "Two others, so far. I'm keeping my fingers crossed, but several other people are critical and it's too soon to relax."

"This wasn't natural, Zephron," Jesse said. "We have to find out what it was and who did it - and how."

"I can tell you what and how. The alarms in the lounge were suppressed manually and this stuff - the lab can give you the formula - was introduced through the converter's injector system." Bell fingered the Defense Command shield in the lobe of his right ear.

"Chief Sheehan's people are taking the converter systems apart to sterilize them and purge the contaminants, and I've assigned most of the Security section and the apprentices to help transport people to the Infirmary and to their quarters. And I assigned a team to go through the residential areas and make sure no one got sick and couldn't call for help."

"Good thinking," Jesse said. "What about Control and Command Systems?"

"As far as James and I can tell, they weren't affected. Whoever it was physically interfered with the injectors, but this time he didn't get into the control systems. I had Valery message the outriders, but whatever it was, it was restricted to us."

Like all the other bugs, Jesse thought. *It's being done in real time, and whoever's doing it is right here. Dragon's breath!*

"We'll have to rearrange the duty rosters, and run some sections short-staffed for a while," Bell said. "I hate to say this, but - well, look at this list."

Jesse took the data card he handed her and read the list of names. "Youngsters."

"Yes. I didn't talk to the docs - they're busy - and all the lab had was a preliminary, but it looks to me as though this is something that mostly targets younger people. I've been thanking the Gods of Space all morning that Mariko and James usually have breakfast in our quarters."

Jesse shuddered and gritted her teeth to control the spasm of nausea that suddenly gripped her from the lower gut to the back of her mouth.

"Command, are you all right? You just went pale."

"I..." she ran her hand over her forehead. It came away wet.

"You shouldn't even be here. The docs told me you got some of it trying to revive Ali. Let me take you back to quarters. The kids and I can take care of things the rest of today."

She shook her head and tried to straighten, but the nausea hit her again and she doubled over.

#

When she woke, she was in her own bed, and the clock told her it was late into the night watches. She felt calm, clearheaded - and weak. *Not surprising, Jesse. No food today, and a bout with - whatever it was. And since it's 0300 and nobody's called or come, either the situation's under control, in which case you don't need to do anything, or hopelessly compromised, in which case nothing you could do at this point would remedy it.* She made sure the alarm was set for 0630 and went back to sleep.

#

"By the One!" Jesse exclaimed, before she could stop herself. "If I ever get my hands on the monster who caused this, I'll rend him limb from limb." It was good, even for a few moments, to feel angry. Anger pushed out the sorrow, the aching sense of failure, the fear she didn't even want to admit to.

I'm glad I got a good night's sleep, she thought. *I almost wish I hadn't gotten up.* She dropped the lab reports on the long table in the command office.

"Tell me again, Zephron, slowly."

Zephron Bell ran his hand over his beard and picked up the data card again. The dark eyes were shadowed and the line from his nose to his mouth had deepened. *He didn't sleep last night, while I was dead to the world.*

"Five dead - Ali Raschid, Julie Summerthorne..."

Jesse felt her gut clench at the thought of the tall, redhaired girl with the pale, pretty face and hazel eyes. The long white fingers would never again fly over a weapons console, and no one would look into the wide eyes and tell her she was beautiful and loved. *Why? Why is it always our children?*

"...Nagiv Engebbi, Alkhanil, Ha-Ti Ki-Tzung. Fifty so ill they're still in the infirmary, although the medics tell me they don't anticipate any further deaths, thanks in large part to Jason. Seventy-five who were treated and released to their quarters. And we don't know how many people got just a little sick and went about their business."

"I don't understand why, if it was a toxin, it didn't affect everyone who got it the same way."

He handed her the lab report. Her vision was blurring, making the letters crawl and twist behind the surface of the card. She blinked, rubbed her eyes, and forced herself to bring the words into focus. "Pseudo-organic? Targeted?" The words blurred again and she handed the card back to Bell. "I'm sorry, Zephron, I'm not focusing too well. Explain it to me."

"A pseudo-organic toxin, something like a virus, targeted at younger systems. In other words, like a virus, different individual systems reacted to it differently."

Jesse nodded, not trying to conceal the exhaustion and nausea she was feeling. *Children, she was thinking. He killed our children. He deliberately set something loose that would hurt our children.*

"Okay, Zephron, I've got it from here. You go get some rest and spend some time with your partners, and I'll see you tomorrow."

The big man blinked, then nodded and rose. "Thanks, Command."

He was barely out the door before it opened again to admit the maintenance chief. She'd always thought the little man resembled the legendary leprechauns of Earth, but today he was a picture of sorrow and anger.

The thin fingers holding the data card he carried trembled. "See here, Command? All it would have taken was a little syringe, and that would have dissolved in the recycler," Chief Sheehan said.

"And the culture?"

"Ask the biotechs to be sure, but I think it could have been freeze dried and condensed, which means it could have been in a capsule that would fit under an earring," the maintenance chief said, shaking his head.

"So there's nothing in either what it was or how it was introduced into the system to tell us who might have done it?"

"Nothing at all," Sheehan said.

"Thanks, Chief," Jesse said, putting a hand on Sheehan's thin shoulder. "I'll keep looking."

"Good luck, Command. We have to catch the bastard, but he hasn't put a foot wrong so far."

The chief had gone and Jesse was glancing at the daily logs when it hit her - "he hasn't put a foot wrong so far." *He hadn't till now, Chief. But he went after our kids, and that means I'll get him if it's the last thing I do.*

She sighed, pulled a flimsy toward her, and started rearranging the duty roster. *And speaking of duty, where are my partners?*

"CC, do you know where the Command Second is?"

"Right here. Sorry I'm late - I must have forgotten to set my alarm last night." The door slid shut behind David and he moved over to the table.

"And the Command Third? Did he forget to set his alarm, too?"

The steel-grey eyes lightened a little, and the look he gave her could have ignited rocket fuel. "Jason is in bed, I hope, asleep. He exhausted himself yesterday, fighting to keep those kids alive, and we nearly lost him with Julie. He is, by doctor's orders, off duty today and probably tomorrow."

Jesse raised an eyebrow, but when David didn't answer the implied question, decided to let it rest. *For now. I'll find out soon enough. Right now other things are more important.*

"All right," David said, "I assume we need to rearrange duty rosters."

Jesse nodded. "Among other things. One of the other things is arranging a memorial service."

David flinched, as though she'd hit him. "I think that was one of the things I was trying to forget."

"I wish I could."

"It's okay," he said. "I'll meet with the chaplain when we're finished here."

At least I can offload the notifications to Quadrant HQ onto the Comm Officer, Jesse thought. There was a standard form for transmission.

They worked for the next several hours, passing flimsies back and forth, seldom exchanging more than a word or two.

No more deaths. It was some small consolation, although the least ill of the affected youngsters - they were all apprentices, the oldest twenty-three - wouldn't be fit to return to duty for at least a week. Rearranging the schedule to cover the gaps was the least difficult task in this long dreary day, and Jesse almost wished it had taken longer, to put off the others.

"Jesse, do you want me to write the letters? Or have Dorothea do it? I know she wouldn't mind." She hadn't realized David had come over to her.

"No, thanks, David. You and Dorothea'll have enough to do with the memorial service, and when Ashe is recovered, he and Zephron'll be busy putting together an investigation." She'd been reluctant to relinquish her suspicions, but discussions with the engineers and the medics had removed Ashe from any suspicion of wrongdoing. He'd been up early, been met at the triad quarters door by one of the night staff with questions and accompanied to the labs; and he'd stayed there with his staff until he'd been called to the infirmary.

Of the people who comprised the complement of *King Kamehameha*, Jason Ashe was one of the few who couldn't have put the toxin in the lounge injectors. Jesse wondered again if he ever ate or slept, then dismissed it from her mind. Other things were more important. She didn't allow the question of why she'd automatically suspected Ashe to enter her conscious thoughts.

With a sigh, she pulled a light stylus and a flimsy toward her and called up the first youngster's record.

The last schedule adjusted, the last letter written, the last report initialed, Jesse threw her light stylus into the desk drawer, piled the day's flimsies into the recycler, and rose. *By the One. I am so tired - I could go to bed and sleep for a week.*

"Get something to eat and go to bed, Jesse. It's been a long day, and I'm afraid tomorrow isn't going to be any shorter."

Eat. Right now, I'm not sure I ever want to eat again, however safe the converters are supposed to be.

"David," she said, before he reached the door, "what were you and Ashe doing in the Infirmary? Zephron said something about, 'it would have been a lot more if it hadn't been for Jason,' and I don't know what he meant."

"He meant we were lucky, Jess. It would have been a lot worse without Jason and Mari. And we came very close to losing the Command Third."

"Explain, please," Jesse said.

David shrugged and complied. "Delores Roberts called us - Jason, me, and Mari. By the time we got there, they had ten people in convulsions and the security people and students seemed to be bringing them in in batches. I helped move people around, set up IVs, draw blood, hold people to keep them from hurting themselves. What Jason and Mari were doing was Healing - pulling the pain away, calming people - and in Jason's case, maintaining people who were in danger of dying until the medics got them stabilized."

At Jesse's lifted eyebrow, the corner of his mouth turned up. "You didn't know a Healer could do that? I understand most can't - they aren't strong enough. Jason can, and he did, and Nick Thassanios thinks there are ten people sleeping in that infirmary tonight instead of cold in the stasis chambers because of him.

"There's another reason most Healers can't - or won't - try what Jason was doing. If they hold on too long and the person dies, they can go, too. We didn't realize Julie was dying. By the time we did, she was gone, and he was well on the way to going with her. A minute more, and he would have."

Jesse shook her head, not sure if it was disbelief or wonder she was feeling. *He's right, I've never heard of a Sensitive, or a Healer, doing anything like that.*

"I'd still suggest you get something to eat, but at least get some rest, and I'll see you tomorrow." He started toward the door again.

"Where are you going?"

"I," David said, palming the control plate, "am going to get stinking drunk."

Jesse stood, gnawing at her knuckles, until the room's echoing silence called her back from the dark place her thoughts were leading. *This won't do at all*, she told herself. *Do something, don't just stand here.*

Workout? She was too tired. Food? The idea nauseated her. Get drunk like David? For a moment that sounded attractive, then she remembered she was on duty in the morning. The forgetting might be alright, but the aftermath was hell. *Not worth it*, she decided.

Hot shower and bed - and on that thought, she wheeled and headed for her quarters.

She hadn't realized how tired she was until the door of her room shut behind her. She pulled her clothes off, for once forgetting the discipline of neatness and letting them lay where they fell, stumbled into the shower and stood under the hot water until she was almost asleep, and slid into bed, glad to sink into the pillow and drift off.

Voices woke her. Thinking something was wrong, she threw back the covers and slid out of bed, grabbing her robe as she headed for the door of her study.

The door slid open and she started into the living room, ready to respond to an emergency, then checked herself and pulled back. David and the junior Pilot, Yuri Kelman, were staggering across the living room, David's arm draped across Kelman's shoulders, the younger man's arm around her Second's waist. What she'd heard had been a collision with one of the couches.

Jesse pulled farther back, shaking her head. For some reason she didn't want Kelman to realize she was awake. *He always seems to be around when things are going wrong.* She waited a few moments, until she heard the living room door open and close again, then went to check on David.

There was a night light in his study, and she noted, in passing, the usual profusion of papers on his desk, the guitar lying on the couch, the flute on the coffee table. She paused before touching the control, then put her hand against it, the other hand on the door to allow it to barely open.

A harsh sob shattered the silence, and Jesse pulled her hand away and stepped back, letting the door close. Gathering her robe around her, she hurried to her room and climbed into bed. "He doesn't need me hovering over him, making it worse," she muttered, pulling the covers up to her chin. "I just hope he gets some sleep tonight."

Tired as she was, she expected it to take her hours to get back to sleep, but the strain of the last two days won - before she could roll over, she was gone.

#

"Dragon's breath," Jesse muttered, rolling over to touch the alarm control in her bedside table. "If this is the way I feel going to bed cold sober, I'm glad I didn't get drunk last night."

She ached all over, worse than she had the night after her last dan level test, and her head felt as though it was full of pre-digested carbon mass. She staggered through the room, swearing when she stumbled on the boots she'd left where they'd fallen the night before, and precipitated herself into the shower while the water was still barely warm.

Dry and refreshed, Jesse checked the time as she pulled a comb through her short hair. Still early - plenty of time to work out. She stretched, pulling her rib cage up. *That's exactly what I need. A workout will get the oxygen going, clear my head, and get me ready to face this day. And a workout will help me forget for a while.*

#

I was right, we did present a temptation to a saboteur. She bowed, took a deep breath, and began the movements of the kata, concentrating on precision and focus.

The creature who did this didn't care how many it killed or injured. It has to be a Tragan. No civilized being kills so indiscriminately, even in war. But how did a Tragan agent get on a Command Platform? And who is it?

I'm still not sure David is right that my suspicions of Ashe are unworthy, but - he doesn't need to impress anyone, and he came too close to dying for all this to be just a sham. She pushed her fist forward against the resistance of every muscle in her body, sweat streaming down her face and making her hands clammy.

No wonder the man seems arrogant. His idea of just doing his job would petrify many people we think of as heroes. He's everything any Intuit dreams of in a Third, and the better he is, the more he shows himself to be the ideal partner, the less I want him.

What's wrong with me?

"Stop, Jesse," she told herself. "Concentrate. Focus. Let the rest of it slip away."

#

"Oh, God! Next time I do that, kill me before I wake up, will you?" David's eyes were puffy and his cheekbones looked bruised, but despite his groans, he appeared otherwise healthy.

"Why, David? To absolve you from the just punishment for stupidity?" Jesse pitched her voice a bare tone higher than normal, taking malicious pleasure in the way he winced.

"Well, you could consider that you were preventing me from setting the apprentices a bad example," he muttered, swallowing a couple of pills with a glass of juice and following it with a large glass of milk. He looked at Jesse's toast and fruit and shuddered.

"Did it help?"

He glanced over and shook his head. "Did you think it would?"

"No. That's why I didn't join you. I hope you at least slept."

"If you can call it sleeping," David muttered, and Jesse decided he'd been punished enough. Getting through today was going to be, if not worse, at least as bad as yesterday had been.

#

The launch bay was crowded - almost everyone who was off-duty and capable had decided to attend the memorial service in person. Jesse listened with her head bowed as David's rich baritone floated over the crowd, amplified by the comm system that carried it through King K's rooms and corridors.

Most of the youngsters had filled in the disposition form with the standard permissions and left it at that, convinced as young creatures always are that death was hardly possible, but Julie Summerthorne's friends had requested that David sing. "She loved Mr. Christiansen's voice - she said it reminded her of her father's," one of the girls said. "I know it would mean a lot to her - and to all of us - if he'd sing for her - for them."

The old song ended and David stepped back. His voice had been strong and true and beautiful to the end - Jesse hoped hers would last. She swallowed, twice, to push down the tears she could feel welling up in her throat, and stepped to the comm pickup to perform her role in the simple service.

"We remember our fallen, by ancient custom, without rank or title, returning them to the universe, as we will all return, as warriors of Prometheus, defenders of the Light.

"Ali Nagani Raschid." She nodded to the solemn youngster who stood at the head of the casket, draped with the flag of the Lyran Hegemony. He gave a soft command, and the six youngsters aligned along the sides lifted the flag as he laid his palm on the fire control. The slim black tube slid along the track until it was encompassed by the ram, and with a rush of compression, launched toward the nearest star.

"Ha-Ti Ki-Tzung." The flag draped on this casket carried the elaborate sigil of the Divine Empire of Duvarei.

"Alkhanil." The night black flag with its single eye for the mysterious nocturnal people other Prometheans called Anharzi lifted and the glossy tube slipped down the launch chute.

"Nagiv Engebbi." A yellow sun circled by nine satellites, the symbol of the Solaran Alliance.

"Julie Summerthorne."

Someone in the bay gasped and was hushed.

Jesse raised her eyes from the flimsy and realized it was Ashe who stood at the head of this casket, draped in the blood-red that was the Ansari symbol of death. Instead of the conventional dress uniform, he and the six youngsters serving as pallbearers wore the crimson formality of Ansari silks, and he held a knife in his hand, the water-blue of the rippled gemstone blade winking in the overhead lights. Ashe lifted his left hand so the loose sleeve fell back and slashed at his palm. The blood ran, gathered, fell onto the sleek black shell. He murmured something, and was echoed by the youngsters who lifted the shroud as he touched the fire control.

"We bless her with the blood of the living, whose life and honor have been enriched and strengthened by her presence among us. May she be gathered into the arms of the Creator," David murmured close to her, and she realized he was translating what Ashe had said.

"We return them to the fire of beginning," Jesse said, struggling to keep her voice even and clear, "young warriors who went into death never knowing defeat, and commend them to the care of the Universe which bore us all."

In the silence that followed, a sleeve brushed hers as David pushed past her and reached Ashe's side in time to support the blonde man as he staggered. As the two turned away, Jesse could see the tracks of tears on the Sensitive's face.

-Chapter 4-
I would a tale unfold...
William Shakespeare—Macbeth

"I can't help it, David. He's too - too..."

"Too not Thom? That's what's wrong with everyone, isn't it? We're all too 'not Thom.'"

Jesse glared, but David ignored her, scooping perfect white rounds from the center of the nilla fruit he held in his right hand and popping them into his mouth. It was infuriating, and she was tempted to shove the fruit into his face. Realizing her hands were fisted and her teeth were clenched, Jesse forced her hands open and relaxed her jaw.

"Too perfect. Nobody real can be that perfect." She dropped the spoon into her cereal bowl and stood, gathering her dishes to take to the recycler. "He never makes mistakes, he never eats, he never sleeps, he never makes jokes, he never loses his temper, he never laughs. He seems to have no human weaknesses, and I don't trust him."

She dumped the dishes in the recycler, wiped her hands and pitched the sanitizing wipe, then turned back to the table. David was sitting, the shell of the nilla fruit in his hand, staring into the middle distance.

I got through to him, Jesse thought.

"I know he never laughs," David whispered. "He used to. His laugh could make the whole day bright." He shook his head and put the fruit down. "He sleeps, but I don't think well. He eats, but not enough. He would tell you that he's clumsy, he makes mistakes all the time, he works very hard to control his temper, and the reason he doesn't laugh at jokes is that he's too dense to get them. He is real, Jesse, and he's human, and he can be hurt. You should have realized that when you saw what the memorial service did to him."

Jesse remembered the way Ashe had staggered, the way David had caught and supported him, the tracks of tears on his face. *So he grieved for the youngsters who were killed. Who among us didn't?*

"He acts as though he's walking on eggs around me."

The dishes clattered as David dumped them in the recycler and wiped his hands. "Damn it, Jesse, almost the first thing he said to me was, 'she doesn't want me here, does she?' He's afraid of you! He's driving himself into the ground trying to please you, and you're barely civil to him." David coughed, reddened, and turned away.

It was like being slapped. *Ashe is afraid of me? Why?* "Why didn't you tell me?"

"You wouldn't listen. You've been so busy trying to find reasons to dislike Jason, you couldn't see or hear anything else. A triad is supposed to be a partnership, Jesse. But you aren't treating either of us like partners. So ask yourself - are you trying to sink us?"

The back of her mouth tasted sour and her gut was churning. Jesse swallowed, concentrating on pushing the nausea down, and straightened her back. "No. I don't know, David. But I don't want Ashe making himself sick, for the sake of our people if nothing else. So help me - tell me what to do."

"Get him to talk to you," David said. "And listen." And before Jesse could ask how, he was gone.

#

The door closed and Ashe paused, data card in his hand, whistling under his breath. David opened his mouth, and Jesse raised her hand and shook her head. He subsided into the couch where he was stretched out, turning his wineglass in his supple fingers.

You told me to make him talk to me, David. So let's see if this gets him to talk. And I hope it works. Because if it doesn't, at least one of us is going to end up on the Unattached Roster - if we don't all end up dead.

Ashe stood by the door, reading, oblivious to anything else, so long Jesse wondered if he'd stay there all night unless one of them disturbed him. She cleared her throat and he jumped and looked up.

"That's the best-pressed uniform I've ever seen on an 'off-duty' officer," she drawled. She let her eyes move from the tips of his shiny boots, past the knife-sharp crease in his uniform trousers, his immaculate tunic and perfect shave, to the top of his head. His right hand lifted, as though he was about to touch the freshly-clipped hair, then dropped to his side. "In fact, it's very nearly the best-pressed uniform I've ever seen."

"Uh, Kwame had a question and I went down for a few minutes..." his voice trailed off.

"And had your hair cut, and checked out the science section, and spent several hours with your analysts, and taught a class — tell me, Third, what do you do when you're working?" Jesse bit the inside of her cheek to keep the chuckle that was rising from under her breastbone from coming out. *He looks as though he thinks I'm about to kill him. Is David right that he's afraid of me?*

"He gets back about four hours later when he's working," David commented. Ashe went bright red.

Jesse let the silence go on as long as she dared. "I see. You do own wearing apparel other than uniforms, don't you?"

"Of course, First."

"Then go change into something casual, please. David and I would like you to eat with us, and I'd like to see if I recognize you without that uniform."

He nodded and reached for the data card he'd put down.

"Leave that," Jesse said. "Please. I don't want you slipping away into your study and 'forgetting' to come back."

"I apologize, First. Kwame thought it was important..."

David snorted and put his glass down. "Don't you recognize when you're being had, Jase? She's giving you a bad time."

Astonished, Jesse watched as a wave of color flooded Ashe, moving from his neck up to his forehead, until the pale skin was a delicate salmon. *Is he angry?*

He dropped his head a moment, then straightened. The color was already receding, leaving him, if anything, paler than before. "I see." He reached for the data card and Jesse shook her head.

"Please - I do want you to come back."

He pulled his hand back and met Jesse's eyes a moment, his dark blue eyes very clear and direct, then nodded. "Then I'd better go change. If you'll excuse me, First."

"Jason," Jesse said as he reached his door.

"First," he replied, without looking back.

"When we're off duty, particularly when we're in quarters, I am not 'First.' I'm 'Jesse,' and that's what I expect you to call me. Got that?"

"Yes, First — uh, Jesse."

As the door shut behind him, David drew a long breath and sank into the couch, until Jesse thought he was trying to hide in the cushions. She picked up her glass, raised it to her lips, and put it down without swallowing. "Will he come back?"

"Oh, he'll come back," David said, twirling his glass and watching the liquid bubble against the sides. "You made it a matter of courtesy, and his manners are impeccable. Besides," he looked up and grinned, "you made him leave his data here."

He sat up, put the glass down, and wrapped his hands around his left knee. "Jesse, the Jason Ashe I knew was a strong, self-reliant, confident individual who wasn't afraid of anything. But that - was a long time ago. Don't - I don't want him hurt."

"Are you in love with him, David?"

He shrugged and sat back. "My feelings are irrelevant. Right now, what matters is that he's working himself to death, and this so-called partnership isn't working."

Jesse let the subject drop, and when Jason came back, barefoot, wearing an open-necked blue shirt and loose slacks, she and David were arguing the tonal values of twenty-second century computer music versus eighteenth century classical. She waved a hand at the third glass. Jason picked it up, slid to the floor by David's knees, and curled up, watching but not commenting.

David dropped a hand to the back of Jason's neck and began to massage it. Jason hunched one shoulder, then relaxed and settled back.

Jesse pretended not to notice. *He may be touchy with other people, but he doesn't seem to mind when it's David.*

They finished the argument, as they usually did, without reaching a conclusion. They ordered food, and Jesse's appetite was decent for the first time in days - but she had no idea what she was eating. The conversation was light, inconsequential; the food was good; and for a long time she would remember Ashe's long, slender fingers playing with his fork or lifting his cup to his mouth.

That's why he looks smaller than David, she thought, watching him wrap those fingers around his cup. *David's bigger boned - he looks sturdy and muscular. They're almost the same height, but Ashe is so fine boned he looks fragile.*

Dinner ended, the table was cleared. Jesse settled back into the corner of one couch, David into the corner of the other. Jason, leaning back against David's couch, drained his coffee cup and set it down. "Thank you. That was very pleasant. Now, would someone please tell me what this is all about?"

David's right eyebrow lifted and the corner of his mouth quirked - he raised a hand and gestured, as though to tell Jesse she had the ball.

"You don't think it's possible the three of us are just spending a pleasant evening together?"

Jason shook his head. "I'm sorry, no. I haven't seen any indication that you enjoy my presence - you put up with me when you have to. So, much as I appreciate you cushioning the blow with the food and the company, I'd like the bad news up front - please."

Jesse shrugged. "All right. One of our senior officers is jumpy, absent-minded, has no appetite, is losing weight, and doesn't seem to be sleeping. It's affecting his performance."

Jason shifted a little. "A senior officer? How senior?"

"Very."

"Me?"

"Something's wrong," Jesse said. "It won't be long before other people start noticing."

Jason spoke without raising his head. "If you want to get rid of me, tell HQ I'm not working out. You don't have to explain. No one would think of questioning you. But don't play games, all right?"

"That was cheap, Jason. I resent that."

He lifted his head. The dark-blue eyes were hard, and his pale skin was, if anything, paler. "What did you expect? I do my job, as far as I know nobody's complained about me, and I know you didn't want me. If you were me, what would you think?"

"I don't know. Maybe I'd think what you're thinking," Jesse said. "And I'd be angry. But I'm not playing games. I'm not just looking for ways to get rid of you. It's becoming more and more apparent that if you go on like this, what I do won't matter. You're going to get sick."

"You don't eat, Jase," David said. "You work too much, and you never seem to relax. And - you're having nightmares, aren't you?"

"What makes you think that, David?"

"Because I go into your study at night to put stuff on your desk. You don't always shut your bedroom door, and you talk in your sleep."

Jason shrugged. "All Sensitives and Healers have nightmares. It's an occupational hazard, like headaches."

"And losing weight so fast it's visible? Is that an occupational hazard, too?" Jesse asked. "Do all Sensitives and Healers try not to sleep, or work themselves so far beyond exhaustion they can't help sleeping? Come on - thick as I am, I can tell something's wrong. David and I are your partners, Jason. We want to help. Talk to us. Please. It can't hurt."

Jason stared into his empty cup, his face blank, fingers curling and uncurling around the delicate porcelain. "Do you know, Jesse," she could hear the slight emphasis on her name, "tonight's the first time you've ever called me Jason. It's always been 'Ashe,' or 'Third.'"

She couldn't sit still any longer. She gathered up her empty glass and David's, but when she reached for Jason's cup, he shook his head. "I know," she said over her shoulder. "But right now, I think we need to focus on you."

She dusted her hands, made a circuit of the room, and returned to the couch, curling up with her feet next to her and draping the skirt of her jade-green dress over them.

Jason glanced up and smiled. "By the way, did I mention that I like that color on you, if that isn't too personal a remark? It's very becoming."

Jesse smiled and ran a hand over the soft fabric. "Once in a while I like to remind myself that uniforms and working clothes aren't all there are in the world, and no, that isn't too personal a remark. Like most people, I enjoy being told I look good.

"Now, to return to what we were discussing."

"The gist of it seems to be mostly that I'm talking in my sleep, which is disturbing you and David," Jason said. "I apologize. The easiest solution would probably be for me to move to the guest quarters on Level Ten."

"Jason, what's disturbing is not that you talk in your sleep," David said. "What's disturbing is all the things that go with it - and the reason you talk in your sleep. So why don't you let us help? What's the matter? Are you afraid we'll uncover your deepest, darkest secret?"

He stiffened, the beautiful, pale face as colorless and expressionless as porcelain. Jess saw his hands curl into fists. "My deepest, darkest secret is not much of a secret, David - you can find it in my Service Record. I've been in Defense Command fourteen years, on active duty nearly ten. I've had three partners killed, been rejected by a fourth, gone from assignment to assignment, never managed to become permanent. This is about my last chance before somebody politely suggests maybe I'd be happier doing research on one of the more isolated stations, and as the two of you have made more than clear, I'm failing at it, too."

Jesse wasn't sure which was more shocking - the bitterness in Jason's voice, or what he'd just said. *The most valued Sensitive in Prometheus, the most decorated soldier in Defense Command, the only living holder of the Lion of Prometheus, the officer with the highest ratings in the Triad ranks, the youngest person in the Command Table - and he thinks he's a failure?*

She was even more shocked when David slid down next to Jason, grabbed him by the shoulders, and shook him, hard.

"You are not failing. We - not just you - will work things out. You did not 'let' three partners die, Jason. Sometimes terrible things happen - you're not responsible for them. And you have never been rejected by a partner. Never." He released Jason, who fell back against the couch, and settled beside him.

"Let me tell you about this 'failure,' Jesse," David said, putting a strong hand on the younger man's shoulder and holding him there when he tried to move away. "Hold still, you, or I'll sit on you. Jesse needs to hear this, and so do you.

"You already know he's the youngest person on the Command Table. Did you know he was the youngest person ever admitted to a Defense Command college? He was sixteen, and he not only led his class academically from the day he started, he taught hand to hand combat and self-defense.

"He says he's 'let' three partners die. I'm not sure what happened when Amari and Sara were killed, but I was there when Mike Reynolds died." The big man pulled in a long breath, and the hand on Jason's shoulder relaxed and fell away. Jason's head drooped, and he pulled his knees up and curled his arms around them.

"You know the *Sagan* story - a raider popped out of random space, probably looking for Talents.

"The pilot died in the shuttle, and as nearly as we could tell, his co-pilot took an energy bolt when the raiders breached the hull. She was dying when we found her - they'd discarded her like..."

"Like garbage." Jason's voice wasn't loud, but the bitter undertone was shocking.

"The other passengers," David continued, "two officers from Fort Joshua who'd been guest lecturers the week before - were in disruptor chambers. One was already dead. The other died three days later.

"Before he died, he told me the kids - Jason and our First, Mike Reynolds - had spent the time while they tried to run from the Tragans setting booby traps. The one that activated *Sagan*'s self-destruct breached the raider's hull and kept them from slipping back into random space - that was how we caught them.

"When we got there, those bastards were using energy whips on the boys - or trying to. The kid, here," he g anced over at Jason, "had been fighting. Trying to get between the brute with the whip and Mike, trying to make them stop. He was screaming at them, calling them names, swearing at them - I doubt he even knew what he was saying."

David stopped, breathing hard. His normally smooth face was hard, the gold skin greyish.

"We - cleaned up the mess, and started back. And Jason fought all the way, trying to hold Mike. It didn't help - he died in my arms. For a while I thought I'd lose Jason too.

"He was in the hospital over a month. While he was still hospitalized, his parents were killed. But he graduated with his class, on time — with honors.

"He's received just about every commendation Prometheus has to give, and he has so many medals from individual systems he could probably sell them for the metal in them and never have to work again. He was one of the best teachers the Point ever had, and the only reason they let him go was that he asked to return to combat. He's been wounded in the line of duty five times."

David turned so he could look at his victim — Jason had ceased to squirm and was sitting dead still, eyes closed, head bowed on his knees. David put his hand under the other's chin and raised his face. It was as white as raw carbon mass.

"You have never been a failure. You have never been rejected by a partner. You did not 'let' them be killed. You can't take on all the pain in the world, you can't rescue everybody, and it wasn't your fault! You couldn't have saved them, no one could. Understand? It wasn't your fault!"

He was gone before either Jesse or Jason could react.

Jesse rubbed her forehead. "By the One! Does that happen everywhere you go, Jason, or am I just lucky?"

"I'm sorry." He looked up. "It's been so long - I'd forgotten David had such a temper. I didn't mean to upset him."

"You should be sorry. It'll probably take him hours to calm down."

The blue eyes glazed over, and Jason lowered his head, pressing his fingers to his temples.

"Head ache?"

He nodded. Jesse got a cup of coffee and a brandy, putting

one on the table by Jason and taking the other back with her to the corner of the couch.

Jason picked up the cup without looking and took a long swallow. "Thanks." He straightened, ran his hand through his hair, and took another swallow. "So, now what? Do you still wish I'd go away?"

"You never heard me say that."

Jason shook his head. "No. But your feelings have been very clear, and they were practically pushing me out the door."

It was Jesse's turn to blush. "No, I don't want you to go. I want you to stay and help me - help us - work this out.

"Why me, God?" Jesse intoned. "All I wanted was a nice, quiet command, maybe a little base in one of the inner systems. I get the most dangerous command in the Service, along with a lunatic and a madman who expect me to keep them attached to reality. Why me? What did I do to piss you off?"

Jason took a swallow of coffee and choked, which brought them both back to reality.

When he was breathing again, Jesse settled back in her chair, exhausted. "I feel as though I've been through the Battle of the Bridge. And the sad thing is, this is probably only the beginning."

"Let's make an agreement, Jesse," Jason said. "You agree to stop thinking of me as an arrogant bastard, and I'll agree to quit thinking of you as a... tyrant. We'll put our priority on the job, where it should be, give ourselves a chance to know each other, and let anything else come with time."

"That's so reasonable I'm afraid there must be a catch. All right - but will you agree to something as well?"

The corner of his mouth and the corresponding eyebrow lifted, giving him an uncanny resemblance to David in a skeptical mood. "May I hear what before I agree?"

"To start, go to bed and get some rest. Then, take a few days off - really take them off, don't just be officially off duty. And while you're off, relax, do some things you enjoy."

"There are things I'm supposed to be working on," he said.

"They'll keep. If you don't get some rest, you won't be any good for anything."

He shrugged.

"I may not have the right to say anything, but I think you should give serious consideration to some counseling. For a man with a record like yours to consider himself a failure, something must be wrong."

He sat, head bowed to his knees, eyes closed, and Jesse felt the silence wrapping around and between them. *Good, Jesse. Put your foot in it again, didn't you. You probably just blew any chance there ever was of making this work.*

When Jason lifted his head, his face was smooth and pale as marble, wiped clean of expression. "Very well," he said, "I'll take some time. And I will do some thinking." He pushed himself to his feet and went to the outer door.

"I thought you said you'd get some sleep."

"I will, but I think I'd better go find David. Good night, Jesse. Sleep well. I promise not to wake you tonight."

The door slid closed behind him.

Jesse finished her brandy. It was quiet, the soft lamplight was soothing, and she could still hear echoes of David's voice. When they died away, she crawled to her feet and made her way to her room.

-Chapter 5-
...that will harrow up your soul
William Shakespeare—Macbeth

Sleep was deep, and sweet, and cool. Jess luxuriated in the blackness until...

"Damn it, now what?" Jesse fought her way up from deep darkness, shoving the covers away to let the room's cool air wash over her. Shivering, she sat up and rubbed her face, trying to scrub away the residue of sleep.

It was cold, quiet. Something in the taste of the air told her it was very late - or very early.

There was a bang, then the sound of a door, followed by rapid footsteps.

Jesse grabbed her robe and pulled it around her, tying the sash as she crossed her study.

Jason's door was open. Another nightmare? She peeked into the study.

"Come on, Bro, wake up. It's me, Jason, wake up." She heard fabric rustling. Jason moaned, and Jesse pictured him pushing David's hands away, opening his eyes, trying to sit up.

"Come on, Bro, get into your clothes and let's get out of here."

Jason muttered something Jesse couldn't understand.

"We'll go down to the conservatory, so you can touch dirt, and lean on a tree, and we'll talk. And when the bot's had time to straighten this up, and you've had time to calm down, we'll come back and go to bed - and sleep the rest of the night. All right?"

Sounds good to me, Jesse thought. *I think I'll invite myself along.* She went back to her room and pulled on a pair of slacks and a sweater, deciding since it was late at night and she was off duty to allow herself the luxury of staying barefoot.

"Is this a private party, or can anyone join?" she said, as Jason's study door opened.

Jason jumped and drew back, then expelled a long breath. "Of course you're welcome," he said, looking anywhere but at Jesse. "David says we're going down to the conservatory." He stepped back to allow her to precede him.

Jesse lifted an eyebrow at David, who shrugged and led the way out the door.

"This was a good idea," she said, leaning back against an artificial rock set in a bed of thick, cushiony moss. The air was cool and damp, and smelled of foliage and flowers. Jesse stretched her legs and wiggled her feet in the moss, feeling muscles relax she hadn't realized were tense.

She glanced over at Jason. He'd settled against a tree and flattened his hands on the ground. His eyes were closed, and Jesse couldn't help noticing the shadows on his eyelids and in the hollows of his cheeks, the lines around his mouth. "Relax. No one is going to hurt you," she murmured.

He jumped and opened his eyes. "Sorry. And while I'm thinking about it, I'm sorry I woke you. Again."

"Actually, I think it was David who woke me."

"After I woke him."

Jesse was saved from having to answer by David, coming back with his hands full of cups. "That's what partners are for.

"Five nights out of the last seven," David said, settling against a log that turned the little glade into a conversation area. "That's a good average. Is it your usual standard?"

Jason looked blank, and Jesse was puzzled until she realized he was talking about the nightmares.

"Seven nights out of the last seven," Jesse corrected. "You worked late and missed two."

"Hmmm, seven out of seven. Hard to beat that. How many nights out of the last – how many, Jason? Do you know?"

Jason swallowed, put the cup down, and pushed himself straighter. "I probably have nightmares on average three nights out of seven," he said, in the same light, casual tone. "It varies, depending on what's going on. I apologize for waking you. It can't be fun being around me."

"Three nights out of seven – for how long?" Jesse said.

Jason looked down into his cup and shrugged. He still wouldn't look at her. "Oh, roughly eleven years," he said.

"Tell us about it," David invited.

"Why?"

"Therapy, maybe," David said. "Nightmares are born of the dark, of loneliness. Pulling them out and looking at them in the broad light of day, or even the broad light of the conservatory at 0300, can sometimes make them shrivel up and go away. Besides, I'm curious."

"They're nightmares," Jason said. His face was taut, his voice a full tone higher than usual. "Variations on a theme. I told you. Can't you just say, 'oh, that's Jason again, he'll shut up and let me get back to sleep in a minute?' Or I could move – I suggested that before."

"There's another way." David's voice was neutral, and for a second Jesse wondered what he was suggesting.

"No." She'd never heard Jason's voice that flat, never seen his lips that tight, his face that stony.

Sorting! she thought, remembering the way Perceptives could use their ability to find pathways to help people work through troubling memories. *That's what they're talking about. No wonder Jason sounds so uncooperative.* Sorting was a useful therapeutic tool, but it was also very painful.

David's bare foot swung and booted Jason in the hip. "Here, here, a little more respect for your elders, Sonny," he said. "What have you got to lose? Or should I ask, what have you got to hide?"

Jason's face went red and he looked down, but David gave no indication he'd noticed.

"Unless, that is," David swung the foot again, and Jason brushed it away, "you like having nightmares."

"No, David, I do not 'like' having nightmares. I also don't like being poked and prodded and examined and put under a microscope." Jesse could tell from his voice and the set of his jaw that his teeth were clenched.

"If you two are going to argue, I'm going back to bed," she said, and started to get up. *I don't know what I'm doing here anyway. He didn't want me here. If he wants to have nightmares, let him.*

David raised a hand and shook his head. She settled back.

Jason glanced over at her. "David, Jesse doesn't want to listen to my sad story, and I don't blame her. Why should she? Why should you?"

"Because," Jesse murmured, "David believes if you talk about nightmares, it helps. He also believes that since we're supposed to be a team, we're supposed to support and help each other.

He has his faults, but he is a good counselor."

At that, Jason gave in. "It isn't that I don't appreciate your concern, I just know it's useless. But - I'll tell you.

"I told Jesse the other night that I dream about my failures - Mike, and Amari and Sarah, and - and Julie. They're what I call 'responsibility dreams' and all Sensitives and Healers have them. It's part of the price of the Talent. If it gets too bad, you go to a Healers' Center and have them purge it." The long, thin fingers played with his cup, turning it round and round. He lifted it to his mouth, swallowed, and put it back on his knee.

"When I'm tired, or I don't feel well, or I'm - upset - I have other dreams - real nightmares. I dream about *Sagan*." He emptied the cup and set it down next to him, leaning back and stretching. "I guess I've been a little - tense - the last few weeks. Since the kids..." his voice broke off and Jesse saw him bite his lip.

He straightened and shook his head. "That bastard chases me in my dreams," he said. "Through tunnels that get smaller and smaller, into dark corridors that turn and twist but go nowhere and never end. It's always barely light enough that I can see, but too dark for me to make out his face.

"Sometimes, sometimes he - laughs at me. I turn to face him and he fades away, and I hear him laughing."

"Go on," David murmured.

Jason pulled both knees up and wrapped his arms around them, resting his chin on his crossed wrists.

"Then I'm alone in the dark. That wouldn't be so bad, the darkness, but I - start to hear things. Engines, and - and people screaming, and shouting, and energy weapons firing. And then - then I'm back. On the raider.

"I can hear Mike, calling me, begging me to help him. But they're holding me, I can't move. Their hands are big, and hard, and sweaty, and they stink of oil and leather - and fear. My fear, Mike's fear. Pain. And blood.

"That's all there is for a long time - pain, and fear, and Mike screaming. Then <u>he</u> comes.

"One of them is holding my wrists, and one is holding my ankles, and I'm naked, but I - I don't remember how. And all I see - it's like a wall of black, moving toward me."

He looked up and met Jesse's eyes. "I suppose I was so terrified I was blinding," he said, in a matter-of-fact tone.

"He had..." his voice grew distant, his eyes far away and

cloudy, "he had large hands, very white – some of them bleach their skin, you know – very soft. His nails were long, filed to points..." he shuddered. "I still remember those – claws, touching me, running down my body..."

Jesse exchanged a puzzled glance with David. He shook his head.

Jason intercepted the glance and a bitter smile crossed his face. "Something you hadn't heard before?" he said. "Some of it I've never admitted, even to myself."

"Tell us," David murmured. "You only forget bad things by pulling them out and letting them shrivel in the light."

"I don't think talking about it is going to dissipate this nightmare, and I'll never forget. But I've started, I may as well finish," Jason said. "Besides, if we turn over all the rocks in my subconscious and chase the worms away, Jesse will be less worried about me weirding out in deep space."

He held his empty cup out to David. "Please – it might help me get my scattered wits together."

When David left, Jesse leaned over and put her hand on Jason's wrist. His arm was tense, but he didn't try to move away. "Are you all right?" she asked.

He nodded. "'Oh, God, I could be bounded in a nutshell and count myself a king of infinite space, were it not that I have bad dreams.'"

"I think that's true for all of us. But don't let David bully you. If you don't want to tell us the rest, don't."

"I like that – the minute I leave you're slandering me. When have I ever bullied anybody?" David handed Jason and Jesse their cups, settled back with his own. "Well, speak up – when have I ever bullied anybody?"

"You're doing a pretty fair imitation of bullying right now, David," Jesse said, "and slander's what you deserve for eavesdropping."

David's face reddened, and he turned away.

Jason raised his cup, took a swallow, cleared his throat.

David and Jesse turned their attention back to him.

He put the cup down and wrapped his hands around one knee. The relaxed posture was belied by the white knuckles. "The – ah..." he cleared his throat, "sorry, this isn't going to come easily. Bear with me.

"No, it's all right," as Jesse started to speak. "If David's right about it stopping the nightmares, it'll be worth it. If he's wrong — I still don't have much to lose."

David shifted and reached a hand out.

Jason seized it. He raised his face and the light caught it. It was as though the flesh had fallen away, leaving the thin, fine skin, stretched taut over uncushioned bones. His face was covered with a film of sweat.

"The raiders practice — what we consider sexual perversion. Some of them have a taste for..." - Jason hesitated, and the knuckles of his and David's clasped hands whitened - "...for rape," Jason finished. He picked up the cup. Two spots of bright red burned high on his cheekbones.

David had gone pasty. He swallowed, licking his lips as though he was nauseated, staring at Jason as though he didn't believe what he'd heard. Jesse was frozen, a small voice in the back of her mind screaming, *no, no, stop, I don't want to hear this* - but she couldn't open her mouth.

"They like their victims," Jason continued, addressing the bottom of his cup and the toes of his outstretched foot, "young, unwilling, and if possible, inexperienced. Mike and I were all three.

"David conceived the notion that since I was celibate I was — untouched. I let him think so, because it was — less shameful than letting him know the truth."

He turned his face away, but not before Jesse saw the tears on his cheeks. "They held me," he whispered, "so I couldn't look away, and made me watch what they did to Mike."

The clasped hands loosened, fell apart. David turned into the log he was resting against and buried his face in his arms.

Jesse saw his shoulders shaking. *Let him cry it out. What Jason needs, I can give him.* She slid closer to Jason, putting herself between him and David.

"Jason," she murmured, "have you ever told anyone this?"

The sapphire eyes were midnight blue. "I didn't want anyone else to know. I was ashamed. I was — defiled."

"You had no choice." *You had no choice. You fought, and you fought, and you couldn't get away, and you did nothing wrong. Nothing.* She didn't know if the voice in her mind was addressing Jason - or Jesse.

"Mike died," Jason whispered, "and I lived. I was so overcome by my own pain, I couldn't take his, I couldn't hold him. They took me, and I lived. I was - I am - dishonored."

"You were a child. You had no choice. The dishonor was theirs. 'I hear him laughing at me.'"

Jason turned his head away, the red rising in his face and throat. She put a hand under his chin and urged him toward her - he met her eyes, and the color in his face receded until he was ghost pale.

"You were a child, frightened, and alone. And because you were ashamed, you never told anyone. And no one could help you learn that the shame was theirs. I tell you now, and I know," the hand under Jason's chin trembled, "I know, you did nothing to be ashamed of. It was not your fault. Do you understand me, Jason? It - wasn't - your - fault."

Jesse let her hand drop from his chin to his shoulder. "It won't be easy, but if you let yourself, you'll heal."

Jason took her hand and pulled it to his mouth. "Thank you, Jesse," he whispered.

He jumped and looked up at her, but Jesse pulled her hand away. *I'm always afraid he's going to pick up a feeling I don't want him to.*

Back in her own room, Jesse dropped to her knees at the side of her bed and buried her face in her hands. "I'm not used to praying," she whispered, "but if You're out there, whoever and whatever You are, and if You're listening, please - help him to heal. No one should have to live with that kind of pain. Help him to put it behind him - and help me, too. Help us all. God, help us all."

She stripped and crawled into bed, exhausted and sure she'd never be able to sleep. Resigned to lying awake, convinced her body needed the rest, she ran her hand over the light control, rolled over, and dropped into oblivion.

The next two days were off-days for Jason and David, and Jesse was more glad than she wanted to admit not to have to deal with them. *We all need time to get over it,* she thought, as she initialed data cards and put them in the stack for her aide. *Time for the emotional climate to settle down.*

She refused to acknowledge the implications of her private conversation with Jason. Like everything else from her past, that was easier to bury than to deal with.

#

Jesse fought her way up through layers of sleep, feeling as though she was wrapped in sheets of cobweb that clung and refused to drop away from her.

Blindly, she reached out to touch the alarm button, and realized it was the comm signal that had wakened her. "What," she croaked.

I can't be awake. "Say again? I don't think I got that."

"I said, Kwame Ngoro has been attacked and the systems lab's been vandalized. Are you awake now, Jesse? Did you understand what I said?"

God, please, what have I done? Are we cursed? "Yes, I'm awake."

"Good. We're on our way up. We'll meet you in your study in five minutes."

"All right, let me see if I've got this." Jesse strode back and forth behind her desk, heedless of the black marks her highly-polished boots were leaving on the cream-colored carpet. Her hands were clenched, and she could feel the tension building in her neck and shoulders with every step she took. Her gut was churning, and she wasn't sure whether it was anger or fear. Anger, she decided. It was easier to be angry. It had always been easier to be angry.

David perched on the corner of the desk, but the big hands wrapped around his knee were so tense the knuckles had lightened and the tendons across the back stood out like cables. Ashe was on the edge of his chair, eyes downcast, hands wrapped around the arms. The fair skin was pallid, with greyish undertones, and a ring of dampness at his hairline told Jesse he was sweating.

"Doctor Ngoro was alone in the systems lab monitoring a data retrieval for you," she glanced at Ashe but he didn't look up, "and was attacked and knocked out. He didn't have a chance to trigger an alarm. The lab was searched for we don't know what, and if it was found it was removed or destroyed, including Doctor Ngoro's notebook. The attacker then left the lab, jamming the door and setting the ventilation system to exhaust, leaving Doctor Ngoro to die of suffocation. Am I right so far?"

She stopped pacing and wrapped her hands over the top of her desk chair. David's right eyebrow floated up, as though he was thinking of arguing, but he nodded. Ashe continued to stare at the floor without responding, but the faint color that had crept into the knife-sharp cheekbones told Jesse he'd heard and resented every word.

"When Mr. Bell called you because he'd noticed the life-support warning, you," she looked at David, "immediately called Ashe and the two of you met a medic and a security team at the lab.

It apparently didn't occur to you that I'd be of use or that I needed to know."

"There wasn't time, Jesse." David's voice was level, but his jaw was as tight as his hands, and his eyes were the color of rain on a cold day.

"There was time for you to call Ashe." *There should have been time to call us both. You had to wait for him to get up and dress.* Jesse was surprised at the bitter resentment she was feeling - it was so sharp she could taste it in the back of her throat.

"It's Jason's lab. Zephron said he couldn't override the door code."

"So you opened the door," Jesse said, "using Ashe's door code?" she widened her eyes interrogatively. *I could kill them both. We're supposed to be a team, and they didn't even think of calling me. David's my partner. This is Ashe's fault.* It was like a litany in the back of her mind, forming a counterpoint and undertone to the vocal conversation.

"No. The lock had been damaged, the door was jammed. Jason cleared the lock and we pulled the door open," David said.

Jesse nodded. "And after you entered the room, the medic attended to Doctor Ngoro, and you initiated a search of the room."

"And asked Zephron to run a system-wide anti-viral, and started diagnostics running on the alarm systems and the life-support systems. And messaged our scouts and outriders to do the same in case he has confederates."

"And you, knowing we had a saboteur in the crew," Jesse dropped into her chair, placed her hands on her desk and leaned forward, addressing Ashe, "left your assistant alone, trying to retrieve data so critical someone was willing to kill to either steal it or suppress it. And you didn't bother telling either of your 'partners' about it, did you?" *It's your fault, you arrogant bastard,* she thought.

Ashe's face drained of color, leaving him paler than she'd thought possible. "It started as a training exercise for the youngsters. They were looking for rare elements, and Josse found a trace of nimidium – enough to be interesting, maybe enough to justify some time here for research.

"It was not critical. Do you think I'd just blow something like that off and risk Kwame's life? Or one of the youngsters?"

"How long have you known about this?"

"That was the data card I had in my hand, the - the other night." It occurred to Jesse, watching him, that the stutter probably meant he was angry, but she didn't care.

"The cleaning 'bot took it before I remembered it, so Kwame was trying to retrieve it. The computer was chewing on the figures yesterday, but we've had a lot of activity in the system and for some reason it seems to have had a lot more to process than it did when Josse found it. We'd have brought them to the command team if it was anything more than one of those traces a stellar disturbance leaves. David called me about three minutes before my alarm went off.

"There's nothing, in the lab or anywhere around it. Chan went through all the access tunnels and vents, as well as lifting everything in the lab and looking under it. They're checking the disposal chutes as well, but if anything went into them, we haven't found it."

"Holy heaven, what a mess," Jesse said, settling into the desk chair and massaging her temples. "Is Ngoro going to be all right?"

Jason looked up, shifted, dropped his eyes. "I don't know."

"Ashe," Jesse murmured, "you might be the best in the service, but right now I don't believe it."

He stood, swayed, and steadied himself against the back of the chair. "If I may be excused, Command, I have data recovery routines running that need to be monitored." He turned on his heel and was through the door before Jesse's mouth closed.

She turned on David. "Something happens and you call him but not me! Is this what I have to look forward to – you shutting me out, letting me find out what's happening after the fact, him being rude like that?"

David sat a moment, head bent. "That was uncalled for and unfair, Jesse," he said at last, "and you know it. It's Jason's lab, of course I called him. I wasn't shutting you out, I was doing my job. And so was Jason.

"I remind you that this is a triad, and you are not his boss – or mine."

Jesse dropped into her chair and put her hand over her eyes. "Sweet, black, dragon-infested Space, David, what's going on? This is the second attack on our people, and we don't even know why." *I'm so tired,* she thought. *I can't handle this any more. I'm not strong, I only seem strong, and I just can't do this.*

David began rubbing her shoulders. "Don't give up, Jesse. If we give up, this base may never be established."

She rolled her shoulders under his hands. "And if we don't

figure out what's going on and stop it, we won't care.

"I thought we might find something in the personal profiles that could give us a lead."

"Not a Tragan – that would be too easy to tell with the medicals. But a plant, from one of the border worlds. I think checking the profiles would be a good idea."

"The problem," Jesse said, "is determining whom we can trust. I know I can trust you, I know a few of the senior officers. Other than that, it could be anyone." *Even Jason Ashe.*

David shook his head. "It won't be a woman. That eliminates half your people right there. And I've known Nick Thassanios since I was a student."

"I'll have him start going through them. Anything else?" Jesse said, sitting up and shaking David's hands off, pulling the console up from its slot in the desk.

David came around to the chair facing her. "Bodyguards. I've assigned my best to Ngoro."

"I'll buy that. Anyone else?"

"Jason, I think. If this attack was to prevent us seeing that data, he'll be after Jason, too."

Hmmm. And if that isn't the case - it might keep him out of mischief. Jesse touched the comm pickup, summoning the security sub-chief, telling him where Jason had gone. "Have Mr. Ashe call me as soon as you find him, Raavik.

"All right – that's a start. You can set up a rota of bodyguards. Next thing, Second," she said, turning back to David.

"Back-trace all the automatic systems, to see if we can figure out how he shut down the life-supports in the lab."

The comm unit chimed and Jesse answered it.

"Command," Jason's voice said, "Mr. Raavik had orders to report my whereabouts as soon as he found me. I am in CC."

"Thank you, Third. I'm on my way." She closed the comm pickup. "Damn! I've upset him again. David? Anything else?" She dropped back into her chair at David's gesture.

He began walking the room, jingling the things in his pockets. He finally came to rest with his forehead against the bookcase, his usual place, but still said nothing.

"That bad?"

"Oh, God," David whispered. "I don't know how it could be worse."

"Then you'd better tell me," Jesse said.

He glanced up, then dropped his eyes. They were misty, almost colorless. "The morning after your little role-play with Jason," he choked and swallowed, "I 'persuaded' him to let me Sort his memories."

"It seems to me," Jesse said, "that's between you two."

"It should be, except for one thing." He turned to face Jesse. "The applicable term here is 'unforced consent.'"

Jesse stared, the color draining from her face. "No," she whispered. "No. He's playing you, David, tormenting you."

"He never said a word. He probably never would have. But when he turned me down like that the other night, I realized I'd taken advantage of our friendship to get him to agree to something he didn't want."

"He refused?"

He nodded. "At first. And I kept on at him until he gave in. And before the process had gone very far he started fighting me - pushed me away." He moved to the straight chair, his back rigid. "You were right, Jesse, I am a bully," he whispered, dropping his face into his hands.

"Dear God," Jesse whispered. "Have you said anything to anyone else? Has he?"

David shook his head.

"Then don't," Jesse said, straightening her back and standing. "Leave it to me. Don't indulge yourself by telling somebody what a bad boy you've been. Let me talk to Ashe, see what can be worked out." She ran her fingers though her hair.

"There's nothing to be worked out," David muttered, hand still covering his eyes. "Except the time and place. Prometheus doesn't make a distinction between forced mental contact and forced physical contact - it's all rape, and it all carries the same penalty."

"Stop that! I told you not to be self-indulgent. We are all adults, we know the laws. I will talk to Ashe, we will arrive at a solution. Do you understand me?"

David nodded. "I understand. But there's only one solution, Jesse."

She shook her head. "David, we have five thousand people on this platform, and a murderer loose among them. We have three scouts and two outriders out there, and only the One knows what else is going on in this sector. This is the third command platform that's been assigned to this sector, and we both know what happened to the first two. We have to have a working command triad. Is that understood?"

"I understand," he said. His voice was flat, toneless, as though he was drained.

"David!"

He glanced up. The colorless eyes were so clouded Jesse wondered how he could see.

She grabbed him by both sides of his collar and pulled him up till they were forehead to forehead. "Think about what it would do to this command, to me, to Jason - especially to Jason, if this came out as you've told it to me. Do you want that to happen? Do you?" She shook him a little and released him.

He ran his hand through his hair and shook his head.

"You will give me your word you won't do anything foolish, or I'll have you confined to the infirmary under guard. Is that clear?"

"Yes, First. I give you my word, I won't do anything else stupid." He stood. "May I be excused? I have duties."

Jesse nodded, and watched as her Second, walking like a very old man, went through the door of her study.

Resisting the urge to crawl under the desk, she followed him.

-Chapter 6-

Oh, much I fear some ill, unthrifty thing... William Shakespeare—Romeo and Juliet

Jesse paused before she came in range of CC's door control, smoothed her hair, straightened her tunic, and took three deep breaths. *All right, Command, time to be strong, upright, and confident. Forget everything that's gone wrong in the last four hours, forget your Second is suicidal, forget you just made an ass of yourself.* She took one step forward and the door slid aside.

Ashe was standing at the console with James McGowan. His back was ramrod straight, and because she was noticing, Jesse could tell his shoulders were tight. *He's in pain,* she thought. *That's why he's so rigid - you've seen his back, and it only just occurred to you. Jesse, why are you such a bitch?*

He didn't turn when Jesse came in. She settled into a chair and picked up the stack of data cards that held the daily reports from the table. No malfunctions, no explanations, no trace. Whoever had left Kwame Ngoro for dead with the ventilation system reversed and the door jammed had covered his tracks well.

"Nothing?" she asked Zephron Bell.

"Nothing at all. It seems to have been done by an invisible man wearing gloves and carrying a disintegrator. I don't know about you, Command, but I'm about ready to start pulling my hair out over this."

"Don't do that, Zephron. We'll get him." *And soon, I hope. Because if we don't find him, his next trick may kill us all.*

She finished the last report, initialed it, and stacked them in a tidy pile. "Command Third, may I see you in the office?"

He looked up and nodded, said a final word to the young Second, and came across to her. Raavik quietly followed him.

"Of course, Command," Jason said, palming the door control and waiting for her to precede him, as though he hadn't seen Raavik.

"Wait here, Mister," Jesse murmured. The security officer nodded.

Jesse went to the converter and returned with two steaming cups. "Please, sit down, Third," she said, putting a cup in front of Jason.

He came around to pull out her chair, waited until she was seated, went back to his place and sat, wrapping his hands around the cup.

His manners were perfect, even when he was expecting the worst. The thought had its humorous aspects. For a moment Jesse fought to control the corners of her mouth. She looked over at Jason, and the look on his face sobered her.

He was on the edge of the chair, leaning forward, arms on the table. The wide shoulders were tense, almost hunched. His face was expressionless, smooth, his eyes opaque. The shadows on his eyelids and under his cheekbones seemed to have deepened in the short time since she'd seen him last, and lines of strain dragged down the corners of his mouth.

He's waiting for me to jump on him again, Jesse thought. *He's closed off like that because he's afraid of me, and this is a defense.*

She said, "I owe you an apology."

Jason raised his eyebrows, then shook his head. "I'm responsible for the science section."

"Responsible or not, I was out of line. It was a thoroughly unprofessional performance, and I'm sorry you caught the fallout. As David reminded me, I'm your First, not your boss."

"It doesn't matter. If the data was that important, I should have known."

"Was it?" Jesse asked.

"I don't know," he answered, running his hand through his hair. "I printed the raw data from the students' scans and went through it - I'd just about finished it when you came in - and I still can't see anything vital. There's that minute trace of nimidium, but it isn't enough to be useful, and the rest is just the usual space junk you get in any scan.

"I can't recover anything from the run Kwame was monitoring — whoever did it tried to wipe the recovery files, and scrambled them. I've set up the scanners to re-create those higher intensity scans."

"Will we find anything?"

The corner of Jason's mouth twitched. "If something's there, we should. I can only think," he said, taking a swallow of the coffee, "there's something there someone doesn't want us to find."

"Or," Jesse said, "a place they don't want us to go."

She looked up, and Jason's eyes were wide. "I hadn't thought of that."

"What a relief," Jesse said. "I feel superfluous enough lately without finding out you also think of everything.

"David and I believe our saboteur is probably a Tragan agent. What do you think?" she asked.

He sat back and looked into the distance for a minute, then nodded. "I think you must be right - someone from the border regions, probably, not Tragan by blood. This isn't just violence for the sake of violence. If it were, I'm afraid we'd have found Kwame dead. I wouldn't rely on our saboteur's stability, though - the fact that he did leave Kwame alive points to the kind of overwhelming self-confidence that indicates paranoia. We may have a Crystal user in our command."

Jesse nodded. "I was afraid I was getting a whiff of that - and we won't be sure until we catch him. All right - let's go over what we've done and what still needs to be done," she glanced up, but his eyes were on his notebook.

"Now," before he could speak, "here's the situation. Neither Zephron nor I can find anything - anything - that went wrong. It was done deliberately - and whoever did it is bright, good with his hands, and familiar with the systems. That doesn't eliminate many people, if any. David says if it's a Tragan agent, it won't be female, and I'll buy that. So...

"We start by assuming the command team is beyond consideration. David and James will rework the automatics, Zephron and I will run command level systems checks, you work on recreating the data, and see what you can do about increasing security on the life-support systems. I'm sorry to dump that on you, but it could be one of your analysts, and I don't want another incident like last night's if we can prevent it. We'll have Dr. Thassanios look for something in the personal profiles. Security will do a thorough investigation of the incident in the lab. That's going to leave Mariko handling Ops alone, but I don't see any way around it. Can you think of anything else?"

Jason tapped some commands into his notebook, folded it shut, put it in his tunic pocket, laid the light stylus down by his cup. "I wish I could. If you don't mind, I'll go through the profiles also. Two of us may have a better chance of spotting something. Other than that, I just don't know - he doesn't seem to make mistakes."

"I know," Jesse said. "Would you be willing to coordinate the investigation?"

One of the mobile eyebrows arched. "Wouldn't that come more logically under David's purview?"

"Under most circumstances, yes. Right now, though, I'd prefer that you handle it."

"As you wish. There is one thing."

Jesse nodded. *Here it comes*.

"Why is Raavik watching me?" Jason said, dragging the words out as though they hurt.

"What?" *Whatever I was expecting him to say, it wasn't that*, Jesse thought.

He stood and walked over to one of the viewers, standing with his hands behind his back as he looked at the display of local star systems. "I thought," he said, his voice strangled, "the only thing I could think, when you sent him after me, was that I must have done something – questionable."

He must have spent a lot of time learning to control his face. When he has that mask on, most sculpture is more expressive. But no undertones in the voice – he's so tense all the resonance is gone. "Do you always assume the worst?" she asked.

His hand came up to his forehead, and Jesse saw his shoulders loosen. "Do I?" he asked. "I don't know. I couldn't think of any other reason you'd detail a security officer to me."

"You never thought he might come after you next?"

He turned, astonishment plain on his face. "Me? Why?"

"You know everything Ngoro does," Jesse said. "If that's what was behind the attack on him, the terrorist is bound to come after you. David suggested you should be guarded, and I agreed.

"From now on, wherever you go, whatever you do, until we know how Doctor Ngoro was attacked and by whom, unless you are with me or David a senior security officer will be with you. He or she will follow you into the baths and stand at your bedroom door while you sleep, sit with you when you read and eat, and if necessary taste your food before you touch it. Is that clear?"

He nodded. "Again, as you wish. But please don't compromise someone else on my behalf."

He blushes like a teenager. How can a man have lived as long as he has and seen what he has and still react like a young boy?

"David said to ask the medics what you did in the lab," she said. "I'd rather hear it from you. What was it?"

"Nothing important," he muttered. "Kwame's heart had stopped. I just held on to him until the medic got it started."

Sweet space. He saves the man's life and says it's nothing important. He drained himself, that's all.

"Something else you'd prefer not to have on your record, Ashe? Another instance of 'just doing your job?'" she murmured.

He looked up and smiled. "You know, it really is my job," he said. "There's nothing brave or gallant about it. I have a Talent, and I'm lucky enough to be trained to use it. I don't need to be commended when I do."

"I'll note that, but I doubt HQ would see it from your point of view. I've never met a Sensitive before who would consider that 'just part of the job.'" *Not even Thom.*

"You have to remember, I'm a Healer."

The simple conviction in the quiet voice, the lack of emphasis, struck Jesse more than any emotional declaration would have. *Dragon's breath*, she thought. *It isn't that he doesn't feel fear, or pain, or doubt. He sees putting his life at risk as his job. How did he get that way?*

"Even Healers draw limits on how far they'll risk themselves, Jason." A faint smile touched the corners of his mouth, but he didn't speak.

"Quit hovering over there as though you expect someone to come drag you away and talk with me a while."

He turned, eyebrows raised, and she held out her cup.

Jason went to the converter, came back with cups, placed one before her, and sat, on the edge of the chair. "I should get back to work."

"I don't think ten or fifteen minutes with me will set you back all that far, will it?"

He sat back and took a swallow from the cup he held. "You're right," he said, "that was rude. I'm sorry — I've been jumpy lately."

"I couldn't help noticing," Jesse remarked. "I realize the last couple of weeks have been a strain, but you aren't exactly at the top of your form. Something you want to talk about?"

"I think I've talked enough, don't you?" he said, the blue eyes coming up to meet hers. "I'm bored with Jason, and I'm sure you must be. Why don't we talk about something else — Jesse, for instance?"

She shrugged. "You know just about everything there is to know about Jesse Larsen."

"Everything in the records about 'Command First Jesse Larsen,'" Jason answered. "Little or nothing about 'Jesse.' I know your taste in music runs to the traditional, you're a martial artist, and looking at you makes it hard for me to breathe."

"What?" Jesse pulled in a deep breath and straightened, trying to slow her racing heart.

"I had a brain," he said, leaning back and staring up at the ceiling, "I was a good officer. Until I saw you. I'm still more or less functional if I don't think about you, hear your voice, or see you. If you're within fifty meters of me, my brain, my knees, and my guts turn into jelly, and all my so-called stability flies right out the nearest airlock.

"You and David have turned me upside down. I never know if I'm delirious with joy or desperately unhappy. Or both."

As Jesse sat, feeling her jaw drop, he settled farther back, still with his eyes on the ceiling, still speaking in a lazy, quiet voice. "The way things are going lately, you could kill me yourself, send me back to the Tragans and let them finish what they started, or ship me to the netherworld - it wouldn't make any difference. I don't believe anything could hurt as badly as this does," he brought his eyes down to meet hers, "and the best I seem able to do is hurt him and behave like a maladjusted adolescent around you.

"I reverted to the subject of Jason," he said, sitting up. "I didn't mean to. But while I'm sitting here with a foot in my mouth, I might as well put the other one in, in case you didn't get my drift.

"I fell head over heels in love with you about ten seconds after I saw you, Jesse. You wonder why I behave the way I did earlier? Sometimes it's all I can do to stand up around you, let alone talk to you like a reasonable being."

It felt as though somebody'd thrown a bucket of cold water in her face. *I didn't even think he liked me.*

"By the One," she said, trying to catch her breath, "when you open up, you pull your heart out and lay it bleeding on the table, don't you? I was thinking of a few minutes of calm in the midst of this madness so we could reach each other as human beings, and you handed me an armed grenade."

He looked away, picked up the light stylus and began to

play with it. "I'm sorry, I didn't mean to fling everything all over you like that," he said. "I can only plead fatigue and stress and ask you to disregard it."

"I'm not likely to disregard it," Jesse said. "But can this wait until a less unsettled time? There just isn't room for our personal feelings now."

He nodded. "I know. I honestly don't spend the better part of my life emoting all over my partners, believe me."

"Fine," Jesse said, trying to project a calm she didn't feel. "Right now we have a job to do, and we have to function optimally. Agreed?"

He nodded, went to the converter and ordered a cup of coffee and a Vanallian brandy.

"Thank you," Jesse said, taking the brandy glass. "I think I need this."

"You're welcome."

Jesse leaned back and sipped the brandy, trying to look relaxed. *I don't want to do this, but I have to. He isn't going to say anything unless I bring it up. I don't want to know this, I don't want this happening. I am afraid to hear what he may tell me. What if David was right?*

"Jason," she said on impulse, hoping to bring him to the subject without having to ask outright, "tell me about David. How do you feel about him?"

He looked puzzled. "Do you know, I've never really thought about how I feel about David," he said, after a long interval while he stared unseeing at the wall. "Thinking about how I feel about David would be like thinking about how I feel about breathing. For me, and for Mike, David was the missing piece in our personal puzzle." Jason smiled, lifted the cup, put it down without swallowing.

"We went to the Point together, Mike and I. The day we got there and checked in - a few days early, because we were both from Outsystem, and the transport schedules ran that way - the medics delayed Mike. I went on to the living quarters alone, to check us in, get our assignments, start unpacking.

"David was a senior - the Cadet Battalion Commander, the assistant floor supervisor - and he'd come back from leave early to get a head start. They assigned us to his quad, and I ran into him in the hallway - literally. I wasn't paying attention to where I was going, and he came around a corner in a hurry.

"I almost started out by saying, 'hello, Second.' He just - just

Felt like everything we'd ever dreamed of. And we were so lucky - it was the same for him.

"When they took him away from me," Jason said, "I knew it was because I'd let Mike die. I stopped caring what happened to me. The only thing that mattered was knowing David was somewhere, that he was alive and safe, that I could talk to him once in a while, if I was lucky I might get to see him. I thought," his voice dropped, and he stared down into his cup, "I hoped, at least he didn't hate me."

He looked up. "May I ask what he told you?"

Unable to keep still, Jesse paced to the viewer, came back and grasped the top of the chair. "David told me," she said, keeping her voice level, "you let him Sort your memories. He said, 'the applicable term is unforced consent.' I have to know if David was right." She felt her wrists trembling, and realized she was gripping the back of the chair so hard her fingers hurt.

"No. Strong as he is, he couldn't have Touched me without my consent."

Jesse pulled the chair out and sat down. "Unforced, Jason. David says he bullied you into consenting. For legal purposes, consent alone might be sufficient, since you're an adult..."

"But David won't accept that."

"No."

He picked up the cup and swallowed the last of the coffee, then got up and took it to the recycler. Instead of coming back to the table, he went back to the viewer and stood there, looking out. "The problem is - what the problem always is. How do I prove - to you or to David - that my consent was unforced?"

"Tell me why. You reacted so strongly the other night - why did you let David Sort you?"

"I trust him."

"That's all? You trust him?" *That's enough for me, but is it enough for David?*

He nodded. "But," he said, rotating the light stylus slowly over his fingers, "it hurt, and I fought him. He blamed himself for *Sagan*. I never realized that before." He smiled, his mouth a little crooked. "It never occurred to me."

Jesse noticed she'd been holding her breath. "So, what now?"

"I don't know," Jason said. "I tried to talk to him - he didn't want to listen to me, and I put my foot in it again. In case you hadn't noticed, I do that a lot. All I can think of is to convince him to let me

Heal him."

"Can you?" Jesse frowned. "I admit, I'd rather not have to take this to anyone else, but – that's asking a lot, isn't it?"

"I can. I think. But," he turned back, "it means having both of us off duty at least one full day – possibly more. This isn't the time."

"It isn't the time to have David suicidal, either. If that's what it takes, we'll have to work around it, and pray our saboteur doesn't decide to pull another of his dirty tricks. Clear your schedule and do it. Let one of your female analysts start on that coding analysis."

Jason nodded. "What if David won't cooperate?" he asked.

"I won't even consider that." She laid her hand over his. "Take care of him, Jason. Don't let him be hurt."

Jason took a deep breath. "Of course, anything you wish. I'll solve all the problems in the universe, fight off all the bad guys. Is there a dragon nearby I can slay for you?"

The hand under hers was shaking. "I suppose you're going to go leap over mountains any minute now?" Jesse said.

The door opened and David walked in, preventing Jason from answering what Jesse later realized was one of the top ten stupid questions she'd ever asked in her life.

David moved in far enough to let the door close and stood looking from one to the other until they were both squirming. "Do you two realize you've been in here for two hours?"

"Did the sector blow up, David?" Jesse asked sweetly. *By the One! I'm not Sensitive, but I can feel the anger he's radiating. He's furious - just because he didn't know where we were?*

"No, but it's no thanks to you," David said crossly, getting a glass of wine and seating himself. "Somebody here is supposed to be on duty, and it isn't me."

Jesse looked at Jason, hoping he'd say something. He was chalk white, his fingers clenched around his cup.

"I can only say, we were busy," Jesse said.

Jason turned his head. Jesse signaled with her eyes and he nodded and rose. "Let me order you something to eat, and we'd better be on our way. We have things to do."

"Thank you," Jesse said, as he placed a loaded tray in front of her. The smell of the food reminded her she hadn't eaten since the night before.

Jason turned to David. "You and I have business," he said. "My study. Ten minutes."

As though he'd forgotten Jesse was there, David rose, turned, and left.

Jason put his hands over his face.

"Are you all right?"

He took a deep breath, exhaled slowly. "So much pain," he whispered. "Pain, and anger – I can't make any of it clear." He tugged his tunic straight. "I'd better go. He'll be waiting for me. You were right - this can't wait, even a few hours."

Jesse nodded. "We need him. I need him. Jason - when I talked to him this morning, his eyes were cloudy."

The mobile eyebrows lifted. "Cloudy?"

"You know how his eyes change color? But they're always clear. This morning they looked - misty."

He scowled. "It may just be that he's overfatigued, but I'll check. He's got classes today, and I have a meeting with some of my teams."

"I'll take care of your schedule. Do you need me to do anything else?"

"Other than keeping us from being interrupted, there's nothing you can do. I should warn you, though - you said yourself, David is a stubborn man. He wants to be punished."

"I know. He usually gets what he wants." Jesse looked at the clock. "He's waiting. Go. Call if you need me."

She sat down and started on the meal - *breakfast, I guess*, she thought - but the look on David's face intruded itself between her and the plate, and her appetite deserted her. She pushed the plate away, then got up and took it to the recycler.

What are they doing? How did this happen? How much of it is my fault?

She paced the room, hands crossed behind her back, until she realized she'd taken the same posture Jason had, waiting for disaster. *He was standing like a man with his hands cuffed. Don't start anticipating the worst like that, Jesse - one of us doing it is more than enough.*

Remembering her promise to clear the schedules, she went out to CC and went through the duty rosters, notifying two of the students that David wouldn't be able to meet them for tutoring sessions that afternoon, calling the infirmary to check on Kwame Ngoro - still unconscious, but out of danger - notifying the analysts that Jason wouldn't be available for consultation, assigning the coding she and Jason had discussed to the senior female analyst.

After a few moments' thought, she called Zephron Bell into the office and the two consulted the schedule. He conferred with his partners, then came back. "Barring disasters, Command, if you'll be on call in case of emergencies, I see no reason why the three of us shouldn't take it for the next couple of days. If you'll pardon my saying so," there was a flash of white teeth through Zephron's black beard, "it's about time you took some time off. You're all looking tired."

"Thanks, Zephron. Ask Mariko what most women think when you tell them they look tired," Jesse said, but she returned his smile. "All right, then - call me if there's an emergency, but Command Second and Third are to be considered incommunicado. And pass that on to Valery, if you will, so he can intercept any calls for them." The big man nodded. "Very well - Mr. Bell, Sector Twenty-Three is yours."

-Chapter 7-
I am in your power, to live or not... Euripides; Alcestis

Raavik was halfway to the door before it was completely open, the chair he'd apparently been sitting in still in the process of toppling.

"You came down with the Command Third?"

The big Kondrassi nodded, the cloud of smoke-colored hair floating around his head. "Mr. Christiansen came out of Command Three's study and went into his own rooms about an hour ago, Command." The soft voice was deep, even for a man that big.

What is he doing? Jesse thought. *I hope he reminded David to eat.*

She explained the duty situation to the security chief, and, "I'm going to be here several hours, at least," she said, "in and out of my study. Go ahead and assign one of your mobile people to the residential levels, and if we need someone here, I'll call."

"Right, Command. Thanks. I'll get my duty rosters set up to provide bodyguards for the Command Third and Doctor Ngoro."

Jesse retrieved a cup of tea from the converter and curled up in the corner of the couch. Her right knee felt stiff, so she shifted, stretched out, and put her feet on the coffee table. She looked around the room, taking pleasure in the sand-colored walls, the slightly darker carpets, the soft gleam of the light oak table Zephron Bell had traded her for the glass one that had figured in Jason's nightmares. It looked off balance. Maybe if she moved it, just a little...

When she caught herself readjusting the big ginger jar that stood on the table by the door, Jesse took three deep breaths and looked at her watch.

"All right, I can't stand it any more."

The door opened to her touch. It was, Jesse realized, the first time she'd been in Jason's study when the lights were on. *Does he have any human weaknesses?* she thought, looking at the meticulously arranged shelves, the gleaming desktop, the precise array of wire gauge, light stylus, laser pen, and notebook to the left of the console. *Judging by this, he probably hangs his uniforms all facing the same way.*

Jason was at his desk, his eyes on a readout on a second console. The slate-grey working uniform had been replaced by a thin silk shirt of dark blue - *of course, the silk irritates his back less* - and loose-fitting, casual slacks. A sandwich, its edges curling, sat on the corner of the desk.

"Are you going to eat that, or are you just keeping it company?"

He pulled in a sharp breath and made a sound that wasn't quite a scream. "Dragon's breath! I think you scared me out of ten years' growth, Jesse." He was halfway out of the chair, hands on the desk. It took Jess a moment to realize the whiteness of his skin was shock and not the lighting in the room.

David was right. I could have walked up behind him and killed him before he ever knew I was there.

"Sorry. I did knock. You know," she said, reaching for a pickle and taking a bite, "David told me you've been known to babysit coffee cups until they grew up and were ready to move out on their own."

"David lies. I've never kept one past the time it was old enough to go to school." He was regaining some color, and the smile that turned the corners of his mouth up lit his whole face, as though someone had turned on a lamp behind his eyes.

"Now that you're here, would you take a look at this? I have this feeling I'm missing something."

Jesse moved around to stand behind him so she could see the data the console was displaying. He touched a couple of controls and the screen brightened, arranging itself into power flows, spectrometry readings, fractional analyses of the debris the scoop had ingested. Jesse made no attempt to catch individual readings, letting her gaze drift from screen to screen and absorbing the gestalt.

"I hate to say it, but I can't see anything but the usual junk, with a slightly higher than average proportion of dark matter - and that's probably because this boy," she gestured in the direction of a nearby blue-white giant, "is very young. There's your Nimidium - you're right, it isn't enough to be significant."

"What about this?" The long finger came to rest just above the screen, underlining a series of figures.

"I've seen something like it before, but that doesn't mean anything. We'll have to keep it in the back of our minds and see if anything bubbles up. Or maybe Doctor Ngoro will have an idea when he wakes up."

Jason shook his head. "I talked to Nick a few minutes ago. Kwame was awake, but the last thing he remembers is eating dinner with Ngaio Chin."

"Did you tell him what happened? Ask him to look at his notebook?"

"Chan never did find Kwame's notebook. And Nick did tell him what happened. He's just blank. We don't think he'll ever remember the rest of that night."

"All right. Ship the data to me and I'll take a look at it later," Jesse said. "Maybe something'll come to me."

Jason sighed and stood, gesturing Jesse to the couch. "Coffee?"

"Tea, please."

He came back from the converter with two cups, handed one to Jesse, and curled up in the armchair with one leg under him and one bare foot on the edge of the coffee table.

He does that to minimize the pressure on his back with nobody noticing. He's probably done things like that so long he isn't even aware of it.

The corner of his mouth quirked, as though he knew what she was thinking. "As you can see, I do own clothes other than uniforms, and I even sometimes wear them without being told."

"Direct hit. I surrender." Jesse raised both hands, then reached for her cup. "If you're trying to tell me that David and I have been fussing you to distraction, I apologize."

Jason shook his head. "Now that I've had time to get over my crotchets, I'm grateful to the two of you for 'fussing' over me. It's been a long time since anyone did. And I apologize for being bad-tempered."

"Do you mind if I ask you a personal question?"

"With the proviso that I may choose not to answer it." He softened the remark with a smile.

"Mmm - I don't know if this is one you'd object to answering or not," Jesse said. "The day of the..." she stopped as she realized what she was about to ask sounded more or less like a delicate phrasing of "why did you try to kill yourself in public?" *Not the best way to keep things on a calm, even keel, Jesse, even to satisfy your curiosity.*

"The day of what?" Jason looked inquiring, open, and then,

as Jesse stayed silent and her fingers wrapped themselves together, his dark blue eyes sparkled. "The day of the memorial service, when I made a fool of myself in public?"

"Oh, I wouldn't say you looked foolish, Jason. In fact, I think a good many of our youngsters thought you looked almost unbearably romantic."

His lip curled and the twinkle left his eyes. "Oh, hell," he muttered. "I never thought of that. I felt like such an ass... So, was that what you had on your mind?"

Jesse nodded. "I gathered that what you did was something to do with Julie being Ansari, but I'd like to understand." *And I'd like to know, if you were that close to the edge, why it had to be you.*

Jason took a swallow and put the cup down. "All right. How much do you know about 'the Ansari?'"

"Aside from the fact that your home planet is called Ansar and that there seem to be a lot of Ansari in Defense Command, I think you could assume I'm pretty much ignorant."

"Actually, it's our sun that's Ansar."

Jesse raised her hands and shrugged. "See what I mean?"

"All right. On the Ansari worlds, to be accepted into Defense Command at any level is to achieve a lifelong dream.

"You may have noticed that a great many Sensitives are Ansari - about seventy percent. Ansar's radiation caused a heritable mutation that allows a very high proportion of us to develop at least some level of Sensitivity."

Jesse nodded. "I guess I knew more than I thought, because I remember reading that somewhere. But that doesn't explain..."

"That's just the basics, Jesse. Now - are you sure you wouldn't just rather check out the histories? We're getting very close to talking about Jason again."

"If you're suggesting that I might get bored - I'd much rather have a personal point of view than read the histories."

"Very well, First. As you wish."

He sat turning his cup in his fingers a few moments. "I hope you'll forgive me if this isn't entirely coherent - you're requiring me to think about things that are so much a part of my background I'm seldom conscious of them.

"It's probably easiest to put it this way - any Ansari could have done what I did for Julie, but I was the first choice because I'm a priest."

At Jesse's look of surprise, Jason smiled, shifted, and continued, "Not like the chaplain. Ansari religious practice doesn't include clergy in the sense that, for example, Hamilton's Worlds do - I'm nobody's spiritual guide, and no one's moral arbiter. The only 'flock' whose spiritual health is my responsibility is me. But humans need community, and the community needs someone to express its feelings. That's where people like me - Sensitives and Healers - come in."

"I'm sorry - it may be ignorance, or just that I've tried to avoid religion since I became an adult, but I still don't understand."

He got up and went to the converter again, coming back with a steaming cup. "Did you want something else?" Jesse shook her head.

"It's a part of the Healing function. All Ansari Healers are priests, in the old sense of a person who may offer sacrifice for the people.

"I'm afraid it isn't very exciting. My primary purpose is to serve my people - to relieve pain, to comfort - sometimes just to be there. I've been lucky enough to bless babies and their mothers, to help them heal from the birth trauma, and to serve at funeral ceremonies.

"Grief is painful, Jesse, and it's usually mixed with anger, and guilt, and regret, and sadness. Mourning helps relieve the pain and comfort the living."

"I understand that, but why did you cut yourself?"

"Blood carries the essence of life, so we use it to bless the dead - to thank them for their lives, to send them into the light with a piece of ourselves. The little bit of pain I feel, the blood I shed, expresses the anger, and helps relieve the grief and comfort my people. The collapsing afterward isn't supposed to happen - that was just stupidity on my part. I forgot to eat that morning."

Jesse nodded. "I see. Thank you - I'd been wondering. That leads to another personal question, and you may not want to answer this one. I don't suppose there's anyone in Prometheus who hasn't heard about the Way of the Blade."

Jason glanced up, then dropped his eyes to the stylus he was rolling over his fingers. "I take it this is about what I told you the other night?"

"I'm sorry. I can tell you don't want to talk."

He shook his head. "No, compared to that, this is easy. I

assume the question is, since I'm Ansari and I told you I'd been dishonored, why I didn't take the Way of the Blade instead of hanging around to become a burden and an annoyance for you?"

"That wasn't nice, Jason. And I suppose it's a stupid question - you were only nineteen."

"Sorry - sort of a bad joke." He leaned back, briefly, then shifted so his back wasn't touching the chair. "I was old enough, by Ansari custom. But we have another custom, one not quite as well known as the Way. If you save a life, directly, that life becomes yours. David Christiansen stepped between me and the man with the energy whip and stopped him."

Jesse realized she'd been holding her breath and the arms of the chair. She pulled in a long breath and deliberately loosened her fingers. "Does David know?"

"I don't know. That's another of the things we never had a chance to talk about."

"Is that the reason you came here? Because I warn you, Jason, I may want to strangle you from time to time, but if you kill yourself I'll murder you."

He looked up and grinned. "That's part of the reason, but not in the way you mean. Custom also says that until and unless he releases me, I should take care of David. This was my first opportunity to put myself in a position to do so."

"And that leads to the most important question - what about David? Did he talk to you?"

Jason shook his head and leaned forward to put his cup on the table. "No. He kept saying I didn't understand, that I didn't want to admit what happened. He was exhausted, hungry, grieving..."

"Grieving?" Jesse leaned forward, resisting the impulse to cover Jason's hand with her own.

"He blames himself - for *Sagan*, for our kids - thinking he could have done more, gotten there faster. And - there's something else, but I can't - I don't know what it is.

"David is angry, and confused, and ashamed, and..." he shook his head. "This has been piling up a long time."

Jesse nodded. "He has nightmares too, you know."

Jason shook his head. "I didn't. I should have."

"Jason, may I ask you a question?"

He grinned. "Why not? I seem to be dumping my feelings all over you, the least I can do is supply you with the answers to your questions - if I have them."

Jesse took a sip from her cup and set it on the table. "I just wondered - as strong as your feelings for David seem to be, and as strong as I know his are for you - why did you ever let yourselves be separated?"

The mobile eyebrow lifted. "We didn't have a choice."

She looked the question.

"When Mike was killed he'd just turned twenty-one, David was - almost twenty-three, I think, and I was nineteen. Then my - my parents were killed, and that left the Point's Commandant in loco parentis. He ordered David transferred." He ran his hand through his already disordered hair. "I wanted him back - I was going to go to Aldrich and demand it, when they let me out of the infirmary - but everyone told me I'd make it harder for David if I caused any trouble, that I was in danger of losing my own commission, I'd been out of so many classes. So I - I wrote him a lot of letters, that he never answered, and I waited until I was twenty-one. I kept expecting him to come, or to call - but he never did. Eventually, I stopped writing." He turned his face away, but Jesse could see the delicate flush rising on the fair skin.

"Would it surprise you to know that he called - or tried to call - every week until you graduated? That he wrote you every week?"

"Ten years ago it would have surprised me very much. Now - I don't know. All those feelings I ran into when I Touched him... But..."

"But why didn't you get the letters? Why didn't you know about the calls?"

He nodded. "Aldrich?"

"Exactly," Jesse said. "When they finally managed to dump Council Member Pukavich and 'retire' Quadrant Marshall Fournier, somebody actually dug into what Aldrich had been doing. He'd been running that college like his own little personal fiefdom, using it to forward his own favorites - and using it to act on his prejudices. You probably won't be surprised to discover that Aldrich - shall we say - disapproved? of the Triads.

"There's been speculation that it was because his own Talent was negligible, and he was bitterly jealous. Believe me, yours isn't the only life he screwed with.

"It won't be much consolation, but let me explain something to you. Since you had a signed pledge, approved by your parents and witnessed by responsible people, when your parents died, your partners became your next of kin, and since you were under age, your legal guardians. Mike's death didn't change that, although Aldrich lied to you, to David, and to a lot of other people about it. In fact, now that I come to think of it, unless you've since made a will designating someone else, David may still be your next of kin."

"Not my guardian?" The mobile eyebrow had lifted again, taking the corner of his mouth with it, and the deep blue eyes were sparkling.

"I think you may have outgrown the need for a guardian by now," Jesse said. "But you never know. And speaking of guardians," *get away from that, Jesse,* she told herself, "what did you do with David?"

"I sent him to his room, told him to eat, get some sleep, and think. And," he glanced at the clock, "I'd better get back to him. I didn't realize it had been this long."

"I'm going to work out," Jesse said, as the study door closed behind them, "I'll station the guard at the door until I get back. Call me if you need anything."

#

Jesse wiped the sweat off her forehead and pulled the fastener loose from the tape, letting the soaked fabric dangle in a wide ribbon to the floor as she unwound it from her hand and wrist. She unwound the tape from the left wrist, then gathered the bundle of fabric and threw it into the bin to be laundered. She walked over to the bench, grabbed a towel and wrapped it around her neck, glancing up at the clock.

More than an hour, she thought. She dried her hands, grabbed the weapons she'd worked with - bo and sai - racked them, and took herself into the showers.

Time to head back, relieve the door guard, find out what's happening. And pray, she thought, as the warm water ran over her body, rinsing away the salt sweat, *that I don't go back to find the scattered remains of my erstwhile partners all over our quarters.*

She went to her own study first, checked with CC to be sure everything was quiet, then pulled up the files Jason had been scanning. The computer had added the results of the last several hours' scans to the data. The small patch of - whatever it was - on the giant planet attached to the blue-white sun's gravity field had increased.

Jesse put her chin on her fist and brooded over it, resisting the itching at the back of her neck she knew was her Talent responding to a suppressed memory. "Something's happening there," she muttered. "And it's beginning to look familiar, but I can't see it yet." She stared a while longer, then shook her head. "Maybe I'll be able to see it with more data."

She checked Jason's quarters - the study was tidy, consoles folded shut, small tools aligned alongside them, his notebook in the center of the desk. He wasn't in his bedroom, so she went to David's rooms.

David was asleep on the couch in his study and Jason was curled in the armchair. Their faces were streaked and sweaty, their hair was rumpled, and Jason's right hand was in David's left, the fingers laced together. As she came in, Jason's eyelids lifted, then closed.

"If you two are going to persist in sleeping together," Jesse remarked, "it would be simpler and more comfortable if we enlarged the bed for you. It looks so messy with you collapsed all over the furniture and on the floor."

"And your Intuit's soul," Jason muttered, "is offended by untidiness. I know." He opened his eyes, repossessed his hand, pushed himself upright.

David pulled the released hand down and buried his face in his arms.

"How is he?" Jesse whispered.

Jason looked at David, laid a finger across his lips, gestured to the door.

Nodding, she went out, and he stumbled to his feet and followed her.

"Gods, what time is it?" he asked, running his fingers through his hair. "Never mind," he croaked, before Jesse could tell him. "Coffee, for the love of the Many."

"What about him?" Jesse said, as she ordered.

"He's a big boy," Jason said. "He'll get his own when he wakes up."

When Jesse brought him the cup, he sipped, put it down and leaned against the table, resting his hand on the satin finish of the light oak. "I like this table," he said. "It makes the room seem warmer."

"Thanks," Jesse said. "The glass one seemed – cold." She ignored Jason's involuntary shiver as they both remembered what made the glass table seem cold. Then she pulled out a chair and sat. "Well? How is he?"

"I think he'll be all right. He'll be jumpy for a couple of days, but other than that, he'll be back to normal. Maybe better.

"I want him to sleep as long as he can. I had to go very deep, and it disturbs some neural connections. The sleep will help them settle.

"Jesse," he said, taking a swallow and rubbing his eyes, "I tested David's blood. It showed traces of a psychoactive."

"What? That's impossible. David wouldn't do anything that stupid."

Jason said, "I don't think he did. The creature who injected the toxin into the food converters wouldn't have had any difficulty rigging the drink dispenser in David's study. Or yours, or mine, for that matter. We may have gotten it, too, although I tested my own blood and didn't find anything. I tested the converters - all three of them - and got negative results.

"We need to take precautions against that sort of thing. I'm sorry I didn't think of it earlier – I should have."

"So should I," Jesse said. "I guess that explains a lot of David's behavior, doesn't it?"

Jason nodded. "I think so. I think he was given something that would intensify his emotions, make him more suggestible. Our fiend's timing was superb - David was on edge, vulnerable - when I blurted that story out, his guilt about *Sagan* got twisted, and you saw the reaction.

"Dragon's breath," he said, running his fingers through his hair, "I feel as though I've spent most of my time here either having my life screwed with or unwillingly screwing with other people's lives. I'd really like to get back to what I always thought of as my job."

"Are you all right?" she asked. "You look more or less dead." His hair looked dry and stiff, his skin was pasty and greyish, his lips looked dry, and the circles around his eyes had gone from purple to almost black.

He smiled, and Jesse smiled back. "Only more or less?" he said. "I must be improving. I'll be fine. Something to eat and I'll be almost human again."

"Food sounds good," Jesse said. "Sit down and I'll order."

"How long has it been since you remembered to eat?" she asked, watching Jason eat.

"Hmmm – yesterday, I think," he replied, after chewing and swallowing. "I'm not sure."

"No wonder you're so thin," she said.

He laughed and pushed the plate away, finishing a large

glass of fruit juice. "That's my metabolism, not anything I do. Sarah used to say I ate like a Mangosian fruit bat – constantly and in huge quantities, none of which ever got digested sufficiently to add to my frame."

"What was she like?" Jesse asked.

"Sarah? I thought you knew her."

She shook her head. "I knew Amari. I never met Sarah."

He smiled. "She was a little thing. Full of energy. Brilliant. She graduated at the top of her class.

"Sarah was a wit," he said. "She teased me all the time. I never knew what she was going to do next. She liked paired gymnastics. I'm about as graceful as a fuel transport, even after four years of required gymnastics, but she liked me for a partner – she used to say I made her look good." He swallowed, got up and cleared the table, walked around.

Jesse watched him in silence.

"We took a hit to CC. It knocked me out. When I came to, Amari was dead, the chief engineer was trying to patch us together and bring *Orion's Bell* home. Then I found Sarah.

"She was cold," he whispered, "and I had two more black pearls. I wish I'd never seen a black pearl."

"I know what you mean," Jesse murmured. "I'd give a lot not to have mine." She shut her eyes a moment, pushing away the memory of the man she'd thought would be her partner through life and beyond.

She pushed the chair back and stood. "Well, I'd better get back to work. By the way, other than in David's room, how long has it been since you slept?"

"Slept?" he said blankly. "I really don't remember. It doesn't matter. I still haven't worked out the pattern in those sensor scans."

"That will wait. Go check on David, then go to bed – and tell him to go to bed, too. Zephron and I cleared all our schedules for the next two days. I don't expect to see either of you before tomorrow. Late. Understood?"

#

I told Jason to go to bed and sleep, and tell David to do the same, Jesse thought as she pulled the gi jacket on and knotted her wide, worn black belt. *But I don't trust him any farther than I could pick him up and throw him – if he can find a way to work, he will.*

She went into the gym, planning to work with the heavy

bag, but found Yuri Kelman working on a kata.

He turned as she came through the door and smiled. "Hi, Sensei," he said. "You're just the person I wanted to see. I'm stuck."

Well, it'll take my mind off my problems, Jesse thought, as she went to show him the next move.

-Chapter 8-
'Tis in vain to seek him here that means not to be found.
William Shakespeare–Romeo and Juliet

"Dragon's breath!" Jesse muttered, "why can't I see it? It's right on the edge of my mind and I just can't get it to come out."

The door slid open and she jumped.

"Sorry. I didn't think to signal," David said.

"I probably wouldn't have heard it. So," she came around the desk and held her hands out, "how are you? Are you back?" He still looked tired, but relaxed, as though he'd been relieved of a great burden no one had realized he was carrying.

The big hands were warm under hers, and then David pulled her into his arms. "I'm fine. I jump out of my skin at the slightest noise, I keep getting this knot in my gut, and I feel as though I've been through a month-long survival course, but I suppose I'll get over it. Otherwise, I don't seem to be psychotic, or delusional, or dangerous to myself and others except in the way I always have been."

He was joking, but since she was listening for it, Jesse could hear the pain under the light tone of voice. "David," she said, pulling him toward the couch where she could sit facing him, "quit blaming yourself. Feeling guilty is not logical, but it's human, and natural. You've been overworked, stressed, worried - and we're lucky you're as resistant to psychoactives as you seem to be."

He got up and went to the converter, coming back with two steaming cups. "You know, of all the things that have happened since this mission began, the only thing I resent more than that is what he did to the kids. I don't think I have an inflated idea of my own worth, but if I'd killed myself it certainly could have endangered this unit."

"He has a lot to answer for," Jesse responded. "And he will, never doubt that."

At the look on his face she changed the subject. "Jason gave me a puzzle to play with while you two were busy. Come look at it."

"That." The long finger came to rest under the data from the gas giant. "It almost looks like bacteria."

"It does, doesn't it? The rate of growth's begun to slow in the last twenty-eight hours."

David raised a quizzical eyebrow. "Out of nutrients?"

Jesse shook her head. "I don't know. I have this nagging itch at the back of my neck that says I've seen this before and I should know what it is, but - my mind's a blank." She sighed and turned away, just as the door chimed.

The cleaning 'bot had cleared the plates, the scanner tracings were displayed on the consoles next to the cups. As he studied the screen before him, Jason rubbed his chin, and Jesse realized he'd forgotten to shave. A trace of a smile crossed his face, coming and going so swiftly it might have been a trick of the light.

I wonder what that's about. It seems to keep happening - and David's doing it, too.

"Okay, this is what we have," Jason said. "Broken carbon molecules, much like the scatter castings from our own engines; minute traces of a rare and expensive element – Nimidium, which is virtually useless unless you're a Duvari jeweler; and increasing amounts, on the fifth planet of this system, of something that looks like an isotope and seems to multiply like bacteria. I think I know what number one is; number two is the sort of trace you could find in any stellar system. Number three – I have a feeling I've seen it before, but I don't know where. It isn't alive - at least, it isn't anything we recognize as organic, but it's been growing."

"Well," David said, "You and Ngoro were right – this Nimidium is not exploitable. It's interesting, though, and it's very rare. Josse deserves a pat on the back for finding it. Did he actually identify it?"

Jason nodded.

"Remind me to note that, if you haven't already - if he's at all inclined that way, he seems to have a gift for research.

"Nimidium," David said, returning to the subject, "is an indicator - usually, when you find nimidium, you find something else. That's why it's valuable. Because the something else is something the Tragans would do almost anything in their power to get. Something they prize above gold, platinum - even above Talents."

Jason looked puzzled, and David turned to Jesse.

She drummed her fingers on the table, trying to clear her mind, the itch at the back of her neck almost unbearable. *Not alive, but capable of growth and movement; looks like an isotope but behaves like a bacteria; extremely valuable to the Tragans. And illegal in Prometheus.* "By the One!" she exclaimed, as the answer flooded over her. "I should have recognized it sooner. Crystal!"

David exhaled and she realized he'd been holding his breath. "Exactly," his tone of voice reminded Jesse of a good teacher congratulating a bright student on solving a puzzle. "A huge growth, almost at the perfect stage. And the Tragans would love to have it. It'll be recoverable soon."

"But how?... That supernova the astrophysicists were so excited about?"

"Probably. They grow it in labs, but it's inferior to the natural form. And we blundered along just when conditions were perfect - a young, hot star; more than usual dark matter in the immediate neighborhood; the perfect growth medium - that gas giant; and the trigger - a supernova relatively nearby that blew out a lot of junk, including the seeds. It's no wonder we've had a saboteur - the wonder is that he didn't call in one of their supercruisers and have them blow us out of space. They've probably been watching that field for the last fifty years."

"Well, gentlemen, I think we've solved the mystery of why our border station in this sector keeps getting destroyed," Jesse said. "Now all we have to do is figure out how to keep from getting that way ourselves."

Jason muttered under his breath and his fingers became very busy at his console. He fitted an earpiece and swiveled the mike to his mouth. "Pull down holographic projection of immediate scan area, using most recent data," he murmured.

A small transparent cube appeared above the table, bright motes of dust and twinkling lights suspended throughout it.

"Enlarge by one."

The cube now filled the center of the table, and some of the dust motes became planetary bodies.

Jason glanced from the cube to his console and made some adjustments to the screen display. The computer mimicked his actions in the holo cube.

"Enlarge by one." The holo cube now encompassed the table. "Refocus. Concentrate display on north northwest of area, using *King Kamehameha*'s location as true north. Reduce by one."

The cube now contained a star system and an area of surrounding space. The star, a blue-white giant, commanded five giant planets and a field of asteroids.

Jason made further adjustments to his screen. "Add tracings of expended carbon by-products from last ten sweeps and correlate," he commanded.

David shifted. "Jason, have it highlight the tracings in fluo red." Jason murmured into the mike and the computer outlined a segment of the cube in angry crimson.

"By the One," Jesse breathed. "Is that what I think it is?"

"A Tragan supercruiser in random space," Jason replied. "We have company. Not the class of neighbor who does much to raise the local tone," he commented.

"I suppose there's no possibility that's at least partly composed of our own scatter castings?"

"Time display of enhanced data from that area since original sweep," Jason murmured into the mike.

They watched in silence as the computer wiped the holo cube and recreated it, showing the ghost of the great battle cruiser. It sidled into the system, just on the edge of scanner range, closer and closer to the gas giant in the system's outer ring – the place the youngsters working with Ngoro and Jason had first found traces of Nimidium – the place the Crystal was growing.

"This may be the first time a ship in random space has been scanned," David said. "Extraordinary, Jason."

"They knew we were here or they wouldn't have come in random," Jason said, ignoring David's remark.

"I think you're wrong, Jason," Jesse said. "They'd have come in random anyway. This area isn't settled, but it's well beyond the Interdicted Areas." *And someone's going to have to find out how they - and that raider - got past the Interdicted Areas without triggering the ADS.* "We've stumbled on a secret they didn't want us to find. They've probably had either supercruisers or gunships hiding in this area off and on for years.

"This must be the reason for the attack on Ngoro," she drummed her fingertips on the tabletop. "It wasn't the data about the Nimidium, it was this. He was trying to keep us away from it."

"I move we run for home while they still think we haven't found it," David said.

"We'd never make it out of the system," Jesse responded. "The only thing protecting us now is they don't know we know they're here."

"And possibly who they are. Jase, can you scan that bastard real-time?"

Jesse raised an eyebrow, but David ignored her. Jason shifted the console so it faced him directly, cutting off their view, and began to alternate subvocalizations into the mike with keyboard work.

"It's not clear," he said, after several long minutes, "and I don't want to push it any more - their screens might catch the scan. This is what I've got."

He rebuilt the display cube, narrowing the focus until the hazy image of the supercruiser floated in the holo cube above the table.

David sat staring at it until Jesse nudged him. "Well?"

He lifted a finger. "This area. Capture and then pull it off so we can enhance it and look at it."

Jason nodded and did as he was asked. When the external scan had been terminated and the image had been transferred to the console, "Now what?" he asked.

"Trade me," David said, pulling the chair out. He sat down in front of the console and began playing with the image, sharpening the focus as much as possible, shifting the perspective to make parts of the image seem to recede while other moved into the foreground. As he worked, Jesse could see that they were looking at a surface. The image focused, sharpened, clarified, until -

"By the One," Jesse whispered. "Ts'Chuk of Sidari."

David nodded. "The Prime Hexarch himself. That crystal field just became the most important location in the universe, and we're the only people available to keep the Tragans from getting it."

"Computer, store display and all related scans in priority locked file, voice access only, Command Team and Operations Team voices," Jason commanded. "All future data from that area is to be placed immediately in the same file until further notice. Repeat and verify instructions."

"What are they waiting for?" Jesse asked. "It's obvious we know where the crystal source is. Yet they're sitting there, taking the risk we'll do what we just did."

David said, "Like I said, nobody's ever scanned a ship in random space before. They think they're hidden. They're waiting to see what we do next. If we notify HQ, they'll wipe us out, move to get what crystal's already matured, destroy the source and get across the Interdicted Areas before another vessel can get out here. They'll wait as long as they think they can, to let more of the crystal mature.

And the growth rate's dropping."

"We can't run, we can't hide, we can't call for help, and there's a terrorist trying to destroy us. If we don't do something, the inner systems where the Tragans never venture may be a matter of legend in the near future. If we do, we may be a matter of legend in the near future," Jesse said.

The cups slid across the table, jangling in their saucers.

#

"We're drifting," Jesse said, reaching for the comm. Before she could activate it, the link opened and Mariko Itosu's voice was broadcast through the system.

"Systems failure is imminent, I say again imminent. Initiate emergency procedures now. All personnel, report to emergency posts. This is not a drill. I say again, this is not a drill."

"Shit!" David glanced down at his jeans, sweater, and bare feet, and stood.

Jesse made it through the door before either of her partners, but they came abreast of her in the corridor and the three ran as a unit, confident passersby would get out of their way.

"Alert, alert," the comm officer's voice was level and uninflected. "Advance to Alert Condition One. Section doors will close in one minute."

By the time they made it through the Command Center's door, the floors had taken on a pronounced tilt, and Jesse was beginning to feel like a very springy rubber ball.

CC was a flurry of activity. Pilots, navigators, computer specialists, fought to recover control.

Jason moved to the central console, his fingers playing over the touch pads, activating the entry points to the computer system. "Third, prepare to go to manual on my mark and hold steady." Zephron Bell, displaced from the console, began moving around the room, belting people in place.

The young Sensitive's hands moved across her console, resetting controls. David moved behind her and belted her into the seat. She nodded thanks, then looked up at Jason. 'Ready, Command."

"Releasing controls to manual - now."

The room lurched, then steadied as the manual control took hold and Mariko grew accustomed to its feel.

David and Jesse finished belting the rest of the people in

CC into their seats, then took their places at the central console. Bell moved to the tactical chair, belting himself in next to James McGowan. Glancing over, Jesse saw the partners wrap their little fingers together before each turned to his touch pad.

Jesse placed her hands on the console, fingers spread so her right hand touched David's and her left touched Jason's. The readouts brightened, flickered, faded.

"Dragon's breath!" Jason muttered. "I think most of the executive systems are fried. Hang on, it's going to be a bumpy ride."

Jesse saw his jaw clench, and beads of sweat popped out on his forehead. The readouts brightened and steadied under Jesse's hands, and information started to flow in the columns and displays in front of her. "By the Many!" she heard Bell mutter. "What a mess."

Protected by the Sensitive's wards from being pulled too far into the system, channeled through the branches of the logic tree by the Perceptive's awareness of energy and matter relationships, guided by the Intuit's instant assessment of outcomes, the three coiled through the master control system, exploring, adjusting, tracing the line of the system failure. It took seconds, Jesse knew, as she also knew they were only gathering information, not swimming through the circuits; but it felt like hours, or days, and when they finished, she was dripping with sweat, panting, her muscles shaking as though she'd just finished an extreme workout.

"The control codes have been wiped at all levels," Jason said, lifting his hands. "We're going to have to rebuild them."

"Second, how far did we drift?" Jesse said.

"Not far, Command," the redhead responded, displaying the sector grid. They were almost within the gravitational field of the blue-white giant, too close to the last location they'd traced for the Tragan.

He doesn't know about the intruder, Jesse thought. *I've got to get us away from that big bastard without showing them we know they're there.*

Jesse exchanged a look with Zephron, David and Jason, then turned back to the pilot. "Third, correct to two-two-nine and stay at dead slow. We're too close to that gas giant's gravity well. First, set up a two hour rotation for pilots, with the two of us on six-hour rotations monitoring them until the Command Third's had time to restore the piloting system. While you do that, the Command Second and I will consult with the construction engineers and make sure we haven't had another section shaken loose."

She turned to the Comm Officer. "Damage reports, Mister Radonov?"

"Command, Mr. Kelman was in one of the maintenance shafts doing routine work when we slipped, and was knocked out. That's all."

"Thank you, people," Jesse said. "Stand down from alert status. Return to normal operations. Gentlemen," she gestured to the office. Zephron, David, Jason, and James followed her.

When the door closed behind them, Jesse drew in a long breath and looked up at Jason. "How long will it take to restore the control codes?"

He thought a moment. "Using what we've got on backups, a total of about thirty hours, spread over – say three full days. That's assuming James can be broken loose to help me, and that David is going to be working on the security systems and then testing the rebuilt codes. It'll take about ten hours, maybe as much as fourteen, to re-build the piloting controls before we even start on the others. James, David and I are the only analysts who have clearance to write, link, and test control codes."

"That isn't long enough," Jesse said. "How long can you plausibly take, putting the piloting console back on automatics as soon as possible and then taking your time on the other systems?"

David moved over and settled on the edge of the table. "I can add another day for testing and verification."

"Is that the longest we can manage?" She intercepted a look and explained. "The longer the executive systems stay down, or seem to stay down, the more puffed with his success our saboteur is going to be, the more likely he is to get careless. It also gives us a chance to drift away from the sensitive area of the sector without appearing to do it deliberately."

Bell said, "I have this feeling there's something out there James and I don't know about."

Jason nodded. "That was supposed to be the next item on the agenda. Come over here." He called up the data files and recreated the holo cube, explaining the situation with no wasted words.

"You know, when we signed on as ops on this platform, I thought it was the big break we all dream about. I'm beginning to wonder if we're cursed."

"Just in the wrong place at the wrong time, Zeph," David said.

"I hope you're right," the bearded man said. "All right, I

agree so far - and something Command One didn't mention. If we appear to be drifting, or at the very least under minimum power, that bastard," he gestured at the holo cube, "will think we're less of a threat. That's a sort of shield in itself."

"It makes sense," Jason said. "We can redistribute those programs, after David tests and verifies them, to come back on line over a period of days – a week or more for the complete sequence."

"Good," Jesse said. "Let's do that. David, you need to coordinate with the engineers on rebuilding the failsafes."

David nodded, pushed himself away from the table. "I'm on it. Jesse, you and Zephron need to do a thorough check of the environmental systems and make sure this didn't corrupt any of them."

Jesse led the way back to CC. Jason, James, and David went their separate ways. After an hour watching the pilot, consulting with Zephron on the shift rotations for pilots and navigators, Jesse signed off on the logs and headed down to eat and rest.

It was the best way to go about it, it might just bring their terrorist out of his hole and give them a little time to think of something to do about that bandit, and it was going to be a very long week.

You've missed something, Jesse, she thought. *I don't know what it was, but you've missed something.* She fought with it, but it wouldn't come. She shrugged and dismissed it. *It'll come back when I need it. I hope.*

Zephron called her half an hour before she was due to relieve him. "Just thought I'd give you a wake-up call, Command."

"Thanks, First. I'll be up as soon as I shower and dress. How's it going?"

"Not too badly, all things considered. It's wonderful practice for the apprentices, but it's wearing. You were right about two hour shifts for the pilots - even Mari was about wrung out by the end of her shift. Environmentals are checking out clean so far, but I'm running every backup test I can think of, and I've got all the failsafes on line. It's slowing things down, but nobody's complaining. Chief Cody tells me they're going through all the locked in sections rivet by rivet, and so far they're tight.

"Oh, Command Three called me about thirty minutes ago and told me they'll be ready to test the piloting system by about 0700."

Good, Jesse thought. *They must have been working constantly since they left. I'll be glad to have the piloting system back on line, but even if we can't get far enough away from the supercruiser to call for help with impunity, the time Jason and David are buying might show us whether he's more interested in what we're doing or in guarding that crystal source.*

The Prime Hexarch's flagship, planted here in an obscure corner of the sector farthest from his territory, staking out a crystal field. I know they value Crystal even more than talents, but what makes this field that important? Why does it matter so much Sidari puts his own flagship here on a stakeout?

I hope this gives us some time to work on finding our terrorist. I wonder why he was planted here in the first place. It can't just have been to keep us from finding that crystal source - no one knew we'd be in this area of the sector. It must have been - of course! New platform, new command - we were a challenge. He was probably planted years ago just in case this opportunity came along. She shuddered as a wave of cold moved up her back, and tightened her shoulders to control it. *I wonder how many more there are, just waiting for the next opportunity.*

The vision of children, brought up and trained so they could test into the Defense Command Colleges, work their way into key assignments, and then commit random acts of terrorism, made her gut twist. Deliberately, using every form of mental and physical discipline she'd ever mastered, she pushed the thought from her mind and focused on the present.

For the next four hours, she monitored pilots, helping a couple of the apprentices when the controls slipped, consulted with Zephron on the environmental systems, and wondered what Jason, James and David were doing.

"All right, Command, and First, let's see if this works," Jason and James slipped through the doorway and Chan followed them, letting the door shut and taking a stance in front of it where they commanded the room.

Jason placed his hands on the central console, waited for the system to recognize him, and entered an access code. He pulled the earpiece and mike from his pocket, slipped them on, and began to talk. For several minutes, he'd murmur a command, wait, murmur another one, make an adjustment, murmur another command. "All right, Pilot, release control to me on my command. Now."

There was a moment when things felt suspended, not quite balanced, then the executive program stabilized and took hold. Zephron, standing behind the pilot, looked up and nodded. Jesse walked over to the central console, flattened her hands on her section, and watched the data rolling across the screens. "It doesn't look quite the same."

"It isn't - we worked from the backup, but we built some safety features into it."

"Good." Jesse glanced down at her watch. "First, let's spend a few minutes rearranging pilot schedules, and then I think we can leave CC to the duty officer and get some well–deserved rest."

-Chapter 9-

It is easy to deal with a situation before symptoms develop.
Lao Tzu—Tao Te Ching

Jesse pulled in a deep breath, initialed the last of the routine reports, and handed the data cards back to Valery Radonov. "Thanks, Mr. Radonov. You've done yeoman service the last several days."

Radonov grinned, not quite baring the tips of his sharpened canines, and flexed his right hand, releasing and withdrawing his fighting claws. "Just doing my job, Command," he said. Jesse nodded and he went back to the comm station.

"Anything else, First?"

Zephron Bell let one corner of his mouth lift in acknowledgement of the attempt at humor, and shook his head. "Not a thing, Command. All lights are green, sensor readings remain at status quo, functions are nominal to optimal."

"Good. It's about time. I'm going to see how the Command Third's doing with that coding, and then I'm going to bed. Unless there's some kind of emergency, I'll see you tomorrow."

Feeling, for the first time in days, as though she could allow herself to slow down, Jesse took time to shower and change before she went looking for her partners. David was curled up in his study, a book in his hand. "Dinner time?"

"I was thinking so. Let me go see if Jason wants to join us," Jesse responded.

Jason was, as he'd been almost constantly since they'd found the Crystal source, at his desk, both consoles open, the lights from the one on the side wing of the desk playing over his face like fairy lights as the function readouts scrolled past.

She slipped into the room and sat down in the chair in front of the desk, never letting her eyes shift from his face. "Jason," she murmured.

He jumped and his fingers came down on the control pad. "How long have you been there?"

"I just came in. I assume you've been there the last three days?"

He smiled, and turned his attention back to the screen in front of him. He swore under his breath and began backshifting, erasing the random symbols he'd inserted into the code when Jesse startled him.

"Sorry. I did palm the door signal."

"It's all right. I think I can finish this in - maybe another four hours. And if you don't mind, after that, I'm going to take tomorrow off and just sleep."

"I don't mind a bit, if you'll really do it. Even though," she glanced over at him, "this took longer than you told me it would." She let the corner of her mouth quirk up a little.

Jason acknowledged the feeble witticism with a faint smile. "I'm afraid 'everything takes longer than you think it will,' is an unacknowledged law of nature. And James insists he can't think if he isn't allowed to sleep and eat from time to time."

"He's human, Jason - and so are you. You're allowed to have a few weaknesses. Even machines need rest cycles. How long has it been since you ate?"

He shut down the side console, then the front one, and lined his small tools up on the desk. "I think - David brought something - I don't remember."

"That's what I thought. James is right. Take a break for a while - you'll work better for it."

Jason nodded and rose, stretching backward, then forward, loosening his arms and shoulders. "You're probably right." He stepped out from behind the desk and went around Jesse to the converter.

"David and Chief Edmonds found some interesting bits and pieces when they went through Engineering," Jesse remarked. "One of the consoles had been run through a bypass into the self-destruct, so it could be triggered without the three-way backup. There was a timer on one of the injectors that could have caused exactly the same kind of meltdown that killed Thom. Among other things, it made me wonder if Thom's death was more than - just an accident." Jesse choked and cleared her throat, willing her face to stay calm, her eyes to stay dry. *I don't want him to know how much it hurts even to think about that.*

Jason put his hands on her tense shoulders, pulled her back against the chair, began loosening the knotted muscles. As the slender fingers moved over her shoulders and up the back of her neck, Jesse felt the tension leaving, and small pains she hadn't been aware of became noticeable, then melted away.

"That sort of meltdown does happen by accident." His voice was smooth, neutral - nothing to suggest anything more than conversation. "This terrorist's intent was to force us to abort this mission before we ever came near this sector. I suspect he was planted here in the first place to cause *King Kamahameha* to fail before we found that Crystal source. Remember, the last two platforms sent to this sector have been destroyed."

"Oh, thanks, I really needed to remember that."

His hands tightened on her shoulders, then relaxed. "We haven't failed, and we haven't turned back. And now we're perilously close to something they didn't want us to find. I think he's desperate. I think he's going to get more and more obvious, and careless," he said.

"With our luck, he'll blow us to kingdom come before his big brother out there decides to have us for dinner. We don't have a clue who he is."

Jason's hands stilled on Jesse's shoulders.

She pulled away from him, turned and stood. "Do you know? Thassanios hasn't found anything."

He shook his head. "I'm beginning to be suspicious, but that's all it is – suspicion. I'm not sure."

"Suspicion isn't enough. We have to have proof. Could we have him watched?"

"If I'm right," Jason said, "if we start watching him he may know it. We may trigger what we're trying to avoid. If he thinks we're still in the dark, he may leave well enough alone. He may even make a mistake."

"I don't like waiting," she said between her clenched teeth.

"I know. But for now, that's all we can do."

"You're right." Jesse forced herself to breathe deeply, slowly. "I don't like it, but you're right. But by the One, Jason, if you do find something, don't keep it to yourself. Whatever he's got going for him, I don't think just one of us can take him." *But I'd like to try. I'd like to wrap my hands around his throat until he turns blue and passes out, and then revive him and tear him limb from limb.*

He nodded and settled on the edge of his desk, the long fingers rotating the cup he'd put there earlier. "I agree. Now if you can get David to agree as well, and you'll promise to do the same, the command team will have agreed collectively to act like a sensible adult."

"Okay, I can tell you're too tired to think straight. Come and eat, and then get some rest before you come back to this. Remember, we're trying to extend the time these codes are off-line, not decrease it."

Jason nodded and drove his fingers through his hair. "You're right. I just don't like knowing they aren't available if we need them. You're also right that I'm too tired to make sense, and food sounds wonderful. I'll go shower and change, and then meet you."

Jesse nodded and sat back down. *Right, Jason, of course. I think I'll just wait right here and enjoy this lovely wine you've given me. Then, when you come out all ready to go back to work and forget about eating, I'll be here to herd you to the table.*

The room was warm and quiet, and the wine was pleasant and refreshing. Jesse let her head rest against the back of the chair and closed her eyes, all too aware that Jason wasn't the only one too close to the edge from fatigue. *David's the only one with any sense,* she thought, and then the vision of David as she'd seen him before she came to Jason's study rose in her mind. Curled up on his couch with a book in his hand - a book in his hand... "Damn it, it was a technical manual!"

"What was a technical manual?" Jason's hair was combed straight back from his face, the soft ends already drying and falling into loose waves. He'd shaved and changed his clothes, and though the circles under his eyes were dark, his eyes were less dull than they'd been when Jesse had come in.

"What David was reading. I thought he'd had the sense to take a break and actually do something pleasant, and he was sitting there reading a technical manual."

"He's probably trying to figure out how to put back-ups on the back-ups," Jason said. "He was very angry about what happened to Kwame."

"We all were." She held a hand out so he could help her up, but he took it and settled on the edge of the desk again, gently running his thumb over the backs of her knuckles.

"Can we talk for a minute, Jesse?"

"Of course." She tried to ignore the sudden chill, like cold fingers caressing her spine. *What do you want to talk about, Jason? And why am I almost sure it's something I don't want to hear?*

Jason reached behind him without looking, picked up the light stylus and began playing with it, rolling it over and through his fingers.

"Please tell me you're not on the verge of confessing something horrifying," Jesse said, trying to keep her tone light. "I don't think I could take another one in this lifetime."

The corner of his mouth turned up at that. "No, I don't think I'm about to confess to anything, and although what I want to talk to you about has its horrifying aspects, they're long since past."

"Oh, good." She settled back a little, making no attempt to withdraw the hand Jason was holding. *I don't suppose it can be much more horrifying than what I already know about him.*

He pulled her hand to his mouth, kissed the knuckles, and released it.

"What was that for?"

"Because I don't think I ever thanked you - for - taking the chance on me."

Jesse shook her head. "You were taking just as much of a chance with me - and David. And sometimes lately, I think you got much the worst of the bargain."

"Oh, no. No, Jesse. They tore me into pieces, and you and David have put me back together."

He settled back and dropped his eyes to the light stylus still winding in and out through his fingers.

"I knew Aldrich was terribly - jealous is the right term, I guess - of the triads. He couldn't hide it - you could Feel it coming off him in waves any time he was near you, like the heat from a boiling pot. But I'd never realized his jealousy had tipped over into madness, and..." he looked up and his face was as cold and pale as marble.

The face he uses to hide pain, Jesse thought. *The face he puts on to make the world think he's invulnerable.*

"... it never occurred to me he would do anything so - cruel. So vicious.

"I spent more than ten years afraid to talk to David, afraid to hear what he might say, afraid to get too close to him in case I'd Touch a bit of what he felt about me. Because I knew - I knew - the only reason he would leave me like that - with Mike and my parents gone - was that he blamed me for losing Mike."

He glanced down at the stylus rolling over and over between his fingers, then looked back up at Jesse. "Sometimes when I - when I was having a very bad day, I thought that was why..."

"And you still came here?" *And what an act of courage that must have been, if he believed David blamed him for their First's death and he could tell I didn't want him. Courage - or desperation?*

"I was desperate," he said, in an almost echo of Jesse's thoughts. "I didn't know what else to do. Being that far from David was like living with a knife in my back. I - had to know, for sure."

He stayed staring down for quite a while. When he looked up, for the first time, she could see the pain he'd hidden behind the calm facade.

"A letter a week, every week, for over a year. Mine - I don't know how Aldrich did it, but they were all returned, marked 'refused.' David's - there was - nothing. Not even that. And by the time I was posted away from the Point, away from Aldrich's control, he'd accomplished what he'd set out to do - I was too afraid to send for David, to have it out with him. Prometheus is a big place," he waved a hand, "it becomes too easy not to communicate."

"But when you're Healing, you have to Touch your patient. After David woke up, we talked for a long time," he murmured. He was staring off into space, over Jesse's head. "Hours, I think. About - that, about all these years, about everything. You, Thom, Amari and Sarah. Mike. My folks dying, and Christian - David's father. And about us. About who we are, how we feel about each other."

He straightened, and brought his eyes back down to meet Jesse's. "Nothing's changed, Jesse. After all these years, everything that came between us, he's still my Second, my David. And I'm his. So I have to thank you again, Jesse, twice - for taking the chance on me, and for - for giving me my life back."

The smile that spread across his face was extraordinary, and Jesse seemed to hear an echo of David's voice; "when he smiled, it took your breath away and made your heart feel like it was going to explode with the joy."

He offered his hand, and this time when Jesse took it, pulled her to her feet. "Meantime, I've probably kept you from eating so long you're getting weak from hunger."

That was what the goofy grin was about, Jesse thought, watching Jason and David at dinner. It was back, drifting from Jason's face to David's, disappearing for a moment, coming back, this time to David's face, then Jason's. The two were in high spirits, making silly jokes and taking every opportunity to make contact with each other.

At last, not able to stand any more, she sent them to bed and retired to her study. The readouts on her console told her nothing new, the text in the book she was trying to read blurred and shifted, her back ached no matter what position she adopted.

Give up, Jesse, she told herself, shutting down the console and standing. *You're as tired as anyone else, you need your rest.*

She put her clothes away, wandered in and out of the shower, fell into bed and turned the light out. And felt her eyes open, her neck and jaw tense, in the dark. Deliberately, willing herself to relax, she closed her eyes.

It was a fight, but she kept them closed. She tried one of the relaxation exercises she'd learned at the Point, concentrating on each area of her body starting with her toes, willing the tension to flow out and away, like water from the low side of a pool. The more she concentrated, the more she tightened up, until she felt like a ball of taut wire, stretched almost to the breaking point.

Exhaling a long, deep breath, she sat up, switched on the light, and wrapped her hands around her knees. *What's the matter with you, Jesse? Too tired to sleep?*

That wasn't the answer. If it had been, images of CC would have been going through her head, and the relaxation exercise would have worked. But what kept intruding on her thoughts, pushing itself into her consciousness every time she started to relax, was the dinner table, the warm evening light on the mellow oak, the gleam of the dishes and cutlery, David's hand lying over Jason's...

Stop it, Jesse. He's an adult - they're both adults, it's none of your business. Just go to sleep, you need the rest, you can't afford to be tired in the morning.

What, are you jealous? You? Of what? You keep telling yourself you don't even like Jason Ashe, and as for David - as for David...

"As for David, you've been doing everything you possibly could to keep him at arms' length since Thom died, haven't you, you stupid woman?" she muttered. "You thought he'd just wait, until you were 'ready.' It never occurred to you that he could still love Jason Ashe, that he'd jump at the first chance of any kind of lasting relationship. And here you are, on the outside looking in. Not fun, is it?"

Not fun at all, she acknowledged, lying back with her hands behind her head. *Not fun at all.*

#

"Command, could you meet me in the Command Office?" Jesse looked across her study at the clock and wondered where the day had gone. She set the report she'd been reading aside and touched the comm control. "On my way, Command Second."

On the way up to CC, Jesse speculated about what David wanted, but then her thoughts returned to the reports she'd spent the day reviewing.

I'm glad it isn't a hundred years ago. At least the kids have been out enough on short trips for the medics to find out if anyone's prone to space-sickness, she thought.

That was the only blessing. The tension was starting to show in the usual ways - partners fighting with each other, roommates requesting assignment changes, scores on combat exercises falling. *We need to consult on ways to relieve the tension and get the scores back up in the optimal range - we can't take a chance that bastard out there will let us get away without a fight.*

"What's up?" she asked, as the office door swung open.

"Well," David said, "we thought maybe we should give you a surprise party for your birthday."

"It isn't my birthday, David, but I could use a pleasant surprise." Jason's eyebrow lifted, and Jesse realized she'd emphasized 'pleasant' without meaning to.

"Well, your control and executive systems are all back on line," Jason said. "Come see what you think."

The pad was already warm, and the system controls came online immediately. Jesse scanned them and, "This is terrific," she said. "You didn't just put them back together, you completely revamped them!"

"Oh, not completely," Jason said, making a minor adjustment to one of the flux readings. "I guess you could say we took the opportunity to enhance them a little. Most system designers are engineers, and they don't have a lot of experience with triads. We just made some modifications from our point of view, since we had the time to do it."

"Well, I have to say, you've done a superb job." She shifted through the scans, taking in information that had never been directly available before, delighting in the play of colors designed to make different systems easily distinguishable, the clarity of the symbols and characters he'd used.

She looked up and five pairs of eyes were fixed on her, with five broad grins on the mouths under them. "I take it I'm the last to have the chance to play with the new toy?"

Zephron Bell laughed and the rest chuckled. "Well, you might say Jason and James used us as guinea pigs," he said, gesturing to his partners.

Jesse nodded. "Well, this is good. All right, I take it this is timed to come back on line in segments?" Jason nodded. "And what about backups?"

"Zephron and I have been working on them," David said. "It's going to be a continuing process, but with what we've got on it now and what Jason and James built into it as they went, our terrorist is going to have a hell of a time disrupting us that way again."

"Very well. Let's get back to work." She waved her hand as though shooing small children, and the five laughed again and turned to leave the command office.

"Third." Jason and Mariko both glanced back, and Jesse indicated that she'd meant Jason. The young woman nodded and followed her partners and David through the door.

"You promised me when this was finished, you were going to take the day off and sleep," Jesse said.

The corner of Jason's mouth lifted. "Are you implying that you think I might not be in tip-top form at the moment, First?"

"No, I'm saying it right out loud. You're even staggering. Go home and go to bed."

The smile broadened, and he straightened. "Yes, Sir. Whatever you say, Sir. Please don't wake me unless it's the end of the world, Sir."

And before Jesse could think of an adequate comeback, he was gone.

-Chapter 10-
Here's much to do with hate, but more with love.
William Shakespeare—Romeo and Juliet

"Do you realize we've had five, no, six whole days without any major upsets?" Jesse asked.

David nodded without looking up from his plate, but Jason put his soup spoon down. "Don't say that too loudly. You'll tempt the gods."

"Ah, superstition. I knew you had a weakness somewhere."

He smiled and picked up his glass. "I have many weaknesses, but superstition isn't really one of them. I'm just afraid any period of relative peace will let us relax enough to be vulnerable to his next nasty trick."

"And the longer we stay in this area with that monster hiding out there watching us, the itchier the back of my neck gets," David said. "Jason, finish your soup or I'll hold your nose and feed it to you."

"I hope you're not going to need a referee, because I'm too tired to pull you apart," Jesse said. "I appreciate the quiet, but it's still tense with so many of the systems offline, and meanwhile, the command responsibilities keep growing. Do you realize no one in this sector seems to feel capable of doing anything without consulting us?"

Jason put his spoon down, and before David could admonish him again, picked up bowl, spoon and glass and took them to the recycler. He came back with a cup of coffee. "I sent the last section over to David for testing this afternoon. The timing sequence is bringing them online a piece at a time, and that one should be in place about twelve hours after David releases it."

"Which means it will be up and meshed with the rest of the system controls sometime tomorrow evening," David said. "I started the tests running before I came down for dinner."

"Good," Jesse said. "Now, much as I hate to eat and run - it's been a long day and I need to be up early. Good night."

"Good night, Jesse," David said.

"You look as though you don't feel well," Jason said, getting up and following Jesse to her study door. "Can I help?"

She shook her head. "I'm just tired enough to have a headache, and that's making me cross. I'll be fine in the morning."

"Do you want me to help you sleep?"

"No. Thank you. I actually get some of my best ideas when I can't sleep." *And I don't want you to Touch the feelings that keep me from sleeping, Jason. I still don't trust you that much.*

"The headache, then. You can't think clearly when you have a headache."

Jesse nodded and closed her eyes as his warm, strong hand came to rest on her forehead. The warmth spread from his hand through her body, and as it spread, the pain drained away, leaving her relaxed and clearheaded. "Thank you," she said as his hand fell away. "I didn't realize how bad it was. Listen, you and David should get some rest, too."

Jason smiled. "I'm fine, but I think David's at about the same point you are. I'm going to put him to bed and then spend some time catching up on my own work. Good night, Jesse."

#

"Jesse. Jess, are you there?" She struggled up out of the warm blackness and opened her eyes far enough to see the clock before she palmed the comm control. *Oh-one-thirty. What does he want at this time of night? I don't want to deal with it, Jason, I don't. Leave me alone. I've only had about an hour's sleep and I'm tired.*

"I'm here." She made no attempt to disguise the fact that she was irritated. "What do you need?"

"Can you come to my room, please? As soon as possible." The comm went dead before she could ask any questions, and Jesse pushed the covers back and began fumbling for clothes. "What in the name of the One does he want? A shoulder to lean on because he had another nightmare?"

"What's going on?"

Jason's room was full of people - a medic, a nurse, a tech, Jason, Jason's bodyguard - and David. The big man was stretched out on the mattress, his body covered with shadows where bruises would be visible by morning. His eyes were closed, the gold skin was sweat-covered and pasty, and his breathing was shallow and rapid.

"What happened? What did you do?" she turned on Jason, who was backed up against the wall, his face paler than David's.

"Never mind. Wait in my study."

He glanced over at the medic, who shook his head, then slipped out of the room. Jesse lifted her chin toward the door and the security officer followed him.

Jesse moved to the wall at the foot of the bed. She kicked into the pile of blankets and sheets and realized they had been shredded. *What happened? Who did this?*

She stayed out of the way as Thassanios scanned David, handed the scanner to the tech, ran his hands over David's head and body, then took the scanner back and read the results. "Well, Mr. Ashe was mostly right," he commented. "That rib is broken, and so is his wrist. The ankle's only sprained. And I'm damned if I know how it happened in here, or at all - he's a pretty formidable fighter when he's conscious."

"You think this was done while he was unconscious?" Jesse made no effort to control her voice, and Thassanios glanced at the nurse and the tech, both going about their business as though they were deaf, then took her arm and pulled her out of the bedroom into Jason's study.

"I think he was asleep. Jason says when he found him, David thought he was having a nightmare."

Jesse opened her mouth, and Thassanios' grip tightened on her arm as he shook her, hard. "If this was what I think it was, we do not, I say again, not, want any more people involved, Command. Keep your voice down."

"How could..." she heard the shrillness of her voice, and its volume, and made a conscious effort to control it, swallowing hard and taking a deep breath before she continued. *Calm down, Jesse, behave yourself. You're supposed to be Command.* "How could someone do that to David and not wake him up?"

"I don't know," Thassanios said, releasing Jesse's arm with a further admonitory shake.

"Ashe said he was going to put him to sleep." *He let David be hurt.*

The medic shook his head. "Having a Sensitive or a Healer put you to sleep is rather like drinking warm milk. It helps you relax and drift off, but it won't keep you asleep.

"Christiansen doesn't seem to have been drugged, but that's only preliminary. I'm going to take blood when I finish putting him back together, and run some tests. I think he did wake up, at least enough to fight a little - there was tissue under his fingernails."

"So you can get a match?" *He was right. We don't want it to get out - it would cause a panic. The Command Second attacked, in the Command quarters - we'd have people killing each other in the halls. And what kind of reaction was that, from the Command First? You should be in better control, Jesse. Maybe you need to back off entirely and leave this one to Zephron.*

"Oh, I could probably match it," the medic said, perching on the edge of Jason's desk. He looked tired, and his face was grim. "But it won't do us any good, unless you choose to believe he was attacked by a couch - what was under David's fingernails was black leather." At Jesse's look of confusion, he shrugged, and pushed himself away from the desk. "Probably Tragan personal armor, but I don't know. And I don't know how someone could wander around, even in the middle of the night, in Tragan body armor and not be noticed by at least fifteen people, but someone apparently did. Now, Command, if you'll excuse me, I need to get back to my patient. This isn't going into the morning report, by the way."

Jesse nodded, and the short, stocky man slipped past her and back into Jason's room. She turned to follow him, then paused. *Thassanios is taking care of David*, she thought. *They don't need me. But Ashe is waiting in my office, and I can do something about that. Damn the man, I think I'm going to start liking him and he lets something like this happen. He let David be hurt.*

The guard at Jesse's door was a tall redhead named Jean Camaretti. "How long have you been with the Command Third this evening, Mr. Camaretti?"

The security officer glanced down at her watch. "I came on duty about fifteen minutes ago, Command. I met Mr. Ashe at his office and came up to the residential levels with him."

"Thank you," Jesse murmured. "Did Dr. Thassanios make it clear this doesn't go on any of the morning reports?"

"Yes, Command." Camaretti nodded and stepped aside, palming the door control for Jesse.

Jason was standing with his back to the door, shoulders hunched, staring at her bookcase, but she suspected he wasn't seeing the small carving he was scrutinizing. *Anticipating the worst, Ashe? This time you might be right.*

"David," she said, seating herself behind her desk, "has a broken rib, a broken left wrist, a sprained left ankle, heavy bruising all over his upper body, especially on his throat where he seems to have been partly strangled, and contusions on his face. He's also unconscious and in shock."

Ashe jumped as she spoke, closed his eyes and drew in a long breath, then seated himself in one of the chairs in front of the desk. "I thought his ankle was broken."

"Well, if you know all that, then perhaps you could explain to me why and how David was attacked in your room, in his sleep, and even more important, perhaps you could explain what he was doing in your room in the first place."

"What?" He sounded surprised, and faint patches of color rose to paint the pale cheeks. The blue eyes were direct, dark, and hard.

"I said, explain what David was doing in your room."

"He was sleeping." Ashe was breathing hard, and the long fingers were white around the light stylus that never seemed to be out of his hand.

What, you're insulted, Ashe? Your feelings are hurt? It's none of my business? I don't care. You let David be hurt.

"Don't take that tone with me, Mister. I am not the one at fault here."

The tense fingers didn't relax, but Ashe's voice was calm. "And I am? Would you explain to me just how and why I'm at fault because my partner is in my room? In case you've forgotten, Command," the slight emphasis on the word was edged with acid, "Mr. Christiansen and I are both adults, and neither of us is obliged to explain what we do together to you - or anybody else."

Answer me, damn you. How did you let him be hurt? If it's your job to take care of him, why didn't you take care of him?

"Just how did that monster get in there to attack him while he was alone and asleep? Where were you?"

"I was, as I told you earlier, catching up on some work. I got back just before I called you - and yes, I did call the medics before I called you - my priority was David. I presume, since he was in my room and no one could have known that in advance, that David's attacker was after me."

"You told me it was your responsibility to take care of David - to keep him safe. So why weren't you taking care of him?"

She hadn't thought he could get any whiter. His lips opened, as though he was about to speak, then he turned his head so she couldn't see his face.

"Don't turn away from me, Jason Ashe, don't you dare turn away. David was in your room asleep, and that son of a bitch got in there, looking for you, and hurt him. How? How did he do it?" She leaned forward, her weight over her hands, until she was as close to him as she could get with the desk between them.

He pulled his head back, but met her eyes. "I don't know. I can't even imagine. David isn't a heavy sleeper..."

"But you said you were going to help him sleep."

He shook his head. "Only to get to sleep, not to stay asleep. If you need to wake up, you wake up. To continue - I don't think you're a heavy sleeper, either, judging by your response to my nightmares. He somehow managed to keep David from calling out, but I don't know how. There's a shadow over David's mouth, and I almost wonder if he was lightly drugged before the attacker started probing for - whatever he was after."

Oh, God, I'm going to be sick. "You mean this attack wasn't - just physical?"

Jason looked up, then returned his attention to the light stylus, rolling over and over his fingers. "I think the physical side effects are the result of him trying to subdue David so he could mind-probe him. Remember, he was after me."

"So now we have to assume that the terrorist knows everything David knows." It was revolting. It was horrifying. Jesse was so angry she felt it thick in her throat, like bile, souring her mouth, her gut - her whole being.

"No. If he'd gotten what he wanted, I don't think David would have lived. The probe alone might have killed someone not quite so strong, but David fought, and fought hard. That slowed the attacker down, and I think my return interrupted him. I doubt he got more than surface thoughts, and most of that would be concerned with resisting the attack. He may not even be sure it wasn't me he attacked. Nevertheless, it would be the better part of discretion to change David's access codes as soon as possible."

Jesse nodded. "Mr. Camaretti told me she met you at your office and accompanied you to the residential levels. Were you alone before that?"

He glanced up, but his face didn't change. "Doctor Ngoro was in the lab and we talked for a few minutes. But if you mean was I unaccompanied, no, Command, I wasn't. Mr. Raavik was with me until Mr. Camaretti relieved him. Please feel free to call the Security Office and confirm that with Raavik and their logs."

Jesse nodded without relaxing. *Don't think I won't do that, Ashe. I will. You let David be hurt.*

"I know you didn't want me, and I know you don't like me

much," his jaw was tight, but his voice was still level and conversational.

Well, his self-control is admirable - if it was me, I'd probably be ready to kill somebody. Maybe he is.

"But whatever my faults, I am not the terrorist, and I wouldn't hurt David under any circumstances. I wouldn't - have..." He choked and turned away again.

Then the slumped shoulders straightened and he pushed himself up in the chair. "There's something else I think you need to consider. For a reason I can't fathom, all the - personal attacks - have been directed at us - me. It may simply be that he hasn't gotten around to it yet, but our operational counterparts have been safe so far. If he becomes frustrated, that may change."

Jesse thought of the monster who had tried to kill David attacking tiny, fragile Mariko, or smiling, freckle-faced James, and felt the same chill she'd had the morning Zephron had been glad neither of them much liked eggs. "I agree. Whoever is doing this, they need protection. I'll arrange it."

"You might consider arranging something for yourself as well."

Jesse didn't answer, and he sat silent for a moment. "Are we finished, Command?"

"Not quite." Her voice sounded thin and cold, and the muscles in her throat felt strained. "Since you're so concerned about protecting us all, I think you should make David your priority until you've done your job and found the terrorist." *I'm being unfair*, Jesse thought, then dismissed the thought. *I don't care. You let David be hurt. You will not let David be hurt again, or I will kill you.* "You've bought yourself a new assignment, Mr. Ashe - you're David's bodyguard. You make sure he isn't alone, you make sure he's covered, and you do it yourself unless it's absolutely necessary for the two of you to be in different places. Is that clear?"

"Very clear, Command. And if you'll excuse me, I should return to my responsibilities."

He was on his feet before Jesse could respond, and the door closed behind him as the vase she threw found its target. It shattered and pieces flew all over the room, but even the tinkle of broken glass didn't relieve Jesse's fury. She dropped her head into her hands and covered her eyes, concentrating on regulating her breathing, willing the pounding in her head and throat to slow, smooth, steady.

Calm, Jesse. Rational. You are not a creature of impulse,

you are not controlled by your emotions. You think before you act, you make decisions based on facts, not on feelings. You will not let your feelings about Jason Ashe interfere with your functioning as the Command First.

When her fingers quit trembling, she pulled the console up and accessed the security logs. Raavik and Ashe had gone to Ashe's office less than ten minutes after Jesse had gone to her rooms, stopping in the science office to consult with Doctor Ngoro, remaining at Ashe's office until about ten minutes before he had called her, when Raavik had been relieved by Jean Camaretti. Once again, on the evidence of the security team, Ashe couldn't have been responsible for the attack. *Well, I knew that already,* Jesse thought. *It doesn't matter. He let David be hurt.*

"How in the Name did he get in here?" she muttered as she cleared the screen and folded the console down. "Why didn't somebody see him? Why didn't David wake up and kill him? What am I going to do?"

Go to bed and get some rest, she thought. *You're ringy, and it's making you irritable, unreasonable, and off-balance. Talk to Zephron in the morning.*

She didn't remember getting into her bedroom and into bed.

Sleep and waking brought no relief from the sick anger that had almost overwhelmed her the night before. She went through her wake-up routine with her teeth and jaw clenched against the threatening nausea, stretching, showering, dressing with her attention focused on what she was doing to keep the image of David away. *He let David be hurt.*

In her office, she opened the console, skimmed the overnight reports, then checked the duty roster. *That's what I thought. David's supposed to be on today. Well, I guess I'll have to find him a substitute.*

As Jason's bedroom door opened, Jesse reached for the light controls and palmed them to full. David muttered and threw his arm over his eyes. Jason, who'd been lying beside him, pulled back the arm that had covered David and pushed to his feet in one move, hands open in front of him.

You're ready to fight. Good.

"I rearranged the duty roster to keep our attacker from knowing he'd succeeded in doing any damage. You're taking David's shift. You have ten minutes to get there."

She kept her voice low. Behind Jason, David stirred and raised himself on his elbows, then began pushing himself up. Jason nodded, glanced back at him, and came toward her. His left hand had gone to his side, as though it ached, and he moved stiffly.

Jesse stepped aside. "Ashe."

He stopped.

"You look like hell. Get yourself cleaned up before you show up in my command center."

"First," he said. His head was bent, and turned away from her.

"If anybody asks, you and David were wrestling in the living room and went over one of the couches."

He said, "Perhaps you could let me know when you get ready to leave. I'll send a security officer to stay with David until I'm off duty." He went out.

"I don't suppose it ever occurred to you that you have no right at all to chase him out of his own rooms?" David said as Jesse went to the converter.

She turned, an eyebrow raised. "Do you object to the way I treat him?"

He pushed himself up, grimaced, and leaned back against the head of the bed. "Would you expect me not to? And since when is it 'your' command center? I'd think, if it were anybody's, it would be Zephron's."

She ordered without answering him, came back balancing a tray with two cups, two plates of toast, and a bowl with a selection of fruits. She set it on the table beside the bed, seated herself, picked up a cup and swallowed.

"What would you suggest?" she said. "Act as though nothing happened, as though everything is the way it should be, as though you being attacked in the middle of the night because you're in Ashe's room is perfectly normal and I shouldn't be angry about it? Last night I… I thought you were dead." Her voice had almost disappeared, and she turned her head, unwilling to let David see that her eyes were wet.

He put his cup down and held a hand out. She slid closer and took it, twining their fingers together and tightening her hold as though the warmth of his hand could keep evil away.

"Try using your head, Jesse."

"I don't want to use my head. I'm so angry all I want to do is hurt somebody."

He shook her a little, then settled back. "Cool down and use your head. Somebody got into this room. Somebody physically held me down and physically damaged me in the course of — what he did." He looked away from Jesse a moment, his lips hard. "How? Even with Jason and his bodyguard gone, you were there, and I'm not the world's heaviest sleeper. Do you think he just walked through three doors, and left the same way, and nobody saw him? Not the patrols, not the visuals, not anyone?"

"I don't know, and neither does anyone else. Thassanios found black leather under your fingernails."

David winced and tried to push himself higher, swearing under his breath as the broken wrist came down, panting with the pain and clutching at his left side.

"Calm down. Do you need some help?"

He shook his head. "No, I just need a new body. When I get my hands on him, whoever he is, he'll wish he'd killed me. Now," he pulled in a breath and some of the tension went out of his face, "did you just say you found black leather under my fingernails?"

Jesse nodded.

"Tragan body armor. And he got in here through three doors, past the security patrols in the corridors, and got out the same way past Jason and his bodyguard, and no one saw him. It's impossible. It'd be easier to believe I did it myself."

David shifted, and Jesse reached to steady him, brushing his side.

He drew in a breath and clenched his teeth. "Careful, those are the broken ones," he said.

"That's where Ashe's hand was when I came in," she said.

He nodded. "I know. Guess whose ribs ached all night? Not mine."

"What do you mean?" she said.

"I mean, a Sensitive experiences the pain he's helping relieve before draining it away."

"Yes, so?"

"Jason fell asleep. In case you haven't noticed, he's been working himself to exhaustion. He couldn't drain the pain away from himself in his sleep, but he could still absorb feelings from me when he was in contact with me. I didn't feel any pain last night, but he did.

"You had a headache, and Jason relieved it. I was tired, and he helped me sleep. He was tired, too, probably more tired than either of us, but he had a job to finish, and he did finish it. And when he came back and found me, he got help, and he watched over me the rest of the night.

"Was he thanked for this care? Was his concern appreciated? Did anyone even notice or care that it could have been him? On the contrary, someone told him he needed to stay awake and guard me.

"Somebody around here's piling up a lousy record in the treatment of partners, and it isn't Jason Ashe.

"If the man in this room had been Thom Isaacson instead of Jason Ashe would you be acting like this? Do you resent me loving him? Why do you care, Jesse? You keep saying you don't want him. Since Thom died you haven't wanted me, either.

"I was supposed to be on duty this morning, and I'm going to work, First." He slid away from Jesse, and before she could answer he was gone.

-Chapter 11-

Much Speech Leads Inevitably to Silence - Lao Tzu, Tao Te Ching

By the time Jesse got to CC, David had taken over the shift and sent Jason, accompanied by his bodyguard, to his rooms. David turned as Jesse entered, and the look on his face was so forbidding she slipped into the command office without attempting to speak to him, retrieved a stack of files from her in-basket, and slipped out. She noticed in passing that Mr. Raavik and one of the youngsters on the Security team - Hakarlu, that was his name - were standing by the weapons controls.

I don't know why he's blaming me. She set the last file aside and rubbed her forehead. *I'm not the one who hurt him. And as for Ashe...* she let the thought trail off, biting her lip and concentrating hard to control the spasm of pain the thought of him caused.

Oh, Thom, why does it hurt so much just to see him? Why does it make me sick to see David touch him, why do I want to slap him if the two of them smile at each other? Why did you have to go and get yourself killed? How could you leave me this way?

Her chest was so tight it was hard to breathe, and her throat hurt. A good cry or a good screaming fit would be a relief - *but I can't cry. I've never managed to cry for you, Thom, did you know that? Not once since you've been gone.*

She pulled in a long breath, stacked the files neatly on the corner of the desk to be returned to the office, and stood. *Down to the gym, Jesse. At least you don't feel as much like tearing someone limb from limb after a good workout.*

It was easier when she didn't see Ashe; when she didn't see either of them. For almost a week, the turn and turn about of schedules made that easy - she passed David in the hallways a couple of times and acknowledged his greeting with grave courtesy, but didn't pause to talk. Ashe she saw once, across the lounge, but when she realized he was there, she turned to go. She noticed in passing that he seemed, if anything, paler and thinner than usual, and that as usual he didn't appear to be eating, but dismissed him from her mind as soon as the door had closed behind her.

She was busier than ever - conferring with Zephron on internal matters, fielding queries and calls for help from throughout the sector, maintaining contact with the outriders, dealing with the traffic from HQ, continuing to bone up on their command and the people in it. From time to time she wondered if David and Ashe were as busy as she was, but had no desire to see either of them to ask. Their share of sector command duties was done, and she told herself that was all she cared about.

The terrorist stayed quiet, and Jesse wondered if his attack on David had somehow weakened him. She broached the matter with Thassanios, but he shook his head.

"I don't know how he's doing what he's doing, Command. The Command Third and I think he must be using Crystal - perhaps there's a frequency that has a hypnotic effect. But I can't speak to whether he was damaged in the attack or not, or if it would weaken him. We can only hope." He'd managed to review nearly a thousand personal records, with no luck - everyone was exactly what he or she claimed to be, nothing more, nothing less.

The intruder was quiet as well, staying in random space, hovering in near opposition to them with the giant planet between. She and Zephron had designed a route through the huge system that had them making no progress out, but looked as though they were exploring - that, after all, was one of the command platform's tasks. That it was usually delegated to the outriders and scouts made no difference - until they assumed permanent station, *King Kamehameha* was mobile.

It was a relief, but it wasn't enough. Down on the nebulous surface, hidden among the toxic gases that constituted a great portion of its diameter, the giant was breeding something far more deadly than poisonous waste. Day by day, as they waited for the interloper to do something, for the terrorist to either break out again or be discovered, the Crystal grew. *Whatever else happens*, Jesse thought, as she closed the file with the precious, deadly data, *we have to make sure they don't get that. That alone could do more damage than all the weapons they've developed in the last hundred years, and cause more misery.*

Face it, Jesse, that's more important than the way you feel about Ashe. It's more important than missing Thom, or hurting, or feeling left out - more important than you are.

David looked up that afternoon and smiled as he came to relieve her, and that seemed to end the matter. No one apologized, but Jesse decided not to push it. *They're too wrapped up in each other. They probably don't even realize what they've been doing to me.*

Thus comforted, she let life resume its normal ways, taking care to be especially polite to Ashe when she thought about it. The rest of the time she ignored him - it hurt less to pretend he didn't exist.

"Jesse, are you off duty?"

She turned. David was following her along the hallway, lengthening his stride a little to catch up with her.

"I was on my way to the lounge to eat."

"I just got off. Why don't you join us?"

She looked up into the grey-blue eyes a moment, trying to discern a possible hidden motive, then shrugged. *It's dinner time, I'm hungry, and company might take my mind off things.*

"Thanks. I'd like that."

"Oh, for the life of a rough and ready border patrol detachment," Jesse sighed, laying down her knife and fork and pushing her plate away.

"I thought your ambition was to command a maintenance base," Ashe said, pushing away from the table and picking up his untouched dishes to return them to the recycler.

"In the inner systems, where the Tragans never venture," Jesse added.

"Well, First, if you're complaining about the blessed and incidentally boring quiet, I'd venture to say life on a maintenance base in the inner systems would be worse."

"One of the ancient writers said life in the service was 'moments of agonizing fear, punctuated by centuries of boredom,'" David commented.

"She must have been a soldier, whoever she was - that's the most perfect description I've ever heard. The problem with me is, I handle the moments of terror better than I handle the centuries of boredom."

Ashe picked up her plate and carried it to the recycler.

Well, why not, Jesse thought. *It's been a pleasant meal, we're all relaxed, and we're never going to get things cleared up until it's on the table.* "Since we've had a few centuries of boredom, I've been doing a lot of thinking lately," she remarked.

Ashe came back and got David's things. The big man looked up with a smile, and Jesse couldn't help noticing the way their fingers touched. She gritted her teeth to control the wave of fury that washed over her, and went on.

"For some reason, I've thought a lot about personal responsibility. Like one's responsibilities to one's command, one's partners. The kind of chaos that spreads when a set of partners isn't getting along, when someone is breaking the partnership.

"Sometimes I think a person who interferes between partners deserves to be treated like a thief."

The table cleared, Ashe had picked up a cup of coffee and seated himself to David's left. The long fingers wrapped around the cup as though to catch the warmth, but he didn't raise it to his mouth.

"Don't you think so, Third?" Jesse asked.

He looked up, the dark blue eyes blank. "I'm sorry, I must have been spacing. What was that?"

"I said," Jesse's voice was as clear and hard as cut glass. She bit off each word. Her jaw was rigid, her shoulders tight - she was furious. "I said, anyone who comes between established partners is at least as bad as a thief, and should be treated as such. Don't you agree?" *Answer me, damn you, you - you - interloper. You interferer between partners. You...*

She pushed back the rising anger that was souring her gut and making her head ache. *I could kill you. I could strangle you with my own hands, and never feel an instant's regret. You let him be hurt, and now you're taking him away from me.*

Ashe dropped his eyes to his cup, picked up his spoon and stirred the coffee. *No sugar, no cream. He's doing that to buy time. That's fine - buy all the time you want, Ashe, but you're going to answer the question. And then perhaps David'll realize what you've done.*

He set the spoon on the saucer and lifted the cup. "I think perhaps," he said, choosing his words, "that a true partnership would not be weakened by a — a..."

"A third?" David interjected, apparently unaware of any double meaning.

"Let's say — another," Jason said. "I think you'd need to look at the circumstances, know the background..."

"You don't think it's a question of moral responsibility, then?" Jesse said. *Circumstances? Background? I thought you were too tired to be anything but straightforward, for once. It must be a reflex.*

"Whose responsibility? It could depend on what you mean by 'established partners.' Or on the intent of the 'other.' Interfering in a life commitment..."

He broke off and Jesse bit her lip to keep from saying anything. *Does he think I'm trying to come between them?*

"I suppose I never..."

He'd gone from pale to chalky; the cup rattled in the saucer and he put it down and stood. "I'm sorry. I don't seem to be tracking very well. If I may be excused, First? May I leave David with you?" She nodded and he turned from the table.

That's all right, Mr. Ashe, Jesse thought, watching him. His shoulders were slightly hunched, as though he was expecting an attack, and the slate-grey uniform hung on him as though it had been made for a Kondrassi and misplaced. *You go on to bed, Mr. Ashe, and rest well. We'll have this out someday, and I'll tell you exactly how I feel about what you did to me.*

He paused at his door and looked back. David went over to him, and Jesse had time to notice that the big man was still limping before she pushed herself away from the table and went to the converter. Keeping her back to the two men, she retrieved a glass of brandy and settled herself in the corner of one of the couches.

David lowered himself into the corner of the other couch, picked up his glass, and sat turning it, watching the light catch the gold liquid. "You mind telling me how long you're going to keep this up?" he murmured. He didn't look at Jesse.

"Explain what you mean by 'this,' David," she finally said. "I'm not aware that I'm doing anything out of the ordinary."

He pinched the bridge of his nose, pulled in a long breath, set the glass down with a thump. "By 'this' I mean this coldness, this closing yourself off. Avoiding us as much as possible, and then behaving as though we're strangers. This extraordinary courtesy that's worse than open rudeness, this anger. By 'this' I mean letting your Third wait on you as though he's a servant, and not even having the grace to acknowledge him. This trying to provoke a fight that will make him apologize to you when you're the one who's in the wrong. This barely controlled fury that makes him so sick he has to leave the room. How long are you going to act like a spoiled little kid in a fit of the pouts?"

How dare you? The heat from the brandy and her anger with Ashe drained away, and as her chest and gut tightened, Jesse felt herself getting cold. She stood and stared down at David, hands on her hips, fingers spread. Her mouth tightened into a thin line. "I think," she said, in a soft, cold voice, "you're forgetting whom you're talking to, Mister. If you have a problem, I suggest you file a complaint." *A spoiled little kid! He tramples all over me, he almost lets you get killed, and you accuse me of acting like a spoiled little kid? What in the name of the One is wrong with you, David?*

"Jesse, this is me, remember?" David said, looking up. "I'm your friend - your Second. Your partner. I love you. If there's something wrong, let me help."

"There's nothing wrong," she said, returning to her place and picking up her glass. "Nothing except Ashe. Nothing you can do is going to 'fix' that. Nothing you can say is going to change my mind. I never should have let them send him here in the first place, I certainly shouldn't have given him an opportunity to impose himself on you. But I will exercise my authority properly in the future, I swear I will. He'll never hurt you or anybody else again." *If I have to kill him with my bare hands. He let you be hurt.*

David stood and grabbed Jesse's wrist, so fast she didn't have time to evade him. "All right," he said, "I've had enough. I told you before, I'm not your personal possession." She tried to pull away and he tightened his grip. Jesse felt the bones in her wrist shift and her fingers go numb. She clenched her fist and her jaw, determined not to let him know he was hurting her, not to be drawn into a fight.

"Listen to me, you bad-tempered bitch," he said, spitting the words out. She opened her mouth and he shook her, hard. "I said listen.

"I do not, I repeat, do not, need to be protected from Jason Ashe. I'm beginning to think Jason Ashe and I need to be protected from Jesse Larsen.

"You have no cause for grievance. I had every right to be in Jason's room, and he had every right to have me there. We're adults, what occurs between us is our business – not yours, not anyone else's. We don't need your permission. Do you understand that?"

He shook her again, and she stiffened her neck to keep her head from snapping back. *I knew David had a temper, but I never knew about this. What has Ashe done to make him this way?*

Jesse struggled to free her wrists, and David tightened his grip. "You're jealous, aren't you? That's what's really wrong. It isn't me getting hurt at all, is it? Since Thom died you can't stand the idea that anyone else should be happy. And since Jason got here, you've done your level best to make sure he and I wouldn't be.

"We are a triad - a partnership, not a hierarchy. Jason and I are your partners, not your subordinates. If you just want the eagles, that's fine — but in that case, take another command and leave Jason and me free to find a First who wants to be part of a triad. And do it soon. And don't waste any more of your time trying to get at Jason, because if you hurt him..." he pulled in a long breath and straightened. The changeable eyes were pale as rainwater. "If he gets hurt because of the way you've been sulking and carrying on, Jesse, you won't have to worry about getting rid of him - you'll have to worry about staying alive long enough to get someplace where I can't get to you. Have I made myself clear?" He released her wrist and before she could recover her equilibrium, pushed her down on the couch.

Jesse pushed away from the couch and started toward him, but David turned away.

"I'm going to my brother."

Jesse sat a while after David left, trying to ignore the echo of his angry words. "You'll have to worry about getting far enough away that I can't get to you. We're adults, what we do together is none of your business. I'm going to my brother... my brother... my brother." Only the very closest partners called each other 'brother,' as well as 'friend,' 'lover,' 'partner.' In all her life, Jesse had only met one triad that did so - Louise Jameson and her partners, Britt and Jenn. And they'd been together since - since...

"Since they met at the Point, Jesse. Since, Jamie once told you, the first time they saw each other." And another faint echo sang through Jesse's mind. "I almost started out by saying, 'Hello, Second.' For us, Mike and me, David was the missing piece in our personal puzzle. Once we found him, we knew we were complete."

It was like being hit in the face by a brick, what her sensei had called a blinding flash of the obvious.

Poor Jesse - no wonder neither of them got it when you were talking about coming between partners - you were the interloper in their partnership. Ashe didn't come between you and your partner, you tried to come between him and his - his life-partner. Oh, my God, what have I done?

Pulling in a deep breath, Jesse pushed herself away from the corner of the couch where David had dropped her and headed for her room, pausing on the way to put her glass in the recycler.

You really messed up this time, didn't you, Jesse? She pulled off her shirt and threw it at the closet door. Her boots followed, then her pants, then her underwear. Naked, she stretched up toward the ceiling, then down, trying to turn her mind off by keeping her body moving. *A shower might help* - she followed the thought into the bathroom, standing under the hot water until her tight shoulders started to loosen up and her knees began to soften.

Thank the One for the person who invented recycling. She rubbed herself dry with the rough side of the towel and headed for the bedroom. *I suspect I'm not the only one who considers our relatively unlimited water supply a necessity rather than a luxury.*

She slid into bed and pulled the covers up, stretching her long legs with a sigh. *Sleep on it, Jesse.* She palmed the touch pad to turn off the light. *You'll feel better in the morning.*

She turned over and closed her eyes, only to open them again to shut off the image of Josiah Clark, the man she refused to call her father, his huge fist descending toward her face. She lay panting, staring up into the darkness, trying to command her racing heart to slow. She stretched out, pulled the covers gently around her shoulders, wiggled her head into a more comfortable position on the pillow, and closed her eyes again.

"Nothing ever 'just goes wrong,' girl," the harsh voice intoned. "There's no such thing as an accident - things go wrong and accidents happen because people are careless. Now do it again, and this time get it right."

"No," Jesse breathed. "That isn't true. It was an accident. It wasn't my fault. I didn't do anything wrong." She curled into a ball, burying her face in the pillow, covers tight around her.

Twenty minutes later she sat up and turned the light back on. *I can't let this go on.* She threw the covers off and went to the closet, grabbing a sweater and a pair of pants.

He may never forgive me, and he's right. Dragon's breath, but I hate admitting that. I've been acting like a bitch since David got hurt, and I knew then it wasn't Ashe's fault - I just needed someone to take it out on. Someone to blame.

Damn you, Josiah. I hope you're finding out what it's like, wherever you are. I hope you're finding out what you did to me.

She gritted her teeth, shook her head, and left.

-Chapter 12-

...tis not so deep as a well, nor so wide as a church door...
William Shakespeare—Romeo and Juliet

"David?" The room was dark, and Jesse didn't want to startle him. She took a couple of steps closer to the bed and stopped, listening. Then she went back and hit the light controls, flooding the room with daylight brilliance.

A music card and a bookcard lay on the bedside table. The bed was smooth, blankets and spread taut, pillows fluffed. The closet doors were shut. The room looked - not unoccupied, but as though its inhabitant had been gone a while, and never spent much time there.

The light was off in Ashe's study. She was halfway toward the bedroom door when he lifted his head from the console he'd been bent over, and the movement caught her eye.

By the One! He looks as though he hasn't eaten or slept for weeks. A sudden vision of him carrying an untouched plate to the recycler slid across the forefront of her mind.

"David isn't in his room." She was surprised to realize she was breathing hard.

Ashe put his hands on the desk and pushed himself up, as though he was too old or too tired to rise without assistance. He tipped his head toward his bedroom door. "He's in my room."

"I told you not to leave him alone." *I thought you came to apologize, Jesse?* the little voice in her head murmured.

The corners of his mouth lifted and he came around the desk, waving Jesse to a chair. "Mr. Camaretti's with him."

"I thought she was supposed to be with you?"

Ashe shrugged. "May I get you something?"

Jesse sank into a chair, the trembling in her legs telling her how she'd felt when she'd found David's bed empty. "Please. Brandy, if you wouldn't mind. When I couldn't find him, I..." she let her voice trail off, hoping Ashe hadn't been listening.

She rubbed her hands over her face, pausing to let the warmth of her palms seep into her temples. The clink as he set the glass down called her back, and she straightened and reached for it. "Thanks. For some reason, this feels like the end of a very long day in a succession of very long days."

Ashe acknowledged the courtesy with a slight smile, the long fingers wrapping themselves around the cup as though to hold and absorb its warmth. He'd settled into the chair with one knee up and the other curled in front of him, and Jesse was once again reminded of the state of his back.

"Why didn't they take care of that while you were in the hospital?" she said, without thinking.

He looked surprised. *Hasn't anyone said anything before, or is it just that he's noticing how rude I am?*

"Nick told me they were afraid to try the surgery when I was first brought in - I wasn't stable enough. And later - there just never seemed to be a time when other things weren't more important."

Jesse nodded and took a long swallow, feeling the heat as the brandy slid down her throat. The warmth relaxed her, and almost as though she was talking to herself, she went back to her earlier thoughts. "They can feel it, you know. They're not sure what, but they know something's wrong. When I walk down the halls, I feel the tension in the air, like unanswered questions."

Ashe nodded. "I know. We keep trying to pretend everything's normal. And I keep looking at them, wondering who he is, what he's going to do next, what he's waiting for. I look into their faces and I find myself thinking, 'are you the one? Are you the bastard who hurt my brother?' Sometimes it's all I can do not to start grabbing people and screaming at them."

'My brother.' There it is again. A description of their relationship deeper, more intimate, longer-lasting than 'my partner,' even 'my lover.' As though they were meant for each other and no one else from the beginning of time. The connection no one has ever been able to understand, no matter how much it's been studied. The chill at what she'd almost done tightened her shoulders and caught her breath in her throat. *Looked at objectively, what I've been thinking and what Aldrich did aren't all that different - but I don't have insanity as an excuse.*

She took another long swallow of the brandy, savoring the aroma, the taste, the glow as it slid down. Ashe was staring down into his cup, the dark blue eyes distant. His face and shoulders were tense, and the long hand that held the cup was almost skeletal, like an armature thinly covered with flesh.

He's been fasting. And now that I come to think of it, to-

night's the first time in at least a week I've seen him and David together, and why was he out here working with David in his bed? Has he been doing penance for my sins?

He leaned forward and set his cup down. "I keep waiting for the next disaster," he said.

"Don't. Don't wait for it, don't think about it, don't even admit there could be one." Jesse sighed and let her head fall back against the chair. "We've had more than enough disasters - I'm tired. I think I'd like to sleep a hundred years and be awakened by a handsome prince's kiss."

"And live happily ever after?"

"Mmm. Why not?"

She was waiting for him to say "because that never happens."

"I'm afraid, if you get bored at the idea of a backwater, the handsome prince would have you screaming with frustration in a week," was what he said.

Jesse straightened and looked at him. He met her gaze, the blue eyes deep and clear, but at the corner of the grave mouth there was just a hint of a curl - the promise of the smile he was afraid to let show.

This is what he's like, Jesse. He'll never give you the conventional answer, never tell you what you want to hear - he'll tell you what he thinks. He'll never lie to you, or play you false - and if you let him, he may even love you. And you may already have lost your only chance to share the gift he is with David.

"We need to talk."

His shoulders loosened, and he exhaled a long sigh. "We do." He stood, and held a hand out to her. "Would you mind if we went to your study so we won't disturb David?"

The moment she touched the door, Jesse felt a wave of blackness that contained all the pent-up rage, fear, and sorrow in the world. It was disgusting. It was obscene. She could taste the bile in her mouth, feel it burning in her throat. She glanced at Ashe and his face seemed suffused with wicked satisfaction, as though he'd caused all the pain she'd ever felt and was gloating. Her hands trembled and she clenched them into fists, trying to control the impulse to smash them into the thin, beautiful face.

Then his arm was around her waist and he was pulling her back into the living room, the door closing behind them, and the wave of fury was receding...

"Dragon's breath! What was that?" Jesse said, when she could talk again. He'd pulled her back to lie propped against the back of one of the couches and knelt beside her, panting.

"Minute." He settled back, and Jesse could see him shaking. "Let me - catch my breath. Never - felt one - that powerful - before." He pulled in a deep breath, another, and another, each slower and fuller than the one before.

He straightened and sat back on his heels. "That was a booby trap, First. A crystal, a potent one, designed to overpower you emotionally and throw you out of control."

"It nearly succeeded," Jesse said, swallowing what felt like a rock and clearing her throat. "I was all ready to smash you when you pulled me away from it."

He nodded. "It's the way alcohol and some drugs work - all the intellectual functions are deadened and what's left is raw emotion. Magnified several times. It could have been very - ugly. That's what he intended."

"And if I hadn't known it before, now I see what makes Crystal so dangerous."

Suppressing a groan, Jesse pushed herself to her feet and went to the converter. Ashe looked up and nodded as she held the tall, cold glass down to him, then shifted to lean against the back of the couch with his knees up. "Thanks. Nice."

"I'm glad to know it wasn't me," Jesse said. "I know I have a temper, and I lose it from time to time, but - not like that."

"I know." He lifted her hand, pressed it to his cheek, touched his lips to her knuckles. His fingers were warm under hers, and she could feel his heart racing. He released her hand and moved away from her. "Sorry. Not the right time. How long has it been since you've been in your study?"

"Early this morning. I walked through it to my bedroom earlier, but I didn't stop."

"And you couldn't get to sleep." He stated it as a fact, and Jesse nodded.

"You never lock your door, and you've been gone all day. Anybody could have walked in. Obviously somebody did.

"You've been feeling negative. Can you imagine what would have happened if we'd gone in there and shut the door? Or if you'd been alone?"

"Thanks," Jesse said, "I'd rather not." She pulled in a long breath, taking a swallow and letting the cold water trickle down her throat. "I feel like I just went through a full-scale combat exercise on a hot, dry, day. And I guess the next question is - what do we do now? Just go back to your study, or over to David's, and wait for it to go away?"

"I wish it were that easy. If we just leave it, it will probably spread - the strength of the effect tells me it's nowhere near the edge of its effective range yet. The fact that you walked through the study earlier and didn't notice anything, but that you had trouble sleeping, tells me it hasn't been there long. By morning it could be all over the suite, if not this whole residential area, especially now that the door's been opened. It'll diffuse, so you won't realize you're walking into it like we did just now, and it'll poison everyone who comes near it."

Jesse bit her lip, trying to hold in the profanity - the string of profanities - that was rising in her mind. "So what can we do? Even if 'move out till it's all over' were an option, I'd hate to give him the satisfaction. I'm assuming this is our terrorist."

"I don't doubt it." He set the empty glass down and walked over to the door, touching it but keeping away from the control plate. After a moment, he turned.

"Someone's going to have to go in there and find it and neutralize it. I can probably do it, but it would be faster and safer with two."

"Fine." Jesse stood and walked over to him. "How?"

"First, we call Security and have someone bring up a specimen box and a couple of pairs of gloves." He called Security and ordered them.

"How do we get back in there?" she asked. "We aren't going to be much good if you're sick and I'm feeling murderous."

He moved around to face her. "I can shield us, for a short time — but you'll have to let me Touch you to do it." At the look on her face, he pulled back. "I'll call David. He isn't afraid of me."

She shook her head. "No. I'm going to have to learn to trust you. Now is as good a time as any. All right," she pulled in a long breath, "do it."

He put his hand on her face. Jesse closed her eyes, heard him draw in a deep breath, and felt warmth spread from his hand, enveloping her. Reaching out with an awareness she rarely needed to use, she Touched the wards he was wrapping about her — strands of his personality, of strengths, of training, of discipline. She'd never Touched the wards, even in the command mesh. She'd never even wondered about them. Now, she was astonished at their fragility, their strength.

She opened her eyes. He was pulling his hand away. "All right?"

She nodded.

He smiled. "What we're looking for is a lump of rock — it may be as small as the last joint of your little finger, or considerably larger. Probably larger, as strong as it is. It will be red, opaque, not transparent or translucent."

"How are we going to find something that small without taking the room apart?" Jesse said. "It could be anywhere, even one of the desk drawers."

"It may be behind something, but not in something. Being in something dampens their effect. That's how they carry them after they're tuned."

"And why we didn't feel it until the door was open?"

He nodded.

A security officer came in with a black box about a foot to a side. "Do you need any help, Command Three?"

"No, thanks," Jason answered. "Command and I will take care of it."

When she was gone, Jesse turned to Jason. "Why a gold-lined box?"

"Gold and platinum are the only things that completely insulate Crystal - remember, this one's still increasing its range.

"All right," he said. "Are you ready?"

Jesse nodded. Jason handed her a pair of gloves. She pulled the left one on and palmed the lock. The wave of blackness poured out of the study, but the wards protected her. Instead of invading her, it flowed past her.

Behind her, she heard Ashe draw in a breath. His hand touched her shoulder. "Above or below eye level, where it won't be conspicuous. Where someone in a hurry, who doesn't know where you put things, would hide something."

"The bookcases," she said, and turned to her left. Ashe set the specimen case down and went right.

Jesse looked for something that didn't belong. She scanned the shelves above her eye level, then down, shifting the small objects she collected. No lump of rock, nothing out of the ordinary, nothing she didn't recognize.

"Here," she heard him say, as she moved to the third set of shelves. "I think this is it."

He held out his hand and Jesse went to look. He held a lump of rock the size of a nilla fruit, irregular, opaque, with none of the depth she would have expected of an object called a crystal. Red — brown-red, the color of dried blood — it lay in his hand like a threat. "That's it?"

"I think so," he answered her. "We'll know when it's cased." He moved to the specimen case, opened it, dropped the ugly lump into it, shut the lid and fastened it.

The lights brightened, objects were clarified, colors warmer, the air cleaner. Jesse straightened her shoulders and eased her back. She hadn't realized she was tense.

Beside her, she felt Ashe relax. The wards he'd wrapped around her loosened and fell away.

"I would never have believed something that small could be that - malignant," Jesse said.

"It absorbs energy from the operator as it's tuned. Our terrorist hates us - a lot."

"That's a pleasant thought. I was hoping at least it wasn't personal."

"It wasn't, before. It is now. I wonder what's changed." He rubbed his eyes, the long fingers covering, then somehow emphasizing, the dark shadows under them, and Jesse wondered if, in addition to fasting and depriving himself of David, he'd also not been sleeping.

"We were going to - discuss the situation," she said, applying her thumbprint to the seal on the box and rising. "Are you still up to it?"

He nodded, and she gestured to the chair in front of the desk and went to the converter. "Drink? I feel as though I need one."

"Coffee, please."

Jesse set the cup on the desk and moved around it. *The couch would be more friendly, but this might help keep things on a less emotional basis.*

She heard a snap, like someone clicking fingernails together, then a hiss.

"No! Jesse, get down!" She froze for an instant, and he dove across the desk toward her, his body's passage closing the console and scattering the objects on the surface.

The impact knocked her back into the chair. Overbalanced by the weight, it went over backwards, taking Jesse and Ashe with it. They landed in a heap, human and chair bodies twined around and over one another, and for a few moments, all Jesse was aware of was the weight of his body on top of her and the pressure of one of the chair's legs on her back.

"Get off me," she gasped, and his hand came down on her mouth. It was wet, and she realized her glass and its contents were also on the heap. *One of us is probably cut*, she thought. It didn't seem very important.

"Shhh," he whispered. "I think it was a movement that set it off, but it may be sensitive to sounds, as well."

"We can't stay like this," she whispered back. "We have to do something. Besides, you're hurting me." It was the chair hurting her, but the pain was becoming so acute she found it hard to make the distinction.

He rolled away, stifling a moan, and Jesse wriggled until the chair was out from under her. Pulling her feet up, she got them against - something - and pushed. The chair slid back, and immediately she heard the snap, this time followed by a hiss.

"Dragon's breath!" she muttered. "What is that?"

He shook his head and scrabbled with his left hand, trying to lever himself to a sitting position against the bookcase. His right hand was curled protectively against his left shoulder, and there was a dark smear growing under the fingers.

"You're hurt."

"Doesn't matter," he said, biting his lip as Jesse helped him push himself up and settled beside him. "No time now. Where is that thing, can you tell?"

She glanced up, then tipped her head back. The snap and hiss came again, and a thin column of smoke rose from her desk. "Right above us," she said, "judging by that. And I think it just destroyed my console," she closed her lips, thinking of the dark smear spreading above Ashe's shoulder and where she'd been standing when he knocked her back. *It'd have gone right into my heart. He saved my life.*

"I suppose there's no chance we could wait this out?"

He moved his head in a negative. "If it's what I think it is, it's powered by a tuned crystal, and at the rate it's firing, we'd be waiting about a hundred years."

The snap and hiss came again, and again a thin column of smoke rose from the desk - this time from the corner farthest from them.

"Shit!" Jesse breathed. "It's moving."

"That's what I was afraid of," Ashe said. "If we don't get it, it could get the next person to come through that door." He put his right hand down - Jesse noticed absently that it was smeared with blood - and tried to push himself up. A film of sweat broke out on his face, and he grimaced and clenched his teeth. "And I'm afraid you're going to have to be the 'we' who gets it. I can't seem to move."

Jesse nodded. "If I come straight up, and keep my back to the bookcase, I should be under the sensor's field of vision." She put her hands under her and pulled her knees up, bracing herself to rise without leaning forward.

During the eternity it took to push herself to a standing position, Jesse found herself thinking prayers of thanks to whatever deity had inspired her to become a martial artist. The strain on her quadriceps and hamstrings was terrific, but years of kicking practice had strengthened and hardened them to make it achievable.

Once up she stood, hands at her sides, back f at against the shelves, and turned her head, slowly, to her left. What she could see of the shelves above her eye level appeared normal, undisturbed. "Nothing on this side," she whispered.

She turned her head to the right and - "There's a bracket on the top shelf."

"Can you see what it's holding?"

"Barely." She edged sideways a bit, then looked again. "That's why we didn't see it. It's painted to match the shelf, and it's between two books. The bracket's an ordinary swivel mount, and there's a - it looks almost like a short club, maybe six or seven inches long, attached to it."

"Black, cylindrical, maybe a couple of lumpy spots?"

"Right," Jesse breathed, and it snapped again. This time the beam hit the chair in front of the desk, and Jesse had to bite her lip to control the surge of nausea. The neat round hole, blackened at the edges, went through the back of the chair at just the level of a tall man's heart.

"All right. It sounds like an energy whip." He was panting, drawing in sharp breaths between short, choppy speeches. "The control - probably on top. Wait - till it snaps again. Grab from the side, above. Don't - point it at yourself."

Jesse nodded. Pulling in deep, slow breaths, she focused herself on the ugly object, shutting out Ashe, fading below her, the vision of David with a hole burned through his heart, the heat on her back she now realized was the bolt, missing her and going into Ashe's shoulder. She flexed her fingers and drew herself up on her toes, stretching for every inch of reach.

It snapped, and she slid her right arm out and up, keeping it against the shelves. Her hand came up, level with the bracket, then over it, barely, and she closed her fingers on the lumpy black cylinder, not allowing herself to think of what might happen if it was secured to the bracket.

It wasn't. It slipped out and she pulled her arm back, holding her breath, concentrating on not allowing it to slip around so it was pointed at her, or down at Ashe, wounded and unable to evade it.

It snapped again and she felt the heat under her hand. The bolt shot out and across the surface of the desk, singeing the fine, dark wood and boring a hole into the opposite wall.

"I think it just killed my control operations manual," she muttered between her teeth.

"I'll get you another one," Ashe breathed. "Try to get it down here so I can disable it before it goes off again."

She nodded and slid down to rest her weight against her heels, concentrating on the hand that held the thing still. Her fingers were going numb, and there was a sharp pain in her wrist from holding the unnatural position.

Ashe's hand came up under hers and she felt his thumb move. There was a sharp click, and he drew in a long breath. "It's disabled. Let me have it, Jesse." She forced her cramped fingers to relax so he could take it, then settled the rest of the way, shaking her hand to restore the circulation.

"I probably destroyed any fingerprints or skin cells," Jesse said, as Jason pulled a slip ring out, turned it, and let it settle back in.

"Doesn't matter," he murmured. "He'd wear gloves. And congratulations, by the way - this was on full. Can you get the bracket?"

She was shaking all over, cold, and she could feel her teeth beginning to chatter. *Adrenaline rush,* she thought. "I think so," she muttered between her teeth. She stood again, ignoring the looseness of her knees, the bitter taste in her mouth, the odd feeling of emotional detachment that was creeping over her. *I'm going to be so stiff and sore in the morning I'll hate myself. And it isn't even a workout.*

There was a small vacuum clamp holding the bracket down. Jesse released the lever and pulled the thing off the shelf, trying not to touch anything but the edges. She dropped to her knees next to Ashe and held it out.

He simply looked at it, then nodded. "If you wouldn't mind getting the box, we'll drop it in with that crystal, and see what we can do about checking it for trace evidence tomorrow."

"It's ingenious," Jesse said, bringing the box from where she'd left it by the door and concentrating on breaking her seal.

"Hmm, yes, but not too clever. If I'd been using my head, I'd have looked for something like this after we found that rock, and it wouldn't have been too hard to spot, even painted to match the shelf. The bracket's something we probably have in stores, and so's the clamp. I wonder where he got the whip?"

"I wonder how he smuggled it in," Jesse muttered. The lid of the specimen case was closed again, locked, sealed with her seal.

"Probably in pieces. The only thing likely to set off an alarm would be the crystal, and that only if it was tuned. I suspect he has a stock of them with him, all or mostly all untuned, and they came in looking nothing like what they really are."

Jesse nodded. "Probably. And if they're going to keep planting terrorists on our bases, we need to change the way we screen the troops - and their personal possessions. There, that's finished. Shall I call someone and have this taken down and put in the safe? And have them bring up a hand scanner and go over this room at the same time?"

He started to shake his head, then stopped in mid-move. "I was about to say no, that's probably it, but I was wrong before. Yes, I think that would be a good idea - you might have them go over your bedroom, as well.

"Meantime," he rolled to his knees and pushed himself up, biting his lip, "I'm going to get something.

"Don't worry, I'll be back," the vagrant smile flickered over his face, "we still have things to discuss."

-Chapter 13-
Be merciful, say "death..." William Shakespeare—Romeo and Juliet

He came back as Jesse was applying her seal to the specimen box. The security officer put the scanner in her pocket, picked up the box, nodded to Jesse, and edged past Ashe, nodding as she passed him.

Jesse hadn't thought he could get much paler, but the edges of his lips were white, and the little color normally in his face had drained away, leaving him almost as white as alabaster. *And nearly as transparent.*

He moved away from the door and staggered, and she realized he'd held the door for the security officer not just because his manners were impeccable, but because he didn't want the woman to realize how weak he was.

"Here," he said, dropping to one knee by Jesse's armchair. The chair behind the desk was broken, the desktop was singed in several places, the console was fried, and the operations manual was indeed destroyed. *And who pays for that, and how do I get them repaired without having it get all over? Or do I let it get all over, and let our terrorist wonder how he failed?*

Jason's fingers on her wrist called her back from speculation, and she looked down into the blue eyes. There were faint lines around them, and his mouth was tight. "Look." He popped the lid off a small white box and dumped the contents into his left hand, ignoring the blood that made the palm sticky and red. "Short course on the Tragan energy whip, arguably the nastiest weapon ever invented."

"Nastier than thermite bombs?"

"Point taken. Let's say the energy whip is more personal, and to me that gives it an additional flavor of nastiness. Anyway," the long, slender fingers were trembling, "this is it. They all run to this pattern - some are heavier, some are lighter, depending on the maker. This," he touched an oval slider, "is the trigger. Slide it forward, you activate the bolt. Sideways, you activate the whip. The bolt has a range of about fifteen yards; the whip is about seven feet long."

Jesse nodded. The control was very simple - *of course, it had to be made so the cannon fodder in the Hexarchs' army could handle it as well as a warlord who'd had years of weapons' training.*

"You control the intensity here," he turned the ugly cylinder over and put his finger at the bottom of a red slider marked as a gauge. "The lowest intensity would have an effect like poison ivy on human skin; the highest can cut a body in two. This setting," he slid the marker about halfway up, "is the one they prefer for the 'death of the whip.' It allows them to do a lot of damage before the victim dies."

This setting is the one they used to tear two boys to shreds. Jesse swallowed the roughness in the back of her throat and blinked - hard. *Enough to cause hours, maybe days of agony before it killed.*

"This is the safety." He pulled out a locking ring on the bottom of the cylinder, rotated it once, let it settle back into place. "Set here," he indicated a notch, "it's deactivated. Pull it out and turn it, like so," he moved it to another notch, "and it's ready to go." He pulled the ring out and returned it to the original notch, reversed it, and handed it to Jesse. He settled back on his heels, breathing heavily.

She put the thing on the desk and held a hand out. He looked up, let the corners of his mouth lift a little, and let her pull him to his feet and help him into the armchair facing hers. There was blood dripping from his left hand.

"You're bleeding."

"It isn't important. You've never handled one of those before, have you?" He dipped his chin in the direction of the black thing on the desk.

Jesse shook her head.

"Why didn't you take Illegal Weapons at the Point?"

"After my time. They didn't start that until..."

"Until after *Sagan*. I'd almost forgotten."

Jesse picked the thing up, turned it over and inspected it thoroughly, turned the locking ring and turned it back, put it back in the box. "Where'd you get it?"

"David had it. I - took it away from him."

"Where did David get a Tragan energy whip?"

He looked down, fingers tapping the arm of the chair. "Under the circumstances, I didn't want to ask."

The moving fingers drew Jesse's eyes down. The blood

beneath the arm of the chair had become a puddle. As she watched, a drop appeared on the ends of Ashe's fingers, thickened, hung suspended, and joined itself to the pool.

"Look, we've got to do something about that," Jesse said. "I'll call the medics."

"No," he said, as she reached for the comm controls. "Don't. If you call the medics, our terrorist will know this trap caught someone.

"He's panicking now, he's doing stupid things. If he thinks this," his right hand lifted in a gesture that implied the crystal as well as the planted bolt, "failed, that we disarmed it before it did any damage, it could push him into making more mistakes. We need him to make mistakes, Jesse."

"Then let me help you down to the infirmary."

He shook his head, then let it drop back against the chair, as though holding it upright had become more work than he could manage. "Same argument. People would be bound to see us, and someone would notice me in the infirmary. We don't know who he is - he could be one of the duty officers who routinely checks logs - he could be almost anybody, except the people we know we can trust."

Jesse thought a few moments, watching the blood gather at the tips of his fingers and fall to the floor. The flow didn't appear to be increasing - but it wasn't diminishing, either. And the One only knew about the volume that, having soaked his shirt through, was soaking into the back of the chair before it could trickle down his arm onto the floor. "Not to be crass, but cleaning up in here isn't going to be fun."

"Sorry," he murmured. His eyes were closed, and his breathing was very shallow.

He's going into shock. Do something. He's absolutely right, but - "Okay. You stay here and try not to bleed too much. I'm going to take my nightly walk - it would be noticed if I didn't. No one will think a thing about me dropping into the infirmary to see who's there, and no one will think a thing about one of the medics leaving."

"If you catch Nick, nobody will think anything about him coming up to see me," Ashe murmured without opening his eyes. "He's trying to teach me to play Go."

Another thick drop fell to the floor, and Jesse suppressed her slight shock at the notion that Jason played games and went to get a towel.

"Sorry, I should have thought of this," he said, as she

opened his shirt and pressed the thick pad to his shoulder. He lifted his right hand, but it stopped halfway, the fingers quivering. Jesse grabbed his wrist and pulled his arm the rest of the way across his torso, clamping the fingers around his shoulder to hold the pad in place. His fingers were cold, and his skin was clammy and tinged with blue.

"Well, I'll excuse you, since you're in shock," Jesse said. "Besides, I should have thought of it sooner." She opened the blanket she'd grabbed from the end of her bed and tucked it around him and headed for the door. "I'll be back."

Did he actually say, "I'm not going anywhere?" she asked herself as the door to their quarters closed behind her. *Probably. It was the sort of thing both he and David would think was funny.*

David. She suppressed the thought of David, refusing to let her mind dwell on the look on his face when he saw Ashe's shoulder - or if he decided she was to blame.

It isn't your fault, Jesse. The long hallways seemed longer tonight. *It isn't your fault. Shut up, you sorry son of a bitch*, her mind screamed at the internal voice of the man she refused to call her father. *I didn't do anything wrong. I'm just not superhuman. And you aren't even my conscience, you're just the residue of that hell-cursed Crystal.*

It took all her concentration to stop in Engineering, in Environmental systems, in Maintenance, as usual, instead of going straight to the infirmary. "He's right, I know he's right," she kept telling herself. *Hurry, hurry*, nagged the little voice in the back of her head. *He could bleed to death while you're strolling the hallways.*

When she got back, having made her entire round, consulted with Zephron, and even visited with one of the Anharzi pilots who was taking a dinner break, Thassanios and a tech were bending over Jason. The soaked towel was on the floor, on top of the ruined shirt, and for a fleeting instant she noticed the beauty of Jason's pale skin and the definition of his torso. *He doesn't have an ounce of fat on his body.*

Thassanios had put on a pair of magnifying glasses and was exploring the mangled flesh of Jason's shoulder with an impossibly tiny pair of tweezers. He probed near the edge, and the blond man winced and bit his lip. "Sorry," he muttered.

"Quit apologizing," the medic said. "I'm the one who's hurting you, and I'm trying not to. Here," he grabbed a small spray bottle and applied it liberally. "If you were anybody else, I'd probably put you to sleep, or at least give you a shot of morphine."

"No." It was little more than a breath.

The tiny tweezers were back in the wound, and as Jesse watched, Thassanios lifted them and deposited something in a glass dish. He placed his hands on Jason's arm and throat to steady him, and scrutinized the ugly wound. Bubbles of blood were still oozing out and trickling down the white arm.

"All right, I think I got them all. Let me scan it to be sure." Jason nodded. His eyes were closed, his breathing was shallow, and his teeth were clamped in his lower lip.

With a wad of fiber soaked in antiseptic, the medic cleaned the blood away from the edges of the wound. He sprayed it with something, Jesse assumed an antibiotic of some sort, and then with a layer of artificial skin. That was followed by a layer of slick gauze, a thick pad of soft fiber, another layer of the gauze, and a spray of adhesive and sealer. "You're going to have to hold still; any movement and it'll start to bleed again. Are you sure you don't want me to give you something to put you to sleep?"

"No. I have - things to do. I won't move it, Nick."

"Very well."

The tech loosened Jason's fingers from hers and straightened, stretching as though her back was stiff.

"Can you clean up here, Mali? I need to talk with the Command First." She nodded, and Jesse followed Thassanios through the door to the living room.

"He's lost a lot of blood," the medic said, settling one hip on the dining table, "but I don't think he's in danger from that at the moment. There are going to be two major problems - the first is that he can't take conventional pain pills, and he needs to rest and heal. The second is that he's underweight, and obviously exhausted, and his resistance is very low - he could catch a minor infection and have serious complications."

Jesse nodded. "I'll consult with Zephron about some schedule changes and pull Jason off duty. I thought of putting it down to that strain of the flu that knocked so many people for a loop last year."

"That'll work." He dropped his head into his hands a moment, rubbing his temples, then seemed to notice the sticky redness and pulled them back. "Now, Command, at the risk of incurring your wrath, I want to talk to you about something else."

He straightened so his eyes met Jesse's and held them. "I was a young Fellow in Combat Medicine, doing a term at the Point, when David Christiansen carried in a mess of bloody flesh they claimed was Jason Ashe. He was nineteen years old - barely.

"We got to be pretty good friends during the year it took him to heal enough for them to send him out to the lines. I was about the only one of the medics who didn't think Aldrich was the law and the prophets, and I did my best to protect him.

"He'd lost one partner - Aldrich took the other one away. After his parents died, he told me once he didn't understand what he'd done that was so wrong.

"He takes the world on himself - if you give him a chance, he'll assume he's responsible for everything that goes wrong.

"He's a good man, an honorable man, even by the standards the Ansari live by. All of us - or almost all of us," he glanced at Jesse under his eyebrows, but she refused to meet his eyes, " - are well aware how lucky we are to have him. Take good care of him, Command."

The tech came out of Jesse's study, and Thassanios turned and nodded to her. "Be right with you, Mali. Here," he pulled a small tube out of his case, "these are a combination sleeping pill and pain killer developed especially for Sensitives. I've tried them myself and not had any side effects. Give him two before he goes to bed, and tell him I said if he doesn't take them, I'm going to come feed them to him."

Jason was leaning back in the chair, hands slack on its arms, his eyes closed. For a moment, Jesse thought he was asleep, and she was tempted to just turn the lights off and leave him to rest, but he opened his eyes.

"Things to discuss," he murmured.

"They'll wait," Jesse said. "You need to get some rest."

He moved his head in a negative, once left, once right. "This is more important." He pushed himself up and straightened his shoulders. "I've watched you get more and more angry with me since David was hurt. It can't go on. It's starting to show in the crew, and - it's tearing David up.

"You didn't want me, Jesse, and David is your Second. In giving in to my own emotional needs, I may have put paid to any chance we had of making this a working triad, but I hope not. I hope you'll let me make amends, I hope the two of us can make a fresh start and at least become working partners, even friends. If not, I'll leave."

"Taking David with you," Jesse said. She was shocked, not

just at the bitterness she heard in her own voice, but at the cold, empty feeling in the pit of her stomach.

The blue eyes were steady, his voice flat. "That will be David's choice – not mine, not yours. If David wants to stay and you want me to go, I'll go. But if there's a way we can achieve – " he licked his lips and hesitated, "balance, some kind of harmony – I'd prefer that."

Jesse settled back in her chair and braced herself. She'd never liked admitting she was in the wrong. "So would I. And it should start with an apology. My apology to you. I've been resenting you for coming between me and David, and I never knew just how deep your feelings are, or how far back they go. I realized this evening, listening to you and David call each other brothers, that your ties must go back to the Point."

She'd thought he was pale before, but the color drained from his face. Even his lips paled. "No," he breathed. "You don't mean that. You can't realize what you're saying."

"I'm saying what's obvious, Jason, that you and David have always been tied to each other."

He slid to his knees before her, his trembling hands over hers. The blue eyes were tear-bright, and his fingers were icy. "Jesse, think, please. David and I were at the Point together eleven years ago. Eleven years."

She nodded and took his hands, trying to warm them. She was more concerned with willing the cold fingers to quit trembling and become warm than with what he was saying. Jason's head drooped, as though it had become too heavy for his neck to hold up.

"And?..."

"Think, Jesse. When we were at the Point together last, I was nineteen and David was almost twenty-four."

It's important. At that time, the difference in their ages was the most important thing about them. What is it I'm not understanding? Why does my head feel so thick?

"You've forgotten." The soft voice seemed to be coming from a long way off, mingling with the drone of the old Professor of Ethics her first year at the Point. "It's called, 'contact with a child under the age of consent.'"

The last five words shocked Jesse into alertness, as Jason's cold fingers tightened on hers. "Please, Jesse, for the love of the Many. I will do anything. I'll leave, and promise never to see or touch David again. I'll..." he pulled one hand loose and reached for the ugly black cylinder Jesse had put on the edge of the desk. "Take this," he held it out like an offering, "use it on me. Do whatever you want - cripple me, kill me - I don't care. Just please, please, don't ever say that again. David is a good man, an honorable man," the highest tribute an Ansari could pay, Jesse knew, "he has never, ever done anything wrong. He never - the first time I felt his hand on mine was after I came here..."

He choked and stopped, sinking back to his heels, exhausted. The hand that had held hers so tightly went slack, and for a moment she thought he'd fainted.

I can't imagine meaning that much to Thom. I can't imagine what it must be like to have anyone care that much for you. It's almost frightening.

"Let me help you up," she said. She put a hand under Jason's right shoulder and lifted and pulled, moving him back into the armchair. He collapsed like a rag doll.

"I think we're both too tired and too upset to be making sense," Jesse said. "Let me say this, and then I'm going to help you to your room and to bed. I did not mean to say or imply anything that would impugn David's honor - or yours. What I meant was - I think there are relationships that go far beyond what anyone can see. It may be reincarnation, it may simply be that you're attuned to each other, it may be something as basic as chemistry. That's all I meant, Jason. It never occurred to me that anyone could think either of you had done anything wrong."

He lifted his head a little and the faint smile touched his lips. "Sorry," he whispered.

"Here. Can you walk? I'll help you back to your room."

He pulled away with surprising strength, and straightened. "No. I can't go to my room. I can't have David see me like this. Help me up and I'll go down to my office." He tried to push himself out of the chair and Jesse pushed him back.

"Absolutely not. You're in no fit state to be moving around at all, and you need to rest. Besides, if you didn't want anyone to see you on the way to the infirmary, what makes you think they won't on the way to the office?"

He subsided, panting, and nodded.

"I should call David." *I should have called him hours ago.* She glanced at her watch and realized it had been less than two hours since she'd first walked into Jason's study.

"No." The blue eyes came up to meet hers, and he articulated slowly, clearly - obviously, he intended her to understand him. "David is tired. David works too hard. David spends too much of himself on other people. There's nothing he can do tonight - let him rest."

And what about us? She ran a hand over her hair, conscious of the weight of her body, the way her mind was beginning to drift with fatigue, the bitter taste in her mouth that was the aftermath of adrenalin, the hollow feeling that told her she was exhausted. *I can't take him to David's room - no one would know he was there, he'd die and we'd never know what happened.* "All right, wait a minute."

She pulled the extra bedding from the top shelf in her closet, forcing herself to ignore the way her arms trembled.

Jason was where he'd been when she left, eyes closed, hands slack on the arms of the chair. There were purple smudges on his eyelids and under his eyes; the shadows under his cheekbones were so sharp they looked as though they'd been drawn with pencil. For a terrible second, she thought he was dead; then he drew in a breath in a long sigh.

Spreading the blanket on the couch and putting a sheet over it seemed to take hours - the soft blankets and sheets felt as though they were made from lead. By the time she had the pillow in place and another sheet and blanket on top, Jesse was willing to fall on it herself and sleep until she woke up. She straightened, with effort, and went over to Jason.

"Come on," she held a hand down to help him up. "If you won't go back to your room, and we can't take you to the infirmary, I guess you'll just have to sleep here."

He blinked like a sleepy cat, and let her pull him to his feet. His body was warm against her as they stumbled to the couch, and it was all Jesse could do to keep him from dropping in a heap. She lowered him gently, and lifted his feet, pulling the covers over him. "Sleep."

"Thank you, Jesse," he whispered.

Jesse started to turn away, then remembered. "Pills," she muttered. She staggered over to the converter and retrieved a glass of water, then retraced her steps, one at a time, afraid if she stumbled and fell she wouldn't have the energy to get up.

"Here," she mumbled, pulling the vial from her pocket and fumbling two of the tablets out. "Thassanios says if you don't take these, he'll come feed them to you."

Jason's eyes were filmy, and his head wobbled as he raised

it, but he managed to get the pills in his mouth and swallow when Jesse held the glass to his lips. He turned his head, and she set the glass on the table, narrowing her concentration to a pinpoint to maintain her coordination.

"Jesse. Go sleep."

-Chapter 14-
If I had to do it again...

"Would you please tell me what in the name of the Many is going on around here?"

Jesse answered without opening her eyes, putting off as long as she could the sight of the face that went with that angry voice. "Do you think it's remotely possible that you could give me five minutes to wash my face and get dressed before you tear me limb from limb?"

She didn't hear him step away, but the door slid open and then shut. Jesse opened her eyes, wincing in the glare of the overhead light David had left on.

He was gone. She pushed herself up, whispering imprecations under her breath, and slid out of bed.

#

"Now," she said, striding into the wreck that had been her study, "what was it you had on your mind?" She settled into the far armchair, keeping her eyes away from the stain on the back of the other one.

The puddle of blood had sunk into the carpet, making a red-brown blob against the pale sand; Jason's shirt and the soaked towel were still in a heap on top of it. *The 'bots are going to have to cut a chunk out of the carpet and replace it.*

David was perched on the end of the couch above a jumble of blankets, sheets, and pillow. His eyes were as pale as rainwater, and the big hands were opening and closing as though he was dreaming about crushing bones.

"When I went to sleep last night," he said, "in Jason's bed, I was expecting my brother to work a couple of hours and then join me. When I woke up this morning, he wasn't there. He wasn't in his study. He wasn't in his lab. He wasn't in CC." He stopped, the muscle in his jaw working and an angry pulse beating in his temple, and Jesse had time to visualize the frantic, uncoordinated search, the fear that turned to panic.

"Why didn't you call me?"

"The last place I thought he'd be was with you. I came here because I'd run out of places to look - I even looked in my room -

and I guess you know what I found." The comprehensive gesture took in the damaged desk, the rumpled bedding, the stained carpet and chair.

A trickle of cold ran down Jesse's spine, and she shivered. "You mean he wasn't here?"

He gave her the sort of look an intelligent child gives a particularly thick adult. "Of course he was here, Jesse, in the midst of this mess, covered with blood and looking like death. I took him back to his room and helped him clean up, and he collapsed while we were eating breakfast."

"Please explain what you mean by 'collapsed,' David." Her irritation at the way he'd wakened her was gone, replaced by a cold shaft of fear. It was an effort to keep her voice steady, and she could feel the faint, hollow undertone of nausea.

"He said," the big man articulated, "he'd stood up too fast. I put him to bed and he fell asleep before I got the sash of his sleeping robe tied - over a particularly nasty-looking wound in his left shoulder that looked like it came from an energy bolt. Since I found him in your study, I assume you must have at least some rudimentary knowledge of what happened to him, and I'm asking - no, I'm telling you - to share it."

The relief was much like the sensation when a high-speed lift started. Jesse closed her eyes and took a deep breath. Then she pushed herself to her feet and went to the converter. "Do you want something? My blood sugar's so low I'm woozy."

He shook his head, but accepted the glass of juice she brought him, and settled into the corner of the couch, shoving the blankets, sheets, and pillow to the other end.

"We were talking," Jesse said. "Or at least, that was what we set out to do." Trying to remember every detail, she recounted the events of the night before from the time she and Jason had left his study and crossed the living room to hers.

"What did you do with the things?" The big hands and broad shoulders had relaxed, and his eyes had darkened to steel grey, but the muscles in his jaw were still tight.

"Put them in the box under my seal and sent them to Security. Incidentally, I had the officer who came to collect the box bring a hand scanner and go over this room and my bedroom, but I think you should have the rest of our quarters checked today - especially your rooms."

He nodded, and put the glass down. "Why didn't you call me?" His voice was neutral, but Jesse could hear an undertone she wasn't sure was anger or hurt. *I meant to wake up first. I meant to go get David, to tell him before he found Jason. I'd still be asleep if he hadn't come in.*

Jesse closed her eyes. "'David is tired. David spends too much of himself on other people. David needs to rest.' Under the circumstances, I didn't want to argue with him."

He nodded, and ran his hands through his hair. "Do me a favor, will you? Next time, don't pay any attention to him. Even better - don't let there be a next time."

"I'm sorry. I meant to be up early and come get you."

Jesse got up and went to the desk, picked up the small white box and held it out. "Do you mind my asking where you got this?"

He took it from her, opened it, looked at it a moment, and set it on the coffee table. "I took it from a man who didn't need it any longer."

David's eyes were very light, and the casual voice had an undertone of - *is that really hate I'm hearing?*

She raised an eyebrow. "Why didn't he need it?"

"He lost interest after I broke his neck," David said. "As I look back on it, I think I was a bit hasty, but at the time I had other things on my mind. If I had it to do again, he'd take much, much longer to die."

That's what I thought. That's the energy whip the Tragans used on Jason. "I think," Jesse said, "it might be as well if you were to dispose of it. There seem to be way too many of them around. Someone could get hurt."

One eyebrow lifted. He picked up the box, went to the recycler, moved the control to incinerate, and dropped it in. "Just remember what I told you, Jesse.

"By the way, if I have anything on my calendar, you'd better plan to do it yourself or cancel it. I'll be with my brother today."

Before Jesse could answer, he was gone.

That was David, that was. I think. It might have been that hurricane I've been anticipating since Jason got here.

She headed for the bathroom and a hot shower she was sure she needed, activating the control for the cleaning 'bot as she went by.

#

"Are you busy?"

She'd glanced up from the record she was reading as the door slid back. She lifted a hand and David slipped into the room. "As a matter of fact, no. Zephron rearranged all the schedules and James took your training sessions, and I'm caught up on all the Sector paperwork for once." She closed the new console and let it sink back into the desk, ignoring the rough edge where the carpenters hadn't finished.

"What's on your mind?" She went to the converter and retrieved two glasses of cool white wine. *I may not have Jen to stock my wine cellar, but I think I did a pretty good job with the wine program myself.*

David settled into the corner of the couch and ran his hand through his hair. "Did I say something I shouldn't have this morning?"

"You were - somewhat threatening," Jesse answered. "I decided to put it down to the fact that you'd had a fright and you were upset."

"Thanks. I don't think I was sparking in every synapse. But I probably owe you an apology anyway."

Jesse considered, turning the glass in her fingers. "I think you probably do. I don't mind you being appalled at either Jason's condition or the room's, but I do resent you thinking I'd hurt him or deliberately neglect him."

"I'm sorry. I don't even think I meant that. I just - I needed to hit something, and you were right there. I was wrong."

"Thank you," Jesse murmured. "Apology accepted." She let the silence lengthen while she thought. *No, I'm not going to tell him that. That was between me and Jason. But he does need to know...* "Did you know he'd been fasting?"

David's eyes went a shade lighter and his jaw tightened. "Not until last night, no. Somehow he's always managed to be 'too busy' to eat at the same time I do."

"He said, he thought it would clear his mind. I've had some time to think about it today, and I think maybe you and I are the ones who need our minds cleared."

David picked up his glass and settled back. "I'm listening."

Jesse considered. "I don't - I don't know exactly how to go about this. I don't think it's ever going to be easy, David. I'm not sure it's going to work at all."

He nodded. "Three strong personalities - we're bound to butt heads from time to time. But I think we can be a good team - a great team. You just have to give us a chance."

What she wanted to say was, "I have been," but instead, "How is he?"

He turned his face away, but she could see the the strain in the muscles around his eyes. "I'm not sure. He's been awake a couple of times, and he keeps telling me he's okay, he's just tired. But when he's asleep, he mutters, and tosses and turns."

"Has the medic been up to see him?" *I'm sure he said he was going to. But I'm also sure I wasn't tracking much better than Ashe was last night - maybe I was supposed to get him down there and I've forgotten. Maybe I told him not to come unless he was called because we were trying to keep Jason's condition a secret - he wouldn't need to come see him if it was just the flu.*

David shook his head. "Not since I found him. I wondered about that. I asked him if Nick was going to come up and see him or if he was supposed to go down to the infirmary, but I can't get a straight answer out of him. He just smiles at me and drifts off to sleep again."

"Will you come look at him? I think he's worse, but I don't want anyone accusing me of mother-henning."

Is that for me or for Jason? Jesse shrugged and followed David from the room.

Jason was worse. The pale face was flushed, and as he tossed, Jesse caught a glimpse of red on the white silk of his sleeping robe. She put the back of her hand against his forehead, his cheek. "He's hot." She pulled the robe aside and heard David hiss as the soaked bandages came into view. "It's all the tossing and turning, I guess. I heard Nick tell him not to move or it would break open again."

"I'll go get him."

She shook her head. "Mr. Lee," she made a hand-sign to the security officer who was standing in the corner, staying out of the way. "Go get Dr. Thassanios - tell him to bring his kit." The tall woman nodded, the light bringing out syrupy highlights in her brown hair.

"I don't understand why it keeps bleeding, David," Jesse said after the security officer had gone.

David settled by the side of the bed and took one of the restless hands. "It's okay, Bro, I'm here," he murmured. "Tragan weapons," he said, in response to Jesse's question.

"I guess I've never seen anyone wounded by one - only killed."

"They don't cauterize - they're meant to shred the flesh. And they drive microscopic fragments of fabric into the wound. He nearly bled to death in the cruiser before we got back to the Point."

"Nick was picking something out of the wound last night."

David glanced up, then turned his attention back to the man in the bed. "Chunks of Crystal. That's what does the shredding. I don't think they made much effort to get them all out of his back."

Jason stirred and moaned. David stroked his hand and adjusted the covers.

"I think we're bothering him," Jesse whispered. "I'll be in my study if you need me."

#

"Well?" She'd heard him coming and settled into a chair, just in time. She didn't want David to know she'd been pacing the floor, waiting to hear.

He dropped into the other chair and ran his hand through his hair. His eyes were still steel grey, but the lines around his mouth were sharp in the evening light, and the broad shoulders drooped with weariness and anxiety. "No, not well," he said. "But at least - it could be worse." He slid down and rested his head on the back of the chair, and Jesse let the silence continue a few minutes, to give him a chance to bleed off some of the anxiety and anger.

"Tell me." She put the tall, cold glass in his hand and settled into the corner of the couch.

He sat up and straightened his shoulders, and lifted his glass to her. "Thanks. I may have needed this." He swallowed, deeply, and set the glass down. "The wound is infected. I suppose that was to be expected. I know you did the best you could last night, but not working in a sterile field - Nick got the bleeding stopped, again, and told him to be still. Did you get him to take those pills?"

For a few seconds, Jesse's mind was blank. *Pills?*

"Oh, those pills. I did - I told him if he didn't take them for me I'd call Nick and we'd hold him down and force feed him. By that point he was so near out of it I think if I'd just put them in his hand and given him a glass of water he'd have taken them without knowing what he was doing."

David nodded. "Do you know what happened to them? I didn't notice them when I found him this morning."

"I think I left them..." she closed her eyes and thought, then looked at the corner of the desk. "There." The little vial was where she'd left it, undisturbed by the maintenance people as they'd made temporary repairs to the desk and replaced the console.

"Thanks. You never know when you might need them." He

put the pills in his pocket and took his glass to the recycler.

"You didn't finish telling me how he is," Jesse said.

"Oh - well, there's the infection. I told you Nick got the bleeding stopped. He said the effect of the wound was complicated by the fact that Jason's exhausted and - and -stressed, I guess."

And something else, but David doesn't want to tell me what it is. Memories of Sagan? The pain could have triggered a whole repertoire of responses from his body.

"So he'll be all right?"

"Oh, yeah, he'll be fine. The biggest problem will be to keep him from overdoing it."

"Good."

The comm unit chirped, and Jesse fingered it. "Yes?"

"Command, this is Ops. I need the Command Second."

David shook his head.

"He's - a little tied up right now, Ops. Is it something I can do?"

"I'm sorry." Jesse could almost see the apologetic shake of Zephron Bell's head. "I don't think so." Jesse glanced over at David and he shrugged.

"I'm here, Ops. What do you need?"

"I need a judicial officer, Command. We have a situation."

"On my way." He ran his long fingers through his hair and shook it back, straightened his tunic, glanced down at his boots. "Jesse, can you stay with him? I'll take Lee with me - if I don't, Jason'll probably wake up and try to follow me."

He was gone before Jesse could respond, but as she went from her study to Jason's bedroom, she thought about it. The tone of David's voice had been sharp - he's angry about something. *What?*

And then, as she settled in the chair by Jason's bed, she remembered. "You've bought yourself a new assignment, Mr. Ashe. You're David's bodyguard." *Something else he's been doing to wear himself out, and you're responsible, Jesse. David was right - you're piling up a very bad record in the treatment of partners, and Sensitives are -* she abandoned the search for the right word and turned her attention to Jason.

He lay on his back, the soft light casting shadows under his eyes and cheekbones and in the hollow of his throat. *He looks like a boy. Not a man who's spent at least nine of the last eleven years in combat. Not a man who's lost three partners. I've lost one partner, and I've spent the last six months feeling sorry for myself, and he's lost three, but he was still willing to try to start over. I wonder if he's ever been allowed to mourn them?*

The sleeping man turned his head and his eyelashes fluttered. "David?" he murmured.

"He'll be back soon," Jesse whispered. "It's all right. I'm here." *That'll probably throw him into a nightmare.*

Jason breathed out, a long sigh, and the fluttering eyelashes stilled. He'd slipped back into sleep from the edge of waking. Jesse wondered how close to the surface his awareness had come, if he'd realized it was her, or if the simple human presence had reassured whatever part of his mind had needed it.

She closed her eyes and settled back, letting her mind drift.

#

"Some bodyguard you are. If I'd been a bad guy, I'd have had you before you even knew it."

Jesse blinked and pushed herself straight. "I knew it was you. There's something about the way the door opens when it's you - I can always tell." *That sounds silly. The door always opens the same, regardless of who it is. But I do always know when it's David.*

"So what happened that Zephron needed a judicial officer?"

David pushed his hair back with the characteristic gesture, bringing his hand back to rub his temple. "Something so stupid I'm ashamed it happened in our Command. Kelman and Josse got into a fight, and some girl with fewer brains than a Kondrassi gut-worm called Security. Since Josse's an apprentice and Kelman's an officer, it had to be adjudicated."

"I thought they were roommates. What were they fighting about?" Jesse realized she didn't really care, but it was something to take David's mind off Jason a few minutes.

He shook his head. "I'm not even sure they know. Somebody said something about Josse messing with some of Kelman's stuff, but - it was that time of day, on that kind of day, and if that little idiot had stayed out of it their friends would have pulled them apart and they'd have settled it peacefully. Now - well, Zephron's assigning them to different quarters, Josse's going to spend two weeks doing dirty maintenance, and Kelman's going to spend a week restricted to quarters and a month restricted to quarters and duty station, and go without a week's pay, for whatever purpose that'll serve. And have a black mark on his permanent record."

"And in two weeks, they'll be asking Zephron to put them

back together."

"Probably. The sad thing is, I can't do a thing to the girl, and she was the one who caused the problem." He sat down on the end of the bed and dropped his head into his hands. Then a slow grin crept over his face, and he straightened. "For a while there, since what they were doing was fighting, I was tempted to just send them down to the ring and sentence the one who was standing at the end to fight me."

"Or me," Jesse said. "I could use a good fight."

She glanced over at Jason, and David, following the direction of her glance, said, "Not him, Jesse. I know he'll keep going until he drops in his tracks, but he isn't strong enough."

She pulled in a long breath and pushed it out again through her nose. "Oh, if I wanted a good sparring match, he's a superb partner, you were right about that. But he won't fight me. You will, Thom would, but he won't. And I don't really understand why."

"Don't you?" His eyes were blue again, like little flowers Jesse could remember from her childhood, and his face was calm.

It's as though just being near Jason rests him and reassures him. "Should I? It's obvious from the way he's survived that he's a fighter, and you told me yourself he was fighting to protect Mike when you found them that day. So why won't he fight me?"

"You're his partner, Jesse, his First. It's the Ansari Way. You can't make him say or do anything he thinks is wrong, but if he thinks it's just - between you - he'll simply withstand until he can't bear the pain.

"When you're upset, he Feels everything you're feeling, including the pain under the anger. Feeling that, how could he fight you? The point of all his training, of his life, is to help, not to add to it. That may be why the Ansari produce so many Sensitives," he murmured.

Jesse shivered. *He'd let me badger him literally to death.* The shame was like warm acid spreading through her system as she began to realize just what her anger, her bitterness, her need to cause someone else pain, had been doing to Jason Ashe. To an Ansari the family, the triad, is much more important than the individual. *I couldn't lose myself in a partnership that way. It's terrifying.*

"He loves you, Jesse," David said. "I love you. But I won't let you hurt him anymore. If you need to be angry at someone, if you need to fight someone - you fight me."

The steel-grey eyes held hers, and Jesse nodded.

"You've been with him all day, haven't you?"

David nodded, dropping a hand to the small hump under the covers that was Jason's feet. The blond man sighed and smiled, but didn't open his eyes.

"Okay, I want you to go shower and change and get something to eat. We don't need both of you going down sick."

"Somebody needs to be with him."

"I'll stay." He glanced up, and Jesse made a shooing gesture. "Go. We'll be fine."

#

We'll be fine, Jesse thought.

"That's my Third - my partner," she told herself, looking at the blond man in the soft light. The strongest Sensitive in Defense Command, the hero of the second Battle of Seior, the only living holder of the Lion of Prometheus. *Maybe the problem is that no one thought to educate me in the fact that he's human. And vulnerable.*

And so very beautiful. She stood and began to pace. *Maybe that's part of the problem, Jesse, maybe you're jealous. It was bad enough with David, and now - well, look at him.*

I never had these problems with Thom. It was always so easy, as though we'd always been together. I didn't have to worry about hurting him. "But Thom wasn't Ansari," her conscience answered.

And Thom wasn't as strong a Talent. Or as beautiful.

You may be right, she answered the voice of conscience. *But I don't want to think about that now.*

The sleeping man shifted and murmured, and Jesse went back to the chair, turning it to put the light over her shoulder and off his face. She picked a data card off the stack she'd brought with her and began reading.

David must have fallen asleep over his plate, she thought a while later, putting the first card down and picking up another. *I'm sure he didn't intend to be this long.* She yawned and let the card droop from her hand, her head falling back against the chair. *I don't know why I'm so tired. I feel as though I could sleep for weeks.*

Her vision was clouding and she blinked, then blinked again to clear it, but the fog got thicker. *My eyelids feel as though they're coated with lead.* She lifted her hand to rub her eyes, and watched as the data card drifted to the floor. Something was wrong, but she was too sleepy and heavy to care.

The door opened and a dark figure slipped in. Black leather uniform, black boots, black helmet with black face guard - *Tragan body armor. How did somebody wearing Tragan armor get past the guards?*

The intruder apparently didn't see her. In slow motion, one step at a time, he approached the bed where Jason lay sleeping.

I need to do something. I have to stop him, or he'll hurt Jason. How did he get in here? Shit, I'm on the wrong side.

She tried to get up, but her body refused to function. *Move, dammit!* She flexed the fingers of one hand, then the other, and willed her arms to lift and grasp the arms of the chair.

It was like pushing through heavy mud. *Come on,* her mind screamed. *Move, before he does what he came for.*

The pressure that had held her gave way, and she came up as though the artificial gravity had been turned off. As she did, the light in the room seemed to brighten, and her vision cleared.

The sudden violence of Jesse's rising threw the chair back, and it skidded into the wall. The noise caught the black figure's attention - the round, featureless head turned in her direction. There was a low growl, then the head turned back and the black-gloved hands reached for the Sensitive's throat.

"Oh, no, you don't," Jesse barked. Putting one hand on the side of the bed, she launched herself toward the terrorist, prepared to kick him across the room. He dodged, but the move took him farther from Jason. His head turned from side to side, as though he was trying to find the door, and he backed away another step.

"What's the matter, you slime beetle? Not expecting to find him guarded? You're very brave when you're attacking someone who's sick and helpless, aren't you?" Jesse edged in, the adrenaline in her bloodstream loosening her muscles and warming her. "Come on, scum, let's see if there's anything under that armor. What do you wear that stuff for, anyway? Is it to protect you from each other?"

The last word brought Jesse into range, and she kicked for his groin. He pulled up a knee and punched. Jesse countered, and ceased to think about individual moves. It became a matter of action and reaction, move in and then out - all thought subsumed in the fighter's ingrained responses.

She edged, then edged again, to put herself between him and the door. He saw what she was doing and tried to dodge around her, but slipped and fell back onto the end of the bed. His right hand fumbled at his belt, trying to loosen something - a black cylinder about nine inches long. Jesse scrabbled after him, feeling something hard move under her foot, and knocked his hand down. He kicked, making contact with the inside of Jesse's thigh, and reached for his belt again. She chopped down at his arm and her hand came across the faceguard. "I'll see who you are, you bastard," she muttered. "I'll see who you are." She reached for the edge of the faceguard, intending to pull it off, and heat sliced her arm.

She pulled in a hard breath and clenched her teeth. He pushed, trying to throw her with his weight, and she elbowed him in the belly and backfisted his arm, noting with satisfaction that the energy whip slipped out of his fingers. "All right, tough guy," she muttered. "You're so brave in armor, when no one knows who you are, when you're armed and no one else is. When the man you're attacking can't defend himself. Let's see if you can fight without that thing."

She didn't get the chance to find out. He shouldered her out of the way, knocking her back across Jason, and ran for the door. Before Jesse could untangle herself, he was gone.

The room was spinning. She closed her eyes and concentrated on getting her breathing back under control.

"Jesse? Are you all right?" the voice was so soft she wasn't sure she'd heard it.

"Mmm - I think so. How about you?" She pushed herself up and turned to face him.

"Thanks to my bodyguard," he answered. In the lamplight, his pupils were enormous, making the blue eyes almost black.

"How'd he do that?" Jesse said. "For a while, I thought he'd paralyzed me."

"Crystal," Jason murmured.

"Jesse? Jason? Are you all right?"

David's hair was rumpled and his eyes were cloudy, as thought he'd just awakened from a deep sleep.

"Jesse's bleeding."

Her arm hurt. There was a jagged tear in her sleeve, and blood was running down and dripping from her wrist.

"I'll get Nick. Jesse, can you try to wake Chan?"

The triplet was collapsed to one side of the door, sprawled over each other as though they'd been simultaneously knocked out. *Maybe they were. He almost put me to sleep through a door, and he could have been standing right here next to them.* She checked their pulse - it was slow but steady, and their breathing appeared normal.

"Chan, wake up." She shook them, surprised at how light

the individual brothers were. "Chan!" The note of urgency in her voice roused the center brother, and he woke the others.

"Sir?" Their eyes were vague, and they rubbed their hands over their heads. "What..." They scrambled to their feet, swaying.

"It's all right," Jesse said. "Not your fault. Check the other quarters and make sure he didn't do any damage or set any booby-traps." *And thank the One they're so discreet - I don't need to worry about this getting all over.*

They nodded and left, merging as he reached the door.

Jesse turned back to Jason's bedroom and caught herself on the desk when the blood thundering in her head wiped out all other sounds. Her hands were shaking, and her mouth was dry and bitter. "You're fine, Jesse," she told herself, clutching the edge of the desk with sweaty hands and concentrating on controlling her breathing. "It's a minor injury and adrenaline overload. Get back in there - you can't leave him alone."

Pulling in a deep breath, she pushed herself up and stumbled across the study. She had to pause again to get her breathing back under control, then force herself to walk, not stagger, through the door, cross the room, and lower herself into the chair by the bed.

She looked up and Jason was smiling.

"I think you just saved my life," he murmured.

"Makes us nearly even," Jesse muttered.

"Didn't know it was a ... contest," he caught his breath and shifted, then settled back. "Do you ... need me to take the pain?"

Jesse shook her head. "I haven't started to feel it yet. By the time I do, Nick will be here, and he can give me something. Don't waste your strength."

"Not a waste," he whispered. His eyes closed and a - it was like a ripple - crossed his face. *Pain. It probably happens all the time, and he's so good at concealing it, the rest of us don't see it.*

She started to reach for him, then pulled her hand back, wincing. *He'd try to absorb the pain even though I told him not to. By the One! That hurts!*

#

"First? First! Wake up! Talk to me!" There was a hand on her shoulder, shaking her.

"Mmm?" She blinked and tried to sit up, wincing when the edge of her torn sleeve caught on the raw spot on her arm. "I'm okay," Jesse muttered.

"She's bleeding," she heard Jason say. "Probably in shock. Take care of her first. I'm fine."

He was nearly too weak to talk a few minutes ago. How does he do that?

"Ouch! Damn it, Nick, that hurt!"

"Sorry," the medic said, pulling out an anesthetic spray. "I didn't realize it was stuck to you."

The spray cooled the heat and sting from her arm, and Jesse drew in a long breath. "Thanks. Sorry, I didn't mean to yell."

She dozed while the medic worked, using the same magnifying headpiece, strong light, tiny tweezers, and meticulous care he'd used on Jason's shoulder. She was aware of soft voices, people moving around, but she let herself drift, leaving it all to David and the medics.

"Jesse? Come on, wake up enough to walk and I'll put you to bed."

She shook her head and pulled away from him. "I'm fine," she lied, wishing he'd left her drifting.

"Of course you are," David said, hauling her to her feet. "We're all fine. Come on, Lady, time for bed."

The room began to spin, but strong arms lifted her and she was cradled against David's broad chest. "Don't - leave him alone," she whispered. "That bastard might come back."

"He isn't alone," David said. "And you won't be, either. Now, sleep."

#

The belt slashed down and Jesse raised an arm to protect her face. Ignoring the pain as the heavy leather bit into her, she ducked, then sidestepped. *Not this time,* she thought, biting her lip to control the pain.

"Jesse! Jesse, wake up."

"What?" She felt muzzy, and her left arm was throbbing.

"You were having a bad dream," Nick Thassanios said. He adjusted the bedside light and sat on the edge of the bed. "Let me see your arm."

Jesse pushed herself up on the pillow and held her arm out. "Sorry about that."

The medic shrugged, his focus on removing the dressing. "Nightmares seem to be a hazard of command as much as they are of Healing. At some stages, I think they're a natural by-product of responsibility." There was a soft hiss, and the throbbing in Jesse's arm was replaced by coolness. Sighing, she let herself sink back into sleep.

-Chapter 16-
Sew the wind, reap the whirlwind...
Hosea, Chapter 8, Verse 7

She glanced down at the card, then at the blonde man, sleeping in the soft light from the bedside lamp. He stirred and murmured, and Jesse set the card down and leaned back, closing her eyes.

Almost a replay of last night, she thought, and shuddered as the soft fabric of her sleeve rubbed across the inch-wide, three-inch long gash the energy whip had dug in her left arm. *And Nick pulled all the crystal shards from my arm before he bandaged it. If this is minor, I hate to think what Jason's shoulder feels like.*

The minor injury had kept her in bed until she couldn't stand it any longer. Despite painkillers, her arm throbbed, she felt feverish, and if there was a part of her body that wasn't bruised and aching, she hadn't found it. It was easier to be awake and up.

"David?" His voice was so soft she thought he was talking in his sleep, but she realized his eyes were open.

"I sent him to bed," Jesse responded. "He was almost asleep on his feet."

"I tried to send him to bed this morning - was it morning? - but he wouldn't listen to me, and I couldn't fight him." He yawned, right hand coming up to cover his mouth, and Jesse could see his eyes watering.

"I should say not. The shape you were in last night, I'd say it'd be a good month before you could hold your own in a pillow fight."

He grinned. "Want to bet?" He tried to push himself up, hissed, and fell back against the pillows. "Then again, maybe not. You might win. Do you think you could help me up?"

She managed, although the injured arm hampered her more than she would have believed. With her assistance, he staggered to the bathroom.

"Thanks, I think I can make it the rest of the way."

"I'll wait here. David would kill me if I let you fall."

She triggered the cleaning 'bot, and it came out and straightened the bed, fluffing the pillows and stacking them, and dusting the objects on the bedside table. As it turned back to its slot in the wall, it paused, as though it had hit a bump, then picked up a small object and deposited it on the table.

"I'm sorry, I guess I need a hand," his voice startled Jesse out of her absent-minded contemplation of the table.

"Your face is wet," she commented, as she helped him sit on the edge of the bed and swing his legs up.

"I washed it. Got a little shaky reaching for the towel - guess I didn't do the best job drying it." He glanced up and the corner of his mouth lifted. "Sorry - did you think I'd broken out in a cold sweat?"

When she looked up from pulling the blankets up, he was scowling.

"What?"

"Nothing." He'd never been that curt, even when she knew he was angry.

"You don't look like that for nothing, Jason."

"Nothing important. Just - this." The gesture took in the bed, the bandage on his shoulder, her arm.

"Just think of it as an unexpected opportunity to get a little rest." She headed for the converter. "I need - something," she looked back over her shoulder. He'd settled back, and the scowl had diminished, but the long fingers of his right hand were crushing the edge of the blanket. "What about you? Some of David's broth? If I can figure out what he calls it," she muttered, staring at the menu.

"Try 'Mama's Secret.' He claims," she heard a snort, and knew Jason was smiling, "it'll cure anything but a broken heart."

Three years with David and I never heard that. What else have I been missing? She set Jason's cup on the table and settled in the chair. "Now, what were we talking about?"

"Balance. Harmony. Living and working together without killing each other or hurting David."

"Was that it. Silly me - I thought we were discussing how long it'll be until you're ready to go back to work."

He grinned. "I'm ready now, but I don't know how much use I'd be."

"Then maybe we should finish our other conversation."

He picked up the mug, wrapped his fingers around it, blew, took a sip. "All right. We only have one problem, Jesse – you don't want me. Everything else grew from that. The question is – do you not want me because I'm Jason Ashe, or do you not want me because I'm not Thom Isaacson? Or - do you just not want a Third?"

She paced, cradling the elbow of the injured arm in the other hand. She stopped at the chest and picked up the light stylus David had taken from Jason's pocket, turning it over and over in her fingers.

"A little of of all of them, I guess. I feel as though everyone is trying to take Thom from me – and you scare me."

"I scare you, Jesse?"

"I - I think it's not so much you as what might happen to me because of you. I can't achieve equilibrium with you – I'm always on edge – off balance."

He looked up as she dropped into the chair. "I don't want to take Thom Isaacson's place. I want my own place, if your life has a place for me. No one wants to take Thom from you, but I think, with the best intentions in the world, everyone forgot that the only person who can decide you're ready to let go and move on is you. This bloody war," he muttered.

"I'm sorry about that. And I'm sorry I keep you off balance. I don't mean to. If it's any consolation, you've had me off balance since I met you."

"So what do we do?"

"You could send me away. You'd have to wait until we reach our permanent station and start receiving transport traffic, assuming we survive, but we could work out some kind of truce until then.

"Or, if the situation becomes desperate, you could give me to the Tragans. I think, given their notorious hunger for Sensitives," the sapphire eyes were steady, "they'd probably be willing to trade King K and her crew for me.

"You notice," he grinned, "I have no illusions about my relative worth. Somebody told me I was arrogant."

She shuddered. "That's insane."

"No, it's pragmatic. The moral philosophers would tell you it's a good trade."

"Sending you away would be cowardly," Jesse said. "Trading you to the Tragans is unthinkable. Besides, the Tragans have no honor. They'd take you and still blow us into the next dimension. And they probably want that Crystal more than they want you anyway."

"Hmm - you're probably right." He smiled. "How about kill me – preferably quickly and painlessly?"

She took a long swallow and put her cup down. "That's crossed my mind. There are difficulties – committing a perfect murder, explaining to HQ, doing it so David didn't think I'd done it, reconciling my conscience. Details. But they make it inconvenient."

"Ouch. I asked for that," Jason said. "You're even more dangerous in a game of wits than you are in the ring." He put the cup down and pushed himself straighter. "We could keep fighting, but I hate it when you're angry with me."

Jesse took the cups to the converter. "If it were just the two of us on an isolated asteroid - but our lives touch other people's. We're making David unhappy, and we're jeopardizing this command.

"Besides," she said, settling on the edge of the bed beside him, "it's getting boring." She took his hand. The fingers were long, tapered, the palm square. His first and second knuckles and his palm were callused from handling the sword and working against the bags. "You won't fight back. Winning doesn't count if your opponent lays down his weapon and offers his throat for your blade."

"Sometimes it's the easiest way to end the fight."

Jesse snorted. "You're supposed to be brilliant at problem-solving, and so far you're a dismal failure. Maybe I should try."

He kissed her fingers and palm, looking up at her. "Maybe you should. I'm hopelessly incompetent. People around me get ideas and attribute them to me, giving me an unwarranted reputation for brilliance."

"We could start over, as though we'd never met before."

"It wouldn't work. Even when we first met, there was a ghost between us. It'd still be there."

She got up and began to pace again. "It's your third question - do I just not want a Third. It - it never seemed like an option. Command equals triad. But how can you lose yourself that way?"

He shifted and hissed.

"What is it? What's wrong?"

He shook his head and opened his eyes. "Nothing. I just moved wrong."

"Nick left some pills," she said, holding up the small bottle.

"No. It isn't that bad. They'll make me sleep." He took the bottle and started to toss it in the drawer. His hand stopped in mid-motion, and the bottle, forgotten, landed on the carpet. "Where did that come from?"

"The 'bot picked it up while you were in the bathroom. Why? What is it?"

"There's a small box on top of the chest. Bring it here." His voice was flat, hard - the command voice. Jesse obeyed without thinking.

"What is that?" she asked, handing him the thin rectangle.

He grunted, struggling to manipulate the lock one-handed, then pushed the box back to her. "Something designed to make me very crazy, very fast. It enhances Sensitivity."

"But how..." she watched as he picked through the medals and bars, extracting a small gold case and emptying it of the three rings it held. "Of course. When he came after you."

"If he's been using that, it's no wonder he's getting reckless," Jason muttered, using the small box like tongs to grasp the dark grey stone and enclose it. "There. Little or no harm done. You didn't touch it, did you?"

Jesse shook her head. "I think I may have stepped on it, but I was wearing boots."

He nodded and sank back against the pillows. Jesse picked up the box and the ring case and carried them out to the study. *Security can take care of them in the morning. If he feels at all like I do, he's not up to any more alarms tonight.* Remembering someone who seemed able to slide through walls, or at least past guards without being noticed, she slid the ring case into one of the desk drawers and locked the drawer, slipping the key into her pocket.

Then curiosity overcame her and she opened the box, glancing back at the bedroom door as if to make sure Jason hadn't followed her. For a few moments she enjoyed the guilty pleasure of snooping through a partner's possessions, looking at and touching the medals from the various systems, lifting the heavy medallion carved in the shape of a winged lion and feeling the weight in her palm, running a finger over the cool hardness of the three black pearls embedded in the lower edge.

"Are you all right?"

She jumped and put the medal back in its place before she looked around. "You shouldn't be out of bed."

"I'm fine. I'm sure fright's good for the heart."

He walked over to her, shifting his weight carefully before each step, and stood looking over her shoulder at the objects in the box.

Well, I'm already revealed as a snoop, Jesse thought. *I might just as well see if he'll satisfy my curiosity while I'm at it.* She picked up the three rings from the small box and held them out on the palm of her hand. "Tell me about these?"

He flattened his hand on the desk top and levered himself into the armchair, gesturing Jesse into the other. The fingers that touched her palm as he transferred the rings from her hand to his trembled slightly, but they were warm.

"These are bond rings - like wedding rings - for a triad. My father, Stephen, had them made in Shipani for himself and his partners." He glanced up, questioningly, and Jesse signalled him to go on.

"This one," he held up an intricate three-strand knot of gold that would lie almost flat around a finger, "is for the First. This one," the knot was the same - similar to the knot of braid the Talents wore on their collars, Jesse realized, but the living metal was red gold, "this one is for the Second. And this one," it was a knot of white gold, warmer and richer looking than silver, "this is for the Third."

He sighed and replaced the rings in the case, then let the lid fall closed. "They were sent to me after my parents were killed." He closed his eyes and settled back in the chair.

"Oh, no you don't. If you fall asleep there I won't be able to get you back to bed, and then David really will kill me. Come on, Jason," she held out a hand, "you never should have gotten up."

They were both shaking by the time they got back into the bedroom, and his arm was heavy over Jesse's shoulder. She got him into bed and pulled the covers up, ignoring the pain in her arm and shoulder.

"There. I apologize for snooping. Are you all right now?"

"I'm fine." He closed his eyes and leaned back against the pillows for a moment, then opened them and looked up at her. "If you wouldn't mind, though, I'd take another cup of David's wonderful broth."

"What," she asked, handing Jason the cup, "cures a broken heart?"

She tried to keep her voice light, but he glanced up and set his cup on the side table. "Thom?"

She nodded. "Believe me, I don't have any desire to spend the rest of my life grieving for him. And he wouldn't want that. But people keep pushing..." She reached to put her cup down as the pressure gathered behind her eyes, and pulled back with a gasp as the fabric of her shirt rubbed over the raw spot on her arm. Even through the bandages, it felt as though someone had touched it with hot metal.

"Here, let me." He cupped his hand over her arm and drew in a deep breath. As he breathed out, the fire went out of the wound, and then the throbbing ache.

Jesse felt muscles relax she hadn't realize were tight. "You shouldn't have done that, but thank you."

"You know what?" Jason said, taking a cautious sip.

"What?"

"For a while, before David got hurt, we were becoming friends. I wish it had stayed that way. I'm sorry everything went so wrong."

"Sometimes I think we are friends," Jesse said. "Other times..."

"Don't. Don't tease me, Jesse. Please," the sapphire eyes were bright with unshed tears. "Please don't keep letting me think you'll let me into your life and then pushing me away. Do it and get it over. Don't let me keep hoping." His hands were trembling. He turned away. "I can't stand any more. Please. It hurts too much."

"Don't," she said, laying her hand over his. "Don't turn away, don't give up."

"Jesse, if you can't forgive me for not being Thom Isaacson, we'll keep fighting, and wanting each other, and hurting David until we've torn ourselves apart. And maybe even that wouldn't matter - but we'll tear this base apart with us."

"What do you want from me?" she whispered.

"I want peace with you." She started to turn away, and he took her hand. "Don't you understand, Jesse? You've wrapped yourself in your grief for Thom and shut everything else out. You don't have room for anybody else – not even as a friend."

"As long as I'm capable of doing my job, why should that matter to you?"

"Because you're my partner. Because healing is my function. Because relieving pain is my function. How could it not matter to me? How could I see you hurting this way and not want to help?"

He pushed himself up. "By the Many, woman, can't you see what you do to me?" He pulled her to him and kissed her so long and hard Jesse felt her lips bruising, then released her and pushed her away. "Get out," he whispered.

"What?"

"I said, get out of here," he said. His voice was hoarse. "Now, please. I'm about to lose any control I have left. Jesse, if you don't get away from me, you won't have to think of a reason for killing me. I can't keep my hands off you any longer."

"Well, it would be a solution, of a sort," she said.

The slap was so sudden and so hard it left her ears ringing. She brought a hand up to retaliate, but Jason's face stopped her.

His hand was wrapped around his left shoulder, and he was as white as undifferentiated carbon mass. "Don't say that. Ever. You can't possibly know..."

I do know, Jason, but I don't want you or anyone else to ever, ever know about it.

"You do have a temper. I was beginning to think you were a saint."

"Most 'saints' had very bad tempers." He fell back against the pillows, still clutching his shoulder, and laughed. "It hurts, it hurts, make me stop," he gasped.

She went to the converter and came back with a glass of water. "Do you want to drink it, or would you rather I throw it in your face?"

He shook his head, tears streaming down his face, and reached for the glass. His hand was shaking; she had to steady it for him to drink.

"Here," she said. "Let me see what you did to yourself." She pulled the silk robe away from his shoulder. A trace of red was beginning to show on the dressings. "You've torn it open again, Jason. I'll get Nick."

He shook his head. "Put a fresh bandage on it. It'll be all right."

He didn't move as she pulled the old dressing away and put a new one on. When she came back from washing her hands, his eyes were closed. The tousled blonde hair was curling around his face. It occurred to Jesse he needed a haircut.

She settled into the chair. "So much for talking it out logically and settling things. I turned a hurricane loose when I asked for you. I don't know why it never occurred to me it would touch me too."

"'Sew the wind, reap the whirlwind.'"

"I thought you'd drifted away," she said.

"Just trying to think. I didn't know it would be like this. Loving David was always so easy.

"It's no wonder I'm afraid of you, Jesse Leeds."

"You're afraid of me? Why? I didn't think you were afraid of anything."

"Oh, Jesse," he murmured. "How little you know about me. But you," he said, turning to look at her. "I'm afraid of you because I cannot be objective about you. When I'm around you, my brain and my guts turn to jelly. I forget to think, I forget everything – I just feel."

Jesse shifted to sit next to him and took the long thin hand in hers. "I'm sorry. It never occurred to me, in all of this, that you might be hurt - that you might - love me."

"How could I not? You're my First, my partner - not to mention that you're beautiful, brilliant, and brave."

"Flattery aside, Jason Ashe, how can you love David and say you love me at the same time?"

The corner of his mouth started to lift, and she saw a glint of mischief in his eye, then he sobered. "Where are you from?"

"Hampton's Settlement. It's in..."

"I know where it is. I'd forgotten. 'Old-time religionists' of the worst sort, and isolationists, too. It's a miracle you managed to make it to the Point."

"I nearly didn't. But I - I ran away from the man... one of my teachers took me in, and when I came of age, my advisor sponsored me for the Point, and my fa... they couldn't stop me. So, what does where I come from have to do with your emotional capability?"

He grinned and kissed the tips of Jesse's fingers. "Because if you'd been raised on most other worlds in Prometheus, or like I was, in Defense Command, you'd know that for the Sensitive, loving both your partners is the way you're built. Especially for an Ansari. My parents were a triad, I grew up expecting to be part of a triad. To me, loving both you and David is simply the way I'm supposed to feel. I can't imagine any other way."

He pushed himself up, and a grimace flickered across his face.

"You must be tired. This isn't important."

"Yes it is," Jason answered, tightening his grip on her hand.

Jesse sighed, looking down at the intertwined hands. "Until I met Thom, I never imagined I could feel so... Sometimes it hurts so much I think I can't stand it any more. Will the pain ever stop?"

"The fabric of your lives was woven together; there'll always be cut ends. But memory will take the place of the hurt, the anger. Instead of aching inside, you'll be able to be glad for your time with him.

"But you have to decide when."

"I think I've begun to realize that," Jesse said, pulling her feet up on the chair and wrapping her arms around her knees. "Can you help me?"

"I'm probably the last person you should ask to help you with this. As I said, I can't be said to be disinterested."

"Maybe that's why."

"Jesse, I can't just Touch you and make it all go away. I wish I could.

"Healing sets the mind and body on the path to mending themselves. I can begin the process, but you have to do the work - you have to decide it's time. And now is not the time. You're exhausted, and I'm not in the best shape myself." He gestured to the other side of the bed. "Come lie down, and I'll help you sleep."

Suddenly glad Jason had pulled back, Jesse kicked off her boots and settled onto the bed beside him. With the warmth of his hand on her forehead, the pain in her arm disappeared, and so did the pain of memory. She drew in a long breath, and slipped down the long dark tunnel into sleep.

-Chapter 17-
We have to have proof...

"Zephron said you wanted to see me?"

Jesse had been absorbed in the report she was reading, and his voice startled her. She jumped and flattened her palms on the table.

"Sorry. I thought you'd heard the door."

"It's all right. Come in and sit down. Get some coffee, if you want."

As he slipped behind her, Jason's hand touched her shoulder. It was like a jolt of electricity - she felt the spark through her whole body. *Did he feel that? I hope not.*

"May I get you something?" His voice was even, cool.

"Mmm, thanks. Tea, please."

Their fingers touched as he handed her the cup, and she felt the tingle again. She looked up, and his expression told her he felt it, too.

"How are..." her voice was hoarse. She cleared her throat and tried again. "How are you feeling? Are you sure you're fit?"

"I'm fine. How are you?"

"I'm fine, thank you."

He put his cup down and reached across the table. His hand was warm over hers, the thin fingers steady and strong. "I'm glad the Command First is fine. How is Jesse?"

She let the corner of her mouth lift. "Jesse s all right. She's been better, but she's been worse, and she'll survive. I just need time."

He nodded. "I'm here if you need me, Jesse."

"Thank you." She straightened, putting on her 'professional' face. "Okay, Third, vacation's over. To work. First, this." She handed him the report from HQ, and when he settled back to read it, pushed another stack of cards across.

"Zephron," she triggered the comm switch, "can you spare us some time?"

"There in a few, Command. Do you need James and Mari?"

"Not just yet. You might ask them to keep some time free in about an hour."

Jason glanced up from the report. "Should I call David?"

"I already did. He'll be here about the same time as James and Mariko."

He nodded and went back to his reading.

"Well," he said, sometime later, "your analysis is, as always, penetrating, clear, and logical. The only problem is that in this case, you're wrong. I assume it's because you have too little information about our opponent."

Jesse was prevented from arguing with him by Zephron's door signal.

"Are you about ready for me?"

"Yes. Your timing is perfect," Jesse said. "Jason was just telling me our analysis is incorrect because it's based on insufficient information - I was about to ask him to supply the missing intelligence."

Zephron retrieved a drink and seated himself on the same side of the table as Jason, picking up the pile of data cards and glancing through them. "Okay. Show us where we're wrong."

Jason grinned and opened his notebook. "Maybe I'm hoping you'll show me where I'm wrong, Zeph."

Zephron stroked his beard and grinned, then narrowed his eyes and shook his head. "Uh, uh. You've already had your vacation. To work, Ashe."

Jason nodded. "We've been lucky he's been inactive lately. Jesse may have hurt him worse than she thought, but I think there's another reason - one I don't want to discuss right now.

"As Zephron said, I've had a lot of time to put things together, and I think I've found a pattern. I think, to start, that our terrorist began by helping the naturally-occurring problems any new platform would encounter to continue and grow. His task was easier because we're still transporting, and that causes problems in and of itself."

Jesse glanced over at Zephron. He raised a brow. "How sure of that are you, Jason? The two didn't seem connected to us."

"I'm not absolutely sure. I think it makes sense. Let me go

on, and then if you think I'm wrong - I'll be relieved.

"I think his campaign of sabotage started with the section that broke loose the day we ran into that raider."

"But the bolts in that section had been weakened."

Jason nodded. "I know, and at first I assumed it must have been done in the construction yards. But if you look at Chief Cody's last report," he handed Jesse a card, "the only place the bolts had been interfered with was in that section. It was a total of about a hundred and fifty bolts - a few hours' work for a single person. Not too easy, not too hard, and in a section where he could work without fear of interruption - possibly even over a period of several days. It's suggestive, and it was too - confined. If it had been done in the construction yards, I think more sections would have been weakened.

"There were a lot of small things we all assumed were because King K's a new platform and we're moving it to station. Targets of opportunity. That was one of them, but..." he let his voice trail off and glanced up.

"As we get the systems cleaned up, the attacks become obvious. They include the toxin in the mass converters, the life support failure in the lab, and the system failure caused by the wiped control codes. None of those could be anything but deliberate sabotage.

"They share a number of other common factors." He tapped the screen with his light stylus, emphasizing each point as he touched it.

"They were impersonal - attacks against systems rather than individuals. Kwame and the youngsters who were killed weren't specific targets - they just happened to be in the wrong place at the wrong time. The main purpose appears to be disruption of operations. There doesn't seem to be any personal animosity, just indifference. He didn't care who he killed, or even if he killed someone or not. That may be why Kwame's alive."

"I think I can see where you're going with this, Jason," Jesse said, "but that toxin in the converter - how can you classify that as simply 'disrupting operations?'"

"What's the first thing you think when you hear the word 'toxin,' Jesse?"

"Poison, of course."

"Of course. And we all associate poison with murder. But a toxin is more simple and more complex than just a murder weapon, especially a biological like this one. Some people were hardly affected, others became seriously ill, and some died. If his primary intent had been to kill, I think he'd have used something more lethal. Looked at in that sense, that attack was a failure. But looked at as an attempt to cause confusion, disorder, fear - it was a roaring success."

Jesse thought a few moments, then nodded. "All right, I see what you mean there. But what was his point? If I were a terrorist, I'd use something like that to weaken the system for further attacks, not just sit back and let it recover."

Zephron grinned. "Lack of follow-through."

Jason nodded. "Indeed. That was my first hint that he was a Crystal-user - he made opportunities for himself and then failed to follow through. And I think there's a possibility that he's one of the people who got sick, which may also explain the lack of follow-through."

"Why would he do something that stupid?" Bell asked.

Jason glanced up from his notebook. "He could be too arrogant or stupid to think he could have been affected, or he could have been using it as a cover - who'd suspect one of the people who got sick?"

"Very well. Continue, Jason. What else?"

"The original attacks were all simple, and the clues, what there were, were dead ends. He was doing a job, but he wasn't emotionally involved."

He went to the converter and refilled his cup. "At that point, he'd made no mistakes. In terms of his own safety, I mean. It didn't matter if we knew we were being sabotaged, as long as we couldn't identify the saboteur."

Zephron caught Jesse's eye and nodded. "All right, I see the force of the argument here. Press on."

Jason grinned, put the cup down, and picked up his notebook. "Next came the attack on David which was meant for me, the booby traps in Jesse's office, and the attack on me that Jesse disrupted. Those also have a number of elements in common, and I think one element is increasing desperation. He hasn't succeeded in doing what he was supposed to do - operations continued, and King K is still moving toward her permanent station.

"Most obvious, all these attacks are directed at the Command Triad, two of them specifically at me. I don't know if he thinks I know something that threatens him, if he perceives me as the weakest member of the triad, or if the motive is more - personal."

Jesse raised an eyebrow, but when Jason didn't respond to the implied question said, "Maybe it's that if you're not functional, we can't mesh. If we can't mesh, we can't access all the command systems. Ergo, we can't command."

Zephron, who'd been making notes, looked up and nodded.

Jason continued. "That's possible. If that's the case, we need to double Mariko's security."

"Shit," Zephron muttered. "I didn't even think about that." He pulled his mike down and started talking to Security.

Jason dropped his head into his hand.

"Are you all right?" Jesse asked. "I know the medics say you're fit, but it's only been a week."

He lifted his head and managed a faint smile. "I'm all right. I'm appalled I didn't think of the danger to Mari."

"Neither did I, and I'm her partner," Zephron said. "And that's one of the best arguments for Triad command I've ever encountered." He pushed the mike back up. "All right, Jason, continue."

Jason nodded. "It's only luck one or all of these attacks didn't succeed. They've become more and more elaborate - he's taking chances. They all contained an element of malice, they all involved a high risk of discovery, and in all of them, he left behind physical evidence. Instead of setting traps and waiting for them to work, he's risked himself. He's gone from cautious to reckless for no apparent reason."

Zephron raised his hand in a 'time out to think' gesture, at the same time motioning toward Jason's notebook. The blonde man handed it over and rose, going to the viewport.

I think he knows who it is. At least he thinks he does. He doesn't want to tell us because he doesn't have any proof. Jesse started to say something, then shook her head.

"Why did the attacks become personal, Jason?" Zephron asked. "If it's just because you're the Sensitive, and therefore he sees you as the 'weakest link' in the command chain, I'd have expected him to go after Mari, too."

Jason shrugged and came back to the table. "I have two reasons, and I'll tell you what they are, but I also have reasons for not wanting to tell you - any of you - who I suspect, and I hope you'll respect them. First, I have no proof - I just have suspicions. Second, he's been using Crystal, and by this time he's paranoid as hell. If he gets even a smell of suspicion, there's no telling what he might do. Is that reasonable?"

"Unfortunately, yes," Jesse said. "I thought Sensitives were supposed to be emotional and illogical. All right, tell us why you think the attacks have become more personal."

He smiled, and began to walk the light stylus over and through his fingers. "I think he thinks I know something no one else does. Somehow he knows about the Crystal source. He doesn't know about this." He touched a control on his notebook, and the ghost ship appeared in the center of the table, above the rotating planet with the growing patch of livid green.

"And that's why he attacked Kwame?"

"Kwame was in the wrong place at the wrong time. He was after the data, and he thinks he got it before Kwame had a chance to see it - but he isn't sure about me."

"And the second reason?"

It's amazing. I've never seen it happen quite like that before. Jesse glanced over at Zephron - the hand that had been stroking his beard had frozen above his chin.

The blood rose from Jason's neck to his forehead, its progress over his face clearly visible. "If my suspicions are correct - and remember, they're only suspicions - I rejected his advances shortly after David and I..."

"That's definitely personal," Zephron said. "And the hint of ego sounds right, too - he'd be angry because he can't understand how you could prefer someone else to him."

"Exactly. At this point, for a Crystal user, anything that doesn't go the way he wants or expects it to is little short of infuriating. The induced psychosis is like the final stages of sociopathy, when reality is almost completely nonexistent. And time is running out for him. When we get on station and settled, we won't be as vulnerable as we are now."

"Are you ready for us?" James stuck his head around the door, grinning, and Mariko peered under his arm. They stood there, like a pair of naughty children gloating at having disturbed their parents, until David came up behind them and pushed James through the door.

"Not playtime, children," Zephron said. "Work to do, plans to make."

Two hours later, Jesse was rubbing her forehead, trying to calm the nerves that were threatening to make her head explode, and voices around the table were tight with tension and controlled anger.

"Look, David, I told you - if I'd been able to think of anything better, I would have." Jason's voice was flat, but Jesse saw his jaw tighten.

"And so would the rest of us, David. Face it - this is a lousy plan, but it's the best we're going to do. We're stuck between a rock and a hard place, and the risks to us don't count as high as the disaster we're trying to prevent." Zephron pulled his beard and threw his light stylus on the table.

"That's easy for you to say," David grumbled.

"Please, people, let's keep the knives in their sheaths," Jesse murmured. "We're very close to forgetting who the real enemy is."

"Speaking of that," said James, who rarely spoke up during meetings of the command team, "can we see where our intruder is, please?"

Jason pulled the microphone to his mouth and murmured a few words; the cube containing the image of the ghosting supercruiser came into being above the center of the table. For a moment, Jesse thought the huge battleship was gone - then she realized it was almost behind the gas giant where the crystal was growing.

The cause of all the problems. If we could mine that without them knowing we'd done it, we could start out of this system and maybe get far enough away to call for help before it blew and they came after us.

"What if..." she let her voice trail off. *I don't see any way we could plant mines without them being aware we were doing it. They have to be monitoring us, whether the terrorist is in contact with them or not.*

"I thought of that too, Jesse," Zephron said, "but we can't take the chance of them seeing what we're doing. That's part of the reason for setting up the fake trail to draw them away from this system."

"Why not?" Mariko asked. "If it's a question of us or the Crystal field, wouldn't it be worth it, whether we succeed in getting away or not?"

"It would, if we could be sure we'd destroy the crystal," Jason answered. "The problem is, we might leave most of it intact, they'd destroy us, and they'd still have enough mature, natural Crystal to cause damage to Prometheus for centuries.

"That's our major problem. Whether our terrorist is in contact with them or not, whether they even know about him or not, they have to be watching our every move. So far, they either think we haven't noticed the Crystal or we don't know they're there - or both.

"And time's running out, people," he said, bringing up one of the readouts from King K's data collection routines. "The growth rate in that field's slowing. When it stops growing, the field will be mature, and they'll move in to harvest it. If we haven't made our move before then, it'll be too late. It's decision time."

"Very well," Jesse said, pulling her hand away from her forehead and straightening. "Are we agreed, then, on Jason and Zephron setting up and transmitting coded messages to Quadrant HQ that we hope will send that supercruiser back across the border and give us some wiggle room?"

She looked around the table, meeting each pair of eyes, and got nods from everyone.

"That's the easy part," Zephron said. "We've been lucky the last couple of weeks - either our terrorist was injured fighting with Jesse, exhausted himself and depleted the Crystal he was using, or he simply got scared off. He'll be back, and he'll be even more desperate - we're only weeks from reaching our permanent station, and he has to stop us before we get there. So the next part of the plan is to try to lure him out of hiding and dispose of him before he can wreak any more havoc."

"So we have to give him something to disrupt," Mariko said.

"Probably more than one thing," Jason said. "If we just set up one juicy-looking piece of bait, he'll smell the trap and pull farther back into his hole."

"I can think of a few things we could do to try to lure him out," Zephron said, "but I think we all need to be aware that our best and most effective bait is sitting right here, and much as I don't like it, we may need to use it. I mean you, Jason." The blonde man nodded, and Zephron continued.

"Okay, here's the way it looks. Jase and I will design the coded messages to draw our bandit off. We'll probably have to pull Valery Radonov in on that, but I've vetted him thoroughly and I think he's trustworthy."

He looked over at Jason, who nodded again, and continued. "David, you and James need to design and implement the traps to lure our terrorist out into the open where we can get him, with Jase in reserve as a last resort. That's going to leave division management to Jesse and Ops to Mari."

The little Third nodded, her dark brown eyes bright.

Jesse looked around again. "All right. We have consensus

on the first part of this operation. We need it on the second. Are we agreed?"

"Yes," said Jason.

"I don't like it, but yes," Zephron agreed.

Mariko looked from Zephron to James, then back to Jesse, and nodded.

"James? David?"

James nodded. "I'm with Zeph. I don't like it, but I can't see another way."

"David?"

His eyes were pale as rainwater, and the muscles in his jaw were tight. He glanced over at Jason, then away, and the light pen snapped in his fingers. "I'm outvoted. I have to go along with the team." His voice was light, even, but Jesse could feel the anger under it from where he sat at the end of the table.

Either he's very angry indeed, or I'm getting a little more sensitive. "And I don't like it either, but I can't see a better alternative. Very well, then. Zephron, is there anything else?"

Zephron shook his head and pushed himself to his feet. "No, not that I can think of right now. We all know what needs to be done - let's do it and get it over with."

#

"You had something else on your mind this afternoon."

I was expecting him. I hadn't thought about it before, but I just realized it. I've been waiting for him all evening.

She stood and came around the desk, gesturing to the couch. "Do you want a drink?"

Jason shook his head and settled into a corner of the couch. Jesse got herself a cup of tea and came back to the armchair. "You're usually more diplomatic."

"I'm sorry. I didn't mean to be rude, but I had this hideous feeling I didn't have a lot of time to be subtle."

Jesse took a swallow of the hot tea and put the cup down. "Did you think I was going to run out and confront the suspected terrorist, thereby causing exactly what we're trying to avoid? Or send a message to Quadrant HQ in clear so if that supercruiser's monitoring our communications they'll know what we're doing?"

He smiled and shook his head. "No, Jesse. I would never accuse you of being stupid. But whatever it is, I'd rather you'd discuss it with me than with David or Zeph. Unless I'm wrong and what you had on your mind was something not to do with the terrorist."

"I'd like to deny it, just for the satisfaction of seeing you wrong, for once, but you're right." She picked up the cup and turned it in her hands, trying to put the vagrant thought she'd had that afternoon into words. "I'm not sure I can be too clear about this - I've been trying not to think about it, in the hope it would sort itself out.

"In the course of your teaching, I assume you've done a lot of one on one work with your students?"

He nodded. "Of course. That's part of the job, particularly in the sword arts."

"So you know how you come to expect certain things from certain students, come to know a way of standing, holding the body, of entering?"

He nodded again. Deep in the blue eyes, she saw a spark kindle.

"That terrorist - the man who attacked you - I've fought him before. He's one of my students."

"But you don't know which one." It wasn't a question.

"I don't know which one. And that bothers me almost more than knowing it's one of my students - that I can't tell who it was."

"Late at night, in body armor, with that helmet and face mask, after he'd dosed you with Crystal - it might be surprising if you did know." The long breath was not quite a sigh of relief.

"Why are you so afraid I'll figure out who it is, Jason?"

"Not just you. Any of you - David, Zeph, James, Mari, you - any of you. Because if you know, or you think you know, your emotional reaction will tell him something's wrong."

"And we can't afford to risk having him move too fast."

"Exactly."

"Well, I don't know who he is, and I promise you, I won't try to find out, except by the means we've already been using."

She put the tea down and curled her arms around her knees. "It isn't just a 'walk in, everyone's welcome' sort of class, you know. They have to apply, and be interviewed, and David and I have to accept them. We're very - particular. And yet..."

He put his hands on his knees and levered himself to his feet. "Don't worry about it, Jesse. What we - any of us - know of him is not what he is. I don't know of anyone who can't be deceived by Crystal.

"Sorry. It's been a long day, and I'm tired. If you need me..."

She nodded. "I'll call. Good night, Jason."

-Chapter 18-
"If I'd never loved, I never would have cried..."
Paul Simon– Like a Rock

"It's taking too long." Jesse shut down the console and pushed herself away from the table.

"It's only been a week," Zephron said, putting down the data card he was studying. "Patience, Command. We only sent the first message yesterday, and we figure it's going to take at least four days before they have them decoded and figure out what we're saying."

"Why did it take so long?" Jesse wasn't in any mood to be patient - the last week had been full of nightmares, broken sleep, small irritations, things going wrong that shouldn't have. Even working out hadn't relieved the tension.

"Well, Valery had to find us a code we knew the Tragans had broken, but that they didn't know we knew they'd broken. That took time - they don't just label the transmissions."

Jesse glanced up, and Zephron looked over and grinned. "Sorry. Didn't mean to sound sarcastic. You're not the only one suffering from the tension - Mari came back to quarters last night and had a mild fit of hysterics because James had left books all over the living room and the 'bot hadn't picked them up."

"I don't know whether the first question should be, 'is Mariko all right?' or 'why didn't the 'bot work?'"

"Mari's used to being able to consult - the last week's been a strain. As for the 'bot, some idiot who shall remain nameless, but whose initials are Zephron Bell, turned the blasted thing off because he came home the night before and fell over it.

"And it's happening all over. People are complaining about their roommates, about not getting mail, about the food - you name it, somebody's bitching about it."

"Including me."

Zephron chose to ignore that, and put another data card in front of Jesse. "Here, see what you think about this."

"What is it?"

"Some of the bait for luring our terrorist out of the woodpile."

She flipped through several pages - data cards to be left "carelessly" on the tops of desks in offices that had 'accidentally' been left unlocked, phony entries for the system logs to show them making more progress toward their permanent station than they were, reports to HQ that were destined to go nowhere.

"This is good, Zephron. Did you do this?"

"Jase and I, with a little help from James. The boy has a devious mind and a way of looking at things from around the corner. I'm looking forward to seeing what he'll be like when he grows up." Zephron grinned.

"I'm a little concerned about the system log entries - it's a crime to falsify them."

"These will be overlays - what's available to the ordinary operating passwords. The real logs will go into a holding file accessible by the command passwords. When we've caught the terrorist, one of us puts in the command password, and the overlays disappear, to be replaced by the real log. David says as long as the real logs are on file and accessible to the command team, we're covered. The same thing will happen to the reports to HQ - the code will throw them into a locked file, and we can disappear them as soon as all this is over."

"Do you think this will work?"

Bell pulled his beard. "To be frank, no. I think he's already far enough gone, or sensitized by that damned Crystal, to the point that he'll see straight through these - or at least, assume most of them are traps. I'm afraid what it's going to come down to is either setting him up with a real opportunity to sabotage a vital system - and for obvious reasons I don't want to do that - or giving him Jason on a platter."

"Sometimes I'd like to give him both Jason and David on a platter."

Zephron's startled exclamation called Jesse back from where her thoughts had drifted, and she realized she'd spoken aloud.

"I hope you don't really mean that."

She shook her head and gathered her things together. "I don't mean it literally. It's just - it was easier... I don't know, Zephron. You'd think I've got the best deal in the Service - they're brilliant, they're beautiful, they're brave - and most of the time having one or the other of them in the room makes me feel as though there isn't enough air to go around. When they're together, I feel smothered."

"I think you're tired, Command. You'll feel better when you've had a good night's sleep."

Jesse nodded and left before she dug herself in any further. *The problem*, she thought, as she pulled off her boots and threw them in the corner, *is that I haven't had a good night's sleep in a long time.*

#

She saw a shadow out of the corner of her eye, and increased her speed.

"Jesse? Hey, Jesse, wait up."

Sighing, Jesse slowed down and let Jason catch her.

"Hi," he grinned. "You're Jesse Larsen, aren't you? I'm Jason Ashe. I think we worked together for a while, but that was a long time ago."

"Is that supposed to be funny?"

He shrugged and shortened his steps to match hers. "I guess it depends - I thought it was funny when I said it. Are you on your way to a meeting, or can I buy you a cup of coffee?"

"Actually, I was on my way to work out." *And I don't want to have coffee with you. I'm fine as long as I don't have to deal with you or David - why can't you just leave me alone to get on with it?*

"Then, would you mind some company? I always think it's more fun when you have a training partner."

She glanced at him out of the corner of her eye, but his expression was neutral. "If you want, Jason. As a matter of fact," *this should turn you off,* "I was hoping to find a sparring partner."

"Ah, good. I've been working on my speed - soon I'll be too fast for you to catch me."

#

Jesse turned her hip, provocatively, inviting the attack, but Jason grinned and shuffled the other way, circling around and forcing her to shift her stance.

"Coward," she mouthed, grinning. There was sweat dripping down her face, she was panting, her heart was racing, and she felt wonderful.

"You bet," Jason answered, dodging under her guard and tapping her midriff. The fine blonde hair was plastered to his head and his face was shining as he backpedaled to evade her answering attack. "The bad thing about that kick is you telegraph it, every time.

The good thing - for you - is that if you get a chance to get it out, it connects every time."

"Ah, I thought you were getting too fast for me to catch," she muttered. She slid in, ready to punch to his midriff, but he dodged and her fist connected with his shoulder.

He winced and backed away, right hand rising automatically to cover the front of his shoulder.

"Sorry, that was an accident. You ducked into it." Jesse backed away and lowered her guard.

"My fault. It's okay," he'd gone pale and there was a faint green tinge to his skin, "it's still a little touchy."

He started to put his hands up again, and Jesse raised hers, open. "Well, even if you haven't had enough, I have."

"Whatever you say," Jason answered. He straightened and turned to face her, hands at his sides.

She returned his bow and turned away, loosening her belt.

"Will you have dinner with me, Jesse?"

"I'm short of time, Jason. This is the day's break - dinner's a sandwich at my desk."

"Please."

"I really am busy."

"You need to eat, and I have something to show you - something we need to discuss. Consider it a business meeting. It won't take long."

"Very well. I'll meet you at our quarters. If you get there first, go ahead and order for me, will you?"

He nodded, and Jesse continued toward the showers.

This is very naughty of you, Jesse, she thought, settling into the hot tub and burying her face in the bubbling water.

I don't care - I need this. Jason can wait. And so can everything else.

#

He rose as she came in, and smiled. "I ordered you a glass of wine. I hope you like it."

"Thank you." She took a sip from the tall glass and the cool, dry wine flowed over her tongue, leaving behind traces of lemon and vanilla flowers, a touch of merinth. "It's very nice." *I don't remember putting this one on the wine list.*

"Thank you. It's an Ansari vintage - one my mother was quite fond of." He gestured to the dining alcove, pulling her chair out and seating her before he retrieved the plates from the converter.

It smelled delicious, and Jesse realized she was famished. Giving herself up to blissful sensuality, she chewed and swallowed, refreshing her palate with the wine, until most of her plate was empty.

"Mmm - that's the best meal I've had in days. Now that I've satisfied my hunger enough to pay attention, what was it?"

Jason pushed his plate aside and touched the control for the menu, turning it so Jesse could see it.

"Grilled Nilgri fish with angel hair pasta and lightly steamed vegetables," it said. "Jesse's favorite dinner."

"I see. So David's choosing your meals for you now - or did you ask him to pick something to soften me up?"

Jason rose, turning away, but not before Jesse saw that his face was bright red. He picked up the plates and took them to the converter, returning with two steaming cups.

"I didn't talk to David - in fact, I haven't seen him since last night. While I waited for you, I looked through the service menu, and when I saw that entry I thought you might enjoy it.

"I didn't realize I needed to 'soften you up,' Jesse." The soft voice had an edge. "I thought we were partners."

"I did enjoy it. Thank you. And now I need to get back to work." *I'm sorry for my bad manners, Jason, but when I'm around you, I feel as though I don't have a skin to cover my nerve endings.*

"Wait, please. I do need you to look at this." He pulled a data card from the fold of his tunic and handed it to her, then picked up his cup and retreated to the couch.

She read it, then read it again, while Jason sipped his coffee and stared into space.

"I don't like this, Jason."

"Neither does Zephron."

"What about David?"

"David hasn't seen it. David won't see it. This is the last resort, what we do if our terrorist refuses all our other bait and hurts David, or Mari, or James." His face was hard, and his voice was flat - a pronouncement, not open to negotiation, not to be changed by argument or reason.

Jesse dropped her eyes to the data card and read it a third time, conscious that Jason was watching her. Her breathing quickened, and she could feel the pulse beating in her throat and temples. She pulled in a deep breath to calm herself, and forced her attention to every detail on the card before her, shutting out everything else.

Jason's voice drifted into her consciousness as nothing more than sound - then she realized he'd asked a question.

"Yes, you're right. This may be the only thing that will work. All right, whatever you think, Jason. Make sure you and Zephron have it on tap, but keep it until we've run out of other options."

She set her cup down and rose, holding the data card out to him. *He looks as though I just slapped him instead of agreeing with him - I suppose even Jason Ashe feels a little fear about being the tethered goat.* "I have to get back to work. Thank you for dinner. And the workout."

Walking down the corridor on the way to her office, Jesse realized the look on Jason's face had not been fear, but betrayal - the look of the lamb whose trusted shepherd had offered it up for sacrifice.

"Come off it, Jesse, you're imagining things. You're tired. Let's get this done and go to bed."

#

"Jesse, what the hell do you think you're doing?"

Of course. On top of everything else, you're just what I needed.

"Did I say come in, David?"

"Did I knock?"

"No, come to think of it, you didn't. Why don't you go back out and knock, so I can say 'go away?' Or, I could just throw you out."

"You and what other man's army?" David's eyes were like chips of ice, and the hands he'd planted on her desk were taut. "You're good, but you're not that good, and I'm just in the mood to tear you limb from limb."

"Or I could call Security."

He straightened. "I suppose you could. I'm trying to think what you could tell them - oh, yeah, how about you've decided you don't want partners, so would they come throw me out the nearest airlock. That way you'd only have Jason to deal with, and you seem to be doing pretty well on him without help."

Jesse sat back and rubbed the spot between her eyebrows. Her head was throbbing, and the touch of her cold fingertips felt good. "David, I'm not in any mood to play games with you, verbal or otherwise. I've had a long day, I'm tired, and I want to get this finished so I can go to bed. If you have something to say, say it. Otherwise, go away."

"All right. Did you or did you not ask Jason to spar with you this evening?"

What the hell is he angry about? "I didn't know sparring had become a crime, but in fact, I did not. I met Jason in the corridor, and when I refused his offer of coffee and told him I was going to work out, he invited himself along and offered to be my sparring partner." She gestured, and David settled into the chair.

"I could be wrong, of course, but I was under the impression that Jason was an adult and didn't need your permission to spar. If I'm misinformed, I apologize, but I think you should be angry with Jason, not me."

David shook his head. "No, as you very well know, Jason doesn't need my permission to spar. He does, however, need a doctor's clearance to fight full contact, which is what you were apparently doing - his left shoulder has a beautifully developing bruise exactly the shape of your fist. His left shoulder, I emphasize - the one that damned terrorist shot him in less than two months ago. The one that isn't quite healed, because wounds from energy whips take a long time to heal. That should be enough, but it apparently wasn't - he looks as though he's been beaten by an expert.

"I told you, Jesse, if you feel a need to hurt someone, don't take it out on Jason."

"I don't feel a need to hurt anyone, David, and we weren't fighting full contact - Jason ducked into me. I apologized at the time, and he told me he wasn't badly hurt. I'm sorry if it was worse than he said, but things happen, and most of us accept that. If you don't want Jason fighting, you need to talk to him and the medics - as you've reminded me before, I am not his boss."

"No, you're not. You're supposed to be his partner, but there's never been much evidence of that. And people don't usually tell their partners it's okay to go out and get themselves killed."

"I haven't told you that yet, David, but I could be persuaded if this goes on."

"You don't seem to have needed much persuasion to tell Jason that."

"What?"

"Not in those words, I grant you." Jesse wondered how he

could talk with his jaw clenched like that. "He said the two of you had been discussing his and Zephron's traps, and he offered as a last resort to let the terrorist kidnap him and take him as a prize to the Tragans - as a diversion, so we'd have time to get away."

That isn't Jason's plan. And David isn't supposed to know about Jason's plan anyway. We'd be monitoring him - Zephron may already have the sensors in place - what the hell is David talking about?

"What the hell are you talking about, David?"

"I just told you - I'm talking about Jason offering to let himself be taken to the Tragans, and you saying - let's see, what did he say you said? Oh, yes, 'Fine, Jason, whatever you think. Set it up with Zephron, will you?'"

"I didn't hear what he said." She had that blank feeling, as though she was staring at a featureless wall.

"If you didn't hear what he said, how could you have answered his question? Look, Jesse, I know you haven't wanted him - or me, lately - but that's - that's..."

"I didn't hear what he said, David. I was reading, and when I realized Jason had asked a question, I assumed he'd asked what I thought about what I was reading. That was what I told him to set up with Zephron, not letting that bastard carry him off to the Tragans so they could finish what they started."

"I don't believe you."

She shrugged. "I told you, I don't have time to play games. That includes lying. I did not tell Jason to go and get himself killed or captured, I wouldn't do such a thing, and if you want to believe I would - it's your problem. Now, will you please go away and leave me alone, David?"

"Why, Jesse?"

"Why, what, David? Why do I want you to leave me alone? I told you - I have work to do, I'm tired and I want to get it finished. And besides that, I don't find having you sit there and abuse me pleasant."

The big man pushed himself to his feet, went to the converter outlet, and came back with two glasses. "I mean," he said, settling back, "why don't you want to be around us? Why do you run away from us, why do you avoid us, why do you act as though we're infected with something horrible? What's wrong, Jesse?"

Oh, please, not tonight, David. Then, straightening, she looked at the man sitting across from her. He was big, and broad-shouldered, and strong - he looked as though he could handle anything. *All right, why not? Why not get it all out - then maybe I can just go back to work and quit worrying.*

"The first thing that's wrong," she said, trying to keep her voice level and clear, "is that Thom's gone. I know," she held up a hand, "it isn't your fault, and it isn't Jason's. I'm not blaming you. But he left a big hole in my life.

"I could live with that. But the two of you are smothering me. When I'm in a room with one of you it's hard to breathe. When you're both there, there's no oxygen in the air. I can't think, I can't reason - and I can't stand it."

He stirred, and Jesse hurried on, wanting to finish before he brought up all the good arguments she'd heard before. "I hurt, David. I hurt all the time. I'm empty, and I'm cold, and I'm walking on the edge of a cliff with nowhere to go but down." Her voice was rising. She paused, swallowed, and took a deep breath.

"I don't want to fall. I want to quit hurting, even if it means not feeling anything. I want it to stop. And I don't want it to happen again, and if I let you and Jason too close, it will."

She was always surprised at how fast he could move when he wanted to. He was up and behind her before she could react, and when the big, warm hands came down over her shoulders, she thought, *well, either he'll kill me or hug me, and at this point, I don't know which would be worse.*

"Relax," David said, massaging shoulders Jesse hadn't realized were so tight. "You're wound up like a watch spring, it's no wonder you're about to fly off in all directions." He pulled her back against the chair, and she gave up and closed her eyes, feeling the warmth from his hands and the big body behind her spreading down through her arms, her chest.

"Stop, David, I'm about to start crying. Stop, please."

He pulled his hands back and moved to the corner of the desk. "Maybe it's time you let yourself have a good cry. It might help."

Jesse shook her head, biting her lip. "I don't think so. I end up with a sore chest, a headache, and a terrible feeling I look ridiculous. I've never found that improves anything."

He grinned. "Well, I think you look stunning when the tip of your nose is pink and your eyes are red, but that's just me."

"And we all know you're crazy."

"Me? I'm the sane, well-adjusted, intelligent one, remember?

"Let me tell you a little story, Jesse. Maybe it'll help." When Jesse nodded, he stared off into space a few seconds, gathering his thoughts.

"I was born on Benetnash Seven - the world the Federates call Gehenna. The people who live there call it Santia, because it was founded by a man named Arnold Santee. He and his people were Tragan sympathizers, back about the time the Hexarchy was getting ready to split off from Prometheus.

"The man who sired me, by kidnapping and raping my fifteen-year-old mother, was one of the local lords, a man with the power of life and death over his people. And he was an underling - his overlord was a minor Tragan warlord, one of hundreds of petty nobles who considered Santia a breeding ground for their cannon fodder. You've heard of him - Sarg of Benetnash.

"Esau Barlow - that was the underlord's name - ruled his people with an iron fist. My earliest memories are of him beating me - with his fist, with a belt, with whatever came to hand. As part of my 'training,' he forced me to watch one day while he beat a man to death.

"He didn't usually beat his women - breeders are too valuable to take a chance of damaging. But the day he told my mother I'd been chosen to be trained as the overlord's j'nar - his personal slave - she went for him with all she had, and he beat her until she dropped - and then he kicked her. I'd have attacked him myself, but I was too scared of him - all I could do was throw myself over her and hope he'd stop. He did, after he'd kicked me a couple of times and broken my arm.

"I don't know how she did it - begging, bribery - Mama got us out of his compound and on a freighter. Their next stop was Sylvanus Major, and we got off there. I was just seven the day we landed.

"Mama got a job, working for the planetary administrator, and worked her way up. By the time I was ten, she was his assistant.

"Those were happy years. I went to school, and the Sylvanian medics worked with me until the nightmares stopped, and I had Mama - and no Esau Barlow.

"Then, when I was ten, Mama brought her boss home to meet me. His name was Christian Holgerson, and he was bigger than I am now - to me, he looked like a building walking. After a few months, they told me they were getting married - Christian was going to be my stepfather.

"It was like the bottom falling out of the world. I knew what fathers did, you see - I remembered Esau Barlow. But Mama kept telling me it wouldn't be that way, that he'd be good to me - good to us both - and I shut my mouth. If he was good to her, it didn't matter what he did to me, and if I lived long enough, I'd grow up and move out.

"So we moved to Christian's house, and for a couple of months, everything was all right. I stayed out of the way as much as I could, and Christian seemed content to have me around as long as I didn't bother him. I almost relaxed.

"Then one day, Mama told me they'd had this brilliant idea. Christian and I needed to get to know one another, she said.

"Christian was going to Sylvanus Minor to oversee some building there, and he'd be away several weeks. I'd go with him. It was a great opportunity - I'd see Sylvanus Minor, we'd do some camping - no boy in his right mind would have turned it down." He shrugged, and slid off the desk to walk the room, jingling the small objects he carried in his pockets.

Jesse sat back and watched him, interested despite herself.

"Mama wanted me to go, so I went. I'd decided he couldn't do much worse to me than Barlow had, and maybe it would be better to get it over.

"His business took two days, and then we went camping. A herd of pack animals, a couple of striders, and us. We'd move from place to place, staying a night here, two nights there - you'd have thought it was a vacation.

"And I waited. I knew it would come, sooner or later - and I wanted it sooner. I wanted it over. I'd never had to do much to provoke Barlow - I'd never had to do anything but be where he could see me when he felt like beating somebody. But Christian - I tried to provoke him, and nothing happened. I was puzzled, angry, fearful - it was almost as though, by not living down to my expectations, he was letting me down.

"One night we were camped on an open plain. Christian had brought along a tent, and he slept there, but I wouldn't sleep in it with him. I rolled my bag out by the fire and slept where I could look up at the stars. But that night, there was a thunderstorm, like nothing I'd ever seen before.

"By the time the thunder woke Christian, the sky had opened and I was drenched. He yelled at me to get in the tent, and I gathered up my things and went, because I was afraid if I stayed outside I'd drown.

"I was dripping, and cold, and shivering, and my bag was

soaked. With Barlow, that would have provoked a beating that left me unable to move for days. Christian took the bag out of my arms and tossed it in a corner. He pulled out a towel and started rubbing my hair.

"'Come on, David, get out of those wet clothes. You're soaked.' But I was paralyzed. Partly being so wet and cold, and partly fear. Nothing Christian had done had met my expectation of the way a father behaved. Like a small animal, I just froze.

"He got me out of my clothes and rubbed me down - by that time I was expecting to be half-killed, because in addition to my things being soaked, a lot of the stuff in the tent had gotten wet. When he pulled out a blanket and wrapped me in it, - I guess I collapsed."

"The shock?" Jesse was keeping her voice neutral. *He's never talked about himself this openly before. But what's the point?*

"Partly, I guess. I'm not sure.

"He put his arms around me and settled himself with me in his lap - no one had held me like that except Mama, and I'd been too big for her to do it for quite a while. And then he started talking to me.

"'David, real fathers don't hurt their sons. They love them, and they care for them, and they protect them. They guide them, and they teach them. I know you don't know what that's like, but if you'd give me a chance, I'd like to try to be a father - your father.'"

"He went on talking - he may have talked all night, I don't know. The accumulated tension of the last several months, the fright, being warm - I fell asleep in his arms.

"When I woke up the next morning, still in Christian's arms, I looked out at a whole new world. It was as though the rain had washed Esau Barlow's touch from my skin."

The big man sighed and straightened. "Christian gave me a great gift that night. But later that year, he gave me an even greater gift. He gave me my name - Christian's Son.

"You're wondering what the point of all this is, I know. It's this - I was afraid of Christian, because what I'd known was abuse and terror. I made it hard for him to love me, because I was afraid he'd hurt me.

"You're afraid of Jason, and of me, because of what happened to Thom. You're doing the best you can to make it impossible for us to love you, because you're afraid of being hurt again.

"But, Jesse, the love is worth risking the pain, even feeling it. Because nothing, nothing can ever take the memories away.

Nothing can take the love away.

"Christian died the spring after Mike was killed, when the Tragans dumped that plague on Sylvanus. To this day, I find myself planning things to do with him, things I need to tell him, and then I remember he's gone. And then I smile, because I remember how much he loved me, and how much I loved him, and what I feel is the joy from the lifetime I had him."

"What do you want me to do, David?" She was exhausted. *I feel as though someone's been beating me with sticks.*

"Just think about it." He started toward the door, then turned back. "Oh, and you might apologize to Jason - I think that hurt him pretty badly. Good night, Jesse."

-Triad Chapter 19-

It is generally accepted that the way of the warrior is the resolute acceptance of death. Miyamoto Musashi - Go Rin No Sho

"Jesse! Jesse!"

The voice seemed to be coming from a long distance. She wanted to ignore it, sink back into the warm blackness. *Go away. Too tired. Leave me alone, I'm sleeping.*

"Jesse, wake up! Please, Jesse, I need you. Wake up!" Hands were tight on her shoulders, and her head rocked back and forth as they shook her. Someone was shouting at her, demanding her presence.

The warm dark receded, and she became aware of the bedside light shining into her face, Jason's hands on her shoulders, Jason's face above hers, Jason's voice in her ears.

"Hi, Jason," she mumbled, still not quite there.

"Jesse, for the love of the Many, wake up!" he demanded, shaking her hard.

She snapped into awareness and pushed him away, sitting up and rubbing her face. "Jason? What's wrong?"

"I can't find David."

"Did you look in his rooms?"

"Oh, please," he shook her again, "wake up and use your head. I said, I can't find him, Jesse. I can't Feel him."

"Dragon's breath. All right, give me a minute." She pushed him away and staggered into the bathroom.

Cold water helped. When she came out, she glanced at the clock, then at Jason, pacing back and forth beside the bed.

"Wearing a hole in the floor won't help, Jason. When did you see him last?"

"After dinner. He said he was going to talk to you. I went down to the systems lab to help Kwame with a project, and when we finished, I came back and went to bed. I didn't even think about it - I just assumed he was with you. But I woke up, just now, and..." his voice trailed off.

Jesse pulled her boots on and gestured him to the door. "All right. He wasn't with you, he wasn't with me, he wasn't in his own room. Did you check CC?"

"I did. James hasn't seen him."

"And Security doesn't know where he is?"

"I didn't call Security." The blankness of the response told her that for all practical purposes Jason was in shock. That he was even functioning under the circumstances spoke to enormous strength of character.

She pulled her mike down and triggered the channel for Security. "This is Command. Have you seen the Command Second?"

There was a moment of background buzz. "Mr. Camaretti saw him about two hours ago, Sir. He was on his way down to his office."

Jason was already running toward the lift. Jesse hurried to catch him. "He's probably just absorbed in what he's doing, Jase. He may even have fallen asleep."

He touched the control and stood back, holding on to one of the railings. "It wouldn't matter if he was asleep, and it doesn't matter where he is. I can always Feel him. The only reason I wouldn't be able to is if he were unconscious or..."

Or dead. No, don't borrow trouble. Don't even think. Just get there.

The door of David's office was closed, and when it didn't respond to his hand on the plate, Jason growled and started tearing at it with his fingers.

"Stop," Jesse said, putting her hands on his shoulders and pulling him away. "That won't do any good. Let me see if I can override it."

How does that bastard do all this without anyone seeing him? she thought, as she struggled with the controls. Her hands were shaking, and her palms were sweaty. *I have the override code, and it's taking me forever, but he seems to skip in and out, change control codes, and disappear without anyone noticing him. We have video surveillance outside these offices, and I'll bet the cameras didn't catch him.*

The door gave, and a breath of cold air whispered past Jesse's face. "By the One! Did he exhaust the air?"

Jason shook his head. "No, he turned the thermostat down. If David's here, and he was here all night, he could die of hypothermia." He went around the desk and stopped, staring at the floor.

There was a pool of blood under David's head, and the gold skin was pasty. Jason dropped to his knees and touched two fingers to his partner's neck.

"He's still alive. Get the medics."

Jesse let out the breath she didn't realize she was holding and turned to the comm unit.

"Emergency medical team to Command Two's office, stat," she ordered. "Security, send a guard detail and an investigative team to Command Two's Office, stat. Zephron," switching to the command team's private channel, "I need you in David's office, now."

"They're on their way," she said, turning back to Jason. He'd pulled his shirt off and put it over David, lifting the big man and holding him against himself. When he didn't look up or acknowledge her, "Jason?" Jesse shook him. He was unresponsive, his eyes half closed, breathing so slow and shallow it was almost imperceptible.

"Dragon's Breath! Jason Ashe, if you don't come back, I'm never going to speak to you again."

What the hell was he doing here? she thought, looking around the room.

It was orderly, in David's fashion. Two baskets of flimsies and one of data cards on his desk gave his aide a place to look for documents. His small tools - light pen, laser torch, pointer, gauges - stood in a pottery cup. His notebook was lying on the desk...

His notebook. What was he doing with that? As she reached to pick it up, she noticed that the console wasn't completely closed, but before she could check it, the room filled with frantic people, making noise and bustling about. She closed the console and shoved the notebook into her pocket.

Nick Thassanios lifted David out of Jason's arms and lowered him to the floor. Relieved of his burden, the Sensitive folded like a wet towel. Thassanios checked David's pulse and breathing, touched his head, gestured a tech over, and turned back to Jason

"David's the one who's hurt," Jesse said.

Without looking up from what he was doing, Thassanios spoke. "Mr. Christiansen is breathing and his vital signs are stable. I can't say the same for Mr. Ashe." He continued to work on Jason, whose skin had a bluish cast in the harsh light. At last, satisfied with Jason's condition, he turned again to David.

Jesse watched as Thassanios and the medical team worked.

The medic sat back on his heels as they wrapped the Pathfinder in a blanket and lifted him to a stretcher. "It's a good thing he has a hard head, Command. He was hit hard, and I think he's concussed, but he'll be okay. Whatever he was hit with broke the skin - that's where all the blood came from. We'll take him to the infirmary."

"Command, what happened?"

"I don't know for sure, Ops." She glanced around to see if anyone was close enough to hear them, then gestured to the door. "Let's get out of the way."

The broad corridor seemed huge and quiet after the commotion and crowding in David's office. "Jason woke me because he couldn't find David."

Zephron nodded, and Jesse continued. It seemed to take longer to tell Bell what had happened than it had taken for them to search for and find David.

"...and when I turned back, Jason was frozen over David."

"By the Many," Zephron breathed. "Trying to call him back. I hope he doesn't get lost out there."

"What do you mean?"

"Isaacson wasn't a Healer, was he?"

Jesse shook her head. "What do you mean, 'get lost out there?'"

"When a Healer holds on to a person who's close to death, or tries to call back one who's deeply unconscious, he goes into a kind of - inner space, I guess you'd call it. The place the mind goes when the body isn't aware. There are two dangers there. If he's with someone who's dying, and they slip away while he's still in rapport, he can go with them. If the person he's trying to call is unconscious, like David, he can get lost and not come back himself."

"I never knew that," Jesse breathed. "Thom never told me about any of that."

"He'd have no reason to, I suppose. But Sensitives who aren't healers can get lost in control systems. That's why they aren't supposed to go into them without a Perceptive along."

"I knew that. I just never - it never occurred to me they could get lost the same way dealing with people."

Jesse pulled in a long breath and rubbed her face with her hands, wishing she felt more like Command and less like someone who'd been awakened after not enough sleep. "We have to use this."

Bell raised an eyebrow.

"Zephron, we don't have a choice. That plan the two of you

came up with was in case David or Mariko or James was attacked. Well, David was attacked and I think..." she pulled the notebook from her tunic pocket, "I think he'd found something. None of us wanted it to happen, but your last resort has been activated."

Zephron still looked doubtful - *no wonder,* thought Jesse, *this is terrible, and it may not work* - so she used her final argument. "Zephron, what if it had been Mariko?"

He winced and paled. "Right." He sighed and tugged at his beard.

"All right, I'll get it going." He turned and left at a fast walk.

Jesse waited, pacing the corridor, until two of the techs came out of David's office propelling a gurney. "He's stable, Command," one of them said.

Jesse nodded and turned to follow them.

"Command, I need you," Nick Thassanios called her from the office door.

"What?"

"I need you to help me call your Third, Jesse," he said in an undertone, glancing at the Security people busying themselves in various parts of the room. "He's gone a long way."

She looked down at the long, thin body, lying next to the spot where they'd found David, and shuddered. *In the Name of the One, let this work,* she prayed.

"Call him yourself, Nick," she said, keeping her face and back rigid. "He let David be hurt. I don't care if he comes back or not."

She left, hurrying to catch the techs and David. *And please let him - let both of them - forgive me when this is all over. Let me forgive myself.*

Hours later, the next part of Jason and Zephron's plan went into action, and Jesse braced herself for what she had to do. She paused at CC's door and brushed herself down, straightened her tunic, glanced at her boots to be sure they were polished. *Do it and get it over with. The longer you wait, the harder it will be.*

The tall, thin figure standing next to James McGowan at the control console seemed attenuated, skeletal. It was as though he'd faded in the hours since they'd started looking for David.

"Command Third," she said, pitching her voice to carry across the room.

He turned, and it was all she could do to keep from crying

out with the shock.

He looked like something out of a horror story. The dark blue eyes were cloudy and recessed into his skull, surrounded by shadows so heavy they looked like bruises. The silver-blonde hair was dull and lifeless, framing his face in what looked like festoons of cobwebs. The thin hands and the front of his shirt were splotched with blood, and - *he's out of uniform, and he doesn't know it. He came straight here from David's office. He doesn't know how he looks, and no one could tell him.*

"Command," he responded.

"You're dismissed. Return to your quarters and stay there."

It was so quiet she could hear the hum of the electronics from the control consoles, and she realized every ear in the room was tuned to her voice. *Well, this will be all over the base inside an hour. No need to do anything else to make sure it gets to the terrorist.*

"Command First." He took a step, then stopped. "How..." he licked his lips and tried again. "The Command Second. How is Mr. Christiansen?"

Does he know? Jesse wondered. *Can he Feel?* "Mr. Christiansen," she said, working to keep her voice level and her face expressionless, "died thirty minutes ago."

The blue eyes dropped and he stumbled out of the room as though he was going to his own execution.

Jesse glanced down at her watch and was astonished to realize it was still morning. *I feel like it's been days.*

She drew in a deep breath, held it, let it out, and straightened her back. There was the day to get through.

When we catch you, whoever you are, I will take great pleasure in killing you, slowly, with my own hands. You will pay for every instant that man has suffered at your hands, pay for it ten times over.

Jesse later realized she'd signed orders and documents she could never remember reading. There seemed to be a haze behind her eyes - outlines were blurred and colors faded, voices were distant and faint - when people spoke to her, she had to strain to understand what they were saying.

She wanted to escape - to her office, where she could be alone and let go control; to the triad quarters, where she could talk to Jason - *but that isn't fair. You just want to unload, and Jason's already carrying too much.* She struggled to maintain focus, to keep her face calm and expressionless, her voice clear and level, her body erect and controlled.

And all the time, in the back of her mind, was the image of David lying in a pool of blood, face slack, the strong hands curled and ineffective. And behind that, another image, one she tried to push away - the image of Thom Isaacson, covered with blood and soot, the side of his head a bloody pulp, the broad chest crumpled...

"Command?" She jumped. The hand on her shoulder was Zephron's - she wondered how many times he'd spoken to her and not been able to get a response.

"First," she acknowledged him.

"May we consult?" he asked, tipping his head toward the command office.

He looks tired. This must be a terrible strain on him, too. David and Jason are his friends, and he's worried about Mariko and James. They're still vulnerable. We're all still vulnerable.

She pushed herself up and headed to the office. *At least, it'll get us away from all the eyes.*

"Are you all right?"

She blinked, then wrapped her hands around the warm cup he'd set on the table in front of her.

"Jesse. Are you all right?"

Spaced off again. I must be tired. "I'm okay, Zephron. Just tired."

"Did you remember to eat today?"

Did I? "I don't remember. Probably not."

"That's what I thought. Here," he slid a plate onto the table in front of her. "Get that down, then we have decisions to make."

She ate without tasting the food, but every bite seemed to bring her feet closer to the ground. When the plate was empty, the cup drained, she looked around again. "Wow. I didn't realize I was that far gone. Thanks, Zephron."

"No problem. Now," he slid a stack of data cards on to the table in front of her. "This is the situation."

She worked her way through them, pausing occasionally to re-read, then pushed them away and sat back. "I can't believe they took the bait."

"Valery made it very convincing - Sliothi enjoy that sort of thing. Jase and I figure we have - maybe a week - before they realize they were suckered and come roaring back to protect their precious crystal."

"And in that time, we need to take care of the crystal field, find our terrorist, and with luck, get ourselves out of here."

"The field's taken care of," Zephron said. "Jason and James planted the mines this morning. They'd just finished when you came up."

Jesse nodded and ran her hand over her face. "Right. I'm sorry, Zephron, I'm not tracking at optimal."

"I'm not surprised." He glanced at his watch. "Why don't you head back home and get some rest? Nothing else is going to happen for a while."

Jesse looked at the big, bearded man, and believed him. "You know, I think I'll take you up on that." She pushed herself to her feet and headed for the door, feeling as though she was wearing lead boots. "I'll take my customary walk around, and then, if you need me - call the quadrant marshall."

At the door she turned back. "Zephron, leave this to the staff and go home yourself. Your partners need you."

#

The lights were off; the only illumination in the room was a single candle, glowing on top of his dresser. He was kneeling on a cushion in the narrow strip of floor between the bed and the outer wall, eyes closed, face serene.

This may be the first time in days - the first time since he reported to duty here - that I've seen Jason Ashe completely relaxed. And that may not be good, because it means he's completely defenseless.

"Jason?" He didn't stir. "By the One," she breathed. *Don't let him be gone again.*

Jesse dropped to her knees in front of him and put her hands over his.

The blue eyes opened and he smiled. "Hello. How long have you been here?"

"I just got here. How long have you been here?"

A tiny frown appeared between his eyebrows, then disappeared. "I'm not sure. I thought about sleeping, but - I couldn't.

"Jesse, how - how is David?"

"David's fine," she responded. "He has a terrible headache, and he's feeling very sorry for himself. It was the cold more than the head wound that kept him out. He and Dolores are in the guest quarters on Level Seven, and - don't ask me how, because I told Nick I don't want to know - there's a chamber in the stasis room with David's name on the plate and what looks like a body in it."

"May I see him?" Jason's voice was soft, but the hands under hers trembled.

"David is 'dead,' and you're supposed to be confined to your quarters. If anyone saw you, it would be disastrous."

"I know." He expelled a deep breath. "I just - I just wanted to say goodbye."

Jesse put her fingers over his mouth. "David said I'd done something terrible, and I didn't know what he was talking about. I wasn't listening, Jason, the question I thought I was answering wasn't the one you asked. You aren't going to say goodbye to anyone - except our terrorist."

He smiled and pulled her hand down, kissing the palm before he twined his fingers with hers. "It was always a possibility. At this stage, it may be the only way to get him out - just thinking he may be able to get at me to kill me may not be enough any more. It's a good trade; one life for five thousand."

Jesse shifted to relieve the pressure on her knees. "It isn't a good trade, it's barbaric. Besides, Mr. Ashe, don't you know Defense Command would consider it a good trade if the other four-thousand, nine-hundred-ninety-eight of us were killed or captured and you and Mariko were saved?"

He grinned that Jason and David grin. "I've always said you don't have to be crazy to be in Defense Command, but it helps."

Jesse smiled back and her heart turned over. Without any warning, the hole left by Thom's death became a gaping wound, edges raw and bleeding, with no sign of healing. She gasped and tried to pull back. Then a pair of strong arms wrapped around her, and she could feel his heart beating.

"It's okay, Jesse. Don't hold on anymore. Let it go."

But she struggled to contain it, terrified that if she once gave in to it, it would overwhelm her. She gasped and fought for breath, chest taut, every muscle in her body tight.

"Jesse, by the Many Who Are One, let go. Quit fighting it. Let go."

He shook her, and she could breathe - then a howl of mingled pain, anger, fear, loneliness and loss rose from her guts and forced its way out. She screamed, and kept screaming, until her throat was raw, her jaw ached, her ribs protested every breath. The strong arms held her, sheltered her, and let the grief rage until it was spent.

Exhausted, she was silent, shaken. If Jason's arms hadn't supported her, she would have fallen and slept where she lay.

"You're all right now, it's all right," he was murmuring. "Everything's going to be fine. It's all right."

She pulled in a deep breath to calm her ragged breathing and tried to push herself away from him, surprised at how weak she was. "That was, that was..." her throat hurt, and so did her jaw.

"That was too long coming," Jason said. He shifted, and propped Jesse up by the side of the bed. "Here. I'll be back."

She leaned back, absorbing the warmth of the room, the stillness, content not to have to respond to anything, to do anything. It was so peaceful just to sit here, let her mind be blank, not think, not feel - not fight anymore.

#

It was a nice party, as parties went - good food and plenty of it, enough variety in drinks to satisfy the most or the least sophisticated, music not loud enough to make conversation difficult, space large enough to be comfortable and small enough to allow intimacy. Jesse got herself a drink and went to lean against the balcony railing, watching people and enjoying the patterns they made as groups shifted, enlarged, shrank.

He was standing on the other side of the room, a drink in his hand, his eyes roaming the crowd. Dark hair, fair skin - not tall, apparently, but strong and athletic. A Sensitive, by the knot of white gold braid on the collar of his dress uniform. Jesse was a little surprised - Sensitives were supposed to be crowd-shy, unsocial. His eyes met hers, and the jolt pinned her to the railing, her heart in her mouth.

"I know you."

"I know you, too. I've always known you." The brown eyes, almost as dark as hers, were clear and bright, like forest pools in a shaft of sunlight. Jesse felt as though she could swim in them forever...

#

"Here, let me wipe your face." His voice jolted her from her dream of the past, and she looked up, startled, to see Jason kneeling beside her, a warm washcloth and a towel in his hands.

"Thanks, I can do it," Jesse mumbled, taking the cloth and rubbing it over her face. "I probably look like something out of a nightmare."

"No, you just look like you have a bad cold," he said, grinning as he handed her the towel and took the washcloth. "You know, red eyes, pink nose..."

"Oh, thank you, Jason. Very attractive - to another rodent." At the image of herself with huge chisel teeth and upstanding ears, she began to laugh.

"Well, I guess I'm another rodent then, because I find you stunning."

Jesse blotted her streaming eyes with the towel and handed it to Jason. He set it and the cloth aside and settled next to her. "How are you?"

She leaned her head on his shoulder and closed her eyes. "I feel as though I just lost about fifty pounds. And I feel - purged. As though the weight I lost was something inside."

"In a way, that's just what you did - you've been carrying around a huge load of grief and anger and guilt, and you finally let it go. You're not healed, Jesse, but you've taken a first step on the road to mending."

"One step at a time," she murmured, "one step at a time."

Above her, Jason nodded - she felt his chin rub the top of her head.

His body next to her was warm, and the arms that held her were gentle and strong. Jesse felt heavy and tired, and relaxed. Her eyelids drooped, closed, and she drifted into the warm dark.

-Chapter 20-
Let me be taken, let me be put to death...
William Shakespeare—Romeo and Juliet

The soft buzz from the comm unit by the bed woke her. She rolled and touched the button. "Yes?"

"'Morning, Command," Zephron said. "I know you said if I needed you to call the Quadrant Marshall, but I thought maybe after a night's sleep you'd have changed your mind."

She grinned and glanced at the clock. Oh-seven-hundred - she'd been sleeping the sleep of the truly exhausted for ten hours.

"All right, First, give me thirty minutes."

As the warm water sprayed her, Jesse closed her eyes and remembered strong arms, soft blankets, lips touching her forehead, her eyes, her lips. The rest of the night was a deep, warm blank - she didn't even remember dreaming.

"Wow! I don't think I've slept like that since - since before Thom died." It was easier this morning. The pain was still there, but it was distant - old pain, remembered pain, not new and sharp. "Thank you, Jason," she murmured into the towel.

Dry and dressed, she pulled the mike down and shifted to the command team's private channel. "Jason?" she murmured.

"Mmm. Good morning. How do you feel?" he responded.

"Marvelous. I should unload on you more often."

"Glad to oblige."

"That was a joke, Jason. That kind of emotional storm isn't something to inflict on anybody."

"It's something you can and should inflict on your partners if you need to - especially me. That's what the gift of empathy is about. And that's what partners are for. That's why you have a Third."

"Well, anyway, thanks. I'm just leaving."

"I'd tell you to have a good day, but I guess the best we can do is hope it's better than yesterday. May I go into the living room?"

"By all means. Just don't try to go out. Get some rest, and I'll see you later."

As the door of CC closed behind her, the room echoed with the repetitions of "Good Morning, Command." Jesse acknowledged the greetings while her eyes sought Zephron's across the room. She lifted a brow, and he compressed his lips and moved his chin in the direction of the command office.

"Nothing," he said, as soon as they were inside, the door closed behind them. James and Mariko retrieved drinks for themselves and the two Firsts, and the four settled at the table.

"No attempts at communication, no unauthorized file access..." James began.

"And no attempt to get at Jason," Mariko finished.

"You're sure about that?"

"I've placed sensors and eyes all along that corridor. No one's been there who shouldn't have, and no one went near your door except you."

"And no evidence that anyone except ourselves, Nick, and Dolores knows about David?" Jesse asked.

"Not that I can find," Zephron said. "Whoever he is, he's pulled back into his little hole and is staying there."

"Dragon's breath," Jesse hissed. "All right, we don't have a choice. Part Two of your plan is going into effect, Zephron. Assemble the search teams and deploy them, and I'll make the entry in the command log."

Bell nodded, pulled down his mike and began murmuring. Mariko and James returned their cups to the recycler. Jesse pulled her mike down and shifted to the command channel. "Jason?"

"Here."

"No action. Zephron's activating Part Two. Be on your guard."

"Understood."

Jesse pushed herself away from the table and took her cup to the recycler. "Zephron, I'm going for a walk, and then I'll be in my office." She glanced at James and Mariko. "You two, take care of each other."

James nodded without speaking, and slid his hand over to cover Mariko's.

The Intuit raised a hand, then murmured into his mike and pulled it up. "All right. It's going to take Raavik about two hours to assemble the teams - one security officer and three or four off-duty people per team - I told him at least one per level."

"Okay," Jesse said. "Call me when they deploy."

She made the walk last as long as she could, stopping to chat with the construction crews as they occupied themselves with blueprints, plans and models; monitoring a classroom where a senior tech was teaching the apprentices emergency damage control procedures in case of meteorite collisions; working her way from the top to the bottom of the mobile platform that would become Sector 23's Border Control Base. *Assuming we live to get it where it's supposed to be.*

Along the way she managed to wander through the guest quarters. David was sitting up, playing games, while Dolores Roberts, the corners of her mouth turned up as though she was amused, worked on an intricate piece of lace.

"Am I glad to see you," David said, closing down the console. "I've beaten this thing ten times, Dolores is trying to pretend I'm not here, and my thumbs are raw where I've been twiddling them."

"How's your head?" Jesse asked, exchanging glances with Dolores.

"As hard as ever, Command," the medic answered, before David could. "And if he doesn't settle down and quit nagging me, I'm going to bop him again and put him to sleep the rest of the day."

"That bad, huh?"

When she left them, Jesse felt better. They were safe, even if David was bored.

She went to her office, where the first thing she did was give the console in the guest quarters system access under her control codes. That would give David freedom of the system and not leave any clues that it was him.

"Command?"

"Here, First."

"Search teams are ready to deploy. Thought you might appreciate a heads up."

"Thank you. I should be here or in the lounge if you need me while they're out."

She shifted to the private channel. "Jason? Search teams are deployed."

"Understood. Take care."

You take care. Someone wants to hurt you, and this would be a good opportunity.

#

Jesse laid the last card on top of the stack and put the stack in her 'out' tray, closed her console, propped her elbows on the desk and dropped her head into her hands. *I don't know whether it's a blessing or a curse that this has at least given me time to catch up the paperwork. Somehow, with all that's been going on, paperwork seems irrelevant at best.*

With a sigh, she sat back, glanced at her watch and wondered what she was going to do with the rest of the day. *Moments of terror punctuated by centuries of boredom. And I suppose, in a perverse way, some of us become soldiers because we live for the moments of terror. Enough that we're even willing to put up with the centuries of boredom.*

Or in this case, waiting. Waiting to see what it is that Jason's going to let them 'find.' To see if they find anything else. To see if this is enough to bring our terrorist out of the woodwork, or if we have to take that final, 'all in' step. And if we do that, will David ever forgive me?

Thinking of David reminded her of the story he'd told her. 'I was afraid of Christian because I thought I knew what fathers did. You're afraid of Jason because you think you know what happens if you love someone.' *Is that what it is?*

It was a temptation to ignore it, to tell herself David couldn't know what he was talking about. Instead, she set herself, gritting her teeth, to test if what David had said was true. *Was it because I lost Thom, or was it something before? And can I look at my life, and learn from it, and let myself go on?*

Her breathing deepened, steadied. She settled herself, making sure her back was straight, and remembered.

#

At the door signal, she looked at the clock. *Two hours.* She was wringing wet, her hands were shaking, and her head was throbbing. *I think I'm beginning to understand what Jason goes through. And I'm not sure I like what I see when I look at myself like that.*

"Come in," she called, running her hands over her face and her fingers through her hair.

The search team that followed Raavik through the door included one of the engineers, Gerry Bean; a couple of students whose names Jesse couldn't remember; and Yuri Kelman, the junior pilot. They filled the small room to bursting, and Jesse was sure she wasn't just imagining the lack of oxygen.

"Chief, I'm going to take myself down to the lounge and find some lunch while your people are going though my office." She shut the console, touched the locking tab, and looked up to find Raavik's eyes on her. "Secure data," she muttered. He nodded and stepped aside to let her through the door.

Not lunch, she thought, as she headed down the corridor. *I'm not really hungry. A workout.*

"Ops, I'm going down to the dojo."

"Roger that, Command. Sounds like a good idea."

#

Not a good idea, a great idea. Two hours of stretching, warming up, working kata, practicing with her weapons, and then fighting with the bags had left her loose, relaxed, warm - and hungry.

Now I'm ready to eat. And now it will taste good.

She sped through the showers, skipping the hot tub and the steam room, and headed for the lounge, planning the meal she was going to compose.

Grilled nilgri fish with angel hair pasta and steamed vegetables, followed by caramel custard, she thought, and then giggled. *And is David planning your meals for you lately, or does he just know you well? I really owe Jason an apology for that one.*

I owe him for a lot of things. She held the last spoonful of the custard at eye level where she could admire the gold and cream colors, the smoothness...

She put the spoonful in her mouth and shoved the plate into the recycler. *Come on, Jesse, let's go.*

"Command?"

"Here, Ops."

"I have something for you to look at."

"On my way."

#

"It's a piece of a couch cushion. Tragan body armor is impregnated with carbon fiber, and this isn't. This was left for us to find - the recycle chute it was in hadn't been set to incinerate, and this much leather would have disintegrated in seconds."

Jesse nodded, turning the evidence bag over and over between her hands. "I know. I rather expected something like this, and I think you and Jason did as well, Zephron. What I want to know is, can we use it?"

"Well, we can't keep it a secret," James said. "There were five people on the team that found it. It's probably all over the station by now."

"You can blame that on your First and my Third," Jesse said. "I think that's what they had in mind. Was this found on the residential levels?"

James shook his head and exchanged a long look with Zephron.

"Jason and I thought something like this might happen. Either he's desperate, and he's trying to distract us, or he's so far gone he's taunting us. I know it's already all over that it was found - but all anyone, including the team that found it, knows is that it was shreds of black leather. Most people are going to assume it's the remains of a suit of Tragan body armor that he didn't have time to finish incinerating after the search started.

"He knows he planted it, and we know he did. I think the thing to do is let the rumors fly and proceed with the next phase. He'll have to go after Jason now."

"What's to keep him from just lying low and letting us keep looking for him?"

This time it was James who spoke. "The rumor that's also going around that Jason had a Crystal. And that reminds me, Command, here..." he handed her an evidence envelope. "It's a Shipai God-offering - a lot of healers carry them as luck pieces. It was a good choice - most people don't know what Crystal really is, and they're willing to believe it could be something like this. If he thinks Jason knows who he is, and has one of his crystals..." James let his voice trail off.

"And that was all they found?" *Damn it, he has to have more. Where is he keeping it? Where did he get the body armor, and what did he do with it?*

"Fifteen people have rock collections," Zephron said. "Any or all of them could have crystals, but as long as they're not activated, we can't tell - and they aren't illegal. No leather impregnated with carbon fibers, no energy whips - I'm damned if I can figure out what he did with them. We did everything but take the folded sections apart, and if he got anything in there, he's a genius."

"Very well." Jesse pushed herself to her feet. "Get some rest. Tomorrow's likely to be a long day."

"Jesse."

She stopped with her hand on the door.

"James and I will be taking the corridor watch tonight."

"Thanks, Zephron. That's a relief. But who's going to be

with Mariko?" *It would be a disaster if he went after Mariko because we left her unguarded.*

"Mari's with David and Delores. She'll stay there until the morning shift, and one of us will walk her to CC. They'll take turns monitoring the sensors she has in the corridor."

Jesse nodded. "I think you've thought of everything. Good night, First."

"Good night, Command."

#

Jason turned as the door opened, like a trapped animal turning to fight its captor. His hands were fisted, his jaw was tight, and Jesse could tell he'd been pacing - he was suspended in mid-step.

"What's wrong?"

He ran a hand through his hair and dropped onto the back of a couch. "I just - I'm not doing very well. I keep feeling eyes on me, watching me, waiting... And what happened today was my idea, but I didn't realize I'd be so angry, so - humiliated. It was worse than yesterday in CC."

"Why?"

He's furious. He's practically shaking with it. What did they do?

"Go look," he said. "I tried to clean it up, but... I finally came out here because I couldn't stand it."

If they'd set out to wreck his study, they couldn't have done a better job. The book cards were heaped on the floor under the shelves; the contents of the desk were strewn about the surface, the drawers themselves on the floor in an unstable stack. She could tell that Jason had tried to straighten things, then given up.

"Dragon's breath," Jesse muttered. "What did they think they were up to?"

The bedroom was just as bad. The bed had been stripped, sheets, blankets and pillows thrown into the corner. Clothes and uniforms strewed the floor in heaps - the mess was enough to confuse the cleaning 'bot into paralysis.

Jesse picked her way to the bedside table and touched the comm button. "Security, this is Command. Who was in charge of the team that searched the Command quarters?"

"That would be me, Sir," answered Raavik's voice.

That's what I thought. "Get up here, now."

Shutting the comm down, she headed back to the living room.

Jason was kneeling against the wall, as though the sustained fury of the afternoon had left him and he'd collapsed. Then Jesse noticed the knuckles of his right hand, spread as though to support him. They were dead white, the tendons in the back of his hand standing out like a bird's claws.

"Jason."

When he didn't respond, she put her hand on his shoulder. "Jason, come on, get up."

He sagged back, then looked up at her. "Sorry. I'm trying very hard to control it, but - I want to hit something."

"Or someone?"

He grinned and pushed himself to his feet. "Or someone. The problem is, who?"

"Whom. And we both know that. You'll get your chance. Come on, I want you out of here."

She led him into her study.

Well, if I hadn't thought that mess was targeted before, I would now. It was as tidy as it had been the night before. *If I didn't know better, I'd think they skipped this room.*

She retrieved a cup of coffee and a sandwich and put them on the table in front of Jason. "Here. Eat, then try to relax. I'll be back."

#

"All right," Jesse said, turning to face the tall Security specialist. "Explain to me where in your team's orders you found the word 'destroy.'"

"Command?"

"Your orders were to search the base, not destroy the Command Third's quarters."

Raavik's face remained wooden. "The Command Second..."

"The Command Second was attacked by a terrorist," Jesse interrupted. "The Command Third is confined to quarters for his own safety. But that's beside the point. The point is that nothing - nothing - excuses this sort of thing," she gestured to the mess around her. "Nothing, do you understand? Officers of the Promethean Defense Command do not behave in this fashion."

"Sir. Yes, Sir."

"Good. Now," she realized she was gritting her teeth, and tried to loosen her jaw, "clean it up."

By the One! No wonder Jason was so angry. I don't even want to think about what happened besides that.

#

"Want to talk about it?" she asked, dropping into a chair and putting her feet up.

"What?" Jason looked up from the sandwich he'd been staring at. "Oh, hi, Jesse. How long have you been there?"

"I just came in. You were supposed to eat that, not stare at it," she indicated the sandwich.

His eyes were red-rimmed but dry, and the flush had receded, leaving his face pale.

"Sorry," he mumbled. "I was thinking."

"You were brooding. Tell me about it."

He shook his head and reached for the sandwich. "I don't think I could stand to talk about it." The red flooded his cheeks again.

Jesse watched him bite, chew, and swallow until she realized she was hungry, too. She retrieved another sandwich from the converter, added a drink, sat down and started to eat.

When she finished, she touched Jason's hand and left.

Raavik was standing inside the study door. His hairline was sweat-soaked - otherwise Jesse wouldn't have been sure he'd even moved.

Without speaking, she stepped past him and went to the bedroom.

"Very well," she said, coming back to face the big security officer. "It's acceptable.

"You realize I could have your rank for this?"

He nodded. "Yes, Command."

"It's going into your record, but you're getting off easy because other things are much more important now. Next time you see the Command Third, you owe him a very abject apology."

"Understood, Command."

"Good. Now get out. And keep your mouth shut."

When she was sure he was gone, she touched the comm plate. "Jase? It's safe to come home now."

He stopped just inside the door and stared around as though he'd never seen the room before.

"It isn't exactly the way it was, but it's close. I figure putting things back where they really go will keep you busy tomorrow."

"It's - fine," he said. "How did you do all this?"

"I didn't," Jesse answered. "Raavik did. He will also apologize to you - don't let him off lightly. You have every right to file a grievance against him."

She gestured to the couch and Jason sat.

"Now, do you want to tell me about it?"

"I - no. It isn't important. I'm strung up, I just made too much of it, that's all."

"Jason, aren't you the guy who told me last night that sharing emotional overloads was what partners are for?"

The corner of his mouth turned up. "It isn't fair to use my own words against me, Jesse."

"Why not? Oh, by the way - here." She pulled out the small crystal pendant and offered it to him on the palm of her hand.

He reached for it, hesitated, then picked it up as though it would shatter at a touch. Cradling it in the palm of his hand, he said, "My dad brought it to me from Shipani when I was about ten. I've carried it ever since."

"James says most healers carry one as a luck piece."

Jason nodded without looking up. His hand was shaking. "I - I'd forgotten I was going to leave it where they could find it. It was in my pocket."

By the One! They searched him. I should demote Raavik to cleaning the sewers for that.

Jesse folded Jason's fingers into his palm and wrapped both her hands around his. His body was tense, the hand she held taut and cold. "Come on, Jason, let go. You can't keep it all shut up inside. I'm here, it's okay."

He looked up, the dark blue eyes shining with unshed tears. "Are you, Jesse? Am I your partner, or am I just an inconvenience you'd sooner be rid of? Because it would be easier to let him take me - to finish it - than to keep fighting..."

She put her fingers over his mouth. "No. We are going to keep fighting - you are going to keep fighting - until we're dead or we've won. Is that understood?"

"Yes, Command."

"Damn it, Jason Ashe! You are the most infuriating man," she exclaimed, shaking him.

He gave a bellow of laughter and wrapped his arms around her. "All right, Jesse Larsen, you win. We'll keep trying till it kills us." He chuckled, and then the laughter erupted again, shaking them both and making him breathless.

"I don't know what we're laughing about," Jesse gasped. "It's been a lousy day, we're using you as bait for a killer, we still have that monster to face down and a crystal field to dispose of..."

"...and we haven't even gotten this platform on station yet," Jason interrupted. He started laughing again, then stopped, gasping, and hiccuped.

"Dragon's breath," he muttered. "Excuse me." He unwrapped himself from Jesse and stood up.

The small explosions continued while he staggered to the converter and retrieved a glass of water.

"Are you all right?"

He lifted a hand, raised the glass, and began to swallow. His face turned red, his hands trembled, and Jesse had all she could do not to start laughing again.

The long exhalation was followed by a gasp, and he leaned against the wall, his hand over his mid-section, and drank the rest of the water.

"Does that happen a lot?"

"No. Only when I laugh hysterically."

"I see. Well, since it's our current rash of problems that made you laugh hysterically, I'll try not to discuss problems with you any more."

"It'd be even better if we just didn't have any more problems to discuss."

"I don't think we can count on that in the foreseeable future of the system. I guess we'll have to put up with you laughing hysterically from time to time."

He came back and dropped on to the couch. "Well, I don't know about you, but I feel better."

Jesse nodded. "I do, too. I guess laughter is good for you."

#

At first Jesse thought she was hearing things, but at the second tap at the door, Jason was out of his seat and on his way to open it.

"Jason, wait..."

He waved her back and cracked the door.

"Jase, is Jesse here? We need to talk."

-Chapter 21-

Through compassion, one will triumph in attack and be impregnable in defence... Lao Tzu - Tao Te Ching

Jason opened the door the rest of the way, grabbed an arm, and yanked. Zephron Bell flew into the room, caught himself on the back of the armchair, and pulled in a deep breath.

"Not that I'm not glad to see you, Zeph," Jason said, "but what are you doing here? I'm supposed to be off-limits, you're off-duty, and Jesse's supposed to be in her study, sulking."

"James is watching the outside door," Zephron answered, pulling a data card from his pocket. "We thought you needed to see this - both of you."

He handed it to Jason, who waved him into the chair, slipped past him, and settled on the end of the couch without raising his eyes from the card. He flipped back to the beginning, re-read it, growled, handed it to Jesse, went to the desk and activated the console.

Jesse watched him talk to the system a few moments, then lowered her eyes to the card - and wished she hadn't.

"How did we miss this?" she asked. "I thought checking for illicit outgoing communications was one of the first things you did after we found our shadow."

"We did, Jesse, but this is so faint it never showed up. The power output must have increased since we sent them off on that wild goose chase - which argues that it's some kind of automatic setup."

"Dragon's breath," Jesse whispered.

"By the Void," Zephron muttered. "If I ever get my hands on that traitor, he'll wish he'd never been born."

"You'll have to stand in line, Zephron," Jesse said. "I've got dibs on him already."

"You're both behind me," Jason said. "He and I are going to have a very long talk - and if there's anything left of him after that, you can have him.

"Come look at this."

Jesse didn't need Jason's long, thin finger tracing the faint line on the energy use graph to see what he was talking about.

Muttering under his breath, Zephron pushed himself away from the back of Jason's chair and went to perch on the edge of the desk.

Jesse said, "Jason, is there any way to tell how long this has been going on?"

He ran a hand over his face and exhaled. "Oh, I can trace it back, and if it comes to a trial, I'll have to. But I suspect this signal's been going out, piggybacked on our regular communications, since we pulled away from the construction yard. I'd almost bet you the transmitter's on - or more probably in—the outer wall.

"This changes everything," Jason said, pushing away from the desk. "It's obvious now that destroying this command platform and setting Prometheus' defense system back by months if not years was why he was put here. Which explains why he hasn't taken our 'bait.' He's at a crucial stage of his operation and I'm not enough of a prize."

"Then we'll just have to go get him, won't we?"

"We don't have anything like enough proof to hold him, Jesse, let alone convict him. If we go get him, we take him out of play, with luck long enough to let us deal with that monster, and then he's right back in action."

Jesse pulled David's notebook out of her pocket, opened it and handed it to Jason. "There were epithelial cells on the crystals from my office and your bedroom, and on those shreds of black leather. They're all the same, and they're a match. With what David had, it's enough. He got sloppy."

Jason went through the notebook, stopping a couple of places to re-read something, then handed it to Zephron and sat a few seconds, thinking.

"Did he see this?"

"I don't know. It was on the desk, but it was closed. David had tried to close the console, but it wasn't locked." Jason was white and tense. "I'm sorry, Jason, I meant to give it to you last night. I forgot I was carrying it until just now.

"Well? Now, before he can do any more damage?"

Zephron raised a hand. "Wait."

Jason and Jesse glanced at each other and settled back.

"Can we be sure he hasn't seen the new data?"

Jason answered, "It's set up to go into a locked file, accessible only to the command team."

"And we don't know if he saw either David's notebook or whatever he had pulled up on the console."

Jesse shook her head. "I'd say not, judging by the fact that nothing's happened since, but he could be lying low and hoping we haven't identified him. And I'm too involved to trust my Talent on this one - what I'm feeling could be what I want, not what's really there."

Zephron picked up David's notebook and read through it again, then set it down. "All right. We have enough here to go after him right now and lock him up. But - Jase's right that it probably isn't enough to stop him permanently. Since he's one of the fifteen people who have rock collections, he could claim to have handled the rocks in someone else's collection; and he was on one of the search teams, which means we have to prove he didn't have a legitimate reason for having handled that black leather. If you can stand one more day, Jase," he glanced over and Jason nodded, "I think we should give him another chance to come after you and hang himself. If he doesn't - we go after him, and at least he's locked up and incommunicado while we handle the monster."

Jesse thought about it a moment, searching Jason's face for something to tell her how he really felt, then went with her gut. "Are you agreeable, Jason? I know the last couple of days have been hell, and tomorrow will be just as bad or worse."

He nodded. "If you two think it's the best option, then yes."

"Good." Zephron was on his feet and walking the room, right hand smoothing his beard. "In case neither of you have thought about it, that gives us a lot to do tonight, and we're without our judicial officer."

"You're right," Jesse said, pushing herself to her feet, "I hadn't thought about that. We'd better go get busy, then."

Zephron put up a hand. "We're not going anywhere."

Jason turned, one eyebrow raised.

"Listen, bud, I don't want you left alone until we're ready, even with the corridor guards and the sensors Mari set. We'll work here, which will also give us the benefit of your mighty intelligence," at that, Jason grimaced and threatened to throw one of the cushions, but Zephron ignored him, "and hopefully, we'll get it all done and not miss anything.

"Chan is taking the corridor watch. In the morning, he'll leave very conspicuously, and apparently not be replaced."

"And what about you, me, and James?"

"We'll leave just before Chan does, and be in your office monitoring the sensors in the corridor and the living room. And that's the other thing, Jase. When we leave in the morning, I want the doors to David's and Jesse's rooms locked, and you stay out in the living room."

"David?" It didn't surprise Jesse that Jason's concern wasn't for himself. "If the terrorist saw any of that, he may decide David's death was faked and go looking for him."

Zephron shook his head. "There's nothing anywhere he could have gotten to that would let him even think David isn't very dead. And I sent Raavik up to stay with them - the next two days are his off-duties, and no one will be surprised if they don't see him."

"All right." The deep breath wasn't quite a sigh. "One more day."

"Something else I want you to consider," Zephron said. "I know this man is a terrorist and a murderer, but that comm line may not be his. It's entirely possible there's a saboteur working in the construction yard, and that the comm line, and the bolts that were sheared, were done there before the platform was ever launched."

"The only consolation in that, Zeph, would be the faint and probably futile hope that our terrorist isn't actually in communication with that monster. Because if it was set up in the yard, they could be - probably are - getting everything that goes over our comm lines."

Jesse shuddered. "But we know that. That's how we got them to take off."

Zephron's eyebrows rose, and then he slapped himself on the forehead. "Of course. Stupid, Zephron, really stupid. All this time I've been worrying about the terrorist being in communication with them, and we were telling them everything they wanted to know."

"Well, not everything," Jason said. "At least, not since we realized they were there. But before that..."

"So we need to find out just what we've told them," Jesse said. *And we still need to know how they got past the Interdicted Areas without triggering the ADS and every alarm in the quadrant. And why - and how - the two platforms before us were destroyed before they even got to the border.*

#

Jesse rubbed her eyes and scrubbed her face with her fingers to get the blood circulating and wake herself up. "I feel as though we've been here for four years instead of four hours," she said.

Jason looked up from the screen he'd been concentrating on and nodded. His eyes were bloodshot. "Only four? - I was thinking it was at least forty."

"I think we need a break," Zephron said, tapping a pile of data cards into a neat stack. He picked up a handful of flimsies and stuffed them in the recycler. "Is anybody else hungry?"

"Hungry? No. Starving's more like it."

#

Jesse set her plate down and took a long swallow of fruit juice. "Well, it wasn't as good as sleep, but it helped."

Zephron grinned around the last bite of his sandwich, and Jason glanced up from his cup and raised an eyebrow.

"Sleep? What's that?" Zephron said, wiping his mouth.

"Yeah, okay you two, back to work. Time's moving on."

Finally, Jason placed his light stylus in alignment with the other tools on his desk and closed the console. "I think that's all we're going to get for now. With luck, we'll get more tomorrow-" he glanced down at his watch and corrected himself, "-today. If not - we'll go with this and pray that it can keep him from doing any more damage. And you were right, Zephron - as far as I've been able to trace that line back, I don't think it's his. That doesn't mean he doesn't know about it, though."

"Now what?"

"Breakfast," Zephron said. "Lots of breakfast. And then we go to work."

#

As the door shut behind her, Jesse glanced back, hoping for one more glimpse of Jason's face, but he'd already turned away.

"I don't like this, Zephron," she muttered. "I didn't like it when you and Jason dreamed it up, and I've liked it even less every day since - and now I really don't like it. I feel as though we're walking into a major disaster."

"Is that your Talent talking, or your gut?"

"It's that cold flutter at the base of my spine talking, is what it is. My gut feels as though it's full of rocks, and my brain feels as though it's made out of dirty fiber soaked in used oil."

"Ah, good - I was afraid it was just me."

#

A rustle, then silence. Had he shifted, or was that someone sneaking up behind him? If he was absorbed in a book, he'd never notice.

"I wish we'd put visuals in there," Jesse said.

James shook his head. "Jason's gone through enough. Besides, if he's right about the way this slime's been using Crystal, he'd hear it. We'll be lucky if he doesn't catch something from the sensors and bolt."

I'd almost prefer that. Then we could go get him and lock him up, and he wouldn't have a chance to get at Jason.

That called up another line of thought entirely, and Jesse pushed it out of her mind. *Later, she told herself. You can't afford to be distracted now.*

There was another rustle, then a sound like a cushion being pulled off the couch. Something hit the floor with a plump thud and slid, then there was a settling sound followed by a sigh.

"He's meditating," Jesse murmured.

The silence continued. Jesse caught herself glancing at her watch every two minutes, and finally took it off and put it away. Zephron had brought a bookcard and read, chin propped in one hand. James divided his attention between the sensors in the command triad's quarters and a console that duplicated the panels in the command center, occasionally murmuring something to Mariko, who was in CC.

Jesse fidgeted, tried to read, couldn't concentrate, tried to work and couldn't keep her mind on what she was doing, fidgeted more. *I wish I could meditate like Jason does, but I never could manage it. Clearing my mind before class is about the best I can do.*

A door sliding open startled her and she jumped, but it was the door of her office - James had gone to get sandwiches.

"Well, I'm seriously considering going and getting the bastard, just to get this over with," Zephron said, snapping his bookcard shut. "And if it's like this for us, I can't imagine what Jason feels like, being the bait."

"I've been trying not to think about that," Jesse said.

#

The sound of the door opening brought Jesse out of a light doze. She glanced around, but it wasn't the door of her office.

"This is it," she murmured.

"I bloody well hope so," Zephron responded.

"Well, will you look at this. The best Sensitive in the Service, or so they say, in the middle of the room with his back to the door, oblivious. Not smart, Ashe, not smart at all."

Who is that? I don't recognize the voice. Were we wrong?

"You don't even know I'm here, do you, you stupid little rilga? I could kill you right now, wrap my hands around your skinny neck..."

"Security teams, move in," Zephron said.

"Position yourselves in the corridor and cover the doors," Jesse added. "Do not attempt to enter the room without orders from Ops or myself."

"Jesse, what if he does what he says? Jason's helpless."

"Jason's a lot more aware when he's meditating than most people realize, Zephron. I think he's letting this drag out so our killer will convict himself." She took off the double headphone and hung a single from her right ear. "On the other hand, I think we should be on our way. We can listen as we go."

I wish I didn't have to listen. I wish I could just close it off. Shut him up. Who in the name of the Void is he?

"Stupid woman, leaving you here like this. But then, all women are stupid, aren't they? And they all fall for that pretty face. That's how you got where you are, isn't it, pretty boy? All you have to do is open those big blue eyes at them and smile, and they'll give you anything you want. They think you're a gift.

"And you do, too, don't you? The Ancestors' gift to Prometheus, all wrapped up in a beautiful package. Only the best for Ashe - after all, he's worth it, isn't he? The best station, the easiest job - the best partner.

"You're too good for the rest of us, aren't you? We're not worthy of your attentions - only Christiansen's that, isn't he, and even he wasn't quite good enough. Not good enough for you to keep him alive.

"Well, you'll learn better, pretty boy. When I get you to *K'l-nath*, the Overlord will have you, whether you like it or not. And I'll have you on the way there, rilga."

The voice was thickening, blurring.

"We need to get there, fast. He's about to go right over the edge."

Jesse nodded and increased her pace. *He isn't about to go.*

He's gone.

"One thing's for sure," James panted. "This is definitely personal."

"I'll touch you with this little black crystal - can you see it, pretty boy? - it's right in front of your face - and you'll let me do anything I want. And I will - you'll wish you'd never said 'no' to me. I'll hurt you till those big blue eyes are full of tears, and then I'll make you beg me for more."

The squad of security officers in front of the door separated, leaving a clear path for Jesse, Zephron and James. She was reaching for the control before she'd stopped, hand out as much to catch herself as to key the lock.

"...such pretty patterns on that smooth, white skin."

They burst onto a tableau, but not the one she was expecting. *I thought we were going to get here barely in time to get his hands off Jason's throat. I never realized Jason's reactions were so quick.*

Jason had risen to one knee, and instead of being helpless in the hands of an armed intruder, he was holding, with no sign of strain, a man who crouched before him, face contorted and covered with sweat.

"Command. First," the intruder gasped. "He's gone crazy. He's trying to break my arm. I just came to see how he was, and he grabbed me. Help me, please."

"No one here is going to help you, traitor," Jason said, in a soft, cold voice. Chill fingers walked up Jesse's spine, and she tasted bitterness. Jason's anger was spilling over, touching everyone in the room.

I thought I'd heard him angry before. That was nothing.

"No one here will ever mistake what you are again. You're a sneak, a crawler, a lurker in dark corners. You put poison in the food and killed five of our children. Five, murderer. Five youngsters who'll never have a chance to see where their lives could have gone."

The angle of his hand changed, barely, and the crouched intruder was on his face, the other arm curled under him.

"You came up behind Kwame and hit him when he wasn't looking, didn't you?" Jason shook the hand he held, and the intruder grunted. "You jumped David when he was asleep, and even then he fought you off. You set a booby trap in Jesse's office, to kill whoever it might catch. You're a coward. You don't have the guts to face an opponent, the honor to behave like a man. You sneak and sneak and play dirty tricks and hurt people who can't defend themselves.

"That was why you came after me, wasn't it? You thought I couldn't defend myself. You didn't reckon on meeting a warrior that night, did you? Jesse nearly had you, and you didn't have the courage to face her - you ran, like the coward you are.

"And then you slithered up behind David and you hit him when he wasn't looking. He was down, he couldn't hurt you, but you hit him again, and then you kicked him, and you left him in the dark and the cold to die."

"Jason."

The single word, in a voice no one had expected, silenced the room like a hand stilling the strings of a guitar. Jason's hands relaxed and fell away from the man he held.

The man on the ground fought to get up, grunted, and rolled away from Jason. "You're dead!" Yuri Kelman shouted. "I killed you myself, you son of a bitch." He pushed himself to his feet and glared around.

"What are you all staring at?" he sneered. "Do you think you've won? Do you think the pretty boy finished me? You'll spend the rest of your lives wondering if you found all the traps I set for you, you drechils."

He looked down at Jason, "As for you, rilga," the word dripped poison, and Jesse wondered for a moment what it meant, "grabbing me that way was a lucky accident. I wasn't ready for you. But that's how you get everything, isn't it, 'pretty?' Either they look into those big blue eyes and give it to you, or it just falls into your hands by accident."

He moved as though to take a step toward Jason, who hadn't moved, but stopped when David stepped forward.

"Do you know what the Hexarchs call him, Kelman? Have you ever heard their name for Jason Ashe? They call him the Shipkiller."

Jesse heard someone pull in a breath, but she was too busy watching Kelman to notice who it was.

The sneer relaxed for a fraction of a second and then returned. "Him? Pretty boy? Don't make me laugh. He's not man enough to be the Shipkiller."

"Isn't he?" David's voice was soft, but it sent a chill up Jesse's spine. "Isn't he?" he repeated.

Jason opened his mouth, but before he could speak or move, David grabbed him and pulled open the soft silk shirt he was wearing, stripping it down from his shoulders.

"Look, murderer, and remember. This is what the Hexarchy does to children - children from peaceful transports moving through their own territory. This is what they did to him after he killed their ship. When you've endured a fraction of this and still not given up and crawled into your hole, you might have earned the right to kiss Jason Ashe's feet."

She'd seen it before, but the soft light of Jason's bedroom late at night and the hard light of the living room in daylight were two different things. There was nothing "pretty" about the network of scars that covered Jason's back and shoulders - it was horrifying, and painful, and ugly.

For a few seconds, Yuri Kelman stood frozen. Then he moved - straight for Jason's throat.

Jesse heard something pop as David grabbed him, and the dark-haired man screamed. She moved to help, but David waved her off just as she noticed Jason was leaning. She caught him as he collapsed.

When she looked up, Kelman was bent forward with his right arm twisted behind him between David's hands, the left dangling at an odd angle.

"Take this rat out of my sight before I kill it," David said.

As the mob went through the door with the prisoner, David gestured. "Raavik."

The big security chief glanced at the door, then came over to David. "Put a double guard on the security cell. Strip that bastard, and search him to the bone. Leave a guard on the outside door here. The Third's in CC. Send someone up there to escort her here. Pull Josse out of their suite, strip him, put him in an overall, and send him to the infirmary. Tell Thassanios to examine him for Crystal, and I want those rooms taken apart piece by piece."

"Understood." The big man turned away, then turned back. "Command Second - I'm glad to know the rumors of your death were - exaggerated."

David grinned and waved and Raavik left.

Jason pulled in a long breath and righted himself, reaching to pull his shirt together. "Thanks for the lift, Jesse. Sorry about that."

"Listen, after the last three days, I'm about ready to lie down next to you," Zephron said. "James, order some food - a lot of food. David, welcome back. Jesse, I'm taking over your dining room table - we have work to do, people."

"No, wait. James, stop." At David's upraised hand, James froze at the converter outlet, and everyone else turned toward the big man.

"Jason, how long was he in the room before you were aware of him?"

Jason looked puzzled. "I heard the door open."

"It was - maybe thirty seconds from the time the door opened to the time he started to talk," Jesse said.

"Thirty seconds is a long time if you have mischief in mind," David said. "Zeph, is there an area we can pretty much be sure he hasn't had a chance to get to in the last week?"

"The guest quarters where you were," Bell answered. "We've had the whole area closed off - I had Chief Cody tell people they'd found a fractured beam and the ceilings could collapse any minute. We put a force screen at each of the entrances."

David nodded. "Good. Once Mari gets here, we're all going there. And Security's going over this entire base with a fine-tooth comb, starting with the triad quarters - both sets."

-Chapter 21-
Persist. You become what you repeatedly do. Peter Hill

Jesse looked around and drew in a long breath. *One crisis passed and who knows how many more we'll have to deal with in the future. But for now... We deserve a break - especially...* She looked over at Jason, now on his feet and apparently steady. The dark circles around his eyes had deepened, and there was a drawn look to his face that Jesse didn't like.

"All right, Zephron," she said. "I'll concur that staying here would probably not be a good idea, and that staying together probably would. While Security is scanning and clearing the guest quarters, I'm going to take my usual walk around. I'll meet you there."

"May I join you? Somehow, the idea of a walk sounds very appealing." The corner of Jason's mouth was turned up, and his shoulders and back were straight.

"I'd enjoy the company," Jesse answered.

Zephron's black brows drew together, and he started to open his mouth, then shook his head. "I think you should take someone with you," he murmured.

"Lee's outside," David remarked. "She enjoys walking."

So they set off, followed by the silent Mr. Lee. Jesse's usual round - Engineering, Construction, Astrophysics, the Infirmary. She'd realized she was tired, but not how tired.

I don't think I can feel my feet.

"Can you make it?" Jason asked. "You're beginning to look a little dragged out."

"I look dragged out? You need to see yourself in a mirror, Jason. I don't see how you're still on your feet after the last two days."

"I have to admit, since the adrenalin's worn off, I'm feeling a little - hollow," he admitted. "But right now I'm reveling in the freedom - being with you, being out, walking around. That helps."

"You make it sound so simple."

"In a way, it is. But remember, Jesse - you know as well as I do, simple doesn't mean easy. And I think," he said, staggering a little and putting a hand out to catch himself, "I may need to sit down for a while."

"There's a lounge down the hall," Jesse said. She glanced back. "Do you suppose it'd be safe to stop for a bite?"

Mr. Lee nodded.

"Come on, Jason. We'll watch people and raise our blood sugar."

#

"I didn't realize I was so hungry," Jesse said, putting her fork down.

"Did you remember to eat today?" The long, thin fingers were wrapped around the usual coffee cup, but he'd at least eaten first.

"James got us sandwiches, but I don't remember how long ago it was," Jesse answered.

"Mmm."

"I could ask how long it's been since you ate."

He looked up, then glanced down into his cup again. "Okay, you got me. I don't remember. And I feel," he leaned back and slid down to rest his head against the back of the chair, "much, much better now."

"Well, don't relax completely. This is only the beginning."

Jason closed his eyes and let out a long, slow breath. "Thank you," he said. "I really wanted to be reminded. All right, you - tyrant -" he lowered his eyes, then raised them to hers, and she could see the twinkle in them "- we'd better get back to the real world." He pulled her to her feet and they left the lounge.

I'm almost sorry I said it. There's no reason we couldn't have had a few minutes more, just those few minutes.

"Do you ever just want to run away?"

"What?" He didn't stop, but he slowed down and then turned to walk backward so he could see her face.

"Don't do that," Jesse said. "You'll hit a bump and fall down."

He laughed and stumbled, caught himself by grabbing at Jesse's hand, and ended up leaning against the wall, breathless. "I think that was a case of the wish being father to the deed."

"I did not wish you to fall - I merely said walking backward could be hazardous. Besides," she narrowed her eyes and tightened her lips, "I think you did it on purpose so you wouldn't have to answer my question."

He widened his eyes and put one finger on his lower lip; Jesse resisted as long as she could, then relaxed into a smile. "All right, you win. I can't stand in a corridor and look threatening any longer. Come on - the others are likely to send out a search party."

#

"Where have you been?" David was standing in the corridor outside the guest suite. He looked cool, calm, and in control, and his eyes were dark grey.

"Were you worried, Bro, or are you just trying to give us the guilts?"

"I wasn't worried," David said, signing thanks to Mr. Lee before he wrapped one arm around Jason and the other around Jesse and pulled them toward the door. "Zeph's getting a little antsy, though."

The person in question was indeed pacing the floor, pausing at the end of each lap to pull at his beard. He looked up as they came in and immediately turned toward the table, where James and Mariko were already seated in front of an array of tablets, notebooks, styli, and flimsies.

"Okay, people, this is what we have to do."

"Jesse isn't going to do anything, Zeph, except get some sleep. And neither am I. For that matter, neither are you and James. We're all dangerously fatigued, and the best we could do right now is make bad decisions."

Zephron glanced over at James, slumped in his chair, and back to Jason. Before he could speak, "Jase is right, Zephron. Mari and I can handle anything that comes up for the next few hours," David said.

The bearded man opened his mouth, gulped, then closed it again and shrugged. "You're right, David. All right, James, up you get," he hauled his red-haired partner to his feet and pushed him in the direction of one of the bedrooms. "Call us if you need us."

David watched until the door closed behind them, then turned back to Jesse and Jason. "Okay, you two - that's your room. Go. I'll call you when it's time to get up."

"Do you mind?" Jason gestured at the bed. "David was being a little arbitrary."

"The only problem I can see at the moment is that I'm too

tired to sleep."

"I think I can help with that." He helped her pull her boots off and slide between the covers. "Good night, Jesse. Sweet dreams." A warm, strong hand came to rest against her forehead, and then there was nothing.

She drifted a long time in the soft darkness, almost surfacing once, but something brushed her face and she slid back down.

Something roused her and she began the long swim to consciousness. Still more asleep than awake, she felt a warm presence and lifted her face to be kissed. "Love you," she mumbled.

"I love you, too." The touch of his lips on her forehead woke her, and she pushed herself away from him. "By the One! I haven't slept like that for - I don't remember how long."

"You needed it," Jason said, rolling away.

Jesse slid out of bed and went to splash cold water on her face. The eyes that looked back out of the mirror were bloodshot but open, and the slight puffiness around them was relieved by the application of a cloth soaked in cold water. Once again, she blessed the inventor of recycling for a virtually unlimited water supply. *Clean clothes would make me feel almost human again.*

When she opened the bathroom door, Jason was gone, and a plain slate-grey uniform lay folded at the end of the bed. *Somebody around here's reading minds.*

Buoyed by clean clothes and a night's sleep, she left the bedroom, thinking breakfast might be a good idea.

"All right, this is too much," she said, as Jason looked up from the couch and raised a plate of sandwiches and fruit. "You aren't supposed to be reading my mind."

"I wasn't - I was reading my own."

He handed her a cup and settled into the armchair. Jesse took a long swallow and reached for a sandwich, realizing that now that the overwhelming fatigue was gone, she was ravenous.

"I feel like I could eat a strider," she mumbled around a mouthful of egg salad.

Jason nodded. "I know, but don't - too much strider meat will upset your stomach." The deep blue eyes were sparkling, and as she watched, the faint crinkle at the corner of his mouth deepened into a smile.

Hunger and thirst satisfied, Jesse put the cup down and shifted to look directly at Jason. "Do we have time to talk?"

He

smiled again. "All the time you want, First."

I like that, the way he calls me First. I'm not alone, I'm part of a team. I have partners.

"I wanted you to be the villain, you know. I kept looking for ways it had to be your fault, reasons to blame you."

"I know." He'd curled up in his usual position, one knee up, the other leg under him. The blue eyes were steady.

"Then why wouldn't you..."

"Fight you?" She nodded. "You hurt, Jesse. And hating me helped you manage the pain. It's like loving my partners - to me, that's just the way life is."

"And now?"

"Us, you mean?"

She nodded again, feeling the tightness in her chest, the knot in her throat. *He's had enough. He doesn't need any more pain. He should take David and go.*

"I think, maybe, we can be friends. Partners. If that's what you want, Jesse."

And the rest? Maybe someday. And maybe not. It doesn't matter, she realized. *I've had love. I had Thom.* And as the warm feeling flooded her, she thought, *I still have Thom. I always will have. Nothing can take him from me.*

"And what do you want, Jason Ashe? And this time I want an answer."

He looked down into the cup a moment. When he looked up, the blue eyes were clear and open. "That's hard to answer, Jesse, because I have most of the things I've always wanted. I have the training to use the Talent I was given, I have a job that lets me do some good in the world I live in, I have partners I love and respect. So - maybe a little peace and the leisure to get to know my friend - and partner?" She could hear just the hint of a question in his voice, "-Jesse."

She felt the tears pricking her eyelids. "Well," she had to fight to control her voice, "I can't guarantee the peace, but we'll work on the leisure."

The door opened, cutting off his reply. "Are you two ever going to come out?"

She leaned her head back against the couch and looked up at David. "No. We're just going to stay curled up in here, warm and safe, while the rest of you run around making the galaxy safe for

Prometheus."

"Yeah, right. Come on, First. Move it." Making shooing motions, David came toward the couch. "If you're not up by the time I get there," he said, "I'm tipping it over."

In the command office an hour later, Jesse looked at the stack of data cards piled next to David and for a second wished she was curled up in the warm cocoon of Jason's arms. *But this is what the job is about,* she reminded herself. *And it's the job you've dreamed of having all your life.*

She looked over at Zephron, and he nodded at David. "All right, Command Second, I think we're ready to begin."

David glanced at the stack of cards, drew in a breath, and straightened. "All right. In the chronological rather than urgency or importance order of this hellacious stack of reports. The false overlays have been removed from the system logs and destroyed. That should relieve Jesse," he glanced at her, "and keep the rest of us out of trouble.

"The scan of the triad quarters didn't turn anything up, so Jason must be right that Kelman was so occupied that he didn't have time to do anything. Which means we can all go home and sleep in our own beds tonight, and I for one will be greatly relieved.

"Josse and Kelman's quarters, on the other hand, were lousy with Crystal and Dust. Josse's clothes, bedlinens, and furniture had all been Dusted - apparently with the idea of gradually addicting him and making him controllable. Fortunately, he doesn't seem to be addicted. Unfortunately, he has a massive Crystal infection. He's stable, for now, and being treated, but we'll be sending him to one of the Healers' Centers as soon as we start having regular transport traffic. I wouldn't count on him being able to come back."

The light stylus Jason usually rolled through his fingers clattered onto the table. He picked it up and continued to play with it without looking up, but Jesse could see that his eyes had hardened, and he was very pale.

David glanced over at Jason, let his eyes drift across Jesse, and resumed his report. "We found the Tragan body armor. It was inside one of Kelman's dress uniforms. I have to admit, it's about the best job of camouflage I've ever seen - one side's a perfectly good dress uniform, with all the right seams, electrostatic closures - you name it. The other side's a complete set of Tragan body armor, including chains and buckles. We haven't found the helmet yet, but I wouldn't be surprised to discover it camouflaged with the pilots' gear on one of the flight decks. I have our espionage specialist going over it for recommendations to HQ."

"I'd recommend going through your security people again, David," Zephron said. "They shouldn't have missed that."

David nodded, and Jesse thought, *he's probably doing that already.*

"Yuri Kelman was found dead in his cell at 0530. The medics are conducting an autopsy as we speak - Thassanios says we'll have results by tomorrow." His voice was uninflected, but the grey eyes were misty and almost colorless.

"I don't want to sound heartless," Bell said, "but I think he's saved us a lot of trouble and further heartache. I'm only sorry he didn't succeed in killing himself weeks ago."

Jesse glanced at Jason, who looked frozen, and then at David. The big man had set his jaw hard, but he caught her eye and one eyebrow lifted. *I suppose we'll have to do a lot of paperwork on it, but I agree with Zephron. The man was a murderer and a terrorist, and he nearly killed both my partners. But I'm not as civilized as Zephron - I regret not having had the chance to kill him, slowly, with my bare hands.*

"Just as a preliminary, Second," James' voice was soft, as always, "do we at least have a cause of death?"

James is afraid someone killed him, or that Jason or David injured him and he died of internal bleeding.

"Thassanios says it looks like Crystal," David replied. "A massive dose - probably suicide. But from what we know of his activities over the last several months, I suspect the real question is why he didn't drop dead a long time ago."

He cleared his throat and picked up the next card. "Our delay here has had one good result. Chief Cody managed to get teams outside to work on the sabotaged section, and he reports that it's been properly locked down. That means," David said, looking around the table, "we have random space capability again. Which is a good thing, because," he picked up the last card from the stack, "It looks as though our bandit's on the way back - and he's in a hurry."

He handed the card to Jesse, who handed it to Jason, who pulled his console up and lowered the mike to his mouth. Jesse's gut began to churn as he murmured commands and the local system built in the air over the table, expanded until it nearly filled the room, then contracted to its original size but encompassing more space. The image of the 'bandit' was clear, and the trail of expended carbon molecules indicated high speed. "I'd say 'in a hurry' was an understatement." The corner of Jason's mouth was turned up, but his eyes were bleak.

"How long?"

James and David had their heads together over a notebook, making entries, conferring, making more entries. James handed the notebook to Jason, who scanned it, nodded and hanced it back.

"A week at most," James said. "We can't be entirely accurate just using the carbon trail when he's in random space, but that's close."

"I'd say figure we have five days, just to be safe," David said.

"All right," Jesse said, "We all know what this means - playtime's over. David, Jason, get your pilots prepped and ready to go. Mariko, make sure the outriders know what's happening. The rest of us will pray - hard."

Praying was the easy part, Jesse found. Getting the constant refrain of 'God help us,' out of her head long enough to concentrate on the things she had to do was the hard part.

She would have spent more time on the flight deck, but the mechs didn't need anyone leaning over their shoulders. Zephron had taken over drilling the weapons teams.

And that leaves everything else to me, James, and Mariko. Which would be fine, if it weren't for this nagging feeling I have that everything else isn't going to matter much if we've misjudged any of this.

She initialed a log sheet, put it aside, and then realized she didn't know if she'd read it or not. *Put your mind back in gear, Jesse,* she admonished herself, as she picked up the sheet and forced herself to read it word by word.

To keep herself from going berserk and banging her head against the walls, she worked on a report detailing everything that had happened and what the command team had done in response since she'd reported for duty.

Time passed in a fog, as Jesse fought to keep herself busy, focused, calm. *I thought the week before we caught Kelman was hell, but that was nothing. Centuries of boredom, punctuated by moments of terror. They forget to tell you sometimes the terror gets sucked into the centuries of boredom, so you have centuries of being bored and terrified at the same time.*

Sleep would have been out of the question without Jason, who simply decided it was bedtime each night and put his partners to sleep, whether they wanted him to or not. *Nice to know some-*

one's in charge here.

"Command, will you meet us in the CC office, please? ASAP." Zephron's voice was calm, and the request was hardly unusual, but the qualifier was like electricity flowing through her veins. To a Defense Command officer, 'As Soon As Possible' doesn't mean 'when you get around to it,' it means, 'drop everything and do it in the next breath.' Jesse dropped everything and made the best time she could without running.

The fluo red outline floating above the table told Jesse everything she needed to know. "It's a good thing you and James estimated five days, David. At least we're almost ready."

David had been staring at the holo, muttering under his breath. "I didn't know anything that big could move that fast," he said. "They must be ridiculously overpowered to be able to make that kind of speed in random space." He glanced over at James, then met and held Jason's eyes. "We can't take a chance on those engines going anywhere near King K. The concussion could take out structural members."

Jason nodded. "We have to pull him away - and fast. He's nearly close enough to see those mines we planted."

The two got up and were out the door before the rest of the command team could react.

What the hell's going on? We allowed for - we didn't allow for that kind of power. They're right.

"Zephron, James. Get everything buttoned up and ready to go, now. If he gets much closer, we're going to have to pull into random space in a hurry."

Zephron nodded and pulled down his mike. James went out to CC and started shifting people from their regular duty stations to battle stations.

Jesse pulled down her own mike and opened the command channel to the comm officer. "Get me a direct line to the outriders, Valery."

"Roger, Command. Putting you through."

"*Mantis*, *Spider*, this is Command. Pull back to defensive perimeter and enter random space, now. Flight Officer, begin launching fighters."

"Flight Officer, *Falcon* is on-line and ready for launch," Jason's voice announced.

"Roger, *Falcon*," the flight officer replied. "You're clear to launch."

"Flight Officer, Alpha Flight is on-line and ready for launch." It was David.

Dear God, Jesse prayed, *make this work. We can't outgun this monster in a straight fight. Please keep the five thousand people I'm responsible for safe. Please keep my partners safe.*

"Command, all stations report ready to randomize."

"Engineering, prepare to randomize," Jesse ordered.

"Command, fighters are away," the flight officer reported.

"Roger that, Flight." She shifted to the operations channel, glanced over at Zephron and registered his nod and thumbs-up. "Randomize, now."

Oh, she's good, Jesse thought, as the gentle shift to random space rippled over her. *Usually the shift makes me want to heave.*

"Comm, shift to the near-space command frequency and begin monitoring our pilots."

"Roger that, Command."

"Emergency medical teams to fighter bays," Jesse ordered. "Prepare to receive incoming wounded."

There was a crackle of white noise, and subspace chatter began to come through on Jesse's earphone.

"Comm, restrict the normal-space channel to yourself and the command team," Zephron ordered.

"Roger that, Ops."

Jesse forced herself to relax and listen. *I wish I were out there with them. Of all the waiting we do, this may be the worst.*

She started circulating through CC, touching a shoulder here, leaning over to murmur a few words there, look at a display there - reassuring, calming, maintaining. *The question is,* she thought, listening to the crackle in her earpiece, *who's going to reassure, calm, and maintain me?*

"Command, I have a tactical image," James murmured, from the secondary control station.

At first, the screen seemed to be filled with nothing but vague, floating mists. Jesse blinked and shook her head, and the patches of color took on shape and coherence. The tiny blips that were the fighters danced behind the sleek shape that must be *Falcon*, and on the very eges of the screen were the fingertip-sized fuzzballs that were the outriders. For a moment, Jesse couldn't see the interloper; she glanced away from the screen, then glanced back, and there it was, in the midst of the gathering of photons that represented King K's defense force - a vicious dagger shape, dangerous-looking even reduced to a dot on a tactical display.

"James, move to holo display and magnify," she ordered.

It's so slow. By the One. What are they waiting for?

It came, like a river rolling over her with the weight of what was about to happen - what had to happen.

Her gut tightened, and the energy coiled at the base of her spine pulsed and throbbed like a spring that had been compressed too much. She rippled with cold heat, and then - she knew.

She glanced at Zephron. His eyes were on her, but his body was still, frozen. It was as though nothing could move until she commanded it, until she released it.

She opened the command channel. "*Falcon*, this is Command. The word is Now. I say again, the word is Now."

-Chapter 23-

When victorious in war, one should observe the rites of mourning. Lao Tzu - Tao Te Ching

No acknowledgement. She hadn't expected it. In all the scenarios they'd discussed, all the contingencies they'd rehearsed, this had been the last possibility. But from the top of her head to the tips of her toes, Jesse knew she was right.

The tingling receded, as though the energy she'd felt building had been released. She felt light, cool, strong - and ready to bounce off the ceiling.

A clear baritone voice began intoning - not quite singing, not quite chanting. Other voices began, in counterpoint to the first. A bass. A soprano. A tenor...

It's a great way to coordinate, but what would he do if he ever ended up with a tone-deaf pilot? I suppose it isn't the tones so much as the rhythm. I wonder who developed this method of keeping a team coordinated?

The tiny images in the screen moved and danced, surrounding the larger point with light. Jesse strained to see clearly, the voices forgotten.

"James, is there any way you can enhance that?" Jesse said. "I'm seeing individual dots of light, but they're so close together I'm not getting any information from it."

"I can dimension it over the console," James said, "but it won't be very large."

"That would be good anyway," Zephron decided.

The image transferred itself from the console's viewscreen to the cube floating above it, and what had been blobs of light that hazed and sometimes obscured each other emerged as individual entities; they didn't look like fighters, scout ships, and a Tragan supercruiser bristling with weapons, but they were at least distinct.

The dot that was the supercruiser was under attack by the slim needle that must be *Falcon*, supported by two chunkier shapes that must be the outriders, *Spider* and *Mantis*. Trailing mist showed the discharge of energy weapons.

"Weapons are expended, *Falcon*," she heard.

"Break off and recharge." It was Jason's voice, calm and unruffled - this might be a training exercise with a target that couldn't shoot back and no more riding on the outcome than who bought the coffee when they got back.

"Roger that. *Spider* is away." One of the chunky shapes drifted farther from the central needle - a plume of mist followed it.

"*Mantis* is away." The second chunky shape drifted behind the dots that were the fighters.

"Alpha flight leader, close in and target the spot I'm indicating."

"Roger that, *Falcon*. Alpha flight is closing." The chorus changed tone and tempo, and the tiny dots began to rearrange themselves.

James sighed and muttered under his breath, his fingers playing over the console, and the scene in the hologram sharpened and resolved. What had been mist became a beam of light, easy to identify as the plasma energy released by a fighter's cannons. Similar beams of light emanated from the central blob - as they watched, one of the smaller dots brightened, enlarged, then dissipated. The knot in Jesse's gut and the lump in her throat told her she'd just watched one of their pilots die.

Jesse became aware of energy flows within the small circle of people buckled in around the command console. Like blood from an open wound, the drain had increased from a trickle to a stream.

"James, back off!" Zephron snapped. "We can't help them if you deplete us."

Jesse pulled her hand away from the console, breaking the circuit. James' face was bleached, freckles standing out against the pale skin in splotches of beige.

"That's told us everything we need to know, James. Thank you." It was a magnificent feat for a Pathfinder as young as James, and Jesse would make sure he knew it.

"Chief Edmunds, prepare to take us out of random space and re-enter on my command."

"Roger that, Command. How long an interval will we have?"

It's going to be hard on the generators and the structure, Jesse thought, as she told the chief how long it would take. *But not as hard as taking fire from that supercruiser.*

She nodded to the comm officer; he ran a finger over his controls. "Prepare to exit random space." The impersonal voice floated through halls and corridors Jesse saw in her mind's eye as empty and echoing; there was a shift, that maddening feeling of not-quite dizziness, and the tactical screen cleared and presented small images of what was happening near the gas giant. It looked so close someone gasped. For a second it seemed the fighters were literally on top of them. Then her perspective normalized.

"Weapons, target the point *Falcon* and the fighters are indicating with fire and focus all available guns."

"Roger that, Command. Target is locked."

"Commence firing."

The beam from *Falcon* and the bursts from the fighters were joined by the shaft of plasma energy from King K's focused guns - the supercruiser shimmered, then refocused.

"The guns are draining their power - they're in trouble," Jesse said.

"Continue fire," Zephron commanded. "Route the charge from the secondary arrays into your focus."

"Flight, recall your fighters."

"Roger, Command."

The supercruiser broke toward the gas giant, apparently with the idea of hiding behind the planet's disc. It was a mistake. One by one, the mines Jason and James had planted came on line, made contact, and blew.

Their huge opponent swerved and wobbled, toward and then away from the gas giant's atmosphere, but it was too late. It had been too late the moment they'd entered this system. One final mine blew, and the gas giant's poisonous atmosphere reached out to embrace and smother the enemy cruiser.

"Randomize now!" Jesse ordered. There was a lurch like a lift dropping, and Jesse felt as though all her internal organs had launched themselves into the back of her mouth. She grabbed for a handhold, fighting to stay upright and in control.

My headset's gone dead, she thought, tapping the earplug. The chant from the pilots was gone.

"Dragon's breath!" James exclaimed. The redhead was bent over the console, face white, mouth twisted, his free hand clamped over his mid-section.

Jesse pushed herself upright and moved to where she could see over his shoulder. "Oh, my God," she heard, and glanced over at Mariko, who was staring at the same screen, tears running down her face.

The center of the explosion was no longer there - there was a blank space in the fields of dust surrounding the giant planet. The hole was expanding, pushing everything out before it except where it touched the planet's gravity field, which distorted the edges of the circle. And none of the visible debris was more than a meter across.

"James, expand your field," Jesse ordered. "It doesn't matter if you lose focus. And pull up a tactical grid."

The young Second's hands were shaking, but it took him only seconds to expand the sensor's field of vision. Jesse swallowed, feeling a heaviness in the back of her throat. *I almost wish I hadn't told him to do that.*

Some of the shrapnel flying from the explosion's point of origin was now identifiable - chunks of metal, shreds of charred and blackened fabric, unmentionable pieces Jesse didn't want to think about.

She shifted her mike to the command channel. "Flight Officer, prepare to launch search and rescue drones."

"Drones are prepared, Command, ready to launch on order." The flight officer's voice was calm and even, and Jesse wondered if it was because she had no way of telling what had happened, or if she was inhumanly controlled.

Jesse felt her knees sagging and her shoulders bowing, and reproached herself. *We're alive*, she reminded herself. *The Tragans will not harvest that Crystal and use it to cause illness and despair. Most of the people on this platform are safe. We can proceed to our designated location and establish a base.* It didn't help, but she forced her knees to straighten and stabilize, her shoulders to lift.

"Concussion wave has passed, Command," Zephron murmured.

"Roger that," Jesse responded. "Prepare to exit random space." This time the transition was smooth, the sickening sensation of the shift minimized.

"Flight Officer, launch search and rescue drones," she ordered.

"Drones away, Command," the flight officer's voice responded. Her voice sharpened. "We have incoming craft," she announced. "Emergency medical teams, prepare to receive wounded."

It took all Jesse had not to start for the door. *My place is here,* she told herself. *I have a job to do. No matter who comes back and who doesn't, we've all lost someone today.*

"Okay, people," she said, "we have work to do. You all know your jobs - get to them. This base is still in transport to its permanent station - and we're behind schedule."

That should do it, she thought, glancing around. Shoulders had straightened, heads had come up, fingers were flying over controls. She exchanged nods with Zephron and turned to her own console. The prayers she was saying in her heart didn't slow her work at all.

#

Her hand was shaking so hard the flimsy she was holding was unreadable. She put it on the desk, flattened it where she'd crumpled it, and spread her hands on either side.

"Go on, James."

He glanced around and got a nod from Zephron, then dropped his eyes to the data card in front of him and cleared his throat.

"Damage to the outer skin was substantial. Chief Cody recommends shutting down everything from Level Ten up until we're permanent and expanded and they've had a chance to make repairs."

"That'll make the astrophysicists happy." Someone chuckled, then covered it with a cough.

"Three sections broke loose and can't be locked down without extensive outside work at a standstill. We're still mobile, but much strain could damage at least one of them beyond repair, so - we can't randomize.

"We took comparatively minor damage to operations and navigational systems - they're being repaired as we speak. Long-range communications are gone, and the engineers can't give me an estimate on when we might be able to get them back. Valery has launched a comm drone toward HQ, but it will take at least a month to get there. We're on our own."

Zephron nodded and looked over at Jesse. His face was drawn, with heavy lines running from nose to chin, a frown between the dark eyebrows, and shadows around his eyes.

"We lost fifteen fighters of the forty we launched, with pilots." Jesse shuddered and swallowed hard, biting down the need to howl out her grief and anger.

"*Mantis* is operational, but incapable of randomizing. We can't even begin to work on repairs to the outriders until we're on station and have repaired some of the damage we took, so I had them couple on and lock down. There's no sense wasting the fuel and doing further damage to the equipment."

Jesse nodded. Compared to the loss of human life, the

damage to the outrider was inconsequential.

"We're going to have to operate with our fingers crossed, people. We still don't know how that cruiser crossed the border without triggering every alarm in the quadrant, and we can't relax until we do."

She made eye contact with each member of the senior staff before she relaxed and looked over at Zephron again.

"*Spider* is in better shape than *Mantis*, and they're operating as a sort of perimeter guard. They have three people out of commission with minor injuries - we've covered with some of the apprentices. Two of the smaller scouts spun out, and search and rescue drones can't find any sign of them."

In her mind Jesse added up the total of the dead. Five from Kellman's poison, fifteen fighter pilots, six from the scouts, two from *Mantis*... *This border fort has already cost Prometheus a very high price, and we've still to reach our permanent station.*

She looked over at two of the empty chairs at the conference table and breathed a prayer of relief. Not dead, not spun out and probably not recoverable. Jason was in the infirmary with a broken leg and bruised ribs; he expected to be back in his own quarters by evening and back on limited duty by the end of the week. David - David was in the stasis chamber, making official identifications of the dead and saving Jesse and Zephron the pain of writing the letters home to their families.

We still have the memorial services to get through. But not till we put things back together; not until we're sure how many we lost. One thing about the dead - they're not in a hurry.

She turned her eyes and her attention back to James and the report he was making.

#

Silence. A whisper from the ventilation system, the sound of her own heart beating. Jesse held her breath, waiting for the clanging, buzzing, smashing, clattering and banging to resume. Thirty seconds, forty-five - a full minute. She pulled the headphones off, glad to free her ears from the pressure, and listened to the blessed sound of absolutely nothing.

Maybe they're finished, she thought. She crossed her fingers and closed her notebook.

"Command, are you there?" It was Zephron Bell's voice.

"I'm here, Ops. I'm even awake."

"Good. Then you might want to meet us in the command

office in - say, an hour?"

"I'll be there."

It's never as simple, as easy as you hope it will be, Jesse thought, listening as Chief Cody went through the after-action report on expansion and stabilization. *No matter how much you plan, how detailed your operation orders are, no matter what contingencies you've planned for - there's always something else.*

Limping to permanent station had taken two months - and at least once Jesse had found a young navigator weeping with frustration at the balkiness of the overstrained control systems. She'd sent for a relief for the girl, taken her to the lounge and bought her a drink, and gone back to her own study with a strong desire to bang her head against a wall.

And that wasn't all by a long shot. Cost overruns - how do we have cost overruns out here? What are we doing keeping track of expenses, anyway?

And surprise packages - *well, that wasn't as much of a surprise as our opponents thought it would be.* With the experience of the weakened bolts, the toxins in the food supply, the way doors could be jammed and ventilation shut down, Chief Cody had proceeded with caution, scanning every section before beginning to open it, scanning again after it was opened, checking specs two and three times. They'd found five bombs, set to fracture section joints and cause depressurization; the fire extinguishers in one section had come on the moment the locking bolts were released, filling the air with unbreathable inert gases - James' quick work at the internal controls had counteracted that before anyone was injured; there'd been more unaccountable glitches in the controls, giving them a week's grief as they chased phantom raiders through the tactical displays. The list was long, but they'd managed to beat them all. *So far,* Jesse thought, crossing her fingers under the table. *So far.*

"...And we finished reinforcing the final panel this morning - only two months behind schedule." Chief Cody let the sheets of flimsy fall back together and placed them square with the edge of the table.

"So we're officially stable," Zephron said.

The chief looked around the table, making eye contact with everyone, ending with Zephron. "We are officially stable, on position, ready for action, Ops," he said. "And I am taking the rest of the week off."

A ring of expectant faces turned to Jesse. She looked back, trying to stay stone-faced, then let the smile break through. "And...?"

"And I think the next job is yours, Command," Bell said.

Jesse held out her hand for the data card, glanced over it, and scribbled her name. Then, while everyone watched, she pulled her mike down.

"Comm, open base communications."

"Line is open, Command."

"Comm Officer, make to Quadrant HQ: Greetings from Fort King Kamehameha, Border Command Post Number Twenty-Three. This base is on-line and ready for action."

There was a moment of silence, like held breath; then the entire base erupted with cheers, screams, yells of triumph.

Jesse let out a long breath, realizing she'd been holding it. No other mobile base had made it to this location, let alone to expansion. *Whatever else we do, we'll be in the history books for this. These two triads brought Fort Kamehameha on-line.*

#

It was a good party, Jesse thought. Good food and lots of it, music not too loud for good conversation, many smiling faces. She leaned back against a railing, a drink in her hand, and watched the crowd.

He was tall, thin, the dress uniform turning his white-blonde hair to a pale flame. The man standing with him had broad shoulders, gold skin, dark-gold hair.

David looked up and caught her eye. He said something to Jason, and the two started across the room toward her.

"Well, Command First, how's life in Sector Twenty-Three?"

"Quiet, for the moment, Command Second," Jesse said, holding up crossed fingers.

Jason looked from one to the other of them and shook his head. "Did we establish a new formality rule nobody told me about?"

"Just setting an example, Command Third," Jesse said. "Maintaining the structure, keeping up the good work - yanking the Third's chain..." she let her voice fade and watched as the look on Jason's face went from puzzled to indignant to amused to calculating. *We're going to pay for that. Oh, well - it was fun while it lasted.*

"You were looking pretty solemn before we came over," David said. "What were you thinking about?"

She took a long swallow from her drink. "I was thinking that this has been a very long few months, and I was hoping our lives will be less exciting in the future."

"It's a nice dream," Jason said, "but I wouldn't count on it. Somehow, I think life on the border is going to entail a fair amount of unanticipated activity."

The clink of metal against glass caught everyone's attention, and all eyes turned to where James McGowan stood, the glass he'd been tapping with a spoon still lifted.

"I hope everyone's having a great party," he said. Several people shouted or whistled, and James raised a hand to still them. "It's customary at this sort of function to offer toasts, and I'm sure there will be plenty, so I hope everyone has a full glass." He waited a moment while people shifted about and refilled glasses.

"First, I want to offer congratulations and good wishes to the Command Triad on behalf of my partners and myself. As we're all aware, two other platforms were assigned to this sector but never made it here, and I think we all know our high survival rate is directly attributable to them."

He waited until the applause died away. The young face was solemn under the short red hair, but he showed no trace of self-consciousness or shyness.

He's done a lot of growing up the last few months, Jesse thought. The James who first reported as the Second of the Operations team was still a boy - this young man was fully adult.

"Before we continue the party, I want to remind you all of our fellow soldiers - the ones who were on those other platforms, and the ones from Fort Kamehameha who didn't make it this far. We wouldn't be here to celebrate if it weren't for them." He raised his glass. "To our fallen."

Every glass in the room was raised, every voice echoed him. Jesse blinked back tears as she, too, lifted her glass. "To our fallen."

To all the fallen.

-End-

Manufactured by Amazon.ca
Bolton, ON